THE SOLARIS BOOK OF NEW

FANTASY

EDITED BY GEORGE MANN

OTHER BOOKS BY GEORGE MANN

The Solaris Book of New Science Fiction *(editor)*
The Mammoth Encyclopedia of Science Fiction
The Human Abstract
Time Hunter: The Severed Man
Time Hunter: Child of Time
(with David J. Howe)

THE SOLARIS BOOK OF NEW

FANTASY

EDITED BY GEORGE MANN

Including stories by

Christopher Barzak
Mark Chadbourn
Hal Duncan
Steven Erikson
Jay Lake
James Maxey
Juliet E. McKenna
T. A. Pratt
Mike Resnick
Chris Roberson
Steven Savile
Lucius Shepard
Scott Thomas
Jeff VanderMeer
Conrad Williams
Janny Wurts

SOLARIS

First published 2007 by Solaris
an imprint of BL Publishing
Games Workshop Ltd
Willow Road
Nottingham
NG7 2WS
UK

www.solarisbooks.com

ISBN-13: 978 1 84416 523 0
ISBN-10: 1 84416 523 X

Introduction copyright © George Mann 2007
"Who Slays the Gyant, Wounds the Beast" copyright © Mark Chadbourn 2007
"Reins of Destiny" copyright © Janny Wurts 2007
"Tornado of Sparks" copyright © James Maxey 2007
"Grander than the Sea" copyright © T. A. Pratt 2007
"The Prince of End Times" copyright © Hal Duncan 2007
"King Tales" copyright © Jeff Vandermeer 2007
"In Between Dreams" copyright © Christopher Barzak 2007
"And Such Small Deer" copyright © Monkeybrain, Inc 2007
"The Wizard's Coming" copyright © Juliet E. McKenna 2007
"Shell Game" copyright © Mike Resnick 2007
"The Song Her Heart Sang" copyright © Steven Savile 2007
"A Man Falls" copyright © Joseph E. Lake Jr 2007
"O Caritas" copyright © Conrad Williams 2007
"Lt. Privet's Love Song" copyright © Scott Thomas 2007
"Chinandega" copyright © Lucius Shepard 2007
"Quashie Trapp Blacklight" copyright © Steven Erikson 2007

The right of the individual authors to be identified as the authors of this
work have been asserted in accordance with the Copyright, Designs and
Patents Act 1988.

All rights reserved. No part of this publication may be reproduced, stored
in a retrieval system, or transmitted, in any form or by any means, electronic, mechanical, photocopying, recording or otherwise, without the
prior permission of the copyright owners.

10 9 8 7 6 5 4 3 2 1

A CIP catalogue record for this book is available from the British Library.

Designed & typeset by BL Publishing

CONTENTS

INTRODUCTION
George Mann

WHAT EXACTLY IS fantasy?

This is a question that has perplexed scholars, readers, philosophers, and publishers for many years, myself included. What is the nature of fantasy? What makes fantasy different from reality? Or, indeed, what is it that separates fantastic fiction from more "traditional" or "mainstream" writing? After all, isn't all fiction, when things are said and done, a form of fantasy, a story conjured up by a writer, populated with made-up characters and created place names? Is it perhaps the introduction of mythical or fantastical figures that help us define a book as a *fantasy*: goblins, wizards, dragons, heroes? Is the fantasy *genre* just a collection of stereotypes, a convenient shorthand for describing a particular type of story that adopts certain literary tropes, whilst in truth, the actual definition of a fantasy story is much, much wider than that? Or is it more to do with the location or the setting, or how the author approaches his or her story; the manner in which he or she creates a schism between their imagined take on the world and the true, natural order of things? What's more, does it even matter?

It may seem strange for me to begin this introduction with a series of questions, more so because I'm not now about to offer you any answers. Asking the questions themselves is enough to help me set the context in which I approached the assembly of this new anthology of fantastic fiction. Fantasy speaks for itself, its boundaries as blurred as the intercises between the new versions of the world it describes.

Fantasy is—I am convinced—as old as language itself, derived from the oral tradition to entertain and inspire, to sit around a fire and tell tall tales of heroes and monsters, both to delight and to educate one another. Fantasy is ingrained in our psyche.

Perhaps, then, it is simply this primal urge to tell stories that underpins the fantasy genre, the *intention* to use allegory and adventure to enlighten and entertain others. Perhaps it is also just about having fun, and that impulse should in no way be dismissed, for it is just as worthy. No matter the literary devices and styles deployed by the author, or the underlying message (no matter how serious)—the intention remains the same: to entertain.

This anthology is a celebration of that entertainment. It is also an exploration of the diversity of fantasy fiction, be it High Fantasy, Dark Fantasy, Comic Fantasy, Magic Realism—the definitions are as diverse as literature itself. Some of these stories will make you laugh; others will break your heart. Some will fill you with awe and inspiration, others with pain and joy.

In the end, though, all of these stories are *real*. In one way or another they are all about humanity, with all its foibles and neuroses and beauty. They are all about placing humanity in a different context and seeing how those people react. And whatever the genre, that is perhaps the most important thing that fiction has to do.

So, in the best oral tradition, imagine yourself seated around a warm fire, each author a different narrator waiting to tell you a story. I know you won't be disappointed.

George Mann
Solaris Consultant Editor
Nottingham, May 2007

Acknowledgments

With heartfelt thanks to all at Solaris: Mark in particular for helping with the acquisition of key stories; Christian for enduring patience as the manuscript kept getting bigger and bigger; Marc for giving us the chance to do something different. Thanks also to Fiona and James for being patient while I spent long hours knee-deep in manuscripts, and to Lou Anders and Chris Roberson for continued friendship and many heartfelt debates on the minutiae of our favorite genre.

WHO SLAYS THE GYANT, WOUNDS THE BEAST

MARK CHADBOURN

Christmas Eve, 1598

THE BORDER BETWEEN what is and what might be changes with the seasons, and with the hour. Homesteads and fields and lanes that have the hard, dusty air of the mundane on a hot summer afternoon can echo to the sly tread of something wild and irrational under the full moon. Whispers uttered by no human mouth are caught on the breeze on All Hallows Eve or Walpurgisnacht. At the great hall of Charlecote Park, lonely in the frozen landscape, the rules of the daylight world have long since dissipated with the setting sun.

There are whispers here too.

"Now?"

"Soon."

And prints made by no human foot in the deep snow that lies heavy against the sturdy walls. Lights blaze in the many windows and the sounds of viol, hautboy, and harpsichord drift out across the still countryside as the merrymakers prepare for the coming holy day.

"THIS IS A pit of debauchery. We should be home in London, Will, not in dismal Warwickshire among these fornicators and cupshotten ne'er-do-wells. I would be at church when the first bell tolls, and keep the devil at my back." Nathaniel Colt huddled beneath the woolen blanket as he peered out of the carriage window at the approaching hall. His breath clouded and he had long since lost the feeling in his toes.

The man opposite did not appear to feel the chill. He lounged across the seat, cleaning his nails with a knife. His boots were polished to a shine, his clothes the latest fashionable cut from the tailors who supplied the court. An urbane air belied his true nature, which occasionally surfaced in the depths of his dark eyes.

"Fornicators and cupshotten ne'er-do-wells, Nathaniel? England's aristocracy may not take to such a description," he replied. "However true it may be."

"I am a God-fearing man. Unlike yourself," Nathaniel added sniffily. "But I would expect no less from someone who has intimate knowledge of every tavern and doxy on Cheapside."

"Life is short, Nat, and we are bounded by misery on all sides. We must seek out what jewels we can."

Nathaniel snorted.

The carriage jolted as it passed between the grand gates and made its way toward the entrance where servants waited to help them from the carriage.

"And when do you plan to tell me why the Queen has dispatched us to this devil-haunted spot?" Nathaniel added. "What could possibly demand the attention of the magnificent Will Swyfte, England's greatest spy?"

"That note of sarcasm is unbecoming, Nathaniel," Will said lightly. "I may have to find another assistant in future."

"My heavenly rewards come early."

The servants led them into the hall where they were greeted by the host, the newly knighted Sir Thomas Lucy, dressed in a black doublet.

"Will Swyfte, England's greatest spy," he said. Nathaniel rolled his eyes. "This is an honor, indeed." He paused. "Is the Queen—"

"Elizabeth has had to cancel her visit for the festivities," Will said. "And Walsingham sends his apologies. I am here on their behalf."

Lucy was crestfallen. He tugged at his beard for a moment and then said, "You will make merry with us, then, Mr. Swyfte? My house and staff are at your disposal. And I for one would take great pleasure in hearing of your famous exploits in your own words."

Lucy directed Will and Nathaniel toward the room where the festivities were taking place, before hurrying to the side of his wife. "I fail to see the value of a spy with a name and a face that is known by everyone in the realm," Nathaniel sighed.

"England needs its heroes, Nat. People must see that all is being done to keep them safe in their beds. It stops them asking difficult questions of their betters. More, it distracts them from the real nightmares threatening to steal their breaths. Philip of Spain was a small ogre in comparison."

"And what are these nightmares? Should not an assistant be trusted enough to know more than the common man?"

"Do not be so quick to shuck off the common life." A note of regret rose briefly in Will's voice. "Enough chat. I have work for you."

The ballroom was thronging with the cream of the aristocracy, dancing and drinking and carousing with the complete abandon of the carefree ruling class. On show were the finest gowns and cloaks and doublets, bright colors glowing in the Christmas candlelight. Each guest wore a mask, so that a man might have difficulty knowing if the woman with him were his wife; an added attraction. In the shadows, kisses were stolen, and dancers would occasionally vacate the floor to disappear to the rooms above.

"Somewhere in that morass of carnality is Sir Edmund Spenser."

"The Queen's favorite poet?"

"The same. Find him, Nat, and bring him to me. But with the politeness befitting his status, of course."

"What would you have me do?" Nathaniel said incredulously. "Snatch off every mask until I find the face we seek?"

"You are a resourceful man," Will said with a grin. "That is why I have elevated you to your high status."

"And where will you be while I risk the stocks or being thrown out into the winter cold?"

"I go in search of true love."

AT THE FAR end of the entrance hall, a hidden door revealed a tight, winding staircase that led to the guest bedrooms. Ice had formed on the inside of the windows and Will's breath plumed in the chill. He had memorized the layout of the house from the plans Walsingham had given him, but it was impossible to know which room had been set aside for Spenser.

The first door he tried revealed a couple in sweaty coitus. Though both naked, the man still wore a devil mask and the woman hid behind a cat's face. Lost to their rhythm, they did not see Will.

The next four rooms were empty, though fires crackled in the grate. The fifth was locked. From a hidden pouch, Will removed a roll of velvet containing a skeleton key. The lock turned with an irritatingly loud *clank*, but as he slipped inside the figure seated at the mirrored dressing table appeared not to have heard. It was a woman, though her reflected face was lost to the shadows of a hooded cloak. Ringlets of brown hair tumbled out on to her breast. She was still, like a moonlit pool, and at first Will thought she was asleep.

But then her voice rolled out, low and honeyed and as warm as the candlelight: "Leave now, uninvited guest, or face the inevitable repercussions." The soft tones betrayed no fear.

"You are the consort of Sir Edmund Spenser?"

She did not reply.

"It is not my habit to intrude into a lady's chamber..." Will paused. "At least, not without some degree of invitation."

"You did not leave your sword upon arrival," the woman noted. "You are expecting a threat? Here, in this house of celebration?"

Will found himself lulled by her soothing voice. "Weave no spells with me," he said. "I am aware of your tricks."

"Then there is no need for subterfuge." The woman turned to him and removed her hood. Though Will had encountered some of the most beautiful women in Europe, his breath caught in his throat. Her flawless skin appeared to exude a thin golden glow and her hazel eyes flashed with an otherworldly light.

"Glamour?" he said.

"'Twould be an insult if I considered your opinion to carry any weight." She stood, and as the cloak shifted around her form the atmosphere became sexually charged.

"I can see why Spenser fell beneath your spell."

A shadow crossed her face. "No spell."

"What, then? True love?" Will expected a tart response to his mockery, but she turned from him and went to the window.

"I could not expect one such as you to understand," she said quietly as she gazed out across the frozen fields.

"You know we cannot allow it to continue."

"Is it so dangerous?"

"A man and a resident of Faerie? If the icy war between our two lands was not close to growing hot, you perhaps could make an argument for such a liaison. But—"

"War? You speak as if that means anything." She turned to him, her eyes blazing. For the first time, Will glimpsed the true power that he knew existed just beneath the otherworldly beauty. He drew his sword.

She strode toward him, the air crackling around her. "The events of tonight must reach their natural conclusion."

"Your profession of love does not ring true. You know well how much the information you both carry is of value to your kind. You cannot be allowed to cross over to the other side."

"My kind?" Her face grew cold and terrible. "My kind are fools and lovers." She snapped open her left hand to release a wild fluttering of wings. Within a second, Will fell to the floor, unconscious.

"YOUR MASTER CUTS a very dashing figure," Alice Lucy noted as she sent the eldest of her thirteen children back to bed. "Is it true he has personally dispatched one hundred Spaniards?"

Nathaniel masked his weariness at her question and the familiar, tiresome sparkle in the eye of the mistress of the house. "There are many stories surrounding my master, some of them even true."

"My husband has done his own duty to deal with the Catholic problem locally. Though, of course, not with the verve of Master Swyfte," she added hastily. "He is a God-fearing man?"

"I believe Master Swyfte does not know the meaning of fear," Nathaniel said with a tight smile.

"And no woman has yet led him up the aisle. How sad that he abides such a lonely existence."

Nathaniel's attention was drawn to some kind of disturbance on the far side of the whirling dancers. "Master Swyfte does not want for companionship. But Queen and Country demand much of him, and a wife would find her days and nights lacking."

A ripple moved across the ballroom as dancers came to a sudden halt. An animated group had grown near one of the windows looking over the formal gardens leading down to the river.

Alice peered at the growing crowd with irritation. "They are in their cups. Do not concern yourself."

"I fear, mistress, there is more to this than wine." Nathaniel deferentially edged through the dancers until he could hear the conversation of the knot of men and women move from jocularity to concern.

"Get him to a bedroom!" a rotund man in a pig mask squealed. "He holds up the festivities and the midnight hour draws near!"

"Hold. His chest does not move. Perhaps he has choked on a nut. Remove his mask."

Nathaniel could see a man prone on the floor, his white ruffle soaked in the red wine he had been drinking so that it appeared he had been shot. Fumbling fingers plucked his mask free and then all those around him recoiled as one.

"The Devil's work!" the pig-man exclaimed. He crossed himself as he staggered back onto the dance floor.

At first, Nathaniel was sure this was some joke to mark the festivities, for the man on the floor was not a man at all. Straw sprouted from ears and mouth like one of the figures farmers left in the cornfields after the harvest. Silver coins were embedded where the eyes should have been. Yet the skin still bloomed warm and the features were more real than any prankster could have constructed.

"Quick!" Nathaniel said. "Where was he before he fell?"

One of the guests pointed toward the window. "He looked out across the landscape as he drank his wine."

Those nearest the window backed away quickly, amid murmurs of "Witchcraft!" As the ripples of what had happened moved swiftly across the dance floor, Lucy rushed over aghast.

"A joke!" he cried. "A Christmas prank!" Hastily, he ordered his servants to remove the straw man. Circulating rapidly, he managed to calm the most anxious guests, but an atmosphere of unease still hung heavily over the hall.

"Is this why your Master is here?" Lucy asked as he pulled Nathaniel to one side. "If so, I would ask for his help before these matters worsen, for I fear they may."

"My Master's motives remain a mystery known only to himself. Though dress me in a cap and call me a fool if there were no connection, for bizarre occurrences follow my Master like a dog follows a wedding parade."

"Then I beseech you, bring him here, now, before we are all turned to straw."

Nathaniel bowed and disappeared into the crowd, though he was now niggled with the thought that Will had been gone for an undue amount of time.

WILL WOKE ON the cold, hard boards of the bedroom, his head filled with one memory constantly replaying: Jenny calling to him across the golden cornfield that lay beside her Warwickshire home. The image stung him so hard it had brought tears to his eyes while he slept. The remembrance had been planted there to teach him a lesson.

"Magicks," he muttered contemptuously.

"Many a time I have found you in such a position, but never without the consumption of wine."

Nathaniel slipped in and helped Will to his feet. "You were attacked?"

"Not in the way you think." Will steadied himself. Jenny slipped from his mind, but she was not replaced by peace. "I fear I have a score to settle."

"I fear you have to listen to me prattle before you do another thing." Nathaniel quickly explained what had occurred in the ballroom. "What transpired here?" he added. "Is this the same threat?"

"In a way. Come—great danger draws near."

In the cold corridor, Will scraped the ice off the window to peer into the snow-bright night. The light from the great windows fell in large rectangles on rolling drifts. "Footprints," he mused.

"Someone is out there?" Nathaniel squeezed beside Will. "Those are the prints of animals," he said dismissively.

Beyond the pools of light, where the trees clustered, darkness lay heavily. Points of light appeared briefly here and there, as though fireflies moved among the branches. Will continued to watch until there was a sudden burst of fire: a torch igniting. Another, and then another, moving back and forth.

Will did not wait to hear Nathaniel's questions. He found Lucy passing brightly among the guests, splashing sack liberally into goblets while attempting to raise spirits with jokes and bawdy comments.

"Master Swyfte. Is the unfortunate incident now contained?"

Will drew him to one side. "The matter is just beginning. This hall is under siege."

Lucy cursed loudly. "'Tis the Catholics. The uprising we all feared has begun."

"You should find some warmth in your heart for the brotherhood of man," Will replied coldly. "There are worse things under heaven than Catholics."

"Moors?"

"We must make the hall secure by the midnight hour."

The grand clock squatting in the corner near the mantelpiece showed twenty minutes remaining. "There is time enow. I will order the servants to lock and bar the doors," Lucy said.

"That will not suffice. I will advise your kitchen servants to prepare a concoction of salt and other herbs. It must be sprinkled along every entrance into this place: doors, windows, hearths. To miss one opening could be the end of all of us."

Lucy blanched. "'Then you are saying this threat is witchcraft?"

"Best not discuss these things here and now for fear of frighting your guests, Sir Thomas. Trust in me and the authority of our Queen and we shall keep your home safe from all enemies." Lucy nodded. "One other thing: keep all guests away from the windows and anywhere they can be spied from without."

Deeply troubled, Lucy hurried off to find the cook. Will turned to Nathaniel. "Did you find Spenser?"

"I searched high and low, and met many who had spoken to him, or believed they had, but he always stayed one step ahead."

"Then back to it, Nat. The urgency is greater still. Spenser and his love must not be allowed to leave this place before the sun breaks."

"You fear for his life at the hands of whatever waits without?"

"I fear for all our lives, Nat, and the lives of every man, woman and child in England."

IT TOOK FIVE minutes for the kitchen staff to prepare Will's salt-based concoction and a further thirteen minutes to draw a line of it before every entrance into the hall, and that was with every servant working fast with small leather pouches of the mixture. The final grains fell into place as the bell on the great clock began to chime midnight, and only then did Will ease slightly. Fuelled by more bottles brought up from Sir Thomas Lucy's cellar, the guests continued to enjoy themselves, oblivious to what was taking place around them, but Lucy himself wandered the party rooms ashen-faced.

And as the final chime echoed, every candle and lamp in the hall winked out.

Whoops and excited shrieks filled the room. "'Tis time for the great unmasking!" someone called. No one had noticed that even the roaring fire in the hearth had dimmed to a faint crackle. Through the gloom, Will quickly snatched a candle from the table and lit it with his flint.

Another cheer rose up. With fumbling fingers, Lucy hastily lit another five sticks in a candelabrum on the other side of the room. The panic was clear in his face.

From an oblique angle, Will watched through the window, but there was no sign of anyone approaching. All around him, the drunken guests tore off their masks with great cheers. The women blushed and curtseyed. The men brayed and kissed their hands.

Except one. Will saw him at the same time the guests closest to him began to laugh and point. A large, fat-bellied man, he staggered around, feeling across the gray-furred surface of the wolf's mask he wore. Yet in his other hand, he clutched the same wolf mask that he had just removed.

"A mask beneath a mask! How novel," a freckle-faced woman cried.

Desperate to stop a panic that might drive the guests out into the night, Will ran to drag the guest to a more private place. He was too late. "This is no mask. It is my face!" the man howled. Those nearest peered closely and saw that it was true.

There was a gurgle and a swell that became a crashing wave as the guests swept toward the exit amid deafening cries for God to save them. Will was closer to the hall and made it to the grand oak door first. He drew his sword and brought the rush to a halt.

"You know me," he said firmly.

Silence.

"Do you know me?" he stressed in a tone that bordered on the threatening.

A few near the front quietly said that they did.

"Then you know that I will allow no further harm to come to loyal men and women of this realm. As long as you stay within my purview, and do not venture outside, for that is where the true danger awaits."

Several were still consumed with dread of the supernatural. They tore at their clothes and tore at their hair and for a moment Will thought they were going to rush him in the grip of their frenzy. But saner heads held them calm until the panic subsided and then the questions began in force. At the back of the hall, Nathaniel was trying to catch his attention. Shaking off the desperately clutching hands, Will left Lucy to maintain whatever calm he could and ran in pursuit of the figure Nathaniel had indicated.

At the foot of the rear staircase, Will caught up with a man with wavy brown hair above a high forehead that gave him the look of an intellectual, but it was marred by the desperation etched into his features.

Will took his arm. The man did not resist. "Sir Edmund?"

There was a long moment of silence before he relented. "Yes."

"You know who I am?"

"I have heard of your exploits, like every other person in this land."

"Then you know I am only charged with the gravest tasks."

Spenser nodded. Will saw no surprise that he was there, just a dismal resignation.

"Your wife, Elizabeth, has displayed remarkable fortitude during your repeated absences from the family home," Will continued, before adding knowingly, "while you were composing your poetry. She fears your latest absence may be longer than the others, Sir Edmund. Is she correct?"

Spenser bowed his head; his hands were shaking so much he appeared to be sick. "What is your intention?"

"To take you back to London. Our Queen wishes for you to spend some weeks... perhaps months... at the court."

"I cannot return." He grabbed Will's shoulders forcefully. "Please, you must understand. This is an affair of the heart. I seek freedom to let it breathe. I cannot return to the stifling fug of the court."

"You have one affair of the heart, Sir Edmund, the woman you wed four years past. There is no room for any other."

"What are you saying?"

"You will not be allowed to see your current associate, under orders of the Queen—"

"Walsingham, more like!"

"She will be returned to her former residence to continue the work she has carried out these last thirty years."

"No!" Spenser began to cry. "Not back to that cell. To the four walls and the gloom and the questions, the endless boredom. To one such as she, that is a living torture. Why do you not kill her and be done with it? Why do you not kill us both?"

The intensity of emotion in Spenser's face brought Will up sharp. "These are difficult times," he said, softening slightly, "and they require difficult measures. The war between England and Faerie has blown hot and cold, and now it is cold, though no less dangerous. What you attempt here tonight will light a fire that could burn England to the ground. You know these things. Yet you persist."

"You call me traitor, but I am just a man in love. Can you not feel what I feel? Do you have no heart?"

"In the midst of this great struggle, there is no place for ones such as you or I to consider such things—"

"Such things? They are the reason we do what we do!" Spenser wrung his hands; he appeared on the verge of falling to his knees.

"You are a poet, Sir Edmund, and I am merely a spy. All I know is lies, whispered secrets, and the caress of a blade across the throat. Now, why here, this night? Why not return to Ireland?"

"There is a crossing point not far from the hall," Spenser said with bleak resignation. "At this time of year, it would allow me to travel with her without suffering the terrible fate of those who have ventured to the Far Lands in times past."

"Will! Come quick!" Nathaniel appeared at the door to the ballroom, his face pale.

"Stay by my side, Sir Edmund," Will cautioned. "Though a peer of the realm, 'twould not be fitting to ignore the Queen's decree." Spenser bowed his head at the implicit threat and followed silently.

In the ballroom, Will and Nathaniel turned one of the massive oak tables onto its side for cover. Outside, the torches were moving. They had emerged from the tree line and were slowly advancing on the house. As the snow flared in the torchlight, figures gradually came into view. Nathaniel caught his breath.

"Can this be true?" Then: "Is it the Devil and his followers, up from hell to claim our souls?"

"Not the Devil in name, Nat." The approaching group was led by tall, strong males with golden-tinged skin and beautiful but cruel faces. They wore black and silver helmets and breastplates that looked more like tropical shells than armor. But beyond them, still half-seen, were worse things that came with hooves and scales and bat-wings and horns, writhing in shadow, eyes glowing balefully. The approaching line reached across the entire back of the hall, and from the way it curved at the fringes, Will guessed the building was surrounded.

"What, then?" When Will did not reply, Nathaniel turned to him. "You knew of these things?"

"For a long time."

"The Unseelie Court." Spenser stood to one side, his face ghostly in the gloom. "To them, humanity is like the cattle in the field. They have haunted our nightmares since Adam rose up in the Garden."

"*Hunted,* is the word, I think," Will said. "For an age, they saw us as playthings, Nat. Objects to torment, like the bears that dance in the inns on Cheapside. They would steal our children from the crib and leave misshapen things in their place. Or they would turn us into the stones that stand proud in the fields, or lure us to their land with the promise of gold, or magickal instruments." He glanced at Spenser. "Or love."

"No lure," Spenser said. "'Tis from the heart, Master Swyfte, I told you that."

"Your heart, perchance. But your paramour who has been at Her Majesty's convenience for many a year—"

"Imprisoned!"

"I would think she nurtures a little bitterness in her heart, would you not? A desire for revenge, say? To spew forth every detail of our magickal defenses that finally helped hold those foul creatures at bay?"

"No!"

Will grabbed Spenser roughly and thrust him behind the table so he could see clearly through the window. Nathaniel gasped at such rough treatment of a member of the aristocracy.

"Look deep into their faces, Sir Edmund, and tell me they would not make demands upon one of their own, even if she is as true and noble as you say. To prey upon us again, they would do anything to gain the information she holds."

Tears rimmed Spenser's eyes. "I could not bear to lose her, Master Swyfte. To you or them."

"Perhaps arrangements could be made for occasional access to her room—"

Spenser laughed bitterly. "Clearly you have never loved. 'Occasional access'? That would be more torment than reward."

"Where is she, Sir Edmund?"

"I know not. 'Struth." He smiled. "She could be standing an inch behind your shoulder and you would not know. Or she could already be away across the fields, free at last. The things she can do! It takes the breath away."

"Will?" Nathaniel's knuckles were white on the tabletop. Outside, the Unseelie Court had come to a halt just a few feet from the windows. Their torches cast a sickening ruddy glow into the hall. "The salt and herbs you spread at the entrances— it will prevent them gaining access?"

"They cannot cross it and survive."

"Then we are safe. We have but to wait till dawn."

Spenser snorted contemptuously.

"Whatever, we shall hold them at bay, Nat."

"They are so far beyond us, they are gods," Spenser said. "Old gods from the days of the Fall. Would you hold back an angel or a devil, Master Swyfte?"

"I would stand against Hell itself if needs must."

LUCY'S GUESTS HUDDLED on the floor near the walls furthest from the windows in the ballroom and the great hall. Some drank heavily to mask their fear, but most trembled and prayed. Will prowled the building in search of Spenser's Faerie Queen, but there was no sign of her in the ringing, empty bedrooms, or the vast, steaming kitchen.

"Perhaps Sir Edmund is right and she is long gone," Nathaniel ventured.

"If she were gone, our longtime tormentors would not continue to wait beyond the walls. No, Nat, she is still here, and we must find her before dawn. For when the Unseelie Court melts away, she will be gone from here, and all hope will be gone too."

"If she is as powerful as Sir Edmund says, what chance have we of finding her?"

A cry followed by a loud hubbub rose up from the rooms below. Will raced down to find several aristocrats wrestling one of their own to the flag-stones of the entrance hall. He had the glassy-eyed look of a sleepwalker.

Lucy grabbed Will's arm. "He is possessed," he gasped. "My wife noticed him, in a dream, walk-ing to the door where he proceeded to wipe away your concoction." Will turned toward the door, but Lucy continued, "We have replenished your magical barrier."

"Good. No barrier must be removed till dawn breaks. Do you hear?" Will heard the unintended lash in his voice, but Lucy did not appear to mind. He nodded anxiously.

Will inspected the glassy-eyed man who appeared to be coming to his senses. Others still pinned his arms and legs to the floor. Will motioned to them to free him. "The danger here has passed. But be vigilant in case others become pixie-led."

"The Unseelie Court controlled him?" Nathaniel asked when they had moved away to one side.

"They have the power to control weak minds for a short period," Will said.

"And unfortunately," Nat added tartly, "we are surrounded by the aristocracy."

Another cry rose up as a woman lurched toward the barrier at the fireplace in the ballroom. She was brought down in seconds.

"I fear it will be a long night, Nat."

By THREE O'CLOCK, the party guests were whimpering and crying. Every few minutes one of their number would attempt to wander off, only to be brought down in a flurry of bodies. They were growing progressively more violent as the anxiety increased. One woman cried constantly with a broken arm. Blood streamed from the noses of others.

Will grabbed Spenser and hauled him next to the fire. "My patience wears thin, Sir Edmund. You must flush out your love."

"Or what, Master Swyfte? You will murder a favored subject of the Queen?"

"No threats. But death is not the worst thing."

"Will! Come quick!" Horrified, Nat appeared at the door followed by billowing smoke and a sickening smell of cooking meat. A tall, elderly

man ran back and forth, squealing, as flames consumed him; he still clutched the lamp he had
poured over himself, his hand now welded to the
metal. Several men attempted to haul a tapestry to
stifle the blaze, but the man in his death throes was
too fast and random. Obstacles added to the chaos
as women swooned across the floor and other
guests stumbled in their crazed attempts to flee.

"They will kill us all!" one woman wailed
repeatedly.

The blazing man was eventually forced to the
ground and smothered by the tapestry, but it was
too late for him. The smoke and the stink of burning filled the hall.

"Is this it, then?" Nathaniel said. "They will
pick us off one by one?"

"They have nothing to gain by that." Will paced
back and forth, attempting to count heads. "It was
a diversion."

Lucy ran up, ashen-faced. "My wife," he said.
"In the confusion, she departed."

"I saw her," a white-haired woman said. "She
went towards the kitchens."

Will thought Lucy would faint. "They have
taken her," he gasped.

Before Lucy could plead for his wife's return,
Will was racing through the hall, with Nathaniel
close behind. The deserted kitchen was filled with
steam and the smell of Christmas spices, and from
the scullery beyond came the sound of scraping.
Hunched before the door that led to the kitchen
yard, Lucy's wife had just finished removing the

last of the salt mixture. Will vaulted the row of empty coppers, but it was too late. The door began to grind open and beyond an insane shrieking rose up that sounded like birds over the autumn fields.

Will dragged the dazed Lady Lucy back and thrust her into Nathaniel's arms. "Take her back, and put another line of the mixture beyond the kitchen door!"

"What about you?"

"They will be on us before we reach safety. I will hold them back as best I can."

Nathaniel looked aghast, but as the door swung open with a resounding crash, he took Lady Lucy's hand and ran. Will drew his sword and waited. Through the door, the dark was impenetrable and a deep, threatening silence had replaced the shriek-ing.

"Come, then, you foul and cowardly creatures," he said. "An Englishman with cold steel awaits."

The lights in the scullery and the kitchen beyond went out as one. The smell of wet fur and rotting fish filled the room. Holding his sword up, Will backed slowly across the room. A queasy dread began to rise in his stomach; he had felt it before, a by-product of the very nature of the otherworld-ly beings. They were so alien that simply being in their presence could reduce someone to tears or laughter or gibbering fear, the emotions pulled unbidden from the depths of the mind. What lay hidden before him was one of the Unseelie Court's outriders, sickeningly vicious but not as cunning or cruel as its golden-skinned masters.

Though he could see nothing in the gloom, Will was attuned to the slightest movement. The scrape of talons on the flags, the shiver of scales over the wooden table, an animal growl deep in the throat. When something lashed out toward his face, he was already responding to the shift of air currents. His sword flashed upwards, biting into meat. A high-pitched howl made his head ring. What felt like a falling tree crashed against his chest, flinging him back across the room. It opened up his shirt and the leather protector beneath, but only grazed his skin.

Rolling and springing back to his feet to avoid snapping, slavering jaws, he muttered, "Thank you, Master Dee, for the hidden armor. Your inventiveness will be my salvation."

For five long minutes, he danced in the pitch black, striking whenever he sensed his attacker near, clattering over pans and shattering crockery. He missed more blows than he hit, and it was clear his attacker was biding its time.

Finally something that felt like a vine wrapped tightly around his ankle and yanked him onto his back. The creature was on him in a second. Pinning him down with the weight of a horse, it lowered those snapping jaws to within six inches of Will's face. Its breath made his stomach churn and the scrambling effect of its nature left his thoughts fractured.

"Ah, Master Dee. One more time, I pray," he whispered. From the hidden pocket behind his belt, he managed to extricate a small pouch of tightly folded velvet. Screwing his eyes shut tight, he flicked the pouch into the face of the beast. With a searing flash, the velvet unfolded and the parchment container within burst to release the phosphorus.

Another deafening howl rang off the walls as the creature flung itself backward. "'Tis to my endless joy that some of your kind cannot abide the light," Will said as he scrambled across the scullery with the after-burn of the phosphorus still stinging his eyelids.

He pounded on the heavy oaken door to the hall. "Nat! Now would be a good time to admit your master! I have ambitions beyond being a tasty morsel."

Will heard the ferocious movement at his back as Nat threw the door wide. He bounded through and bolted it behind him as a tremendous force crashed against it. Nathaniel threw himself on to his back, but the hinges held.

"Come, I have had more than enough of these games," Will said.

Nat noted the many cuts visible through Will's ragged clothes. "You are hurt."

"Others will hurt more, trust me."

Will returned to the cowering, whimpering aristocrats where Lucy held his wife tightly to him. "For your own safety, you must retire to the bedrooms where I will lock you in," Will said.

"Never!" a man with bovine features exclaimed. "I will hear no such thing! Locked in? That will make us easy prey for those devils."

Will's hand fell to the hilt of his sword. The bovine man watched it uneasily. "You put each other at risk by roaming free. You must trust me to keep you safe."

The bovine man made to protest once more, but several hands pulled him back toward the stairs. "Look in his eyes," another hissed into his ear. "Best not to argue. Take this up with the Queen if we survive this night."

As Nathaniel herded the group up the stairs, Will called out politely, "Not you, Sir Edmund. We have unfinished business."

Hesitantly, Spenser returned to Will's side. The noises outside the house had grown louder, not just the menagerie cries but clanks and rattles as the Unseelie Court tested windows and doors or scurried up the walls to clatter across the roof.

"We have done well to survive till now," Spenser said as he eyed the torches moving past the windows. "They will not relent."

"Did you expect it to end like this when you fled London, Sir Edmund?"

"It has not ended. Not yet, at least."

"Oh, it has, Sir Edmund. For you, and your love. Sit." Will kicked a chair next to the dying fire and pressed Spenser into it; all pretense of deference for his station was now gone. Will pulled up a chair next to him.

"This is a damnable job I do, but to bemoan it is pointless. I accepted the responsibilities long ago, and there is no going back now," Will said as he looked deep into Spenser's face. "My service to

Queen and Country precludes a life of my own. I live only to keep safe England and the Queen's subjects. Do you understand?"

Spenser nodded slowly.

Will laughed quietly. "I think not, Sir Edmund. There has been no sacrifice in your life. No loves lost. No good friends killed for reasons that always appeared trivial. I miss my Jenny with all my heart, and I miss Kit, murdered all those years ago in a small room. I regret so many things. Yet here I am."

"I fail to see where you are going with this, Master Swyfte."

"I speak by way of apology, Sir Edmund, for you should know that what I do is in no way personal, or colored by malice or bitterness. Though I have suffered hard, I have given my own happiness freely for the sake of great things." Will removed a small dagger from the back of his belt, and then he gripped Spenser's right wrist forcefully. "I am about to remove your little finger, Sir Edmund. And then I will move on to the next, and the next, and so on, until you have no digits left to write your grand works. And then I will take your ears, and your nose, and then your eyes. I will leave your tongue till last in the hope that at some point you will stop me to tell me of the whereabouts of your love, and then to order her to return with me to London. You will, then, of course, be free to go."

"I am the Queen's favored poet," Spenser gasped in horror.

"And I am the Queen's right arm, for better or worse. We are small people, all of us, and our individual lives are meaningless against the continued safety of all the good men and women of this land. They deserve to sleep soundly in their beds, and to raise their families, and earn their crust, free from fear and pain of death. I would gladly sacrifice myself for that cause. And so should you."

Will placed the blade against Spenser's finger. Spenser attempted to wrench his hand free, but Will's grip was too strong.

An aroma of honeysuckle filled the room. In one corner stood the Faerie Queen, her face terrifying.

Will quickly moved the blade to Spenser's throat. "He will be dead before you can act."

Tears rimmed Spenser's eyes. "Let him kill me. You must be free!"

The agony in the Queen's beautiful face was almost too much for Will to bear. He softened his tone. "Give me your word you will cause me no physical harm and he will live."

"I so do," she replied icily.

"No!" Spenser cried. "He will take you back to that cell! You will never see the sky again—"

The Queen raised her hand and Spenser slumped unconscious. Will hid his shock. "I see in your face you will not relent," she said. "I believe you will even follow us to the Far Lands."

"I do what I must to prevent all you know falling into the hands of the enemy."

She looked out at the flickering torchlight and the constant insectile movement. "I care nothing for the demands of my people. For this war, which has dragged on for so long. I want to be free." Her gaze fell fondly on Spenser. "The only meaning I have ever found has been in his presence."

"You are their Queen, and they want you back."

She nodded. "But even a Queen must do her duty or pay the price. They would extract the knowledge from me one way or another, however much I resisted. "Who slays the gyant, wounds the beast,' that is what my love wrote, and it is true. Slay me, now, and you wound my people forever."

"You are more valuable to us alive. You have helped keep your people at bay for many a year. *My* Queen needs you."

She came over and gently caressed Spenser's neck. "If we are separated again, my love has only a few short days to live." The Queen's face remained impassive, but in her eyes Will saw raw emotion; human emotion, and this in itself was shocking. "He will die, at Westminster, on January the thirteenth. Three days later he will be interred at the Abbey, a burial fit for a true hero of the nation. And so easily is guilt assuaged," she added acidly.

"You know this?"

"I see it. There is no doubt." She smiled sadly. "Love is a terrible weapon. It can end a life as well as begin one."

Will hesitated.

"I was harsh," she continued. "I set the memory of your Jenny hard in your mind so it would haunt you every time your thoughts stilled. I wanted to show you what love truly meant."

"I know what it means," he snapped.

"How long since she died?" When he did not reply she continued, "I can remove it. Give you peace."

Will closed his eyes, and there was Jenny, smiling beneath the blue summer sky. His lips tingled from their final kiss. Her perfume filled his nose as if she were still there, close enough to take into his arms.

He opened his eyes. "Pain is the price we pay for what we do. I thank you for your gift, good lady. My Jenny will stay with me, and I will never know peace. That is how it should be. And in that I find some absolution."

Slipping the dagger back into his belt, he offered his chair to the Queen. "Dawn is not far away. Sit awhile, and make the most of this time."

With resignation, she took the chair, and Will knew from her face he had just consigned Spenser to death in a few short days.

THE HIDEOUS SOUNDS beyond the walls grew to a crescendo as dawn approached and then faded away like mist before the sun. The snow rolled out thick and heavy, now virginal as if no foot had ever touched it. As the Christmas bells tolled, Lucy and his guests descended, wringing their hands and crying their thanks to the Lord. Will watched them with contempt and then made his way to the main door where Nathaniel waited.

"Another victory for England's greatest spy," Nathaniel said with a tart smile that failed to mask his relief. "The tale of this night will only add to your fame."

"No one will speak of this again, on pain of death. The Queen will convey her wishes to her subjects herein. Let the people be content with stories of swordplay and rescues and assassinations foiled. They deserve no less."

Spenser still slept in his chair by the fire. The Queen, now hooded to hide her features, rose and came over.

Nathaniel cowered a step behind Will. "She is coming with us? Of her own free will?"

"Her love is fading and will soon be gone. There is nothing for her in this world or the next. Why should she not come?"

The Queen's eyes met Will's and an understanding lay between them. She walked silently past and across the snow to where the carriage awaited. Nathaniel followed, but Will stood on the threshold for a moment, listening to the words of his own love, seeing her smile, always dead, always alive. Only there when his thoughts were still, the Queen had said. There would be little of that. The war would continue as cold as that harsh winter, and there would be little rest for any of England's spies.

"Hurry up, Nat!" he called. "There are great works still to be done! No rest for the likes of you or I! To London, and the rest of it be damned!"

REINS OF DESTINY

A WARS OF LIGHT & SHADOWS STORY

JANNY WURTS

The fate of a land and the history of a people are not always determined by the confident hands of the great. So wrote the historians who risked death to chronicle the massacre that dethroned the clan High Kings in Third Age Year 5018. Many a brave act memorialized by their pens became lost to the next generation. Raging mobs destroyed the royal seats. They burned the old libraries to ashes. Lives and heroes' names vanished in cinders and smoke, or fell into the shadows as legend.

Some, unremarked, were never recorded to be remembered at all...

PREDAWN, ON THE day that Telmandir's streets ran red with the blood of the slaughtered, the outlying countryside stayed unaware, still blanketed under sea mist. Kayjon lay curled in the hay barn at the royal stud, jostled awake by his head groom's boot, digging the small of his back.

"Up with you! Hustle. We've got a king's rider pacing the yard. He's got a writ, demanding young stock to be driven down coast straight away!"

Kayjon sat up, blinking. Though muscled enough to strike down his oppressor, he was too mild natured, or, some said, too lazy to bother to curse in offense. He also hated to move in a hurry. He shoved back a tangle of tea colored hair and glared through a dusting of hayseeds. "The herd was thinned once." His mild frown deepened. "Which high court donkey has dispatched the writ?"

The colts they had gelded for couriers' mounts were just barely broken to saddle.

"Didn't ask!" the groom snapped. "For all I know it's a sorcerer's draft, wanting a fresh string to supply the defenders in Falwood."

"Fellowship wouldn't!" Kayjon declared. Still grumbling, he stood to his full height and stretched, cracking the joints in his sturdy shoulders. "No help, to push us for unfinished mounts. Best we have are still green." Flighty enough to toss a new rider, or cause mayhem and start a stampede. "Unsteady horses can't be expected to hold their nerve on a conjurer's battle front."

"Well then, some vaunted clansman might break his head!" The head groom sniffed, self-righteously irritable. "Since when do the high and the mighty take pause for anyone else beneath their birthborn entitlement?"

Kayjon's raised eyebrows professed no opinion. Contention of any sort seldom moved him, although these days feelings ran strong between townsmen and those designate families appointed to serve the free wilds.

"High time that somebody challenged such arrogance," the groom carped. "Counter their claim with the idiot line that's being bandied about in the taverns."

Kayjon grunted, intent on plucking the stubbed straw from his stockings before he shoved on his boots.

"Well who's to say that this vaunted war on the Mistwraith is more than a fraud to strangle the guilds from expansion?" The groom ranted on, though the man he accosted was older, and never his underling. "We've suffered from fog off the ocean for years. That, and the damned drizzle that rolls off the mountains. Could attacking vapors from Southgate make my aching joints any worse? I say not. Sun's so rare here, anyhow; blink and you miss it."

"Such rain greens the pastures," Kayjon dismissed. "Strengthens the dams, and for that, your curse is a plentiful blessing."

Whatever the great ox of a stableman thought of the nascent horror whose leaden murk threatened West Shand, no one knew. If some voices claimed the High Kings and the sorcerers were milking the towns that upheld the realm, Kayjon never took sides. He yawned through the rebellious talk and shrill fears, even as the Fellowship

Sorcerers summoned the cream of five kingdoms to bolster their warding defense. Clear nights, when their uncanny bolts of raised power streaked the southern horizon, Kayjon sipped his usual tankard of beer. He retired to his hayseed's niche in the loft, oblivious as a halfwit.

The head groom sniffed again, pitched to fresh irritation. To watch the man twitch his mussed clothing to rights and shamble his way down the ladder, who would know him as a masterful handler of horses, perhaps the best in the realm?

As appearances went, Kayjon sen'Davvis cared for nothing else beyond equine bloodlines and foaling. His creased face and placid, brown eyes displayed no alert spark of intellect, no curiosity, as he stepped from the darkened barn to meet the disruptive clan harbinger. His wide, ploughman's shoulders held nothing of tension as he sized up the argumentative knot surrounding the royal spokesman.

That one, in the flood of the stableman's lamp, was a young man furled up in a travel-stained cloak. He had tousled blond hair, fancy breeches, and a rumpled appearance that suggested a night without sleep. His pale, clean cut features might have been personable, if not for his withering arrogance. The staff who received him kept their polite distance, warned off by his stiffly crossed arms. They had little choice. The rolled parchment couched on his sleeve like a weapon bore the crown seal of Havish.

Kayjon blinked. Apparently dazzled under the light, he stuck out his hand for the document.

"Your ten best!" snapped the messenger, blind to all else but the urgency of his errand. "The fittest of the young stock that's available, along with one mare in milk on a lead rein."

"Every suckling we have needs his dam." Kayjon cocked his head. A scatter of straw winnowed out of his hair as he finished, town bred drawl poured on thick as molasses. "This spring's first filly is just four months old. I see no wisdom in rushing her." His unhurried fingers accepted the writ. He surveyed the inscription, peered askance at the seal. The knot was picked from the king's scarlet ribbon with the same air of dismissive indolence.

"Move along!" the courtier prodded, sharp edged. "You're wasting time. Even defying your crown sovereign's wishes!"

Kayjon paused. "Am I so?" His slantwise squint abandoned the effort of reading the official script. Limpid eyes sized up the courtier again, from his drawn, sweating face down to mud splashed spurs and dandyish, silver stitched boots. The stableman stated, "Not for fire and storm has the Teir's'Lornmein ever weaned any foal in this stud before solstice."

The crown rider bristled. Balked as though hit by an unfired brick, he choked down the fury that would only confound the mind of a blundering idiot.

A safe distance aside, the head groom licked his teeth. A skinny horseboy stifled amusement. Their master of horse was not roused by quick temper.

Jabbing words, even insults, were always ignored. Outsiders who tried him with shouted demands mistook such staid calm at their peril.

Where the issue at hand concerned his hoofed charges, Kayjon missed nothing at all.

He perused the writ through, while fog streamed like wool past the gateman's flickering lamp. More minutes passed while he surveyed the signature, then the treasurer's stamp on the document. While the clan rider fumed and fidgeted, Kayjon sucked in his unshaven cheeks. He stared for a moment at nothing.

Then he said, "Wake the wranglers. We're cutting out ten. The best of our three-year-olds, get them under light tack." Then, into the stunned silence that fell after a thunderclap, he gave up the stud's most reliable dam without protest. "Catch Shirah as well. Shut her colt in the paddock. Since I'll be handling her lead rein, myself, my saddle's to go on Hazard."

The scarred warhorse had been a dead champion's mount, steady with years, and strong enough to snub the rope against a broodmare pitching a tantrum.

Kayjon continued his list of instructions. "I'll want the winter blanket roll. Also the satchel we take with the field kit."

"No help goes with me!" the clansman burst in. "I've an escort waiting on the main road, and no moment to dawdle for stragglers."

"Then eat my dust, stripling," said Kayjon, unmoved, while around him, his grooms pelted, scrambling.

No one attended the courtier's protests. His arguments hammered on Kayjon's deaf ears, then became drowned in the battering noise as the string of fresh geldings arrived from the fog shrouded pasture. Boys rushed through the press, bearing halters and gear, their paned lamps casting wheeling shadows. Hooves cracked on the yard's puddled cobbles. Horses snorted and shied, while the soprano distress of the foal being weaned gave rise to his dam's frenzied whinnies.

Hazard's white nose towered over the press, a fixed bastion amid tossing heads. Kayjon directed the whirlwind activity, disheveled still from the hayloft. No one had seen him fetch his great knife. But the worn sheath was threaded onto his belt when he set foot in the stirrup and swung onto the warhorse's back. He took Shirah's lead rein from the head groom. Then a piercing whistle through his clenched teeth sent the milling, four-legged fracas clattering out of the yard.

The flushed clansman was caught flat-footed. Still howling objections, he rushed to unhitch his mount from the rail, clawed astride, and made haste to keep up.

"You can't come along!" he shouted at Kayjon, while the herd of young stock kicked up frisky heels and poured at a trot through the outer gate.

The king's master of horse did not turn his head. Fixed as a post astride the retired charger, he rode with straight back and soft hands. While the anguished mare twisted and screamed, he played her along with experienced gentleness. Then the damp darkness closed in like a shroud, and the loom of the barns fell behind. The lamps dwindled, veiled under sea mist that spat chilly rain. The band of young horses was a moving patchwork of shadow until the brightening dawn lit the dew spangled downs leaden silver.

By then, the forlorn foal's distress was past earshot, leaving the mare's neighs unpartnered. No other sound disrupted the day but the squelch of shod hooves chopping turf.

A league passed, then another. The dam's wrenching bellows found no more relief than the courtier's snarling objections. Kayjon refused to listen. He had no speech to spare any man, and no sympathies beyond his horses. Those, he bunched close with his effortless skill. The distraught dam settled, resigned to the pace. Her plaintive fretting still tore at the heart, while the muddy track wound away toward the trade road, and the pewter fog broke under shimmering sunlight.

No quiet interval lasted for long.

"Your help is not welcome!" the clansman ground on. Jaw clenched, pale and sweating, he rode in stiff fury, hunched beneath his wrapped cloak. "More than one rider will draw hostile notice. Stay stubborn, you could see a knife in your back."

"As you have, already?" Kayjon drew rein. A spoken, "Hold hard!" stopped the horses around him as he scanned the clansman's stark face. "Whatever your mission, Shirah's noise will flag down your enemies' attention much faster."

The clansman stared, sharp features now ashen. He jammed in his heels, pushed his tired mount forward, and hissed through clamped teeth. "Shut up, fellow! You don't know anything."

Kayjon shrugged. He moved Hazard out. The distracted mare gave way at his whistle. Around him, the geldings surged forward by rote, a moving torrent of brown, black, and red bay that jostled in spirited company. The roan dam twisted her neck to look back, caught firmly short by the lead rein.

"*Kiel'liess, e'Shirah,*" her handler murmured, an old tongue diminutive. His velvet tone changeless, he ignored the offense and pushed his dialogue with the young man. "I know more than you think. The writ that you bear never came from my king. Nor was this mare any part of your imposter's faked consignment."

The clansman's dark gelding jerked to a stop. Not from pique, this time: the reins had slipped loose. His haughty carriage swayed as he crumpled forward into a faint. His off balanced mount crab stepped, caught short by Kayjon's grip on the bridle. The stableman's firm arm also salvaged the rider before he pitched into the dirt.

AN UNTOLD TIME later, the unconscious clansman awakened, face down upon sun warmed grass. The stained rags of his jerkin had been tossed aside. The shirt underneath had been cut away without care for silk cuffs, stitched with seed pearls. Cooler breeze fanned across his fevered skin, while firm hands probed the crusted wound on his back. No knife, but a crossbolt, had stabbed his left shoulder blade. The quarrel was gone, largely spent when it struck, or he could not have drawn it unaided. But torn flesh and scored bone had exacted their toll. Weakness ripped out a tormented breath, as he measured his sorrowful failure.

"Fool," murmured Kayjon, warned by his flinch as he soaked the scabs free with a compress. "You're in trouble enough, son. Past time you tried talking." The leather satchel unpacked by his knee held pots of horse salve and rolled bandage. Strong remedies, and rough, but effective. Equine or human, Kayjon's field care was thorough as he dressed out the deep laceration. "You can start with why you were shot from behind, bearing twice falsified papers."

"Twice?" grunted the clansman. "The crown seal is genuine."

"The writing," snapped Kayjon, "was not penned by my liege. The postscript that appended the mare was struck in by an unschooled hand; let's not mention the bloodstain that clotted the ribbon was probably yours."

The prostrate clansman pinched his eyes shut, though the pain in his back was now easing. "If I begged for your help, would it make any difference?"

"Depends what you ask for," Kayjon replied, wiping the salve from his knuckles. "You know mare's milk is too thin to replace a wet nurse? The babe you would save cannot thrive off the breast."

"Avenger's death!" The clansman tried to shove upright, and lost, forced flat by a fist at his nape. "Did I spill my fool guts when I fainted?"

"No." Kayjon eased his grip with the same wary reflex that pinned yearling colts down for gelding. "Stay still! If you don't, then your wound cannot set. Tear my work loose and start bleeding again, I'll have to set you in hobbles. Let's not force me to ruin my knife, heating the blade for a cautery."

"You should leave," raged the clansman. His voice was too shrill. A blind man could tell he was desperate.

Kayjon's calm stayed unshaken. He sat, leaking straw like the salt of the earth. But the patience behind those honey brown eyes sorted details with harrowing clarity. "Talk first, boy," he stated. "What's gone wrong in Telmandir? Who sends a forsworn nobody onto my turf to betray the realm through a forgery?"

The injured man shuddered. "What's crown business, to you? You're not clan!" he accosted.

"No." Kayjon's admission sidestepped the antagonism. "My birthright's no fault. Not if you don't cling as another man's dupe and drive yourself silly with differences."

"These differences kill!" the hurt man lashed back. "Why should I place trust in a stranger?"

The prisoning hand snapped away as though stung. "Because I've trusted first that you're saving a child! Forsworn, or king's man, whoever you are, believe that I don't traumatize a colt's mind, or wean beforetime over politics!"

"Grace above! You're flat obstinate," the clansman exclaimed. "My 'allies' would stick your own knife in your gut. If you stay involved, you're a dead man."

"Without me, you'll not last the day on your horse," Kayjon observed, almost cheerful.

The prone man subsided, sapped beyond pride. He was not field hardened, unlike his close kin. The ascetic stamp of his ancestral breeding was scraped to flint by exhaustion.

Shame loosened his tongue, finally. Telmandir's royal seat ran red as an abattoir, and he was beyond hope already. "There's no crown to betray. Your High King is dead, lost to the Mistwraith's invasion. Word reached the crown council only last night. Treasonous factions seized on the confusion and threw the trade guilds into savage revolt."

Small surprise that high feelings should boil to a head. New petitions had been frozen for twenty-five years, with martial law and the strain of an encroaching threat driving fright and frustrations to snapping. The upset that trampled down sane credibility was the horrific swiftness of the attack.

"Enraged mobs are murdering clan folk on sight," the clansman admitted, distressed. Hoarse with agony, he continued. "A rabble stormed into the palace by dark." The ruthless account emerged in chopped speech. The heir, the royal family—all cut dead in their sheets, as the brunt of the assault hacked through the bodies of trusted retainers.

Where another man, hearing, might have interrupted, or recoiled in stark disbelief, Kayjon just listened. His weathered hands scarcely paused in their task. The grievous pause hung, and then stretched, while he repacked his remedies into the battered field satchel.

"You came and went," he stated, finally. "Saw all of this. Helped someone lay hands on the royal seal to forge today's requisition for mounts. Where did you fall out with your fellow conspirators?"

As the clansman jerked in a breath to respond, Kayjon ran over him roughshod. "No more lies! Don't pretend to me that wasn't a clan crossbolt stuck in your back as you bolted!" The spare question followed, a spear's cast to the heart. "Since you weren't struck down with the rest of your kind, why should your own try to kill you?"

"Because of my cousin, who died today because I fell in with bad company." The rest spilt in a torrent, though the stableman's style of brazen simplicity could scarcely stem the riptide of disaster.

"Unlike me, Shassa was gentle and brave. She never spurned her clan heritage." Tradition demanded an affirmation of lineage from each aspirant, before coming of age. Alone, the children who acknowledged their birthright must withstand the exalted presence of a living Paravian. The trial was no pittance. Each generation mourned its losses: sons and daughters who wasted and abandoned life, or went raving mad from the surfeit of ecstasy. "After her testing, Shassa lived at the palace as wet nurse to the infant princess."

Served Kayjon's sharp glance, the distraught young man was forced to crush outside hope. "The little one was knifed in her cradle. I'm sorry." Ragged with grief, but not for that child, whose suffering was brutally ended, his shattered account struggled onward. "Shassa bore a son in the same season. A fine babe, but no seed of her husband's."

"Gierdon," Kayjon ventured, again with that startling, razor perception.

Head spinning, the clansman affirmed the name of the Crown Successor's rakish young brother, a flirt who cut a swathe through the ladies with his wild charm and gallant's discretion.

Yet no claim of fatherhood tarnished that name, as Kayjon was also aware. "The gossips insist that one's planted no bastards."

"Shassa's child is his," the bereaved clansman whispered. "Conceived last year by the falls of Lind'stair, where Elkforest borders the lowlands."

The thick pause let in the grim understanding. That site lay deep inside the free wilds of Carith-wyr. No happening ever occurred there by chance. Paravian decree, and the wood's centaur guardians, would not sanction trespass where the flux of third lane's mystical energies crossed the confluence of the watercourse. Nor would any man who bore the blood royal join with a woman on sacred ground in pretentious ignorance.

Kayjon gave the matter his measured thought. "You have reason to think Shassa's infant still lives?"

"He could be the last s'Lornmein survivor." Teeth set, the young clansman pushed to arise. "A helpless target, if he's escaped the knives of my cousin's assassins."

Again, Kayjon laid on firm hands in restraint.

"Ath above, it's my fault!" the hurt man confessed, undone by his anguished remorse.

Kayjon was not moved. He checked the bandage, but found no fresh stains. "You can't ride, yet," he warned. The cleaned wound underneath was responding, but no stableman's compress would hold against unwise exertion. "Lie still, young fool! Spend what strength you have wisely. Tell me everything, from the beginning…"

THE ROLLING DICE clattered across the tavern's uneven trestle, bounced to a stop in a pool of spilled beer. The town-born pack of roisterers whooped and pounced. They were faceless shadows in the whiskey and smoke scented dimness, mostly clad in trade leathers, with the odd merchant scion's effete velvet and lace glittering with jewels among them. Never his own kind, yet the heedless young man played in their inimical company. The winner's pleased shout let him know he had lost. Now the stake he had promised was forfeit.

Nothing mattered. What was another binge upon rotgut gin to a man already past shaming?

Young and alive, sunk in rambunctious pleasure, he found it easy to drown out the pain brought about by his rejected birthright. Why suffer the hatred endured by his kin? Clan presence was resented in every town enclave. As if the blood-bound obligation to mediate between mankind and Athera's Paravians had ever been subject to matters of human sovereignty; or that the dangers of unshielded contact between races could be moved by competitive traders and their venal bribery.

The exalted beings that nurtured the mysteries were a force unto themselves: no man's to interpret, either for change or convenience.

The loser swallowed his fiery liquor, too merry to care that his present companions would never award him their friendship. No difference, to them, that his legacy was tainted, his heritable strength in all likelihood weakened by a sentimental progenitor swayed to marry outside of clan lineage. His family had already been devastated by the cruel price of that outbred match. At ten years of age, he had watched his weeping parents set the torch to the pyre of his older sister. The unearthly peace on the dead child's face stayed acid etched into memory.

While the cooper beside him recovered the dice, a guild henchman clothed in costly brocade cuffed his shoulder, demanding the prize. "Cat got your tongue, fellow?"

Moist hands gripped his collar, shaking him from his slouch, to an outburst of ribald laughter.

"Too soused to speak, is he?" somebody scoffed.

"Say again!" another bystander declaimed. "Four rounds of rotgut can't mask the wolf, or unmake his bitch bred, incestuous birth!"

"Yon's forest-whelped baggage!" a priggish craftsman agreed. "Slinking and sly with his word as the rest, if he isn't a spy, sent among us."

The burly cooper resorted to threats. "You gambled a promise on the last throw. Deliver the stake. Say where the Fellowship Sorcerers stash the gold they've been skimming off the king's tax shares."

That stunning presumption should have raised contempt. In fact, no such cached wealth existed. Fellowship Sorcerers had no use for coin; just as clansmen possessed no superior motive for secrecy. Well drunken, now surly, the loser slapped off the ringed fingers that badgered him. Another rebellious swallow of gin, and he gave the location they asked for. The bargain seemed just. If anyone dared put the knowledge to use, their comeuppance would rip the blustering guts out of their complacent ignorance.

The guilds and these sheltered town tradesmen might believe their petitions were spurned out of grasping tyranny. The contrary truth could never change. In fact, kingdom law would not be compromised to appease their disgruntled fury.

He drank, before bearing the unfair brunt or owning up to his shrinking cowardice. Not for him the harsh test of Paravian presence. Beside his lost sister, he had lived his mother's care taking grief for his aunt. Fetched and carried for her witless fumbling; endured through her fits of light-blinded raving, after one too many encounters with the unicorn herds that grazed Carithwyr. Few mortals were fit to engage the land's mysteries, still bearing the cloth of the flesh.

Self righteous, he wallowed in his drunken bitterness. No firsthand witness might argue the truth. The harrowing price of Paravian service cost his people altogether too much.

"Why not throw again!" he taunted, flat reckless.

But unlike other nights, the throng of boisterous dicers abandoned the table before cock's crow. The packed taproom emptied, and left him alone with a filled jack of gin and his conscience. Outside in the street, the derisive shouts of the crowd turned more than usually vicious. Prudence suggested he should saunter home. A more upright citizen would summon the watch, before the late round of brawling unrest shortened tempers and battered the innocent.

But by then, he was too far gone on cheap spirits. Sitting down, his sloshing head reeled. No question which way his preference ran: he chose the numb course toward oblivion...

HORROR STOPPED WORDS. He could not continue. The throb of his wound and the shackling distress of his own culpability strangled him.

Still, Kayjon was patient. He rested, cross-legged, a stem of plucked grass in his teeth. He looked beyond any care in the world, immersed in his guileless detachment. The fact he appeared too lazy to care made the pent up burden of horror too crushing a weight to endure.

The clansman drew breath and recounted his shock, as his buzzed stupor started to lift, and the raw urge to spew sent him staggering out of the tavern...

THE JAMMED STREET was a hideous torrent of chaos. Rioters vented their seething resentment, breaking windows and bashing in doors to lay violent hands on clan enemies. Enraged merchants threw rocks, while craft folk and women shouted for blood to redress the strictures of charter law. In terror of discovery for what he was, he hid his face in the shadow. He kept his mouth shut, shaken and hoping his town styled clothing would make him seem part of the uprising. He had not cried protest as triumphant hands slapped his shoulder, or voices reviled the names of the king's company. Had not tried to stop the unspeakable acts that raised choked off screams in the alleys. Even when his feet splashed through streaming gore, spilled by frenzied men savaging bodies: fallen liegemen, gutted defending the children torn out of the arms of their wives. The gutters were glutted. If anyone knew him, he would be butchered just as thoughtlessly as the rest. His tavern acquaintances hazed the pack on, charged with hatred and run mad on bloodlust.

Doubled with nausea, he let the rank fury of the rebellion sweep him along. Spineless fear did not think. Stranded, alone, where his unclaimed birthright threw him headlong into jeopardy, he had been jostled into the wake of the insurgents storming the palace...

FOR WHAT CAME after, words failed him, again. Some grave mistakes could never be shared; some regrets were too poisonous to swallow. As the sun beat down and fevered his skin, and the pain in his back sucked him dizzy, he wept. The cross-bolt of a kinsman had spoiled his last chance to absolve his guilt-wracked part in the wreckage. Futile despair clamped his laboring chest and made stabbing remorse into mockery.

Kayjon stirred, then flicked the grass from his lips. "I don't need to know what weighs on your heart," he said in due time, without censure. "Whatever you were, whoever you are, however you tally your failures, only one purpose counts. Something made you party to a traitor's forged writ, which you altered to include a broodmare. That's my concern, now. Those words are the ones that should be spoken."

WHERE DID LANGUAGE fail the condemned? The devastation that met him in the royal quarters had shown him cruelties beyond all imagining. The heaped dead were past mourning. Even the savaged corpse of his cousin and her infant charge paled beside the enormity of the murder enacted before his shocked eyes on arrival.

This belated defender never bore arms. A corpulent shape in a scholar's robe and wide belt, he tumbled unbreathing into the tangled mat of his beard. His pale eyes were open, but not surprised. The stab wounds that killed him thrust through his broad back while he knelt in mage trance, fingers clasping Shassa's dead hand.

Could a mere mortal even grapple the stakes, having witnessed a Fellowship Sorcerer's death? Luhaine's presence had come too late to spare the acknowledged crown family. Why had he lifted no hand in prevention? The toll of the slaughtered was beyond healing recourse. Why should a mage of such stature and power hold his staid ground as a suicide? Why let his flesh be hacked down by a mob, if not for extreme expedience?

A Fellowship Sorcerer stood guard for the land, his sealed loyalty forged by the dragons. He would strip his spirit out of breathing flesh to preserve the last royal offspring. Here was chilling proof Shassa's bastard still lived. Lone s'Lornmein survivor, the babe was left orphaned by fire and sword, an innocent thrown to a misguided rising pitched to destroy charter law. To abandon that one life along with the rest was to wreck mankind's legacy of keeping harmony with the world's mysteries...

BEFORE SUCH A crisis, Kayjon's sage outlook seemed of little use, except to lay bare the visceral depths of a scapegrace fool's sorry conscience.

"I had to turn coat," the shamed clansman blurted. "The faction that's risen to end the king's justice learned about Gierdon's bastard. I don't know who talked, or how they found out. But the dice throw I lost was no act of chance. I never imagined when I yielded the path to the meeting glade that Shassa's twelve year-old sister fled there to shelter the babe until help came. I learned of my folly when my gambling companions cornered me and demanded I bear their false writ to your stable. I played along. What choice did I have? The brutes have three palace pages held hostage. Those children will die if I fail to deliver the mounts to give chase before noon."

"No broodmare was ever a part of the plan for an infant that's slated for murder," Kayjon said.

How plain words could cut to the core of a failure. The injured man shivered. "Merciful Ath! So I nursed a fool's hope? I thought to hide the dam in a thicket. If I served the conspirators with untrained mounts, luck might grant me the moment to circle ahead and spirit their quarry to safety. Find Gierdon's son ahead of the killers. Then ride hell-bent, and sustain him on mare's milk inside the free wilds, upon sacred ground."

Kayjon's quiet regard absorbed what that meant: that a clansman who had turned his back on his legacy now dared to attempt his deferred initiation. If he braved the unshielded face of the mysteries, he might save a newborn child and, perhaps, redeem his disgrace and recoup the realm's threatened succession.

Two men matched glances, that moment in time, and met fate in the eyes of the other.

First to speak, Kayjon warned, "If you ride on for the sake of those palace hostages, you have to realize they're already dead. Worse, your wound will tear open. The trauma will kill you. Already, you have lost too much blood. If you abandon the victims and strive for the baby alone, without proper rest for recovery you aren't going to live to see sunset."

The clansman swallowed. "The killers will have me long before then. You need to be gone when that happens."

Kayjon said nothing. The clipped gestures he used as he secured his satchel suggested he was not complacent.

"You're not thinking of sacrifice!" the wounded man gasped. "Take the mare for the royal bastard yourself? Ath above! That's too dangerous for one not birth gifted! Hear me, I beg you! You won't survive whole. I tell you, even the sorcerer's stripped spirit can't possibly spare you from raving insanity."

Kayjon's practical nature stayed fixed. "Luhaine's shade can't see a starving babe fed."

"Exposure to such power will burn out your mind," the clansman insisted in agonized argument. "Derange your life, as you lose your purposeful will to the blazing surfeit of ecstasy."

"Then that risk must be taken." Kayjon arose, brisk as he attended the final details. "You asked for green horses to hamper pursuit? Then I can further that effort. A saddlecloth wrinkled in just the right place will make even a steady mount cranky. Here and there, a torn stitch in the tack could result in a rider's rough spill in the roadway."

Too quickly, the stableman had his field kit strapped behind Hazard's cantle. No motion was wasted, and no breath expended in empty assurances. He helped the prostrate clansman to stand. The same quiet strength and unflagging character boosted his wounded bulk into the saddle.

"I don't know your kin name," Kayjon said at last. That rare accolade of respect had been earned as he settled his best horse's reins into another man's unsteady grasp.

A headshake denied him. "If the s'Lornmein crown lineage lives on, that will become my life's legacy. And yours. The babe can't be rescued without you."

Kayjon slapped the younger man's knee in acknowledgment. Then he whistled for the gelding that bossed the string, and tied that one's lead rein to the clansman's saddle. "As you asked for the mare, so you will go in grace."

The dam's halter in hand, Kayjon mounted Hazard. The clansman returned a stiff nod in salute. Once again, he divulged the secret pathway that led to the King's Glade in Lithmere.

The pair parted company with no backward glance: one to ride herd over ten head of geldings and spend his life to buy a delay; the other to challenge the heart of the mysteries, guiding the milch mare to salvage a prince.

TORNADO OF SPARKS

James Maxey

VENDEVOREX STOOD BEFORE the trio of sun-dragons, juggling a white ball of fire between his foretalons playfully.

"All fire is subservient to my will," he said, allowing the flaming orb to fade into a coal-black lump, which he crumbled to dust. Though he didn't mention it, light was also Vendevorex's plaything. The wizard bent light in a dozen subtle ways to enhance his appearance. The sky-blue scales of his hide glistened like wet gemstones. The diamonds that studded his wings cast rainbows with every movement. The silver skullcap that adorned his brow was wreathed in a shimmering halo. Vendevorex hoped to impress the king by looking more like a being from another world than a humble sky-dragon.

"Your so-called magic has an odor to it," said Zanzeroth, the sun-dragon who stood behind the king. "It reminds me of the scent of a storm cloud heavy with lightning. It smells like... trouble."

Zanzeroth was the king's most trusted advisor. Vendevorex knew it was vital to win him over. "Your senses are finely tuned, noble Zanzeroth," Vendevorex said, in a flattering tone. "Only a few dragons are refined enough to detect the aroma of true magic. Of course, magic *is* trouble... trouble that may be directed against the king's enemies."

Though he delivered his comment to Zanzeroth, Vendevorex carefully watched King Albekizan for a reaction. King Albekizan was a giant bull of a sun-dragon, a creature who, even resting on the azure silk cushions of his throne pedestal, looked like the embodiment of raw power. Sun-dragons were the unquestioned pinnacle of the food chain, beasts with forty-foot wingspans and toothy jaws that could bite a horse in two. With symmetrical features and muscles that seemed sculpted beneath a hide of ruby scales, Albekizan looked down on Vendevorex with the assured poise of a creature confident he could kill everyone in the room.

Vendevorex was not even half the size of the king. It was the height of arrogance for him to seek admittance as a peer in the court. Sky-dragons had places of respect in the kingdom, as scholars and artists, but they were seldom found in positions of true authority. Vendevorex knew it would be a challenge to convince the king of his value. So far, he'd demonstrated abilities that he was certain the king would find useful in a personal wizard. He'd turned invisible, he'd populated the room with doppelgangers of himself, and he'd conjured fire from thin air. Albekizan had greeted these feats with a look of indifference, even boredom.

Vendevorex looked toward the king's two companions. Zanzeroth, a dragon over twenty years the elder of the king, was looking at him with suspicion. To the left of Albekizan sat Kanst, the king's younger cousin, who was openly scowling. Vendevorex had studied all the residents of the palace invisibly before requesting an audience with the king. He knew that persuading either Zanzeroth or Kanst would lead to acceptance by Albekizan. Alas, all the sun-dragons were proving more skeptical than he'd hoped.

"Other conjurers have come before us," Zanzeroth said. "They attempt to dazzle us with mirrors and juggling and dare to call it magic. What makes your claims any different?"

"Better mirrors," Vendevorex said, as he willed his eyes to appear as dark pools full of stars. "I have journeyed to the abode of gods and stolen their secrets."

"Your talk of gods falls on deaf ears, little dragon," Kanst said. "What use has the mighty Albekizan for your illusions?"

"Illusions?" said Vendevorex. He spread his wings wide, to show that he had no hidden devices. It was true that most of his magic was mere illusion, but he possessed genuine power as well, the ability to manipulate matter with but a touch. "You misjudge me. The king is indeed mighty. I, however, am master of an unseen world. I hold power over fire, and wind, and stone. I am no simple conjurer. Behold."

Vendevorex leaned down, allowing a wreath of white flame to envelop his foretalon. He touched it to the marble floor and melted his talon-print into the stone. He stood up, the outline of his claws in the marble still spitting jets of flame.

He looked the king once more in the eyes. "You sit there," he said, aware of the arrogance in addressing the king so brusquely, "the proudest dragon ever to have lived. Your pride is well earned. In faraway lands I have heard of you, Albekizan. I have heard of your hunger for power. What I have done to this marble tile I could do to a mountain. There is no fortress your enemies can hide within that I could not burn to ash. I am power, Albekizan. And for a price, I will be a power at your command."

To his relief, Albekizan looked more intrigued than angry at his bold display.

"What price?" the king asked, in a deep, rich voice. It was the first time Albekizan had spoken to him.

"An appointment to your court," said Vendevorex. "A home within the confines of your castle, and a position of authority as your chief consultant on all matters of magic."

Zanzeroth, sounding skeptical, asked, "With your boasts of power, why would you desire these things?"

"Noble Zanzeroth," Vendevorex said, with a slight bow. "When I say I have been to the home of the gods, I do not speak metaphorically. I have traveled outside the ordinary world to gain my knowledge. The price I have paid is great; I can no longer return to the land of my birth. My choice is now to wander the world, an eternal stranger, or seek a new home. King Albekizan is the mightiest of earthly dragons. It is only natural that I desire to serve him; he is the only dragon alive who can grant me the wealth and status that I feel are my rightful due."

"Why would you need wealth?" Zanzeroth scoffed. "Instead of defacing the king's floor, couldn't you have turned the marble to gold? And those diamonds in your wings... are they mere glass?"

"I measure wealth not in gold and jewels," said Vendevorex. "There is also the wealth that comes from being valued in one's work and knowledge. Using my powers in service to the king would be a position from which I would no doubt be challenged daily."

This answer seemed to please Albekizan. His eyes brightened as he said, "I can think of many uses for a dragon who may become invisible."

"Such as a spy?" Kanst asked. Kanst was a dragon nearly as big as Albekizan, even more heavily muscled, but with a certain blockiness to his features that made him look less intelligent than his companions. "How do we know you aren't one? Or an assassin in league with the Murder God?"

"If I were a spy, would I not simply linger in your midst invisibly to learn your secrets?" Vendevorex said, deciding that Kanst's question was too dangerous to leave unanswered. "And if I were an assassin—"

"If you were an assassin you could have killed us unseen," said Zanzeroth. "Or made the attempt, at least."

Vendevorex tried to judge from the older dragon's tone whether he was leaning in support of him, or simply annoyed by Kanst's poor reasoning.

"No," said Zanzeroth, narrowing his gaze. "You are no assassin. You are, however, a liar, to come here and speak to us of gods. I do not know the source of your 'magic,' but I know a falsehood when I hear one."

"Lie or not," the king said, glancing toward the imprint in the marble, "I am intrigued by your abilities. You could burn a stone castle?"

"I call the flame I control the Vengeance of the Ancestors," said Vendevorex. (In truth, until that exact second, he'd only called it "flame," but he'd made the snap decision that his presentation needed a little dramatic flare.) "There is nothing the Vengeance will not consume, and it responds to my will alone."

The king rose and moved toward the far end of the hall, which was open to a night sky full of stars. He spread his broad wings and said, "I'd like a larger demonstration. I'd also like no further harm done to my floor. Follow me."

The king leapt into the air. Winds swept the hall, buffeting Vendevorex, as Zanzeroth and Kanst joined the king, beating their enormous wings. Vendevorex, unsure what the king had in mind, turned invisible. He found the large leather satchel he'd hidden behind a pillar. This bag contained all his worldly goods, including the true source of his powers. He opened the satchel and dipped his right foretalon into a jar of silver powder, coating it with a fresh dose of the miraculous stuff. The dust immediately vanished into his hide. Then, he closed the jar, slung the satchel over his back, and gave chase to the king.

The head start the sun-dragons possessed proved little challenge for Vendevorex to eliminate. Though sky-dragons lacked the sheer physical power of sun-dragons, they were much faster and more graceful in the air. Invisibly, Vendevorex drew to a glide behind the royal party. When the sun-dragons flapped their wings, it sounded like gusts from an enormous bellows. Vendevorex's own flight was utterly silent as his sensitive wings rode on the turbulence left in the trio's wake.

Kanst flew directly beside Albekizan, which came as no surprise to Vendevorex. In his days of surveillance, the roles of the king's closest companions had become evident. Kanst possessed an arrogance that came from knowing he was related to the king by blood. Zanzeroth followed behind the king, perhaps slowed a bit by his age. But as the elder dragon looked back over his shoulder, searching the sky, it soon became apparent that the true reason Zanzeroth lagged behind was to watch the king's back. From what Vendevorex had learned, Zanzeroth didn't boast any sort of royal lineage. He'd lived the earliest years of his life feral, a wild young dragon surviving purely on wits and instinct, before being discovered by Albekizan's father. The old king had treated the task of civilizing the savage beast Zanzeroth had been as an obsessive hobby. It was said within the halls of the castle that the civilizing hadn't fully taken. To this day, Zanzeroth was respected as the most effective hunter in all the kingdom, the only dragon who dared to best the king during recreational hunts. Zanzeroth was, at heart, an untamed creature ruled by instinct, and Vendevorex knew that the elder dragon's instincts were not to trust him.

Albekizan led them to a nearby field of corn. It was late summer. The night was still sultry with the day's heat. Corn stalks fluttered in great waves as the wind of the king's wings beat down upon them. He was coming down for a landing near a stone cottage. Vendevorex had spotted the place during his flights around the castle and knew something of its history, as the residence had been discussed by the king's tax collectors. Until recently, the cottage had sat empty for years; the king's soldiers had killed the former residents for reasons Vendevorex had yet to discover, and in the aftermath no humans claimed the abandoned property. That had changed in the spring, however, when a new human family had moved in and begun repairs. Apparently they were migrants, with no true claim to the place. Within the king's bureaucracy, there was a debate as to what was the wiser course—to allow the humans to return the farm to productivity, or to kill them for their presumptuous use of the king's property.

The king tilted his wings up to use the air as a brake and landed before the cottage, allowing his shadow to loom over the place. The moon was a dim sliver; the stars were cottoned by the humid air.

As the sun-dragons landed, Vendevorex swooped in front of them, coming to a gentle landing. He allowed his invisibility to fade away and gave a deep and dramatic bow of greeting. With his unseen and silent approach, it looked as if he'd known the destination and had been waiting here all along.

"This cottage is no castle," Zanzeroth said.

"But its walls are made of stone," said the king. "Since I've chosen it on a whim, there is no way our would-be wizard can have prepared the structure with any trickery."

"Clever," said Kanst.

"You'd like me to burn this hovel?" Vendevorex asked. "It's hardly a test at all. I'd prefer to demonstrate on something more impressive." Vendevorex instantly regretted saying the words. He could see a look of skepticism flash through the king's eyes. "Still, if it is your will, I will obey."

He turned toward the cottage. It wasn't much to look at. The walls were slightly off plumb, and the roof no doubt leaked in a dozen places. The whole structure was tiny by the standards of sun-dragons, and far too cramped for even a sky-dragon. Though he was no taller than most humans when he stood on his hind claws, if he stretched his wings they would reach from end to end of the dwelling. While the cottage was fashioned from thick slabs of river rock, the walls were so badly constructed that, from many yards away, Vendevorex could hear a man snoring within. He pondered if he should do something to alert the humans. Living in such poverty was bad enough; to die without warning on the whims of a king only added to the unfairness. Then, looking back at Albekizan, Vendevorex steeled himself.

He turned to face the stone dwelling. He concentrated, forming giant orbs of glowing plasma around his foreclaws. With a thrust, he threw the flames against the stone. Instantly, the walls ignited in bright orange gouts of flame. Seconds later, a woman began to scream.

"Step back," Vendevorex said to the king as he walked away from the cottage. "The smoke created when the Vengeance burns certain materials is poisonous."

"Poison is the tool of the Murder God," said Kanst.

"The poison is a necessary result of the basic chemistry," said Vendevorex. He worried for a brief instant that he'd revealed too much, then decided that the word "chemistry" was probably as strange and open-ended to the sun-dragons as the word "magic."

Within the cottage a man's screams joined the woman's. There was the sound of frantic activity, until, after only a few brief seconds, both voices trailed off into hoarse coughs before falling silent. The smoke already affected them. At least they'd be dead before the flames ate their flesh.

"I thought you could control this," said Zanzeroth. "Yet your own magic creates poison fumes you fear?"

"I have no fear of poison," said Vendevorex. "The flames are completely under my control. It is only your safety I have in mind. Flames create their own wind. The smoke moves in ways that are difficult to predict."

"I am pleased to see the flames eating the stone," said Albekizan. "Still, if the poisons would endanger my own armies..."

"My king, you will no longer need armies to lay siege to a castle. The heat and smoke are no hindrance for me. Watch."

Vendevorex walked back to the cottage. The flames were spreading aggressively across the roof. The wooden door was completely ablaze. With a wave of his wings, Vendevorex caused the flames eating the door to flicker out, leaving only glowing embers on the edges of the blackened wood. Before he could open the door he noticed a sudden movement in the field behind the castle. There was an old barn perhaps twenty yards away.

Something moved near it. It was difficult to make out clearly through the haze of smoke, but it looked like a human running from the barn toward the field of corn. A man, if he wasn't mistaken, or at least an older boy.

Vendevorex looked back, wondering if the king had seen the human. Albekizan was focused solely on him. Only Zanzeroth seemed to be gazing beyond the house. Still, he'd been charged with the mission of burning the cottage, not killing every last human on the property. He decided it was best to carry on as if he'd seen nothing.

He pressed forward, reaching out to touch his foretalon to the charred wooden door, which disintegrated at his touch. He stepped into the burning room, the smoke pushed before him in a perfect arc by the bubble of fresh air he gathered. He moved further into the cottage, his heart sinking as he looked upon the ragged possessions of the family that dwelled within. It was the lot of humans in the kingdom of Albekizan to live modestly, but this family had been especially impoverished. He moved into the next room, at the rear of the cottage. The flames had yet to reach this far, though the heat made the air shimmer and the smoke from the other room rolled across the floor in a thick black cloud. Vendevorex's eye was caught by something rising above the smoke—a crib. He crept closer, afraid of what he would find. His worst fears proved true. There was a baby in the crib, a girl if he judged correctly, though human infants mostly looked the same to him. She lay still as death. Then, as he drew closer, she coughed. Though still alive, she was pale and looked weak. He reached out and placed his claws on her chest. The silver powder he'd covered his foretalon with swirled from his skin, coating the infant, before vanishing into her flesh. He closed his eyes in concentration as he looked inside her body. She'd inhaled trace amounts of smoke, knocking her unconscious, but had suffered no permanent damage. Now that she was within the circle of clean air that followed him, her breathing grew more comfortable.

He decided that the only merciful thing to do was kill her.

He placed his foretalon over her mouth.

Her tiny fist moved reflexively in her sleep to grasp the claw that lay against her cheek.

He changed his mind. Killing this child would do nothing to bring him favor in the king's eyes. He scooped her up and placed her into his leather satchel. She was bundled tightly in a gray, fibrous blanket. She looked, atop the jars and pouches and notebooks he carried, more like a neatly packed provision than a passenger.

He willed the stones around him to burn even faster and headed toward the front door once more. He moved his wings to fill the doorway with smoke to make his exit more dramatic. He stepped into the doorway just as the walls began to moan and crack. The whole structure collapsed behind him, filling the night sky with a tornado of sparks. Vendevorex strode forward confidently, emerging from the wall of smoke unscathed. Albekizan looked pleased with the drama of the moment. Even Kanst seemed impressed. Only Zanzeroth still wore a scowl.

"I trust this has answered any doubts you had as to my power?" Vendevorex said.

"Sire," said Zanzeroth, leaning in close to the king before he could answer. "We should consult further on this matter."

Albekizan glanced toward the older dragon, looking ready to argue, then nodded in agreement.

"Return to my court tomorrow at midday, wizard," said Albekizan. "You shall have my decision then."

Albekizan leapt into the air and headed toward the castle. Kanst stood for a moment, studying the mound of burning stone, before turning to give chase to the king.

Zanzeroth lingered, his red scales even redder in the flickering light. He drew close to Vendevorex and said, in a low hiss, "I don't know who you really are or what you really want. The only thing I know with certainty is that you don't smell right. To be blunt, I wouldn't enjoy the atmosphere of the castle with you in it. Do us both a favor… fly far from here tonight, little dragon."

Vendevorex kept his face expressionless as Zanzeroth turned away and launched himself with a mighty down thrust of his wings.

As the king and his entourage vanished into the night, Vendevorex opened his satchel and removed the baby. Laying his foretalons upon her once more, he used his abilities to mend the small damage that had been done to her lungs. The girl responded by drawing a deep breath, then unleashing a loud wail. She continued to scream for the next half hour as Vendevorex moved to the barn in search of any other survivors. He found no one. He waited a while longer, thinking that soon neighboring humans might turn up to investigate the blaze. Unfortunately, anyone who had seen the fire must also have seen the sun-dragons. No one came.

Vendevorex cradled the baby and stroked her tiny pink cheek, trying to comfort her. It didn't work. She cried all the louder. He thought for a moment about simply leaving her in the barn. Sooner or later, someone would come and discover her. Then, he sighed and placed her into his satchel once more. He moved to investigate the cornfield and discovered footprints and a trampled stalk near the area where he'd spotted the human. He flapped his wings and lifted skyward. From above the cornfield, his sharp eyes could spot the bent and broken stalks that marked the path the human had taken. He swooped across the corn, arriving soon at the distant edge of the field, which was bordered by a large stream. As he circled the area, searching for any signs of movement, the baby's cries fell to a few half-hearted sobs. Seeing no one, Vendevorex landed gently on a well-worn pathway that ran along the stream. To his relief, the baby settled into silence.

He searched the site, at last finding the scrape of a footprint on the sandy pathway. The object of his pursuit had headed toward the forest that lay upstream. Vendevorex remained on the ground to follow the trail, keeping a keen eye for further clues. The path was apparently popular with humans and cattle. He wasn't certain he was following the right footsteps until he found a cow patty that had been deposited at some point the previous day. The whole of the patty was swarmed by beetles, save for a flattened section at the edge, where a foot had stepped quite recently. Beetles hadn't yet disturbed the newly exposed dung.

Soon, he found himself at the forest's edge. It was dark beneath the trees. Spotting footprints was no longer possible. He moved ahead, following the path, feeling certain that the human wouldn't be able to see any better than he could and was unlikely to stray far from the stream.

At last, in the distance, he heard the sound of someone crying. He turned invisible and crept forward. Seated by the stream, on the thick root of a tree, a teenage boy sat, his arms limp at his side, his face twisted in grief. No doubt, this was the person he sought.

Remaining invisible, he asked, "What's your name, boy?"

The boy stopped crying and snapped to attention. He jumped up, brandishing a fist-sized rock. "Who's there?" he said, his voice trembling, with fear, or rage, or both.

"I asked first," Vendevorex said.

"I'm Ragnar," the boy said, turning toward Vendevorex's voice, then twisting his head further, searching the shadows.

"Ragnar, I mean you no harm," Vendevorex said.

"Where are you?" Ragnar said. "Who are you?"

"A friend," said Vendevorex. "At least, not an enemy. I'm here to return something you value."

Ragnar spun around, raising his rock to throw, then spun around again, still seeking a target. "Are you one of them?" he demanded. "A dragon?"

"That isn't important," said Vendevorex. "Did you live in the cottage in the cornfield? Were you in the barn?"

"You *are* a dragon," Ragnar snarled, his face becoming a mask of rage. "You killed my family!"

"Did you have a sister? An infant?" Vendevorex said, keeping his voice calm, swaying his long neck to make his location harder to pinpoint.

"Jandra?" Ragnar said.

"She's alive," Vendevorex said. "I've brought her to you. Put down the rock. Turn around. I will place her at your feet. I will also leave diamonds. They cannot replace what was taken from you tonight, but they will help you flee here and begin a new life elsewhere."

"This is a trick!" Ragnar screamed, lunging toward Vendevorex's voice. With a violent grunt, he hurled the rock. Vendevorex easily leapt aside. The sudden jolt caused Jandra to start crying.

Ragnar picked up another rock from the stream bank and threw it toward the sound. Vendevorex jumped from its path, but it was followed instantly by another, then a third.

"Stop!" he cried out. "You'll injure your sister!"

"I don't care!" Ragnar cried, finding a large, dead branch near the path. He lifted it with both hands and wielded it like a club. He chased toward the sound of the crying baby. Vendevorex ducked and darted among the trees as Ragnar shouted, "I'll kill you! I'll kill every damn dragon in the world!"

Ragnar swung his makeshift club with such force it splintered against a tree. The end of the club spun through the air and caught Vendevorex on the cheek. He let out a hiss of pain and Ragnar charged toward the sound. He dodged away at the last second, then, with a flap of his wings, vaulted to the other side of the stream.

"Calm yourself!" he shouted. "Think of your sister!"

"I'm thinking of your blood!" Ragnar screamed, twisting and turning, searching both for the source of Jandra's cries and a new weapon. He spotted a sharp stone on the ground and lifted it, then eyed the far side of the stream. Vendevorex took a deep breath. Ragnar wasn't an adult, but he was still big and in good health, a farm boy with a body chiseled by labor. Judging from the force with which Ragnar had splintered his own club, he could no doubt injure Vendevorex with a lucky blow, or kill Jandra with an unlucky one.

Then, to his relief, Ragnar made the mistake of stepping into the stream, wading into knee-deep water. Calmly, Vendevorex leaned forward and allowed the dust from his talon to fall over the stream. With a thought, he nudged the water into a simple change of state. Instantly, the stream turned to ice, trapping Ragnar.

Ragnar gave a cry of alarm, then began to beat the ice around his legs with the rock he carried.

"You'll injure yourself if you're not careful," Vendevorex said. Invisibly, he loosened his satchel and removed the screaming infant. She was still swaddled in the blanket, a neat, if noisy, bundle. He laid her on the ice, placed three diamonds on her chest, and shoved her toward her brother.

"Take care of her," Vendevorex said.

The bundled infant slid across the ice until she came to a halt against Ragnar's knee. Ragnar looked down, confused, seeming to calm a bit. Then, he raised the rock over his head.

"I'll take no gift that's been touched by a dragon!"

He plunged the sharp stone toward the infant's head.

It never connected. From nowhere, a thick red tail flickered out and knocked the stone from Ragnar's hand. In a flash, the tail whipped back, catching the boy full in the face. He fell backward, still frozen at the knees, completely unconscious.

Vendevorex looked up. In the tree that towered over the stream, Zanzeroth crouched. Vendevorex had never seen a sun-dragon resting in a tree before. Their size and weight normally made them unsuitable for such perches. Zanzeroth moved gracefully as a cat as he leaned down and swooped up the infant with his foreclaw.

He brought the screaming infant to his face. The baby looked tiny against his giant jaws. He could devour her without bothering to chew. He sniffed her, the delicate white feathers around his snout fluttering like smoke. The baby instantly grew wide-eyed and silent.

"She's soiled herself," Zanzeroth said. "She'd probably be quieter if you kept her dry."

In the dark, his eyes seemed to glow with an emerald flame as he turned toward Vendevorex and offered the baby to him. Vendevorex took the infant and clutched her to his chest.

"I can't believe he would have killed his own sister," Vendevorex said.

"Human's aren't like us," Zanzeroth said. "They are beasts driven by primitive urges they cannot fully control. Fear, anger, hatred, lust... they have the same emotions as dragons, but lack our ability to keep them in check. They are all instinct and no reason."

"I've known humans who would prove you wrong," said Vendevorex.

Zanzeroth shook his head. "Think what you wish, but I've hunted humans for many decades. A good hunter understands his prey with a certain... intimacy."

"Why did you save the baby?" Vendevorex asked.

"Why did you?"

Vendevorex sighed. "I'm not a creature who enjoys needless killing. I killed her parents only as a consequence of proving myself to your king. But I do not regard humans as prey. I saw no need for her to die when there was a possibility of reuniting her with a family member."

"I knew you had seen the boy flee the barn," said Zanzeroth. "Your body language betrayed you. Yet, I was curious when you didn't mention it. And when you exited the house, I smelled the baby in your satchel. Again, you kept it secret. I've followed you to find out why."

"I had no idea you were following me," Vendevorex said.

"I am the most experienced stalker in all the kingdom," said Zanzeroth. "Your invisibility doesn't much impress me."

Vendevorex once more placed Jandra into his satchel. By now, the water of the stream had backed up over the dam of ice and was flowing over its surface, half submerging Ragnar, who was still out cold. Vendevorex waded forward carefully. The ice beneath the water was slick; he dug his sharp claws in for traction. He reached Ragnar and melted the ice around his legs, then dragged him to the riverbank.

"I'd as soon not see him drown, or lose his feet to frostbite," Vendevorex said.

"You're going to let him live?"

"Why not?" said Vendevorex. "He's more a threat to himself than to me. Still, I'm not going to leave Jandra with him. I'll have to care for her a bit longer, I'm afraid, until I can find a suitable home."

"The king wouldn't look kindly upon this softness, wizard," said Zanzeroth.

"I will kill for the king when I am his subject and obeying his orders," said Vendevorex. "For now, I am a free dragon. I will be as soft or as hard as my conscience commands."

Zanzeroth slinked down from the tree, standing next to Vendevorex, drawing up to loom over him.

"Within the castle, the king keeps hundreds of humans as slaves. They do the menial labor of the place, the cleaning and cooking. You can find someone there who will care for the infant."

"As long as I've saved her life," said Vendevorex, "I'd prefer not deliver her into slavery. And besides, what does it matter how many humans live within the castle? You've told me to stay away."

Zanzeroth stared at Vendevorex for a long moment. "Use your own judgment as to the baby's fate. It isn't our tradition to hunt human females, so I honestly do not care what her eventual destiny may be. And yet wizard... you should know I have something in common with this child, no matter how improbable that may seem."

"Oh?"

"I, too, was an orphan. I endured many years on my own, but I have no doubt I would never have survived to adulthood had I not been shown kindness by a dragon who had every right to kill me.

Albekizan's father had compassion; Albekizan does not. It would be useful, perhaps, to have a voice in the king's court willing to stand for mercy."

"I can be that voice," said Vendevorex.

Zanzeroth nodded. "Perhaps you can." Then he said, "Kanst doesn't trust you. I saw him back at the cottage after you left, poking through the ash."

"Do I need Kanst's trust?" Vendevorex said.

"No," said Zanzeroth. "The king likes his cousin's company but is wise enough not to listen to his counsel."

"The king listens to you, though," said Vendevorex.

"On occasion," said Zanzeroth. "Come to the castle at the appointed time. I can tell the king leans in your favor. I will not raise my voice in opposition."

"Thank you, Zanzeroth," Vendevorex said.

"Save your thanks, wizard," Zanzeroth said, turning away. "I still don't like the way you smell. My instincts tell me that the day will come when I'll be the dragon that guts you."

Vendevorex wasn't certain what to say to that.

Zanzeroth stepped over the body of the unconscious boy and glanced back at Vendevorex. "Fortunately, unlike our sleeping friend here, I'm a being whose reason is in control of his instinct. As long as you don't give me an excuse to kill you, you may yet die in your sleep."

The giant dragon leapt toward the sky, his massive wings knocking aside branches as he rose into the night.

Vendevorex let out a long, slow breath. He looked down at the little girl in his wings, who stared up at him with big dark eyes. "Perhaps he's right," he said to her. "Perhaps, in this kingdom, there aren't any humans who've been raised to value reason over instinct."

Her mouth moved into what he interpreted as a smile. He stroked her pale cheek with the back of his scaly talon.

"At least," he said, gently, "not yet."

GRANDER THAN THE SEA

T. A. PRATT

"DR. HUSCH IS here," Rondeau said, stepping into Marla Mason's cluttered office, where she sat poring over an eye-watering pile of expense reports from her spies abroad.

"Who's Elmer Mulligan, and why did our agent Brandywine spend $400 buying him lap dances at a strip bar in Canada?" she said, brandishing a piece of paper.

"I think Mulligan is the one who did that thing for us in Newfoundland," Rondeau said, shutting the door behind him and knocking over a pile of true-crime paperbacks with the covers ripped off. "You know, with that guy who had the ice palace?"

"Right," Marla said, rubbing her eyes. "I guess a lap dance is a small price to pay. Grizzly-polar bear hybrids are weird enough without some lunatic uplifting them to human intelligence. And did you see *this?*" She held up a flattened piece of seaweed, scrawled over with luminous green ink. It dripped briny water on the carpet. "It's from the Bay Witch. I can't even read it. Get somebody to go talk to her, will you?"

"Sure," Rondeau said. "Like I said, Dr. Husch is here, from the Blackwing Institute. She says it's urgent. But, ah, if you want me to keep her entertained for a while, I don't mind—"

Marla wrinkled her nose. "Rondeau, she must be a hundred and fifty years old."

He shrugged. "She only looks about thirty. Don't be ageist. And I've heard, when she was younger, she used to be quite the party girl."

"Yeah, I've heard that, too." Rondeau didn't know a fraction of the weirdness and debauchery in Husch's past, but Marla did, because the Felport archives went back a long time. "Is she here to beg for money?"

Rondeau shrugged. His attention was already wandering, and he riffled through a pile of back issues of *The Instigator,* which Marla still needed to comb for secret messages in the personals. On days like this she wondered why she'd ever agreed to become chief sorcerer. She was made for creeping around in shadows and kicking her enemies in the knees, not shuffling paperwork. Maybe she should hire an assistant. Rondeau was useful for many things, but alphabetizing wasn't one of them.

"Send her in," Marla said, wishing, not for the first time, that she had a better office for meeting people. When she had advance warning, she used her consigliere Hamil's office, all sleekness and modernity. But her working office, above Rondeau's nightclub, was an explosion of unfinished business, furnished with shelves, desks, and chairs scrounged from curbsides.

Rondeau went out, and Dr. Husch entered. "Leda," Marla said, leaning over her desk and extending a hand to shake. "Always a pleasure, assuming you aren't here to pester me for more funding."

Dr. Husch was only five and a half feet tall, rather shorter than Marla, but her presence was considerable. She had the body and face of a classical nymph, which she tried to de-emphasize, her curves restrained by a dark tailored suit jacket and skirt, her platinum-blonde hair pulled back in a severe bun. Her heels, though, were so high Marla felt unbalanced just looking at them. "The institute could always use more money," Husch said. "Since we *are* the only thing preventing the destruction of the world. But, no, that's not why I'm here. One of our inmates would like to see you."

Marla raised an eyebrow. "I'm not in the habit of visiting criminally insane sorcerers, Leda."

"It's Roger Vaughn, and he's quite insistent. I take him seriously."

Marla shook her head. "Vaughn? The name doesn't mean anything to me."

"He's the one who sank the ferry in the bay a hundred years ago, killing everyone aboard."

"Ah." That was one of the big disasters in Felport's history, though the details escaped her memory. "He must be getting on in years."

"Some of us do not age as rapidly as others," Husch said, without apparent irony. "More importantly, Vaughn has been in total seclusion since the disaster, without any contact with the outside world. I am curious to discover how he knows you *exist*."

"Maybe one of the orderlies mentioned my name?"

Husch gave a sniff, contemptuous enough to make Marla blush in embarrassment, which pissed her off. "Sorry, I forgot your staff was all wind-up toys," she snapped.

The doctor waved her hand. "Mr. Annemann's creations are tireless and loyal, and I couldn't afford to hire human staff with the pittance you provide me anyway. No, Roger Vaughn must be acting on other information. He is quite lucid—his delusions only extend to certain, ah, fundamental aspects of worldview—and you would be in no danger. I think you should see him. He says the fate of the city is at stake."

If Felport was in danger, Marla had to go. Protecting the city was her one and only responsibility. "Crap," she said. "Okay, fine. I assume you want me to go *now*?"

Dr. Husch only smiled.

"You could've called first," Marla grumbled, rising from her creaking chair.

"One of our inmates discorporated and attempted to escape into the world via the phone

lines last month, prevention of which required ripping out all the wires. I submitted a request for
repair to you a week ago—in the meantime, we
have no phone service." Dr. Husch reached down
and plucked a sheet of pale green paper, with the
raven logo of the Blackwing Institute at the top,
from a heap on Marla's desk. "See?"

Marla groaned. "Fine, I'll have Hamil write you
a check. Why don't you get a cell phone?"

"Because they're vulgar," Dr. Husch said, and
Marla didn't have an answer for that.

"Must he come?" Husch said as Rondeau
approached.

Marla drummed her fingers on the roof of
Husch's silver Rolls Royce. "Yep, he must. You
wouldn't believe the trouble he gets into if I leave
him behind. You know, you could sell this car and
get a nice chunk of change to buy extra blankets
and Thorazine."

"The car is not mine to sell. It belongs to Mr.
Annemann, and if he ever recovers, he will doubt-
less wish to have it. He graciously allows me to use
it in the meantime."

"I thought Annemann got half his head blown
off. I doubt he'll be driving anytime soon."

"His brain is not like that of other men. It has
been regenerating steadily for the past several
decades, and I expect it will be whole again someday."

You sound pretty cheerful about that, Marla
thought, *considering you're the reason he got his*

skull broken apart in the first place. She'd read about *that* in the archives, too.

Rondeau arrived, carrying a plastic bag. "I brought a bunch of leftover Halloween candy for the patients, doc," he said. "Hope that's okay. I know they don't get many treats or visitors."

Husch's aspect softened, and she nodded. "Very thoughtful. Many of them will appreciate the kindness." She gestured, and Marla and Rondeau climbed into the cavernous back seat. Husch got into the passenger side. One of Annemann's creations—which seemed human, if you didn't look closely enough to notice the lack of pores and breathing—was in the front seat, dressed as a chauffeur. It probably wouldn't even know how to drive if you took off its hat and driving gloves. All Annemann's creations (with one notable exception) were fundamentally mindless, but acted like whatever you dressed them as.

"What do these guys eat, anyway?" Marla said, leaning forward to poke the chauffeur in the shoulder.

"Lavender seeds and earthworms," Husch said.

"That's messed up," Marla said.

"*De gustibus* or whatever," Rondeau said.

"It is the traditional meal," Husch said. "As you might imagine, it is quite expensive to feed twoscore homunculi a sufficient quantity of lavender seeds and earthworms. Even with the worm farm in the basement and our extensive gardens."

"I can tell this is going to be a fun drive," Marla said, sinking back into the leather seat. "You know

I'd give you more money if I could, right? But, I mean, it's not like the mayor can tax ordinary citizens to pay for this stuff, considering most of them have no idea people like us even exist."

"And it drives Marla nuts," Rondeau said. "Because nobody ever thanks her for protecting the city from ravaging bands of wendigos or rat people from another star or things like that."

"I don't want *thanks*," Marla said. "Just… a little help. The mayor knows about us, but he's an ordinary, and he doesn't *like* us. He can't decide if I'm a mob boss or a vigilante or a superhero. He knows without me the city would have been destroyed a few times, though. Anyway, for something like the Blackwing Institute, I have to tax the other sorcerers… and no offense, Leda, but nobody wants to give money to the place where crazy sorcerers get locked up. It *worries* them."

Dr. Husch just sniffed.

The Blackwing Institute was an hour outside the city, and an hour outside Marla's comfort zone. She resisted the urge to turn around and press her face against the back window, to watch Felport diminish as they passed into the suburbs and then the fields and sleepy little towns beyond. Felport could be a pain in the ass, but it was *her* pain in the ass. She wasn't comfortable anywhere else.

Especially places that had cows and trees and shit like that. Fludd Park in the city was enough nature for anybody. It even had a creek and a duck pond and a botanical garden.

"My buddy Paul taught me this road trip game where you take the letters from license plates and make dirty words out of them," Rondeau said. "Anybody want to play?"

Marla groaned and tried to go to sleep.

"YOU WANT ME to wear a *dress?*" Marla said, stepping back to put a chair between Dr. Husch and herself.

Husch held a ghastly long white affair embroidered at the neck and sleeves with lace flowers. "It will save a lot of trouble if you do."

"I like trouble better than dresses."

"Don't be stupid," Dr. Husch said. "Just put it on. Mr. Vaughn is from a different era. Do you really want to listen to him go on about the evils of women in pants for an hour?"

"I don't think I've ever seen you in a dress," Rondeau said. "Hmm…"

"Stop imagining it," she snapped, then sighed. "Yes, fine, all right. But I'm not wearing any of the petticoats or whatever. I wouldn't know where to begin."

"You've battled psychopomps and snake gods, but wearing a dress daunts you?" Husch said.

"It doesn't daunt me. I don't daunt. It's just unpleasant. Picking up a big handful of dog crap doesn't *daunt* me, but that doesn't mean I want to do it." Marla hadn't worn a dress in almost ten years. Her old mentor, Artie Mann, had made her dress up for a party once, when she'd first met the city's other sorcerers, but that was the last time. And at least that dress had been short enough to make kicking people easy, when it became necessary.

Dr. Husch and Rondeau left the room, and Marla shed her loose cotton pants and shirt for the dress. It was tight in the waist and bigger on top than she needed, and she wondered if it had been one of Dr. Husch's—it seemed more suited to her curves. Marla tugged the fabric fruitlessly away from her belly. "All right!" she shouted. "Let's go see the wizard!"

Husch reappeared with a heavy iron key-ring and beckoned. Rondeau tried not to stare at Marla, without much success, and she tried to ignore him, with similar results. "Seeing you like this just isn't natural," Rondeau said. "It's like putting a dress on—"

"You'd better stop right there," Marla said. "What have I told you about rehearsing what you're going to say silently in your head first?"

Rondeau looked upward, moved his lips briefly, then squeezed his mouth shut. He nodded once, then kept his eyes on his feet.

Husch unlocked a large iron door, incongruous in the wall of a formal sitting room. A wide white hospital corridor waited beyond. "This door divides my apartments from the Institute proper. This whole building used to be a private residence, of course."

"Mr. Annemann's mansion," Marla said.

"Yes," Husch said.

"Wow, so it wasn't always a hospital?" Rondeau said. "Huh. Wild. So, before we go into the dark corridors filled with madness and all that, I was wondering, how do you keep sorcerers *in* here? I mean, are there some kind of magical barriers that prevent them from using their powers, or what?"

Marla snorted. "Magical barriers? Right. Those *always* work. Nah, the doc just makes sure they don't get any books or chalk or skulls or bells or potions or whatever they liked to use for making magic when they were sane. A necromancer isn't much good without corpses to animate, and a pyromancer's not dangerous if you keep her in a chilled concrete room. It's like how you'd stop an ax murderer. You just lock them up someplace and make sure they never, ever get their hands on another ax."

"But sorcerers carry their axes with them inside their heads," Dr. Husch said, lingering by the door. "And while many of them do depend on props and tools and rituals, some are quite capable of working dangerous magics with only their hands and voices. Those are kept restrained and gagged, as necessary, for their own protection."

"What about the ones who can just, like, *look* at you and make you burst into flame?" Rondeau said, glancing at Marla. "The really powerful ones?" Marla wasn't sure whether to be flattered or offended. She wasn't sure she *could* do something like that—not without preparation, at least—but it was nice to know Rondeau thought she could.

"Ah," Dr. Husch said. "For those rare few, we keep a great many drugs on hand." She gestured, and they went past the iron door, which Husch carefully locked behind them. "But the house actually is well protected. The land here is magically neutral."

"Really?" Marla said. She hadn't realized that. "No ley-lines? No ancient Indian burial grounds? No restless ghosts of past atrocities? No psychic residue left over from epic battles or blood vendettas fought on this spot?"

"No monsters in caverns below ground, no eerie petroglyphs drawn by pre-human civilizations, no local spirits still clinging to sentience," Dr. Husch confirmed. "Mr. Annemann chose the location very carefully. He didn't want outside magical influences to affect his experiments. There's not much inherent magical energy in this area for our patients to draw upon."

Marla opened up her mind, and it was true, there weren't that many deep vibrations here. That *was* rare. Most places had *something* occultish about them. But… "Of course, now a dozen crazy sorcerers live here, and a couple have died in their rooms."

Dr. Husch sighed. "Yes. It's true. In another hundred years, this will be a *very* magically potent location. But for now, the effects haven't soaked into the earth."

"Only a dozen patients, huh?" Rondeau said. "In this big old place?"

"Not counting Mr. Annemann. We try to give each of them as much space as possible."

"Anybody famous locked up here?" Rondeau said.

"Once Mr. Vaughn was famous, or rather, infamous," Dr. Husch said. "One of our newest inmates is our escape artist, the one who tried to get out via the phone lines, Elsie Jarrow. Perhaps you've heard of her."

"I don't—" Rondeau said.

"Marrowbones," Marla said, shuddering. "That's what they called her. They still told stories about her, when I first came to Felport. How she'd suck all the fluids out of your body with a kiss."

"Hyperbole," Dr. Husch said. "But only just. We have others. Gustavus Lupo, the skinchanger, who lost track of his flesh one day and built a new body of the angry dead. A powerful psychic named Genevieve with a mind broken by trauma. Norma Nilson, who did not so much kill her enemies as crush them with despair until they begged permission to take their own lives. Others." She shrugged. "They all have special needs. I serve them as well as I can."

"Charming," Marla said. "Let's meet Mr. Vaughn. What's his mental malfunction, anyway?"

"He wants to raise a dark god from the sea and destroy all human life," Dr. Husch said. "Come along, his rooms are just down here."

VAUGHN'S ROOM WAS crammed with bookshelves made of driftwood, and dried starfish dangled on strings from the ceiling. Despite the nautical theme, the room smelled of dust, not ocean. "Mr.

Vaughn!" Dr. Husch called, and a small old man bustled in from another room. He wore an elegant gray suit, and his eyes were the darkest blue Marla had ever seen. Hands clasped behind his back, he bowed, and said, "Thank you for coming to see me, Miss Mason. We have much to discuss." He nodded curtly to Dr. Husch and took no notice whatsoever of Rondeau. "Thank you for bringing her, doctor. Hail Xorgotthua, and good day."

"Come, Rondeau," Dr. Husch said. "We'll take the candy you brought to some of the other patients."

Rondeau looked a question at Marla, and she nodded. Little old men who hailed Xorgotthua—whoever or whatever that was—weren't necessarily harmless, but if he were too dangerous for Marla to handle, Rondeau wouldn't be much help anyway. They left, and the door shut behind them. Vaughn gestured to an armchair, and Marla sat down, remembering to keep her legs demurely together. Stupid dress. Marla rubbed her hand on the arm of the chair and said, "Is this sharkskin?"

"Oh, yes," Vaughn said, sitting in an identical chair of his own. "Sharks are Xorgotthua's hand-maidens, of course."

"Right. Why did you want to see me, Mr. Vaughn?"

"I need you to stop me," he said. "Kill me, probably. Well. Not *this* me. The other me."

"You're going to have to clarify that."

"Yes, I see." Vaughn took a handkerchief from his pocket and dabbed at sweat on his forehead, though it was cool in the room. "I assume you know of the sacrifice I made to the great god Xorgotthua a century ago? The ferry I sank, so that the screams of the dying might nourish the lord of all depths?"

Marla suppressed a shiver. So he was a religious fundamentalist. They always creeped her out. "Yeah, I know about that." Details were slowly coming back to her. "You were trying to conduct some ritual and raise some ancient god from the sea, right? But it didn't work?"

"Oh, it worked." Vaughn fingered a silver chain around his neck. "But it was only the first part of the ritual, you see. To raise Xorgotthua, I made a sacrifice to the waters, to wake the god. Then, a hundred years later, there must be another sacrifice, as large as the first, to entice the god to the surface, and onto the land. It is a long time to wait, but the attention spans of gods are not like those of men, and a hundred years is but a moment to Xorgotthua. The time for the second sacrifice is only a few days away."

"And you want me to... stop you from making the sacrifice?" Marla said. "Shouldn't be a problem, with you locked up here."

"Ah, well, no, not exactly. I want you to stop the *other* me. My reincarnation." He looked at her expectantly.

"Ah. So do I ring a bell or something to get Dr. Husch back here?" Marla said.

Vaughn sighed. "I know what you're thinking. Death is generally a prerequisite to reincarnation."

"Yeah. That's part of what I was thinking."

"I use the word as a convenience. It is not true reincarnation. You know the technique of putting your soul in a stone, to be retrieved later?"

"Sure. It tends to turn the soulless sorcerer into a pretty unsympathetic bastard with no sense of proportion, but it's a way to preserve your life." Marla was wary of the word "soul," but she knew a technomancer who talked about uploading personalities into computers and making backups of your mind, and he said the principle was the same.

"I did… something similar. But then I made a perfect copy of the stone where I kept my soul, through a certain alchemical process. I restored my original soul to this body, and left the copy in a safe place near the docks in Felport, with instructions to activate a few months prior to the centennial of my first sacrifice. It was a backup plan, you see. If I died or became incapacitated, my backup soul would be there to complete the ritual and raise Xorgotthua."

Marla frowned. "What do you mean 'activate?' Souls floating around loose aren't good for much. They need bodies."

"Oh, well, of course, the soul had instructions to seize control of the nearest suitable vessel."

"Vessel. You mean a *person*." Marla gripped the arms of the chair. "You made a backup of your soul with instructions for it to *possess* some random passer-by?"

Mr. Vaughn nodded. "Yes, exactly! Such an honor for the vessel, too, being given the opportunity to help raise Xorgotthua."

Marla closed her eyes, counted to ten, and opened them again. The urge to strangle Vaughn had not passed, but it was under control. "So this person is wandering around Felport now?"

"Not *wandering*," he said, offended. "He is *me*—or me, as I was a hundred years ago—and he has been learning all he can about the city. That's how I found out you were the, ah, person in charge."

"You're in communication with this double of yours?"

"I see and hear and smell and taste what he does." Vaughn frowned. "It is a side effect I had not expected, though I admit, it is good to smell the sea again. But I do not think this communication goes both ways. I've had no indication he sees what I see."

"Good. Where can I find him?"

Vaughn wagged his finger. "No, no. I will not help you stop him unless you help *me*."

"What, do you want to go on a field trip? Deep-sea fishing or something? I can talk to the doc."

"No. What I want is for you to stop my reincarnation, so that I can be the one to raise great Xorgotthua. It should have been me. I cannot bear the thought of this *copy* of myself raising the god while I languish here, to die with everyone else when the waves cover the land. My copy was meant as a last resort, if I was dead or in a coma, but I am aware, and here, and quite capable of completing the ritual on my own."

"Uh huh," Marla said, standing. "So you want me to stop your copy from killing lots of innocent people, and help *you* kill lots of innocent people instead, and either way the result is a risen god who wants to destroy all human life? Sorry, doesn't sound like something I want to pursue."

"If you help me, I will intercede on your behalf with Xorgotthua. I can make sure you and your city are spared. My copy will show no such mercy, I assure you. But if you let me be the one who wakes the god, I will use my influence to convince it to spare your home." Vaughn rose to his feet and stood facing Marla. He extended his hand. "Do we have a deal?"

Marla contemplated. If a great dark god really *was* rising from the sea, such bargains might be necessary, but she wasn't ready to concede defeat yet. "No, thanks. I think I'll look for your copy on my own."

Vaughn closed his hands into fists. "Listen, *woman*. I brought you here to make an arrangement. You'll never find him without me. If you don't help me, the death of your city is a foregone conclusion. I offer your only hope. Take it, or face the consequences."

"Yeah, let me get back to you on that," she said, opening her cell phone and calling Rondeau. When he picked up, she said, "Hey, tell the Doc I'm done here."

"You can't 'get back to me,'" Vaughn said, his face getting red. "You will make this bargain *now* or—"

Marla snorted. "Please. Like you won't jump at the chance if I come back in two days and tell you it's a deal. What, you're going to turn up your nose and refuse to help me because I snubbed you today? As if."

Vaughn sat down. He glowered at her. "You will regret the way you've treated me. When you return to beg for my assistance in a day or two days, I will know I have the power and will drive a much harder bargain."

"I look forward to negotiating with you," Marla said. "But don't expect me to wear a dress again." The door opened, and Marla slipped out.

"You DIDN'T TELL me he was the priest of a dark god," Marla said, hurrying down the hallway, with the shorter Husch striding quickly to keep up. "You might've mentioned."

"He's not," Husch said. "I told you, his fundamental worldview is delusional. He believes in the great god Xorgotthua, but no such god exists."

Marla stopped walking. "Are you sure about that?"

"Quite. There is no record of such a creature in any oral or written tradition I have consulted. Vaughn claims the god has inspired countless followers through the ages and has been worshipped by many societies, but it's just not true. Vaughn began talking about Xorgotthua after he nearly drowned in the mid-1800s, and his delusion intensified over time, becoming ever more baroque and sophisticated. It was considered a harmless eccentricity, until he arranged the ferry disaster. Then

Felport's elite sorcerers realized he was a danger and had him put away here."

"Huh," Marla said, resuming her walk back to Husch's apartments. "That's reassuring. You wouldn't believe the stuff he told me."

Husch unlocked the door. Rondeau was on the other side, sitting on a couch, watching a television screen. "We heard it all," Husch said. "The guest rooms are under surveillance, of course."

"That dude is batshit," Rondeau said. "Now he's walking in circles and talking to himself and, I shit you not, *cackling*."

"So you brought me here to listen to a crazy guy's pointless babble?" Marla said.

"No. He did know your name and your position among Felport's sorcerers, and other details of daily life in the city he should not be privy to. I think he is probably telling the truth about this double of his, and his plans to conduct a sacrifice in a few days."

"So there's no giant sea god to worry about," Rondeau said. "Just the issue of a bunch of innocent people getting killed."

"Huh," Marla said. "How many people died in that ferry disaster?"

"Over a hundred, most bound for a family reunion on Bramble Island," Husch said. "And it sounds like Vaughn wants just as many people to die this time."

"Crap," Marla said.

"Indeed," Husch replied.

* * *

"GOOD MORNING, BAY WITCH," Marla said, sitting on a bench on the boardwalk with a view of the bay's gray expanse.

The Bay Witch—who'd once been named Zufi, back when she was a surfer girl, before she became a student of the hidden arts—sat at the other end of the bench. She was blonde and dressed in a black wetsuit, a puddle of seawater spreading all around her.

"Nice of you to visit," the Bay Witch said. "You got my note?"

"I got an incomprehensible smear of goo on seaweed. But I needed to talk to you anyway. What's up?"

"Bay's getting more polluted every year. I've sent reports. You don't answer me."

Marla nodded. "I've been busy, but I'm taking bids to deal with the pollution. Unfortunately the best bid is from Ernesto, who wants to gather all the pollutants to create a filth elemental to smite his enemies. I'm thinking of accepting it, but I need to find out who his enemies are first."

"Fair enough," the Bay Witch said. "There's another thing. Probably nothing, but there's—"

"Let me guess. There's a crazy guy hanging around, talking about raising a dark sea god named Xorgotthua?"

The Bay Witch laughed. "They told me you have tentacles everywhere. Yeah, that's him."

"Where might I find this crazy guy?"

She shrugged. "He's been a regular in some of the bars these past few months, bothering people, but he hasn't been around lately. He was pretty irritated when nobody wanted to join his cult. He promised they'd all die if they didn't join him, the usual. Nobody took him seriously. He's just a kid, can't be more than seventeen. I felt kind of bad for him, but he was creepy, too."

Marla nodded. "I've got sort of a weird question. Let's say I needed to get a giant squid in a few days. Just out in the bay, you know. Waving tentacles around, the whole deal. Think you could hook that up?"

"I'm not Aquaman," she said. "I'm not friends with all the creatures of the sea."

"Yeah, but I bet you've got methods."

"A giant squid?" She frowned. "They do like cold water, but they're not exactly common, and they prefer deep water. If it's doable—*if*—I'd need some serious payback. I'd have to burn a lot of power and influence over something like this, and I'm guessing you don't even want to tell me why."

"True," Marla said. "Do it, and you'll be taken care of."

"I'd need the *bay* to be taken care of. You're the chief sorcerer of Felport, and the way you feel about the city? That's how I feel about the bay."

"We'll work it out," Marla said. "You know I'm good for it."

"Okay," the Bay Witch said. She shook her head. "I'll see what I can do. Meet me back here tomorrow." She walked to the edge of the boardwalk, climbed over the rail, and leapt gracefully into the sea.

Marla spent the afternoon talking to her various friends and informants by the boardwalk, the docks, and the boat harbor, but no one had seen the crazy guy lately. If Marla was going to find him, she'd have to get more creative.

"ONE GIANT SQUID, coming up," the Bay Witch said, looking pleased with herself. They sat at an outdoor café a block from the water, enjoying the mild spring air, though the Bay Witch was dripping water, as always. It was an occupational malady. "The thing's the size of a school bus. Where do you want it?"

"A few hundred yards from shore, two days from now, midnight, waving its tentacles around, splashing a lot, making a spectacle. Can you handle that?"

"I can hijack its brain for a little while," the Bay Witch said. "Squid are too big, and their anatomy is too weird, for me to control easily, but if all you want is flailing, I can manage that. What, are you trying to scare away a sperm whale or something?"

"Not quite," Marla said. "I need your help with something else. Where can I get a lot of seashells and other ocean crap like that?"

"YOU LOOK LIKE a kitschy seafood restaurant exploded all over you," Rondeau said.

Marla examined herself in one of the long mirrors in the dressing room of Rondeau's nightclub. It had been a strip club, once upon a time, and still had all the backstage facilities, though these days the only performers were DJs. She adjusted the bit of fishing net she wore as a cloak and tugged the cascade of shell necklaces around so they didn't drag quite so heavily on her neck. "That's the look I'm going for," she said. "You have to admit, the sword made from narwhal horn is pretty cool." It was useless as a weapon, but the long, spiraling horn on a hilt hanging from her belt was a nice bit of flash.

"I still don't see why I have to go," Dr. Husch said, emerging from the bathroom. Even dressed in sailcloth, net, and shells, she managed to look regal. She had a wicked whip hanging from her belt, a scourge with ends tipped by fishhooks.

"I might need backup," Marla said, "and the homunculus orderlies don't listen to anyone but you." She picked up two half-masks made of horseshoe crab shells, which, along with some drawn-on abstract tattoos, would serve to disguise their faces. Better if the original Mr. Vaughn didn't recognize them while looking through his copy's eyes.

Dr. Husch ran her finger along the top of a vanity, wrinkling her nose at the dust. "I don't think this place has been cleaned since last time I was here."

"You've been here before?" Rondeau said.

"When it was a burlesque house," Husch said. "Once upon a time, Mr. Annemann owned this place. I... worked for him."

Marla didn't say anything. Husch *had* worked for him. Sort of.

"Wow, you were a dancer?" Rondeau said.

"It was a long time ago," Husch said.

"I think we look suitably crazy and ocean-themed," Marla said. "Let's hit the bars."

"Why do you think he'll come here?" Husch said. They were in the back of an empty dive bar near the docks, sipping drinks and trying to ignore the smell of old beer and fish. Marla felt a little self-conscious in her sea-witch getup, and the mask cut her peripheral vision down more than she liked. The bartender clearly thought they were nuts, too, but image was important in situations like this.

"I started spreading the word that a priestess of Xorgotthua was in the area, planning the ritual that would raise the god, here to replace poor Mr. Vaughn." She shrugged. "I said this was her hang-out. If Vaughn's copy is paying attention, he'll hear word. And if he does come in, well, we're kind of hard to miss." Marla grinned. "In the meantime, girl talk. You know Rondeau likes you."

Husch pursed her lips. "You don't mean to tell me I should be flattered? I doubt he's very discriminating in his tastes."

"Rondeau usually likes body-pierced college girls with flexible attitudes toward morality," Marla said. "You're not his usual type, so sure, be flattered."

"It's been a long time since I've been interested in what men thought of me, Marla," she said, looking at her levelly. "Given your position, I assume you know the… details of my origin. You can understand why I might be wary of men?"

Marla nodded. "Sure. Just making conversation. But Rondeau *doesn't* know your origins—I promise—so you don't have to worry so much about his expectations."

"I'll take that under advisement."

"Speaking of men," Marla said.

A young man in a T-shirt and swimming trunks came through the door, sunlight streaming in around him. He saw them in the back of the bar and started coming their way.

The bartender shouted at him. "Hold on, kid, I told you, you're under age, you can't come in here!" The kid gestured at the bartender and muttered a guttural incantation, and the bartender fell, eyes rolling back in his head.

"Well, well," Marla said. "Reckless and unnecessary use of magic. This must be our zealot."

"You!" he said, striding toward them. "You claim to worship Xorgotthua?" His hair was wet, and he had a large pimple on the side of his nose.

Marla sipped her beer before answering. "I claim nothing. I am the priestess of Xorgotthua, yes. And who are you, child?"

"I am no child. I am the reincarnation of Roger Vaughn himself!"

"Madness," Marla said. "Vaughn has not been seen in a century. I have come, with my followers, to complete the work he began so long ago." She gestured at him lazily. "Away with you. Enjoy your last days of life before the waters swallow you."

He crouched by the table. "You don't under-stand. I *am* Vaughn. I have pledged my life to Xorgotthua! How have I never heard of you and your followers?"

"We have lived in seclusion on an island," Marla said. "Waiting for the stars to come right. That time is now. The sacrifices are prepared, and the god will rise tomorrow night."

He frowned. "I've arranged a sacrifice. There are bombs, on a ferry bound for Bramble Island, and tomorrow—"

Marla snorted. "The bombs were discovered, you fool, and removed. Did you think the secret ruler of this city would fail to check the ferries, so close to the centennial of Vaughn's first sacri-fice?"

The kid grimaced. "Marla Mason. Yes. I did not realize... I had heard she was effective. I should have been more careful. But surely I can still be of service—"

Marla waved her hands. "It's all arranged. The orphans have already been prepared."

Dr. Husch's eyes went wide, and she made a snorting noise, and after a moment Marla realized she was trying not to laugh. Dr. Husch, laughing—that would be something to see.

"Orphans?" the kid said.

Marla nodded. "Yes. Xorgotthua enjoys the taste of orphans. Something *Vaughn* would know very well."

"Of course I know," he said quickly. "I just... where did you get orphans?"

Marla turned her most withering glare on him, hoping the half-mask didn't dim its power. "They're *orphans*. The essential fact of orphans is that no one much misses them. Now, please, be gone. We are discussing preparations for the ceremony."

Vaughn stood up. "I... please, Xorgotthua is my life... how can I serve?"

Marla sighed theatrically. "Very well. Vaughn, if that is your name. Come to the boardwalk tomorrow, before midnight. You may watch the great god rise with the rest of my followers. Perhaps Xorgotthua will choose to spare your life."

"Thank you," Vaughn's copy said, and left the bar, looking punch-drunk and dazed.

"You'd better go check on the bartender, Doc, and make sure the kid didn't kill him." Marla cracked her knuckles. "We're on for tomorrow."

"Why didn't you just have me summon the orderlies?" Husch said. "They could have seized him, and he would have been safely housed in the Blackwing Institute before nightfall!"

Marla shook her head. "Then him and the *other* Vaughn would just keep plotting and planning and probably causing me more trouble in ten or twenty or fifty or a hundred years, gods forbid I'm still around then. No, we need to put an end to this, or at least build in a long delay." She opened her cell phone and called Rondeau. "Hey," she said. "Send some of our pet policemen to check the Bramble Island ferries for bombs. Yes, I know, I don't know why I didn't think to check there. I guess I expected Vaughn's copy to be more original. Make sure our people keep an eye on the copy, too, in case he decides to cover his bets by throwing firebombs at a yacht or something." She closed the phone. "When they find the bombs, we can say it was terrorists and get some of that sweet Homeland Security money. The mayor would totally owe me for that."

"How nice for you. So what happens now?"

"Squid happens," Marla said.

"ARE THE ORDERLIES in place, Rondeau?" Marla spoke into her phone.

"Yep."

"And you talked to the Bay Witch?"

"Zufi says we're good to go," Rondeau replied.

"Good." She hung up. Dr. Husch and a handful of Annemann's homunculi—dressed in their own seashell-and-face-tattoo cultist disguises—stood on the boardwalk, by the railing, looking at the moonlit water. The air was cool, the tang of salt strong in the air. A good night for a ritual.

"The bay is really very pretty," Dr. Husch said.

"It's a good deep-water port," Marla said, with her usual civic pride.

"I hope we aren't mistaken about Mr. Vaughn and the accuracy of his ideas," Husch said. She swung her fishhook-tipped scourge idly over the railing. "I'd be very upset if a great sea god did rise tonight."

"Eh," Marla said. "The bombs were disabled, and I didn't *actually* sacrifice any orphans. I wouldn't worry about it. Even if Xorgotthua does exist, which he doesn't, he'll just slumber on." She glanced at her cell phone. Five minutes to midnight. "I hope he shows."

"I am here, priestess."

Marla and Dr. Husch turned and saw Vaughn's copy. He wore his own cape of net, woven with seaweed, and a ridiculous profusion of shell necklaces. His face had markings just like Marla's... only his were real tattoos. Marla winced under her mask. Damn. That must have hurt. She felt bad for the kid who'd been possessed. He'd probably never get his body back, and if he did, he'd have to walk around with that stuff on his face.

"Good," Marla said. "Then observe the water, where Xorgotthua will rise."

They all bellied up to the rail. Nothing much happened; moonlight, wind, waves. Then, slowly, the sea began to bubble and roil, and after a moment something vast broke the surface out in the water, and great flailing tentacles, each over fifteen feet long, whipped into the air, flinging water. The "cultists" dropped to their knees, and after a moment's hesitation, so did Vaughn's copy.

"Great Xorgotthua!" Marla shouted, still standing, raising her arms overhead. "We come to welcome you!"

The squid rolled, revealing an eye the size of a dinner plate for a moment before slipping back under the water.

"Yes!" Marla shouted. "I understand, great one! We live to serve you!"

The squid sank beneath the waves, and the cultists rose.

"My people," Marla said, her voice appropriately bleak. "Great Xorgotthua thanks us for the sacrifice, but says it is not yet time to rise. Xorgotthua wishes to wait until the ice caps have melted and the seas have risen to swallow the coastal lands. We are not to disturb its slumber until that time. We must keep the god's sacraments and teach the next generation of followers." She shook her head. "Our time will come. It only seems long to our pitiful human minds. Another few centuries are but moments to great Xorgotthua."

Vaughn's copy remained kneeling when the others rose. He looked up at Marla, stricken. "I can wait," he said. "I have no choice. I will wait. That glimpse of the god will sustain me through the centuries."

Show 'em a few tentacles and they see a squamous god of the outer darkness, Marla though. "I have discovered something," she said, placing a hand on the copy's shoulder. "It seems Roger Vaughn did not die, as we all assumed. He is resting in a hospital, where all his needs are looked after. Would you like to meet him?"

"He—I—he lives? When I woke, I thought he must have died, but…" The copy stood up. "Yes. I'd like to see him very much. I wish to know what happened to my life in the past hundred years."

"Perhaps you and the older Mr. Vaughn can await the return of Xorgotthua together," Marla said. She nodded to Dr. Husch, who summoned her orderlies to lead Vaughn's copy to the car.

"THEY BICKER LIKE an old couple," Rondeau said, watching Vaughn—both Vaughns—on Dr. Husch's closed-circuit television. The two mad sorcerers shared a new, larger suite of rooms in the Blackwing Institute, and spent most of their time arguing over fine points of Xorgotthuan theology. They might have had the same mind, once, but you can't put one soul in two bodies without a little divergence.

"I'm just glad they're locked up," Marla said.

Rondeau nodded. "It was nice of you to bring all this stuff," he said. Marla had loaded a truck with blankets, drugs, and food, donations from the sorcerers of the city. Marla had told the other sorcerers that Dr. Husch was the one who saved the city from destruction by a great ocean-dwelling deity inimical to human life, and had encouraged them to show their appreciation with material goods. They had. No one liked to contemplate the coming of great indifferent gods, and Marla hadn't bothered to tell the sorcerers that Xorgotthua was imaginary.

"Where is Leda, anyway?" Marla said. "I thought she was coming back to the city with us."

"Yep. I'm taking her to see one of those homemade robot demolition derbies," Rondeau said. "It's going to be awesome. She said she had to take care of something before we go, though."

Marla rolled her eyes. She'd done her part to encourage Dr. Husch, but she doubted Rondeau would make it past one date with her.

Rondeau went back to watching the screen, snorting laughter as the two Vaughns argued about whose turn it was to clean the toilet. Marla went looking for Dr. Husch and found her in a room at the end of a short hallway, sitting beside a hospital bed.

Marla stood in the doorway for a moment, then said, "I don't understand why you still tend him."

Dr. Husch adjusted Mr. Annemann's catheter. He was hooked up to a number of machines, his head wrapped almost entirely in a thick padding of bandages.

Marla cleared her throat. "I mean, when you consider…"

"The fact that he created me?" Dr. Husch said. "You might expect me to be grateful for that."

Marla shifted uncomfortably. "But he created you to be his, well, his concubine, right?"

"I was created as his living sexual fantasy," she said, covering Mr. Annemann with a blanket. "Yes. And he used me as such. I was the most sophisticated of his many homunculi, the only one capable of independent thought. At first, I appreciated his attention. Even when he sold me to the highest bidder as a courtesan, and later, when he had me dance in a burlesque house and sold me more prosaically in the alley behind the club, I felt he deserved to treat me any way he wished. But as time passed, I began to resent him and to wish for my own life. The worst part was, I still loved him. He could be very kind, you know, and he loved discovery and knowledge more than anything, something I respected very much. And then one day, I began to wonder if perhaps Mr. Annemann *made* me love him. What if loving him was not a choice, but merely a spell he'd cast on me?" She stroked Annemann's hand.

"That's why you shot him?" Marla said. "Because you thought he'd cast a love spell on you?" The Felport archives had reports about the shooting, but not about the motives.

Dr. Husch bowed her head. "Yes. I thought he must be a monster, to cast such a spell. I thought I would kill him and free myself. He did not die, but his brain was... severely harmed. Any spell he cast on me would have failed, then, after the damage I inflicted." She looked up. "But I didn't stop loving him. I realized the love was not the result of a spell at all, but a true feeling. And so I have been caring for him ever since. Someday, he will wake, and I will tell him I'm sorry. Perhaps then he will realize I am more than his creation, and he will see me as a woman, and his equal."

Wishful thinking, Marla thought. "I'm not saying it was right to shoot him. But you probably never would have had your own life otherwise."

"No one's life is solely their own," Dr. Husch said. "We are all bound by our devotions. Mr. Vaughn would understand that. I'm sure you do, too."

Marla thought of her own tangled allegiances, the web of obligations that made protecting the city possible... but that was the point, wasn't it? To protect Felport. She had devotions of her own and couldn't fault Dr. Husch for hers, however misguided they might be in Marla's eyes.

"Thanks for all your help, Leda."

"You can thank me by doubling my annual budget."

Marla laughed. "I'll see what I can do."

THE PRINCE OF END TIMES

Hal Duncan

Fool of Dreams

ACROSS THE YELLOWED vellum of the book, across its pages thin and dry as parched skin, the black ink of the bitmites crawls in scribbles, scrawls a texture of text upon the parchment that the prince's fingers, drifting over living Braille, cannot make smooth, cannot unrumple meaning from. Here all the curlicues of Arabic, there the restraint of straight Roman, here the kaballababble of Hebrew, there mute mathemantics of the Greek, the bitmites spell out an entrancing dancing gibberish, that *must* mean something, so he thinks, *but what?*

A LICK OF finger, a flick of digits, and a page turns. Outside, in the midnight furnace, shadows burn with questings, calls and challenges, with rumblings of rumors of a way. Outside, in this Möbius city where they dwell, the dead or dreaming war for towers built higher than any heaven, pits dug deeper down than any hell, demon humanity and unkin angels in a firefight for the rock of ages. Inside, in the still of his sanctomb sanctorah, the darkartist flicks through mysteries of myths and histories. A prince of end times, fool of dreams, he tastes a touch of fingertip to tip of tongue and turns—

–A WAY. THERE has to be a way, the darkartist whispers to his sylph. He turns another page, unfurls the map bound into it and smooths it straight. He tries to trace a way in or a way out of the city. The book contains it all, they say, explains it all, the carter's tale of how the world fell to the bitmites, how they came here, the beginning and the end. But his hands are all fingers and thumbs, too clumsy to follow every intricate articulation of this pidgin tongue of Creole nations, the bitmites' twisted, twisting Cant. He thumps the book closed, clenches his frustration into a fist of silence. Has to will his hand back open to rest it, palm flat, on the leather binding of the book. A bitmite artifact itself, the book seems somehow still—so warm it is to touch—alive.

—There are copies of this everywhere? he says.

The consul, standing by the window, nods; he can hear the motion in the stillness.

—The book is spreading through the mob, m'sire. Like wildfire.

No, the young lord of the unkin thinks, not fire but ink drips soaking into sodden paper, blotches smeared to clouds of gray, like mist or mold.

Light catches ice-gray eyes as he opens them and stretches from his hunch to rise back from the black ash desk and hurl the book he's holding at the window where, outside, the city slouches in a silhouette he sees but also hears in the echoes of the Cant, hears as a bestial roar over the waste.

The book explodes to shreds of brown and yellow, leather and vellum, and black powder. They call it angel dust, the humans, the nanite ink that writes their world.

Anarchaic Arachnidae

THE BITMITES SCRABBLE a babble across the window, obscuring the city in a screed of indecipherable creed. They eat, excrete designs like frosting on the pane, strewing an archaic and anarchic glass graffiti in their wake.

Anarchaic, he thinks.

Across the glass they etch the fine delineation of two circles, one inside the other. At equidistant points around the inner circle, ticks appear—at twelve and six o'clock, at two and four, at eight and ten. At each of these, two arcs diverge from the same point, moving toward the outer rim, but curving from each other so they merely touch that rim as they turn in upon themselves in spirals like ram's-horns.

* * *

HE LOOKS AT the empty circle in the center of it, wondering if they're trying to tell him something. The semes they spin seem senseless, but the bit-mites are the artificers of the city, weaving the loose threads of all their afterlives into one wide web of a world, a city at the end of time.

Anarchaic arachnidae, he thinks, *and unkin archons.*

All of them are caught up in that web in one way or another, unkin just as much as any human. As the court's darkartist he's, perhaps, the most enmeshed of all. So they should know him, might well have a message for him. They might understand the questions that he's asking himself now. The bitmites crawling in the city-streets and every book scrawl also in the shadows of his mind.

His consul, footsteps echoing solid in the maze of volumes, crosses to the window, lays his hands upon it, gathering the swarm of logos locusts and semantics ticks, all the burrowing bitmites, into his own metaphysique. Veins in his hands, like vines pulsing alive under his skin, flow black a second and then fade. As he turns back to face the prince, his hand still up, a faint line races, traces a half-remembered scar across his palm. The scraps of book fallen at his feet crumble to dusts and breezes; they dissolve, engrain themself into the smooth line texture of the wooden floorboards.

–THERE HAS TO be a way.

   —A way to where? the consul asks.

That's what he doesn't know though. Where they are. Where they might be. There are maps all around him, in his books and in the city, in the world. But he has no idea now how to read the world. The Cant that was once so clear seems to be... evolving; it's as if the bitmites are developing their own tongue, wiring words together into new sense—nuisance nonsense most of it. He gathers papers on his desk, squares them into a sheaf and adds them to a pile six inches deep, six inches high. He turns to gaze coolly and blankly at the consul.

—Are they waiting for me in the Hall?

—The wake can't end without you.

Are they still a wake, he wonders idly, still awake at the wake? He pushes his hair back from his face, as if to clear the bitmites' chaos with it.

—Let them know I'm coming, he says. I'll be down there soon.

A Gaunt Construct of Tensions

As THE CONSUL leaves, the prince of end times wanders to the window, to a vision of night streets lit with a volcanic light. He's strode the city, dwelt and dealt with rebels, studying the tumbleword litter in the rumblestreets rolling, steel graffiti in the sanctuaries of teaching, temples strewn with rubble of illuminated stone, all broken, all defiled. It took him years to find the book the reacher talked of, in the mob's hands now, bought from a market stall of T-shirts, texts and postcard after postcard, anarchist pietàs of the fallen heroes of the revolution. And the book amongst them. Bought by the future king of all this... carrion. The very dark prince in the tower himself, the bastard prince, the crown prince to be now.

Clown prince.

MIRRORED IN THE glass dark with the night behind, he sees himself, reflection of a shadow, crisp in white silk shirt, black suit, and tie. Roundwound in overcoat of fine black wool, his pale grim surface skin is stitched over a frame of bone, a gaunt construct of tensions. For a moment in the dark his graving shows, wiring his face with lines of onyx black as fine as filigree, a mask of tribal tattoo like some ancient worm-faced deity. He rakes fingers thru his crow-black hair and spits a word of Cant at his reflection, shatters the window and its indecipherable sign, scatters the shards of glass out to the night.

We drift back in as dust too fine for him to see.

READ HIM, WE say to you, ridden by riot, graved in black on bleak. His rage is a book written in wrath, wrought on his skin, a book of bones all wracked with shattered spine, soul skinsuit ripped off page by page, stitched back to hide his hollow soul. Read him. The graving that marks him out as monster, villain, is the tracks of tears unshed. This thing is sorrow, walking in the night, gone wild, a furious massacred slaughterhouse child.

He has walked through the madness of the city, watched as his angel kin swooped down on wings of synthe, disruptors blazing, to... *disperse* a crowd to dust. He has walked through the madness of the city; now it walks through him.

He puts his hand upon the pile of papers on the desk and, as his eyes burn bright with ice-gray light, he whispers just a little word. The notes ignite. The writing burns beneath his hand, the wasting of a lovetime's learnings, journals full of all the names and all the games his blooder played with him when they were younger. All the same: infant dances of death and love; diaries of a fallen dove; snapshot of a boy with glasses and flowers, straight out of the sandpit, in his finest hours. These are the pages of his years, given to cold fire and dark ash, sorrow and hate.

The Kith of Destiny and Fortune
Ash flits from the desk into the breeze that blows in through the broken window. The prince runs a finger through it, smears the gray with a thumb.

When did he become this prince, this dark son? What was he before? He can't be sure. There was a time he had another name, a home, a human aim, before his blooder and the others found him, called him out and made him unkin; but that was too far ago to recall much more than snatches, too long away to rebuild more than a handful of images. He might have been fireteen or twenty-yore when he heard the Cant for the first time. All he remembers is stepping out into the Illusion

Fields, feeling bonesands acoarse his skin, awireness flowing in his nerveins, bloodlust of eternal regenerations. All he remembers is how his first scries pierced his airdreams.

He was on his knees when they came to him, shadows like crows in the blue sky above the corn, and raised him to his feet.

ADAMANTIUM ARMOR GLEAMING; hair the color of the corn; words that made the world shimmer like summer: his blooder. Others behind him.

—Join us, he'd said, graving the Cant into his soul.

So he had sailed the skies with them on silvery steely wings of synthe, and come into the holy city as a newblood gathered to the host. He had flown over streets built out of song itself, raised from the symphonaesthesia of the Cant. He had wondered that this whole confugued musaic of consonance did not crumble in dissent, every man or woman or child seeking to sing a palace for themselves.

—The mob? his blooder laughed. Can they speak the language of the angels, shape the shadows with a word? No, they need us to do it for them.

Glint in his eyes and in his grin, his blooder thought that they were heroes.

–THE GULF THAT sifts humanity and unkin, said his consul once when he was still a mentor, is not one of time and space, but tame and spice. It is an altaring of perspective that comes only to the few, the kith of destiny and fortune. You are a lord of the Illusion Fields, m'sire, both born and borne to this beyond.

But even as he followed his golden blooder's rise up through the ranks, shadowing his footsteps, he was never happy with the rule of the role, more of a wordman than a birdman, more concerned with the humanist than the numinous.

—That's why I'm proposing you for darkartist, his blooder had said.

Lightprince already by then, he'd said he needed someone used to standing up to him, staying his arm, speaking for peace. No more street-battles with ruptor-wielding children, no more razing demon strongholds, just devotion to a study of the Cant itself—he could hardly refuse.

And now? Centuries of his life within this room he's spinned, researching, searching for some sacred secret—*secret,* he thinks—that could tale him the truth about the unkin and humanity. And found nothing that could salve as answer, sooth his senses, not even in the book that was supposed to answer all.

WE TRY TO hissper it into the tomb and womb, the grave and cave, that is his broken head. We try to code it in the peaks and troughs of enformation, in the emanations of identity. But, lost, seeking a refuge in his fugue, he sees only the black ink of us, not the white space between that gives us meaning, the clear quiet absences where voices silence and we simply are. Find the me hidden in themes, we try to tell him. His face is the very image of this shattered city of shadows, does he not see? Ink and vellum. Black line and white space in tension. All awareness is a whereness, is intension and release.

Your rage is only sorrow trying to break free.

The Hero As Destroyer

WONDERING IN TRASH of books pulled down from shelves, the prince stalks strictures of the cage that traps him, kicks disguarded tomes across the room as if he kicks the whole hurled world itself. There are no words to write the wrong of it, to show that unkin are akin to clay humanity. There are no words, only the rotted names of tomes long since corrupted by their age—Toran and Korah and Holy Babble. Angelisch translations of diabolistic grimoires. Apocryptographia of old golem gods with faces never seen, names never spoken. Pseudopaedia full of illustrations of idols with feet and hands of clay, gemstones for eyes. All lies.

HE PULLS A copy of Wolven von Escherpack's *Partsevil* from the shelf, a tale of a poor fool who fell, who fought to pierce the veil, who sought to feel the grail, and failed, got only a glimpse of golden chalice, a scrap of salvation for himself alone. He thinks of Fieryvice, the hero's halfcast brother with his mask of face graved in black lines as if to chart the faultlines of the wounded land.

He spits a word, giving the book to flame. Let the fire revise it. Make the hero not the widow's son, the hinter's knight, but his half-brother, yes,

his kin, the other with the graven skin. Fuck Partsevil. Let Fieryvice, moorage of light and dark, find
the philosopher's keystone, bring it to base humanity. Let him leave Chapel Perilous in ruins behind,
not just the hero, but the hero as destroyer.

The hiero as deustroyer, he thinks.

HE DROPS THE burning book, looks at his hand
unharmed by flame. He turns it, flexes it, awed by
the biomechanism. Under a sensurround of worled
skin veined by rivulets of green, he sees the mus-
culature of his metaphysique, the stone of fossil
bone adjutting at his wrists and knuckles, all the
jointing and articulation of his hand. Icefire,
bloodwine runs in his veins, and words are wires
in his brain, lines of black ink under his skin, the
Cant, the power of the unkin, of the Great Beyond,
the Deep Within. It is the song of a cunning vox
and an orphan liar, the tangle of tones played on
his bones.

He is a pattern of us, we try to tell him, bitmite-
built as all are now, unkin or human, but he does
not hear, unwilling to admit that this eternity of
flesh was his own fantasy once far ago and long
away.

HE GLARES AT all the little flares of fires around the
library. His eyes shimmer to mirrors of the flames,
cold orbs silvered as metal, an impassive gaze of
nickels shining with a cool lucidity. Inside, in all
the fine mechanics of his agital emotion, dialog of
intellect, still, he feels impervious *nothing*. He's far

off course, of course, insane. He should feel something on this day of all days, on this night of all
nights, of the wake.

No heart, no hurt, he tells himself.

Full Fierce

A DOOM OF rod on wood resounds, a formal call.
He snarls a blast of chilling Cant to still the fires,
leaving just half-burnt scrappings, flutterings of
ash, and turns toward the doors.

A set of stelae, smooth, of wet-slate-gray synthe,
solid and impervious as tombstones, cool to touch,
are set into the wall, illusion of a doorway. Two
pillars framing it are the true portals, two columns
of light which seem just one more feature of the
architexture of the library's urnate illuminations,
near identical except... one fire, the other flame,
one burns, the other blazes, the so subtle sense of
such a difference hinted in the quality of color that
reflects off the dark double-doors, a quiet comment that not all would note. The prince has
something of an artist's eye for light.

–ENTER.

The pillars shift and flicker in the air. Two mes-
sagers in blacksuit formal wear step out and stand.
Each clicks one heel hard on the deepwood floor.
Each bows his head. He notes the solid jut of jaw-
bone on them both, not square but wedge, cuneate
with softening curvation, not Neanderthal but...
anubian, a delicate strength. They are almost identical... not quite.

He and his blooder were once messengers like this, the prince recalls.

—M'sire, says one. There are disruptions in the Litan Quarter. The sandminers rise in open riot. We're quelling now but we require consent to use full force.

FULL FIERCE, HE thinks, *the farce of fools, full force.*

—The reacher's soldier is with them, the other says, arousing rabble. Word is that he has some champion named in this book they follow, that they're gathering to strike while we're… weakened.

The prince slicks his lips and sniffs, nods, not affirming but considering. These are the calls he'll have to make after tonight, after the wake and the ascension. After the craftsmith's graved the crown prince to his new role, his new rule. But he has freedom for these last few hours.

—Why are you questing me? he says. Am I the warrior my blooder was? Get your consent from any of the higher host, from one who fights and gives a fuck.

—M'sire, the higher ranks are gathered in the Hall awaiting…

The messenger trails off.

–ONLY YOU ARE still allowing access, says the other. M'sire, it is imperative the measures needed are consented to. We need to use full force.

—No, says the prince.

—M'sire?

—Give mercy.

He says it like it is an unfamiliar concept, as one studying a stranger in the shadows, and—for all the times he's argued in the past for truces, treaties with the rebels, for humane solutions—it's not empathy that shapes the words this time but something else, a pitiless decision born of hate. If they want someone bold and firm to take his blooder's place, to make their rules for them, to call their fates, maybe he'll cater to their taste, give them a ruthlessness they can't imagine. Just aimed at another place.

—Mercy? says the messenger.

He nods and waves the man away. Maybe he'll give them kingdom with the king himself as traitor to his race.

A Fun-For-All Wake

THE HOLLOW WAYS of gallowries and hallways echo with his footsteps, echo empty as the void, the void, the void he would avoid. If duty is to be fulfilled, he thinks, does that not mean it's empty? Oh, but there would be talk. The court's darkartist is a role that brings suspicion as it is. Student and scholar, poet and painter, devil's advocate in matters of debate, he's made few friends since his ascension to the rank. If he were not to play the role of the begrieved to their content, not show his face to all the mourning mass, to satisfy their empathy and sympathy, their sim of pity, their suspicions would become…

—Open, he calls.

* * *

HE STRIDES INTO the modern marble temple of authority, vast valor hall of unkin, the regal court filled with the city's lords, the senators and centurians of the soul. The high echelons of the empyreal city form a complex system of blooder dynasties and house vendettas, notable in the tableaux of tables but refractured and confugued by a more subtle politics of individuals intermingling in covert and overt companies and corps, alliances and betrayals, here a huddle of young warriors from different houses, there a clique of grand dams sat together. To ignore it is to let it win but then to challenge it is to be drawn in. Out in the streets the rebels reject all rule, rise up in revolution, but... to fight the Empire is to become it. The darkartist knows there has to be another way, some way away.

FROM HIGH VAULTS of an artificial sky, cerulean light sheens down upon a full feast slain out on the silk-draped tables. A zodiacal mandala of snow-white chariots and cherubs, radiant signs and sigils, wheels across the ceiling, a living cornicing of cloud. Walls of tall mirrors alternate with weights of azure draperies and intricate screens, fractal tapestries of ever-changing details. It's a vivid, velvet room, its scents of banqueting, its sounds a bold and bawdy Rabelaisian rubble, sunk in cacophonous ruin. The unkin drown their sorrows in lush liquid light. They fight the night with vibrancy of painted glamour.

He remembers his blooder's ascension to light-prince, the glory of the sun that shone in his words

when the craftsmith stepped back and he rose, the
new graving burning in him, and gave the call.

A SUMMARY OF all he sees, then: a hall of Babylon's barbarians, a fun-for-all wake of chaos, and
above it all the table of the Seven, the high table
where the warking and the craftsmith and the
lawscribe, the songweaver boy and the wildhunter
girl, sit waiting. There are two seats empty still, his
own to the far left, the other to the right. The seats
of the darkartist and the lightprince.

The masque goes on, a neverending feast of celebration, low but loudening laughter. Howls and
hails sound at his entrance as they rise to meet
him, greet him. But he knows foul well that even
as they welcome him they cannot look him in the
eyes; they cannot like him in the role.

Well, fuck you all for being here, he thinks.

The Velvet Gauntlet

INTO THE SEEMING chaos of the company he
strides, through all the angels of the secret kingdom, through the belohim and cainan, the
damnonii and athenatoi, the stonebuilders, truthmillers and soulfishers, all the leaders and
officiates of the houses, castes and guilds, the
sweating, seated, standing, sobbing, sodden mass
of them, all gathered in this place by the new
names that bind these gods of history now to one
grand host, all here to show their loyalty to the
slain. He walks the velvet gauntlet of their opulent
and splendorous show of dolor.

He sees it on their faces, how they hate that he's the only choice to take the role—the craftsmith and the lawscribe both too old and the songweaver just a boy. The wildhunter would have worn the glory better but she's needed now to lead them in the hunt. He doesn't like it any more than them, but this is how it is, how it has always been.

ONE BRAVE STEPS out into his path.

—M'sire, our hearts are with you. Will you ride with us to hunt the killers? When the glory's yours, I mean?

He remembers the change in his blooder, from songweaver to lightprince, stepping into the identity the present warking filled before him.

—Don't look so glum, he'd said before the ceremony. I'll still be me; it's just that my song will be light on steel and stone instead of… shapes in the air. You know I think revenge is… ugly. That won't change.

It had.

—Blood for blood, m'sire, another youngblood says. We are all broken on this day. There must be blood for blood. Have you scried your blooder's murderers, m'sire?

—Tell me, his blooder had said to the old dark-artist, as he stood there, newborn in the glory. Have you scried the old warking's murderers?

And they'd all turned—even the warking, one-time lightprince, gray and silent in his new authority of resolve rather than action—toward the old dark-artist, who had laughed, broken and bitter.

—Who do you fucking think put that old dog out of his misery?

THEY STAND ACROSS his path now and he hears the testing in their voices. Not all darkartists fall so fully and so finally as his predecessor, but it seems to be a risk of the role, in trying so hard to understand the twisting logic of the bitmites, to become twisted oneself, to turn. They want to hear his sorrow as a proof of innocence.

Voyeurs and vultures, keep your misery, he thinks. Spite in my face, with honesty.

He shakes his head. His voice is forced but firm.

—Not all deaths are murders, he says. It was an accident.

He sees suspicion flicker in their faces, incomprehension of his mood of speech, the soft restraint of spartan tenderness with something of violence underneath, intense in its tension. They have no shadows in their words. Desolumn-eyed, he simply stares down both the braves in front of him; one first, and then the other, they lower eyes, step to the side.

THEY WILL NOT face the features that resemble all too finely the fair figure of his golden blooder. Slight and sleek, he almost carries the same grace, but he is pale against the memory, dark night to his other's day, winter to his summer, ice to his fire. Still, when he was blooded, when his blooder sang the Cant that graved a new truth in his soul—*join us; you're unkin*—something of the other's self passed into him, rewrote him as a dark reflection; and the comparison of appearancies disturbs them all.

He is the ghost at his blooder's wake.

—Come ride with us in raptor's rapture, calls another from behind him as he walks on through the hall. Come fight with us. Come claim your right.

He doesn't even turn.

—It was an accident, he says.

A Bowl of Ash

HIS BLOODER MET the truth that he was looking for all his afterlife, as angel warrior, as song-weaver, and at last as lightprince, out in the fields, far out into the hinter. Blinded by sunlight and his golden hair, the wildhunter had told them, weep-ing, he stepped out where the cool sleek silver chrome of a synthe bolt from a disruptor took him down. A haunting accident. Three young men out in search of fun and game, burning the road of all dust with their ruptors, hounding through the grain. The hinter had built up a thirst though, and his blooder's gathering made rain, warm rain.

The killers fled, and talk of murder bred.

HE STANDS AT the high table now, ready to take his seat.

—Harpies, furies, valkyries await your call, warns the wildhunter. A whole armory of angel anger calls you out. If you deny your loss... the murdered future, murdered past... the blood cries out. They call you out into eternal now, to slay, to ride with them in wild infinity. It is the way it's done. For every one of us they kill, we slaughter one in ten of them.

He sits down in his blooder's chair. They need fire in the hinter's night. There has to be a light-prince. So, to end the wake, after his eulogy, the craftsmith will bring out a vial of bitmite ink and grave the glory on his chest, right down into his heart. If they can find it. Then...

He remembers watching the old darkartist's slaughter from his seat down with the annunaki, seeing his blooder's haloed face look out at him, a hint of doubt in his decision. But still he said it.

—Decimate the demons.

His mouth dry of all saliva, he chews without appetite on harvest hog, forestalling the inevitable, the toast and what comes after. He feels almost feverish, knowing what he's about to do. His mind blanks out the sounds of banquet in vin blanque and rich red wine, stonebuilders' talk of how the rubble must be crushed to dust, truthmillers' talk of sifting grain to sort it from the chaff, to grind it, leave no seed to spread the weed, soulfishers' talk of throwing out lines of inquiry, talespinners' talk of weaving webs to trap the killers. Dreamwhores' and heartweighers' talk of seductions, small transactions of the soul, of weights and balances and reckonings.

—Name these animals who killed him, the wild-hunter says. I'll send my best to bring you back their heads and hides from the most intimate of slayings.

She leans in close to speak only to him.

—Don't fight what has already been decided.

He dips a finger in a bowl of ash that sits to one side of his plate, the remnants of a funeral pyre that burned so high, so bright.

—WE DO NOT need to kill them, says the craftsmith. Once you're lightprince... there are tools to take these men apart and make things right, if this is what you want.

The darkartist looks at him. Of all of them, the craftsmith seems the only one with any grasp of... *what you are,* we whisper to him, *only humans raised to flesh fears and desires, servant divinities.*

—Enough, the warking says.

The hall falls into silence. It is time to make his toast, smear ash across his face. The others hold their hands poised over their own bowls, ready to join the howling of his sorrow. He scrapes back his chair and rises, bowl of ash held in one hand.

In the empty hall, his voice echoes, a growl.

—My blood is dead, he says. I wear the customary black and join this gathering of grief. What more is there to say? Should I wear words for you as well? Or should I strip my soul to satisfy your doubt? Write your own elegies.

He raises up the bowl of ash. And turns it upside-down over the feast.

—All I will say is that this is a hollow hall without him.

* * *

A Rebel Bound Less Than His Captors

THE COURT ROARS outrage, rising cries and toppling chairs. He listens to the drums of fists on tables, watches angels stagger drunkenly toward the table, pointing, shouting at his insult to the dead. He tears a fistful of carved meat powdered in ash and throws it out at them, as scraps of flesh to feed on, scraps of sorrow thrown to dogs, to beggars, with disgust. He fiends, he fends, he finds in his new attitude a power that makes them stop short of the table. Contoured by tragedy, he cuts a razorhewn new silhouette, standing before them as the scheming bastard.

Only one of them steps forward.

—There are those who say our enemy is among us, he says.

Or your enmity within you, thinks the prince. He leans forward, fists upon the table, full of haught and deignity.

–SAY IT. SPEAK what every one of you all thinks. Say it.

The unkin comes to stand in front of him, an old warrior, old guard. A veinous scar carves slaughter in the left side of his face, from forehead over missing eye and down to beard.

—There was a cry, he says. And with his death, with his last breath, they say he called your name.

The condemnations muttered through the crowd mix with confusion, consternation. They don't *know* his name, cannot; such things are guarded secrets in the city of the soul, where words are binding. His blooder would know it, yes, might even speak it at his death, but who would know who he was calling on? The darkartist scoffs.

—Who says this?

—This! a second voice calls out. This *thing*. We found it at the scene and bound it. You should hear it sing.

THE CHOREOGRAPHY IS perfect, planned precision, accusation waiting in the wings for this old fucker's wave of hand, and now the doorway facing him is opening and closing, and a path is clearing in the hall. The young man struggles as he's brought before the table. Flame-haired, sky-eyed and dressed in drab of khaki epauletted jacket, he cocks a sneering grin, a rebel bound less than his captors. The prince of end times pushes his chair back and walks around the table, unmoved by the warking's silent judgment, the wildhunter's gaze of satisfaction. The one who found his blooder. All of this, he's sure, this trap, is her undoing of him. He wonders if the man is in her pay or if she actually believes him; either could be true. The prisoner is shoved down to his knees in front of him.

—M'sire, he says.

A strange tone in his voice. The stranger takes his hand as if to kiss his ring in supplication, but then twists it in his grip to give a tender sensual press of lips to skin of inner wrist. The prince jerks his hand back, grabs the fucker's chin to raise it. Echoes, shadows, memories of scents. He slips his grip down to the larynx, muses, pictures the neck snapped between his fingers, the throat torn, the skull cracked on the marble floor.

Heads fall, hang heavy in silence in the hall.

—STAND, SAYS THE unkin prince. You say you heard the lightprince's last word?

—An invitation to you, says the prisoner. Come out and play.

There's whispers underneath his voice. *Laugh. Love life with me in the fields. We'll wild our bodies, glory in the dance, as idolescent and anubile ancients come of age, invernal in our grace. We must recover the sexual idyll of our race.*

He steps back in shock to clear the wild, weird resonances from his head. The Cant. The man is unkin, *rebel* unkin, unbound to the court. This isn't the turned treachery of a darkartist, but bloody freedom in a rogue graved only by his nature, unimaginable in this city at the end of everything, inconceivable. He glances back at the wildhunter. There's no way she can know this. There's no way that any of them can know this. There's no way.

A way, we hiss his thought. He gathers himself.

—An invitation? says the prince. Addressed to me by name?

—Invitation? Accusation? All I know is he desired your company in his death.

Light Coiled In Upon Itself
THE CROWD MURMURS this confirmation of suspicion through it as a ripple of grim certainty, proud

nods and noises. The stranger simply waits for the next question, a wild god playing some game unknown, so the darkartist walks round him to face the others of the broken Seven in their seats at the high table, the lawscribe at the warking's ear, the craftsmith studying the wildhunter who looks out at him, inscrutable. The poor songweaver's eyes dart this way, that, the nervous observations of a boy trying to take his signals from his elders.

All of them will fall.

—He called my name then, did he?

Straking fingers through his crow-black hair, the prince turns back to prowl around the stranger. Damn it, but there's something so familiar to his cocky grin, that kiss. In an eternity of lost lives, *could* they know each other? Could he know the name that the darkartist wears still under all the layers of graving? The man matches him step for step, daring his judgment with a taunt, a taint of innocence both steady and seductive.

—He called it loud and clear, he says. Trust me; you'll know it when you hear it.

–SAY IT, THEN, the prince says.

Underneath the sinuous surface of this, he's aware of a strange sexual alchemy at work, a necromance between his own rage and this other's appetence. They circle, fascinated, fastened in harmonious tension, as if searching for a chance, enwrapt, in hate or lust. Smooth in luxurious detachment, there is something about them of felines stalking, poised to pounce in animal uncoiling leap, to fight or fuck.

Two panthers in the skins of men, caged for an emperor's delight. The darkartist tries to remember who he was before, before the Cant called him out into the Illusion Fields.

—Say it, he says.

The stranger drops his grin, purses his lips as if to whisper, spreads his arms wide to his audience and says…

Nothing.

The cold truth slowly settles on the court, as one by one they realize that they're waiting for a word that will not come… all but the prince of end times who knows all too well this silence in his soul.

THE CRAFTSMITH'S NEEDLE graves the glory in his chest. The rebel kneels down, one hand on the floor, the other twisted back and up behind him by a warrior with blood upon his knuckles. More youngbloods stand around him, spatters on their white shirts, smears across their faces. Red streaks the prisoner's face, seeps from a gash above his eye, spits from his mouth with crack-toothed grin and cut lip, trickles from his broken nose to drip from chin to marble floor. They would have killed the stranger there and then if he'd not called for them to grave the glory on him *now* and let the fucker face a student reborn as a soldier. From the wildhunter's nod, her mouthed *at last* and curt command to *hold the rebel liar,* he understands now that her trap was only aimed at this, at pushing him to break, surrender to the role, the rebel simply goad or bait.

But as the craftsmith's needle writes that new role on his chest, as sunlight dances on his golden skin, and bone and flesh and hair and eyes, even the blood of him, shifts and reshapes beneath the graving of the glory, he studies this stranger who still grins through his red mask of ruin, his bloodied eye closing and opening, a wink.

THE LIGHTPRINCE STANDS to speaks to the assembled throng with his new-found authority, and every voice is still, in awe of this... pure force now facing them, not gold but white as virgin snow, whiter than bone or ivory, white-hot as burning metal. A rebel plot, he tells them. Murder and deceit. A ruptor bolt to bring his blooder down, a lie to topple *him*. Now is the time, he tells them, for the old tradition of the hunt, the decimation of demon humanity. They cheer, exultant, the wildhunter loudest of them all. He slaps a hand upon her shoulder, tells her she must lead them, sound the call. Thinks to himself of how he will arrange her fall, how he will turn her dogs upon her.

Under the glamour, as they'll never understand, his dark is there still, not an absence of the light— it never was—but light coiled in upon itself, an energy more fierce because it's twisted, wound and sealed into a ball of matter. Glory? True glory is a sun so vast that it's collapsed into itself, falling for-ever inwards to a point of zero size, infinite density, a black hole where all laws are shattered and all craft undone, all songs unwoven to a single ever-falling note. And now to start a war on war itself, he thinks.

He orders the prisoner let loose, sent back to give his rebel masters notice that they're coming, that the new lightprince is in his role, and burning brighter, fiercer than was ever known.

—Go to your taverns and your drinking dens, he says, and tell them that we come to slaughter every one in ten. And then...

He holds the stranger's eye, the two of them sharing a crystal moment from eternities ago, without words, without breaking from their chosen roles, remembering a split of paths.

—*Can't you hear it? Can't you hear it call my name?*

—*I can't hear anything, mate. Nothing.*

—*Exactly.*

—And then, he says, we slaughter every one in ten *again*, and then *again*, and we *keep* killing them until we're hacking pounds of flesh from a few men.

Until there is no human left, he thinks, who will not rest until they've had revenge.

Across the Cold Sandscape

ELSEWHEN, IN A helter skelter duststorm, a behemoth like a mastodon on tundra is starkweathering its age of ash across a world of desert night. A shape with lion's mane, bear-face and giant body of a man on hands and knees, it haunches its low descent into the burning hail, shambling through the hounded land, crawling on as a pilgrim turned dumb brute. Around it, bonesands drift around the shells of ghost towns long since boomed and shattered, dead in the dust and empty of the beat of empire's drum.

To reach the dawn from midnight in this after-world, the creature crawls through hinter's hell, so lost to survival it's forgotten that it's only chasing its own tale, dawn walking on in front of it across the folds, ever westward, ever returning. If he were phased with it, a man could seek the hidden empire of the equinox forever, ever the stranger come to slay the temple's guardian chimera, marry with the morningstar princess, in haven after haven across the Vellum's hinter. But this creature follows all the cities' falls, seeking something it's become too much a brute to even imagine. All it can do is slouch on through the desolation of its dreams, hoping for...

The creature that was once a hero lifts its hoary head.

A scent of spring or summer.

THE BILLOWING BONESANDS lift in the dry wind they call the maja, blow across the cold sandscape, and scour the hands of the lightprince. His face masked in a jackal-helm of alloyed gold and adamantium, he sails his sloop out of the western sands, the onyxidian sigils on his breastplate glinting jet-black on the gold, his gauntlets held in one hand with the reins so with the other he can stroke the wind and signal it to his command. The wild-hunter and her hellhounds far behind, he rides alone over the waste.

He sights the beast, swoops round and down, sloop shining as a chariot sun and spraying sand in landing. Ruptor blazing at the beast, he hits it hard and true with each shot, and it bellows, staggers. He leaps out to slide his way down dunes that sprout beneath his feet with wheat, with grasses bursting into life to mark the golden hero's passing. Pride of lions in his walk, swoop of an eagle, of a hawk, by the time he's reached the beast the very world around him is an idyll singing his praises.

THE ROUGHEST AND most bestial of the ancients slumps down in the wilderness, falls to one side, breath steaming from its nostrils, sandscape slowing all around it, shimmering. Hunger, thirst and other lusts billow away. Long-dormant memories rise and fall in the dust devils, settle into place. Lines of force and fields of truth come clear and, in the shifting desert dunes, it glimpses lives in grains that seem to glint with sunlight: a caverned rock; an underriver; and a city lost and sunken where lush garden green clings to the golden stone and draws its liquid life from dead soul deeps, a city at the end of everything, graved in the antique song, the Cant, the Cant it too once sang. It hears it now over the rasp of its own dying breath, the last gasp of this slain apocalypse creature, even as the flowers spring up around it as the lightprince walks into the meadow of its death.

He crouches down to close the dead thing's eyes then rises, looks around. A glint in the distance, a flash of his own sunlight sylph reflected, and he turns in curiosity, stepping forward, hair flown in his face.

The bolt hits him.

HE LIES IN the grass looking up at a blue-black night sky turning paler, through azure toward cerulean, with dawn sweeping in so fast, time speeding up, his heart slowing down as it empties his blood onto the red soil through the hole in his neck and the fingers clutching it, three shadows standing over him, the one with flame-hair asking if he's dead, no, and another pulling him away, a third in silhouette saying they have to go, but, no, he wants to stay, to wait and see him slip away, but it sounds like he's whispering for him to stay a wake, no, stay *awake*, to stay awake, he's saying, as a way to… no, no, it's too late, no, there's no hate, all that's already slipped away, but wait, he has a message, he has words to say, he has to stay, wait, no, don't go away, you have to say to him, tell him to find a way, a way to say we cannot stay, to say his toast to all the host, when they arise for me, when they full feast on roasted beast, ask him to say, to drink the red wine down and all away, and say there is a way, there is a way, a way away…

No, wait.

He feels death's kiss. Silence. A hiss.

Say only this…

KING TALES

Jeff VanderMeer

I. The Trouble with Bears

ONCE UPON A time the King of the Bears found a girl named Masha wandering through the forest looking for wildflowers. Her parents had told her not to go out into the woods, but she'd ignored them. She was very surprised to see the bear— almost as surprised as the bear was to see her.

"Hello to you," said the King of the Bears. Admittedly, he was the only bear in this particular forest.

"Hello," said Masha, with a tremor of fear in her voice. For the bear was huge—golden brown, with enormous claws on its padded feet and sharp, pure-white fangs bigger than her hands, and eyes a startling blue. He smelled like mint and blueberries for some reason.

"How lucky am I," the bear said. "Now have someone cook and clean for me. As befit King of Bear. Cottage big mess. I spent lot of time teaching self to talk so no time to clean up. From now on you be my servant."

"That'd be nice," Masha said, getting a little angry now that she'd forgotten her fright. "But I've got to get home to my parents."

The bear shook his head. "Naw. That not happening. My name King Bear, by the way. I'm bear." And so saying he scooped up Masha, shoved her over his shoulder, and went back to his cottage, where Masha spent the next week cleaning up after the messy bear.

IT DIDN'T TAKE long for Masha to get sick of toiling away, especially since King Bear hardly seemed like royalty. Not only did he leave huge crumbs of bread and sticky pieces of beehive all over the place, but the sink was always full of dirty dishes and he was forever tracking paw prints of ash out of the fireplace. At Masha's house her father and mother split the chores so she wasn't used to doing so much, either. She was also sure her parents were worrying about her.

Whenever she pleaded with King Bear to let her go, he just shushed her and said, "Go on cleaning. When cleaning's done, you go home."

But the cleaning was never done! Because no matter how hard she tried, she just couldn't keep up with the messes the bear kept making.

"The rain in Spain falls mainly on the plain," King Bear would say, strutting around the cottage while practicing his English. "The bears at fairs play mostly on the stairs." Every time he took a step, some crumb would bounce off of his fur onto the ground, or he'd knock over a lamp or something.

At night, King Bear would sleep on his ridiculously tiny bed, haunches hanging off of it, in his ridiculous pajamas, complete with a little cloth hat with a tassel on the end of it. He snored so loudly, she never got more than three hours' sleep. This made Masha even angrier. But even if she'd run away, she didn't know where she was, or how to get back to her parents, so she stayed and did the cleaning. All the time getting more and more furious with the bear.

Things only got worse when King Bear began to insist on holding court. With a broom for a scepter and a bucket for a crown, he'd sit in a ruined rocking chair. Masha would be required to curtsey and say, "Your majesty is so powerful and wise. You speak so well."

Then one particularly difficult day, under a huge pile of dirty bear clothes, Masha found a basket. It wasn't a normal-sized basket. It was a bear-sized basket. About as big as she was. When she saw it, Masha smiled. Suddenly, she had a plan.

THE VERY NEXT week, Masha baked some pies and then told the bear, "You need to let me go back to my village. I want to take my parents some pies to eat. I promise I'll come right back. Just show me the way."

King Bear laughed, revealing his snow-white fangs. "Naw. That not happening. Who would clean all day? This place is mess. King Bear need servant."

"Well, then, you take them. You can just set the basket on the doorstep and come right back here."

"Naw, that not happening," Bear said. "Now, go back to clean up."

At that, Masha began to cry.

The sadness on her face was so great that something unfroze in the heart of the great bear. Confusion spread across his features, and he realized just how terrible his thoughtlessness had been.

"Okay," King Bear said. "I King Bear takes pies to parents. But you stay here."

Masha smiled through her tears. "I will, King Bear, your highness. I will! But I'm going to climb that tall tree outside of your cottage to keep an eye on you. I don't want you eating any of those pies along the way!"

King Bear smiled back, which for the bear looked more like he was about to devour Masha. "Whatever you say."

Masha said, "Now, I'll just go and pack those pies."

As soon as King Bear had left, Masha crawled into the basket and covered herself with pies.

When King Bear came into the kitchen he found it empty but for the basket. On top of the basket was a drawing of Masha's village showing her parents' house. King Bear smiled to himself. At heart, he was not a bad monarch, just a thoughtless one. Nor was he a stupid bear, despite his bad English.

KING BEAR SET out for the village through the thick, deep forest.

After awhile, he sat down on a tree stump and yawned. "His Excellency am tired, hungry," he said. "I have pie…" He reached over to open the basket.

Masha's voice, muffled and distant, came to him: "I see you! I see you from the tree. Don't eat any of those pies! Those pies are for my parents."

King Bear grinned a toothy grin. "Uh oh," he said loudly. "Masha must see me from tall tree. I guess I not eat pie."

Then he picked up the basket and continued through the forest. The basket, he had realized a long time before, was a lot heavier than it should be if it contained just a few pies.

The bear and Masha repeated this charade two or three times before he got to the village. King Bear found himself getting a little grumpy. *Just how stupid Masha think me am?* he thought.

By the time King Bear reached the village, it was dusk and not many people were out. He was able to walk down the street without fear of discovery. Soon, he came to Masha's parents' house. He set the basket down and knocked on the door.

Slowly, Masha's father opened the door and stared up at the great bear.

"Who are you?" Masha's father asked. He didn't sound frightened, probably because Masha's mother was hidden behind the door holding a shotgun.

"I'm King Bear, King of all the Bear," said King Bear. "And I, his Highness on high, bring your daughter home and pies. She's in basket right there. All in return is you help me, King Bear, with English."

Masha's father looked at the King of the Bears. The "King of the Bear" looked at Masha's father.

It is not clear that either thought much of the other.

But after a moment, Masha's father motioned to his wife to put down the shotgun, and said, "We will be happy to help you with your English, but for a month, no more. Is that sufficient? We are grateful you've brought home our daughter... regardless of the circumstances."

King Bear bowed and said, "Yes," just as Masha shot out of the basket and into her father's arms.

AFTER A MONTH, King Bear's English was so good that he gave up his title of King of the Bears and ran for mayor of the village. After he won, he renamed himself "Just a Plain Old Bear of the People." He bought a fancy three-piece pinstriped suit and a hat that looked remarkably like a crown. He never returned to his messy cottage in the woods.

As for Masha, she never went out in the woods again, or did anything that her parents told her not to, and eventually she grew up to be a smart, talented woman—although she never was any good at outsmarting talking animals.

II. The Unreliability of Cats

ONE EVENING FARMER Jones was lurching his way back from the pub. He had a wheel of cheese under his right arm for his wife, Greta, and a bottle of milk in his left hand for his cat, Tom. He'd had two pints too many of a good stout and lost half of the money he'd made selling vegetables by playing dice, badly. Still, he was happy with himself, whistling an old tune from when he'd been a boy, and eager to tell his wife the bar gossip. (Which included new insight into Old Man Bobbin's gold and the whereabouts of a certain mother-of-pearl hairpin.) There was a brisk chill to the air that made it seem like he wasn't old and drunk. And he'd called out "Britch" Perrin, who'd been claiming Farmer Tom's vegetables were half-rotten, only to have Britch sit himself right down again and shut up.

As he walked, he did an awkward shadow box, reliving that moment of indecision on Britch's face, convinced that if it'd come to blows with Britch, he'd've been able to take him.

"Stupid cow farmer," he muttered to himself, his ruddy face a little redder than usual. "Don't even own a cat. What kind of farmer doesn't have a cat?!"

Halfway home, with the farmhouse a dim shadow on a hill in the distance, and a glowering full moon lighting his way, a strange sound cut through Farmer Jones's whistling.

Now what could that be? It was muffled yet sharp, and it sounded like many, many voices. Coming from where?

Farmer Jones stopped walking. He stood in a field of wildflowers and grass. The fireflies had come out. The crickets had begun to fidget. The smell of pollen was thick as honey. But, there was that sound.

"Oooooh ooooh ooooh! MMmmmm. MMmm-mmm. Mmmmm."

Farmer Jones had good ears. He could hear one of his kids doing something wrong from miles away. "Why, he can hear a mouse fart in a thunderstorm," his wife was fond of saying, for no particular reason and much to his embarrassment.

"Now, woman, why would I want to hear a sound like that?" he'd snarl.

But this sound confounded him. Where was it coming from? He couldn't tell.

That's when he saw the light coming out of a hole in the ground.

"What in the name of Hell and Ireland?" he said.

There it was, a light shining out of a hole in the ground a little to his left.

His first thought was to run home as fast as he could and forget he'd ever seen a shining hole in the ground. His second thought was, *Maybe the sound's coming from in there?* His third thought was, *Maybe the little people are having a party and throwing their gold around.*

If not for the drink or the vivid memory of Britch backing down, he might have listened to his first thought. As it was, he put down the milk and the cheese on the soft grass and knelt beside the hole.

"*Oooooh oooooh ooooh! Mmmmmmm. Mmmmm. Mmmmm,*" he heard again, louder.

The sound was definitely coming from beneath the ground.

Slowly, on knees creaky from years of milking cows, Farmer Jones lowered himself against the grass, put his eye to the hole, and saw: a cavern hollowed up beneath the hole, twenty strong mice holding up a slow-moving coffin. Around the mice cats prowled, singing out, "*Oooooooh ooooooooooh oooooooh. Mmmmmmm. Mmmmmmm. Mmmmmmm.*" The coffin was decorated in gold and silver and had a shiny black metal mask of a cat's face atop it. The mice were all weeping. The cats wept, too, even as they held up tiny torches.

Farmer Jones started, got to his feet. Suddenly he felt old again. Too much beer. Too much time gambling. It had rotted his brain right out of his skull.

Coffin. Mice. Cats. Crying. What?

He looked off toward his house. It wasn't that far. But he couldn't just pick up his cheese and milk and continue on. Not now.

So instead he bent down and looked again.

The mice were crying as before, but now the cats were singing, "The King of the Cats is dead. The King of the Cats is dead."

As Farmer Jones watched, the strange procession passed out of view, leaving the cavern beneath silent and dark.

Farmer Jones had never seen anything quite like it. Maybe he ought to join old Britch in applying buttocks to seat.

He sat in the long grass for awhile, looking up at the moon, before picking up his milk, his cheese, and continuing on to his house.

INSIDE, GRETA TOOK the cheese and milk from him and set him down at a cold dinner.

"Eat your vegetables," she told him while Tom the cat curled around his legs under the table. Tom was a gorgeous, muscular tabby with huge emerald eyes.

"I'll eat my vegetables," Farmer Jones said. For some reason, all of his bar tales had fled from his thoughts.

"And you'll tell me how your day went and how much money you made," Greta said, wiping her hands on her apron. She'd made meatloaf, boiled carrots and cabbage, and a nice salad.

The fork in Farmer Jones's hand felt leaden.

"I saw something amazing just now," he said to Greta.

"Oh—and what might that be?"

He ate a boiled carrot, said, "A funeral. On the way home. In the field of wildflowers."

Greta looked at him sharply. He could tell she thought it might be the drink telling the tale.

"A funeral you say. Anyone we know?"

"No," Farmer Jones said. "At least, I don't think so."

"Hmmm," said Greta.

"Did I tell you I faced down Britch today," Farmer Jones said in a distracted voice.

"No, no you didn't. Nor did you tell me what happened to all our vegetables. How much did you get?" Greta asked.

"There was a funeral."

"Yes, dear, you've said that already."

"A funeral for a cat."

"A funeral for a cat."

Her tone told him what she thought of that story.

Around his feet curled Tom, meowing for scraps.

"Yes. With weeping mice holding the coffin. And the cats were singing, "Oooooooh ooooh ooooh. Mmmmmm. Mmmmm. Mmmmmm.""

"Is that so? And was Britch one of the cats? And was another one of the cats a pint of stout? And were the mice all shots of single malt?"

Farmer Jones seemed to shake himself awake. This wouldn't do. He was falling into a kind of haze, a kind of *other place* and once there he might not get out again.

"I tell you, Greta, I saw a funeral for a cat."

Greta sat back in her chair. "If this is your way of saying you gambled all the vegetable money away…"

Farmer Jones stood up and pounded his fist against the table. He wasn't really angry, but he felt like he had to do something forceful.

"No! It's not my way of saying I gambled away the money. I saw a funeral for a cat. Let me finish. I saw a funeral, yes, but not just for any old cat." Farmer Jones drew a great breath. "I saw a funeral for the King of the Cats!"

Whatever Greta thought he was going to say, Farmer Jones could tell this was not it.

At Farmer Jones's feet, Tom made a growling sound at his feet.

"What?!?! The King of the Cats is dead?" Tom said. "Is this true, Farmer Jones?"

From a long way away Farmer Jones heard someone say, "Yes, it's true."

"Why then," Tom said with a yip of delight, "That means I am now the King of the Cats!"

Tom stood up on his hind legs and began to dance as Greta gasped. Then he ran into the cold fireplace and up through the chimney. They could hear him yowling his delight for many minutes before the sound faded into the distance.

"Well," said Greta after a little while. "I think I might just believe you."

Farmer Jones started to say something—he wasn't sure what—but Greta shushed him. "That doesn't mean I want to talk about it anymore. And I tell you what—I never want another cat around these parts ever again. Now, eat your salad."

So Farmer Jones ate his salad, very slowly, and eventually he told Greta about Britch and about the rumors in the town and they never discussed the cat funeral or Tom's amazing speechifying ever again. Nor did they ever see Tom again.

But at dusk of a day, coming back from the pub a little tipsy, Farmer Jones from that time forward would always look for a shaft of light coming from among the cool grass and the wildflowers—look for it, sometimes he would say, long for it—but never find it.

III. The Indecisiveness of Birds

A LONG TIME ago in Africa, the lion was made the King of the Animals. This made the birds very angry. After all, lions cannot fly. Therefore, the lion could not be the rightful king of the birds.

So the birds held a meeting to decide who should be the King of the Birds. The forest filled up with birds in all shapes and colors, chattering, chirping, and cawing their opinions of who should be named king. Flamingoes and storks came to the meeting; so did eagles and owls, finches and king-fishers. There were so many birds in one place that the air was dark with them, the branches of the trees bent over with the weight of them.

Finally, when they were all assembled, Nkwazi, the fish eagle, spoke up.

"For too long the lions have claimed to be our king," Nkwazi said. "Lions have no wings and they cannot fly. I say, if you cannot fly, you cannot be King of the Birds! Er, no offense to our cousins from the south," he added, noting a couple of dejected-looking penguins that had swum and waddled to the meeting.

"Further," Nkwazi said, "as the most 'kingly' of all birds, I believe I should be your leader."

"Now, just wait a second," said the eagle owl, whose name was Khova. "You certainly look like a king—especially when you've got your butt up in the air while diving for fish…" All the birds starting laughing at that. "But I think I should be the King of the Birds. After all, I have the largest eyes, and I'm very wise. Since I know best, I should be king."

Kori Bustard laughed at that. "Ha! An owl and an eagle. Thinking they should be king. But I am the biggest bird in Africa. I am the strongest. I should be king!"

The birds all began arguing about who should be king, making so much noise it annoyed the lions napping on the ground below. They didn't care who became King of the Birds—as they saw it, every bird had to land on the ground someday, which meant every bird would become a meal someday—but they didn't like their nap being disturbed.

A very quiet but clear bird voice piped up. "If no one can decide, I'll happily be the King of the Birds."

The bird that had spoken flew into the middle of the gathering. It was Ncede, a southern warbler—a small, drab bird that had never before spoken up at any of the bird meetings.

Nkwazi, Khova, and Kori all started laughing at Ncede.

Amused, Nkwazi said, "Fine. If you want to be the King of the Birds, you can compete with us."

"A competition?" Khova said. "That's a splendid idea."

"Yes," said Kori Bustard, looking hungrily at the succulent little warbler. "A contest is the best way to settle this."

THEY SOON DECIDED on a very simple contest, with the kingfisher as the referee.

"Each of you will fly as high as you can," the kingfisher said. "The one who can fly the highest will become the King of the Birds."

The kingfisher didn't bother to enter the contest. The kingfisher was already King of the Water Birds. He didn't really want the added responsibility of being King of all the Birds. Most days, he couldn't stand to be around the other birds, anyway.

So, on the count of three, Nkwazi the fish eagle, Khova the eagle owl, Kori the Bustard, and Ncede the warbler, shot into the sky, flying as fast and as far as they could, right up into the sky.

Nkwazi took the lead right away. Looking down, he could only see Khova and Kori. "Why, the warbler is already out of the race," he thought to himself. "Not as if he could have won any-way…"

Up and up Nkwazi went, faster and faster. No bird could fly as high as he could. Below, Khova struggled to keep up. Kori had gotten closer, but still couldn't get into the lead.

But the next time he looked down, he could tell that Kori was shouting something up at him.

"…you have… bird… back…"

"What?" Nkwazi shouted down at Kori. "I can't hear you. Speak up."

But Kori's voice only got fainter. Nkwazi was very high up now, and Kori could not follow. Still, Nkwazi climbed into the air. He wanted to prove to everyone just how much better he was.

Finally, he reached as high as he could go. His wings were tired. His lungs were straining. This was high enough. He had beaten them all. He began to glide, high, high over the earth.

It was then that Ncede the warbler flew off of Nkwazi's back and up into the sky, even higher than Nkwazi had gone, and Nkwazi could go no higher—already he was falling lower, just too tired to do more.

"Ncede!" Nkwazi screamed. "You trickster! I'll get you! You'll never be the King of the Birds!"

Ncede did not reply, just kept flying.

Ncede wasn't the kind of bird who could stay up high for long, though. Soon, he had to come down, and when he did, the fish eagle, the eagle owl, and the bustard were waiting for him. They pecked at him with their beaks, lunged at him with their talons. But he was speedy and elusive. He flew between them and back into the forest, hiding in a hole in the ground.

By now, the other birds had left, for none of them wanted to face the anger of three such dangerous birds as the fish eagle, the eagle owl, and the bustard. Only the kingfisher wasn't afraid of those three, but he had some fishing to do, so he'd taken off at the start of the race. He really didn't care who won, so long as they stayed off his turf.

* * *

FOR THREE DAYS and nights, Nkwazi, Khova, and Kori took turns guarding the hole Ncede had hid in.

For three days and nights, one of them would say, "Ncede, come out of that hole. We won't hurt you. Just come out and talk to us."

To which Ncede would reply, "I'm the King of the Birds now. Leave me alone. I command you to leave me alone. Besides, I'm not coming out. You'd just eat me."

Finally, on the fourth day, Khova the eagle owl fell asleep while guarding the hole. Ncede noticed this and darted out of the hole and flew away into the deepest part of the forest. The whole way, as he flew, he kept singing, "I am the King of the Birds. I am the King of the Birds." To this day, Ncede claims to be the King of the Birds.

But the fact is, dear reader, no one could ever really decide who would be the King of the Birds, and so there is no King for the Birds alone—only the King of the Animals, which, as we all know, is the lion.

As for Nkwazi, Khova, and Kori, the fish eagle went back to doing what he most liked—hunting for fish—and the bustard went back to doing what he most liked—watching Nkwazi hunt for fish and then waiting to eat whatever parts of the fish Nkwazi didn't eat. But poor Khova could never get over falling asleep while guarding the hole. To this day, Khova is so ashamed that he only comes out at night, so that the other birds will not see him. And to this day, at twilight, he hunts for Ncede the warbler, searching for him everywhere, with his huge eyes and his sharp talons. Sometimes he finds Ncede, and sometimes he does not.

IN BETWEEN DREAMS

CHRISTOPHER BARZAK

I'M POLISHING THE coffee table in the living room when I hear the man moan behind the door again. I look up, my hand still gripping the cloth on the table, and stare at the sliding door. I've already spent an hour listening to him recount his memories and dreams this morning before I made myself leave his side to do what I have been hired for. That is, to clean this apartment and take the yen left on the coffee table after I am finished. I'm to leave the bedroom untouched, unlooked at even, and if I happen to hear something strange occur behind its door, I am not to pay it any mind. The yen on the table is a separate amount from what I'm paid by my agency. It's left behind to pay for my ignorance of the man in the next room, the foreigner who speaks his memories and dreams as he remembers and dreams them. If the owner of this apartment ever suspects I've done more than stand by the door and listen to the sleeping man's mutterings, I'm not sure what would happen. I think he would do more than fire me. That is, I think my life would be in danger.

I should never have taken this job.

Or rather, I should never have slid the door open and peered in on the man that first time, a month ago, as I do now, creeping in on tiptoe to watch the man moan in what seems like pain even though he has no sign of fever when I touch the back of my hand to his forehead. His eyes are open (they sometimes are) but he's unable to see. They are so blue I think I could fall into them and drown. His lips are so soft. If I kissed him, they would turn purple and bruise as soon as my mouth left his.

"You're home again," he says. I snatch my hand away from his forehead. "Is that you? Please say something. You never speak to me anymore, except when it pleases you."

I understand most of what he's saying. These simple words and grammars are easy, high school English mostly, unlike when he tells stories and becomes intense, his words racing, and I can only make out how heartbroken he is, I can only hear the plea in his voice to be released. I don't say a word though. After all, I don't know what he says when my employer is with him in the evenings. Never trust a sleep talker. If you reveal your secrets to them, they can be your undoing.

"I don't know what to do," he says, "how to live like this. I tell myself you still love me, that you'll come home one day and see the mistake you've made, that you'll wake me from this, that something will change. Something *has* changed. I felt it. I feel it even now. Some time ago—a week? A month ago? I can't keep track of time any longer—you put your arms around me and carried me through the house like a bride. I know that sounds ridiculous. A bride. It's not as if we can even marry. I never expected that really, but maybe I had something like a dream a long time ago, at our beginning, before we came to be who we are now. I had a dream that, even though it's impossible in this world for us to marry, we might still do something like it. An approximation. We could have shared our lives as one. Did that ever occur to you too? Did you ever want something more than what we are? You do know what I mean, don't you?"

I do understand a little, but after high school I stopped studying English and sometimes he uses words I've never heard before. It makes me angry. I should have gone to college. But how could I? It's not as though my parents could have paid my way. Still, I might have been more responsible and studied on my own. If I'd done that, I'd understand his English perfectly. And I can tell by what I do know of his words that he is a romantic. Someone who would understand my soul.

He lies on a futon on the tatami floor, cradled in a heap of blankets, his cheek on the pillow, his lips fluttering as his words flow from his mouth like the gurgle of a clear stream. I saw a stream like that once, when I took the train on a whim one day from Tokyo to the countryside and caught a bus to an area full of rice fields and gently curving hillsides. I walked until the fields became forest, and then through the forest I walked until the land began to slope upward and I found myself at a stream. There I sat back on my haunches and looked at my reflection in the glass of the water and wondered why I was so weak. And, moments later, was given an answer.

His words are like that stream. If I understood all of them, I'd see myself as clearly as I did that day, in that other stream.

"Do you remember the day you introduced me to your parents? You weren't worried at all. And there I stood beside you, the blue-eyed devil, as your grandmother used to call white people, worried about not being able to understand what your parents and brother and sister-in-law said, worried I'd make you look like a fool. I was surprised you even wanted to introduce me to them. I know that what we are isn't talked about openly here. I know that it's best kept a secret. And yet you didn't keep it a secret from anyone.

"Your father spent the night plying me with sake while he told me stories of your childhood. Whenever I understood what he said without your interpretation, he'd hold his hands over his head as if we were playing American football and I'd just kicked a field goal. Afterward he'd make me drink more sake and settle into another story, telling me about how silly you were as a boy.

"Your brother and sister-in-law disappeared at some point in the evening with their newborn son. They were taking a bath in the bathroom together, getting ready for bed. You said it was custom for children to spend the night in their childhood home on New Year's Day. But we weren't going to do that, even though your father had asked you in private if we would stay and have a bath together too. He was a dear old man. An ex-railway worker, proud of his former career. How I miss him when I think of him now.

"It was New Year's Day, that day. We'd known each other for barely a week, and I somehow already knew I loved you. After I met your family, though, I loved you even more."

Love, love, love. Half of the words he says are love. He doesn't change, and I've been working in this apartment for over a month, listening to him almost the entire time. I feel like I know him even though he's never seen me. It makes me want to tell him my story, for him to understand me as well. He makes me want to tell him about the day I went to the stream in the mountains without knowing where I was going, or why I went in the first place.

When I found myself at the stream by chance or fate that day, I was eighteen and had been working at the Seven-Eleven for two years. I'd finished high school though. Mother made sure I had at least that much education. She worked herself to death to keep us fed and with a good roof to sleep under, and to pay for my father's medical bills. Always it was Father's medical bills, his medicines, his visits to the hospital. Always it did him no good. He sat in a wheelchair at the dining room window all day long, no matter what treatment they gave him, staring at nothing, saying nothing, hearing nothing we said.

He'd been in that condition since I was ten. He was one of the unfortunates who, on their way to work that fateful morning over a decade ago now, breathed the fumes of sarin gas left by Aum cult members in the Tokyo subway trains. A woman found him on a platform in the underground, his body flipping about like a fish pulled onto a riverbank. She had breathed the poison too, but she'd quickly noticed something was wrong and left her train as soon as it pulled into the next stop. It was her that called the ambulance to help my father.

At the hospital, his doctors told us he'd get better, but the only thing they did was help him breathe on his own again. Afterward, whenever I knelt in front of his wheelchair and said, "Papa, it's Ai. Papa, please say something," he'd only looked over my shoulder at something too far away for me to see.

I took the train after my shift at the Seven-Eleven was over on a spring day. I went into the countryside and walked through the fields and woods up into the mountain without any knowledge of what I was doing. It was not until I arrived at the stream that I returned to myself and knelt by the water and saw who I was again.

My head tilted to one side, I examined the dark curve of hair along my jaw line. I was eighteen, wearing a Seven-Eleven smock as if it were my uniform outside of work as well as during work hours. Even in that uniform, though, I realized for the first time in my life that I was a little bit pretty. I hadn't understood before, but suddenly I understood why boys had always made lewd comments to me in high school, why old men hung around the store everyday staring at me while they pretended to page through manga and magazines. One day a salary man I often saw at the store brought condoms to the counter, and when I put his money in the register and returned his change, he quickly closed his hand around mine and whispered, "Could you help me make use of these?"

I pulled my hand away and shook my head, but I didn't say anything. I went to the back of the store and cried until my coworker found me and said to pull myself together, there are fates worse than working at Seven-Eleven after all. And though it was a bad moment, I knew what she said was true.

I saw the softness of my skin in the water, the fine bones in my face, the roundness of my eyes, the lilt in my hair. I tried to smile, but for some reason the smile didn't look right on me. It seemed more natural if I stared, showing no emotion at all. Perhaps I had grown used to making that sort of face, so I didn't know what to think when I saw a me that appeared happy.

I smile down now, as I kneel beside the dreamer's futon. I try to smile like a lover might, or like a mother as she stands guard over her child.

"It was after meeting your family at New Year's that we decided I'd move from my little apartment in Ibaraki to your apartment in Nagoya. And for the first time in a long time, I was truly happy. I didn't think it was possible to be as happy as I was when I was with you. You tricked me into letting you inside my heart with stories of your childhood, and then on top of that your father had confirmed how wonderful your childhood had been. But perhaps we are all biased in such a way toward the lives of those we love. Perhaps we all see our beloved as a child and ourselves as their caretaker. How you and I have twisted that relationship beyond recognition. How we have tainted love.

"Before we met, I'd decided my life in Japan would be the life of an amnesiac. I would cast my memories of America into an oubliette and live as if I'd never lived a day before I set foot in Japan. But after we met, after that first meeting at the shop window during the winter holidays, after you took me home and made love to me, after you warmed me with the warmth of your childhood memories, I was suddenly able to see the warmth in memories of my own past as well. And soon I, too, wanted to share my past, my memories, with you.

"At first you listened when I tried to tell you about why I'd come here, but as I persisted in speaking about my brothers, my parents, my old friends from college, you became suspicious. Why did I speak of my past so often now, you must have wondered, when at our beginning I had offered nothing but my body, a blank slate upon which you could imagine any past you wanted me to have.

"The truth was, the truth is, I wanted you to be able to love me the way I'd come to love you. I wanted you to know who I was and still want me. But you found my desire for this sort of love dangerous. I think, for you, if I had a past in America without you, it meant there might be a future for me there that you would have to acknowledge as well."

It was in that moment of staring into the stream, realizing my own beauty, that something even more amazing happened. As I lingered over my features, touching my cheekbones and the curves of my lips as if this was the first time I'd seen anything like them, another woman's face suddenly appeared in the water beside mine. She blinked her long lashes then smiled, and I let out a yelp of surprise. Startled, I fell backward, wheeling my arms in a futile attempt to regain my balance. But despite my best efforts I landed on my backside and, when I opened my eyes, I found her face hovering over mine, smiling down.

"Oh, so sorry!" she said. "Please forgive me. It was not my intention to frighten you."

She wore an old, blue silk kimono with a pattern of cherry blossoms swirling around white moons, and inside each moon was the rabbit who lives there and watches everything that happens here on earth. He had an evil-looking eye, so I looked up at the girl's face again. That was worse, though. Her eyes were green, and I found a scream rising from my throat once again.

"Be calm," she said. "I mean you no harm. If you look past my difference, you will see I am the same as you."

She was Japanese, certainly, but no Japanese girl I knew had green eyes. Unless they wore colored contacts. I asked if that was the case, but she only laughed and said I was a lucky girl, though if I didn't shut my mouth my luck would soon run out. "How am I lucky?" I asked her.

"That's better," she said. "That question is intelligent. Now I can begin to like you a little."

"I don't understand what you're saying. Won't you stop speaking so oddly?"

"It isn't me who's odd," she said. "You're the one. Oh, now don't make such a face. It's not as if we're old friends and I've tried to hurt your feelings. And it's not just you. It's the others too. Everyone. You see, that's what is odd, how everyone thinks they are normal and the truth is no one in the world is normal at all. Isn't that wonderful?"

At this she sprang up and darted away, laughing, her kimono dragging behind her as she navigated among the trees. When she finally circled back, panting like a dog, she said, "Well then, you can ask me a question, one question only, and I'll tell you its true answer. I have that power."

"What power?"

"To tell the truth."

"Don't we all have that power?"

"Oh no. That's not so. I'm sad to say it, but if people could tell the truth, the world would be a completely different place from the one it is now."

"I don't know what to ask."

"Of course you do. Just open your mouth. You can do it if you try."

So I did as she said and opened my mouth. And from my open mouth a question slipped out, quiet as the cherry blossoms that fall in swirls at that time of year.

"Who am I?"

She smiled wider, apparently pleased.

"That question is easier than it seems. But it's difficult to know the answer before everything is over. So I think you may become wise one day if you had the sense to ask it." She kneeled to pluck a cherry blossom from the forest floor, then slipped it by its tiny stem behind my ear. Leaning in closer, her lips brushing my ear, she said, "Listen carefully. I must speak low or someone might hear the answer to your question. If that happens, it will do you no good at all. Okay? Okay. So here is the truth to your question. This is it, so listen well. We wear our masks in between dreams. It's one of the rules of living here. You can't not wear a mask in those spaces of time. But if you want, you can change the one you've been given. All you have to do is be strong and make it so."

Be strong, I want to tell the dreaming man now. If you are strong enough, you will wake up and walk away from this place forever.

"I wouldn't have thought you capable of this," he says the following week when I come in to kneel beside him. "How long do you plan on keeping me? I must be like a plant to you by now. A pet. If I stopped talking, I wonder if you would tire of me more quickly. But no. It was talking that got me into this, so it must be talking that will get me out. I'll keep my faith in words, even though you used mine to betray me."

He speaks like that woman I met at the stream. In riddles. I wonder sometimes if he's a spirit or a ghost. I once knew a man, a foreigner like this one, with white skin and soft hair (yes, I have touched hair like his on occasion) who said there was no difference between ghosts and spirits, but I told him he was wrong. Perhaps in the West there is no difference between ghosts and spirits, but in Japan they are two separate kinds of beings. A ghost is a soul who died in such a horrible way that they cannot leave this world until someone brings them to peace. Spirits, though, were here long before people. They are older, wiser, than any of us. They are not quite human.

That woman at the stream was difficult to decipher. Sometimes I think spirit, due to the truth she offered me. At other times I think ghost, because she seemed too much of this world in many ways. She had a step and a smile, she had a way of laughing, she had a body she seemed used to using. Spirits never seem comfortable when they come in the clothes of humans. This is why I think she must have been a ghost. But if that's so, could what she told me even be the truth? Ghosts are never able to help others. They are always thinking of the pain that roots them here. If she was a ghost, why did she not set me on a path to help her?

He moans a little and I lift his blanket. I think he may have urinated in his sleep. This has happened before. I poke my head under the blanket and sniff. Yes, he's definitely wet himself. I roll the blanket back so I can pull off his pajamas. "I'm sorry," he says. I want to tell him no, it's nothing, that this isn't his fault. But I can't speak. I must work around him if I am not to be discovered by the man who owns him.

I take the pajamas and put them in the washer. I'll dry them and put them back on before I leave. "Aren't you sick of taking care of me like this?" he says when I return. I kneel beside him and wipe his penis and thighs with a warm washcloth. I lift his penis so I can clean under it as well. It begins to grow in my hand, slowly at first, then faster. With each pulse it's suddenly a little bit bigger. I feel something stir inside me and am overcome with a mix of desire and shame. I let it go after I finish cleaning him, but it stands up on its own for a while before beginning a slow melt back to its normal condition.

I sweep the front room and do the dishes then. I dust the corners and take out the trash. I wipe down all of the kitchen surfaces. And when his pajamas are dry, I struggle to pull them over his legs and up to his waist. When I'm done I look down at him in his nest of blankets and wonder how the man I work for could allow such beauty to be shuttered behind closed doors in a dark room, away from the eyes of the world.

"Goodbye, my love," he says as I slide the door to his room closed.

I take the yen spread out on the coffee table, count the bills, then leave, locking the door behind me.

"ALL YOU HAVE to do is clean the living room, kitchen and bathroom. You needn't worry about the bedroom. That room I take care of myself. It is strictly off limits. If you cannot accept this proposal, I will ask your agency to send someone else. What do you think? Can you do this?"

I said that I could, but I wanted to know if I was in any danger at all.

"None whatsoever. Simply leave the door to that room closed and never open it, even if you hear something occurring behind it. Even if you hear someone calling out."

I shivered, but I managed to say, "And how will I be compensated for pretending as if that door does not exist?" I was being strong like the woman at the stream had told me to be. I was making my life happen as I wanted it to become. No one would ask me to help them use their pack of condoms again, unless I wanted to be asked that.

"Well I can leave some money here on this coffee table, and when you are finished you can take it and not say anything about it to your agency. If that is satisfactory to you?"

"Yes, that's fine. And we will never speak of this again?"

"You have gotten ahead of me. I'm sorry. What was your name?"

"Miyamoto," I said. "Ai."

"Well, Miyamoto san, you are correct, we will never speak of this again."

You see, it was so easy at first! I thought I was doing something strong. Why should I care about what happened beyond that closed door? The woman at the creek had said to be strong and I could make a mask to my own liking, not wear the one I'd been given. This is what I was doing then, when I came to work for the man who kept the dreamer locked away in his room. I was shaping my future. My future came in the form of yen left on the coffee table. I told myself each time I took the yen that one day I would not have to live a life controlled by anyone but me. That's strength, I thought. That's what the vision the woman at the stream showed me must have meant.

After the woman at the stream had given me my true answer, to be strong and forge my own mask to wear in between dreams, she said she had one more gift for me, and asked me to let her kiss my eyes so I could see my future. I closed my eyes then and felt her hands hold my head. Her lips touched each of my eyelids a moment later and a spark came to life after each kiss, blue-white fire dancing before me, and soon I fell asleep on the mossy earth.

I dreamed then. I dreamed I saw my father sitting in his wheelchair, staring out the dining room window. I dreamed I saw my mother working in the bento factory, back hunched, slopping curry into the slot of the bento plates as they passed by on the conveyer belt. I saw the dark rings of sleeplessness under her eyes. I saw a young girl near my age, her face terribly bruised and bloody. I looked at her face, afraid I would find my own, but breathed a sigh of relief when I saw it wasn't me. It was the woman by the creek. Ghost, I said in the dream. Her eyes fluttered, suddenly open, and I stumbled away screaming.

"Ghost I am," she said in a mangled voice, as if something was lodged in her throat, making it hard for her to speak. "But I am more than just a dead thing. Before I lived a human life I was what I am now, beyond human vision, so you cannot see what I am unless I show you."

The blood and bruises on her face began to heal then, and fur sprouted all over her. Red fur, white fur, and then a long, bushy tail appeared, curling around her waist.

"I have traveled far from the place that holds my human death, and not everyone can do such a thing. I've walked miles from my death and am walking miles beyond the form I hold now also. One day I will walk so far, death will no longer be able to find me. One day I will leave all this behind."

I hold my breath, afraid, while she looks at me and says: "Walk your own way, little Ai, or be lost to the way someone else has given you." Then she closed her eyes, those terrible green eyes in a red-furred face, and I opened mine to find I had slept the night by the creek in the mountains. It was morning. The birds sang in the trees. And the woman who was neither spirit nor ghost was gone.

She had left something behind though. Her kimono. The one with the cherry blossoms swirling around the moons that carried the rabbit who watches everything that occurs here on earth. I got up, kneeled to fold the kimono and tucked it under my arm. Then I walked back down the mountain into the woods and fields.

I walked until I found a train station, where I took the train back to Tokyo and made my way to the Seven-Eleven. I took off my smock and handed it over the counter to the manager, who looked at me as if he were confused. "This is no longer mine," I told him. Then I walked out the door into the bright streets of Tokyo, beginning to consider what mask I wanted to wear.

IT WASN'T EASY, making that decision. There are so many masks to choose from, and after a while I began to think, which one will do? I could be the bosozoku girl, riding a motorcycle, causing trouble with her tribe of wind riders. But that kind of girl is like a piece of broken glass. She can cut if you touch her, but she can also be shattered if you approach without her knowing and I could not be someone with a weakness now. I could be one of those girls who wear Renaissance clothes, I thought, layers of leather and lace, a Gothic Lolita or a saintly Mary, spending my hours walking the bridge near Harajuku Station. But really, those girls, they are too sweet, like peppermints. Not strong at all, I thought.

It's when I passed by a shop window in Shibuya that I saw her. The woman I would become. She was a kokujin, her skin the color of chocolate, her hair dyed blonde and dredded so that it piled up on her head like a bush. She danced wildly, wearing camouflage pants and steel-toed boots with a white vest over her black sports bra. She was rapping. Waving her hands, shouting. But I couldn't hear because she was behind the shop window on the television screen. So I wandered in to watch her and listen to her shout. She was so fierce, so beautiful, all at once I knew this is what I would be, what I was inside already maybe. A kokujin. A black woman.

Of course now I wonder, Ai, what were you thinking? How stupid could I be? But at the time it was the best I could think of. When I saw Black American women, I saw how strong they were and how, if I were black too, I could be strong as well. I could learn from them, I thought.

So I bought the clothes, the music, the makeup. I dyed my hair blonde, painted my lips red, fitted my arms with bracelets, slipped rings onto each of my fingers. I wore a gold necklace with a charm of fake diamonds that spelled out my name: Ai. I took a job in a hip-hop fashion store in Shinjuku and watched the black women in the videos playing on the store televisions, studying them, looking for new ways to be strong.

I bought a temporary tattoo set and drew the word love on my arm in print block letters. (I didn't trust myself to write in cursive, I never did get good at that.) I surrounded the word with thorny vines so that it looked as if Love, as if Ai, as if I, was the sleeping beauty at the center of the thorn-covered kingdom in fairy tales, who no one but the boldest of knights could ever reach.

I went to hip-hop clubs. I danced with who I wanted. I grew bold. I took men and fucked them. I was the one who did it to them. I didn't let them fuck me. I made them lie down below me and do as I said. I began to drink ridiculous amounts of whiskey. Once I even stopped a man on the street, opened my purse to show him the condoms I kept in there, and said, "Would you help me make use of these?" He held up his hands to wave me off and said excuse me, assuming I would ask him for money, but I said, "Look, I'll be the one to pay. Not you." He narrowed his eyes at first. Then he grinned.

I took him to a love hotel and pulled the salary man suit off him like the clown costume it is, then fucked him hard until he complained. "It hurts," he said. "Won't you slow down, go nice and easy?"

"No," I said. "I'm paying for you. Now lay back and do as I say."

I'm not sure where this Ai came from. Suddenly in a matter of months the mask I had placed on my face had become more than I'd intended. I hadn't realized that could happen. All that strength I thought I'd acquired wasn't strength at all, I soon saw. It was just another illusion. I realized this when I went dancing with a man I met in Shinjuku station one evening, some late twenties jobless guy with a nice smile and a decent sense of fashion. We went to a love hotel and had sex in a room that looked like the bottom of the sea. I liked the looks of him and decided to let him be on top at first, so I could look up at the digital fish swimming across the ceiling.

What an old room that must have been! These days love hotel rooms aren't so tacky. But this room was the old style. It relied on the gimmicks of love hotels from the eighties and nineties, the flash of spectacle that makes not only love but sex an absurd thing. That's when I realized I'd taken someone else's path, even after the woman by the stream had warned me against doing that.

After he came, I took beers from the fridge and tried to make light of the evening. I wanted to make this man into a person now, not allow him to remain someone I had used to feel strong. I thought I could salvage something now that I'd woken from that terrible dream. But he was like me. He couldn't see the path he walked always led back to the place where he began. So I left him alone on the bed and paged through the room's diary.

Love hotel diaries are interesting things. People who come to love hotels leave messages in them. Who they are, who they came with, why they came. Sometimes they're silly, sometimes they're sweet, sometimes they're crude, and sometimes they're sadder than a hundred nights spent weeping. But usually nothing out of the ordinary will be found inside them. While I paged through this room's diary, though, I came upon an entry that stopped me cold.

A man who had come by himself had written the entry. He didn't live with anyone, he had no children, no lovers, not even a friend. He had no reason to come to a love hotel at all. He wrote that he came to that room to think about the lovers who had been there before him, that he imagined himself being one of them, imagined himself having someone to hold. Being in that room helped him imagine what it is like to be loved. He wrote that he stays for an hour, sometimes two, that once he spent the night when he was terribly lonely. He said to whoever read this diary that he was grateful for the love they shared without knowing each other.

I couldn't help myself. I cried before I even realized I was crying. The man on the bed who I'd just had sex with asked what was wrong. I tried to explain but he didn't understand, and then suddenly he got up and was leaving. My heart pounded. No, I thought. Don't leave like this, don't leave me alone. I stood up and took his jacket from him. We had a stupid argument about

Hitler, whose name was written on the back of his jacket. I couldn't read it well because it was written in cursive, but when he told me what it said I was shocked back to my senses. Who had I slept with? Someone who admired Hitler? I'd seen *Schindler's List*. I knew what that man did.

So I let him pay the room fee and parted ways with him on that Shinjuku street to walk whatever path it was he walked. I was crying in the entrance of the love hotel as he disappeared around the corner. I didn't cry because he left me. I cried because I had abandoned myself months ago, and it was only then I realized what I'd done.

Snow fell around me. I shivered and held my fur-collared jacket close to my body, took a taxi home and fell asleep in my bed. In the morning, I told my mother I was going to leave the hip-hop fashion store where I worked so I could take a job at a cleaning company instead. "You'll never find a husband that way, Ai," was all that she said.

I looked at my father sitting in his wheelchair by the dining room window and wondered what he would have said, had he been able to say anything at all. I couldn't imagine though. It had been too many years since he'd spoken. I didn't know who he was anymore. I wasn't sure if he was even thinking anything at all inside the silence that surrounded him like a tomb.

That afternoon I went to three cleaning companies and was offered a job after a quick interview at the third one. Someone had quit that morning and they were in a pinch. "When can you start?" the manager asked.

"I can start now if you like," I told her.

Two hours later I found myself bargaining with the dreaming man's keeper. How much would it take to keep my mouth closed?

Let's just say the pay for cleaning is much better than selling hip-hop clothes. But the guilt is much, much heavier.

"I WANT YOU to let me go," he tells me the following week. "Can you do that? Please. If you ever loved me even a little, you'll release me from this. From this spell you've put on me."

Witch, I think. The man who keeps the dreamer deals in some kind of magic. That isn't good. If that's so, he could watch me from wherever he is. He could send a spider to spy on me, a cockroach or a mouse. He could watch me from the other side of the mirror that stands in the corner of this room. A long time ago, I didn't believe in such things. But I've seen enough unlikely things happen in my life to know it is those who don't believe in such things who are the truly unwise ones.

It's an early morning in summer. The sun is lost behind the spires of Tokyo, and beyond them it is lost behind the smog and clouds. An hour ago I was waiting across the street in the shadows of a store entrance, watching, waiting to see the witch leave his building. I decided to start a few hours earlier than usual today. Something has had hold of me for the past few days and I've spent night after night sleepless, tossing and turning in my futon. A grip of ice is on my throat, choking me. It is how I felt the night I realized I'd been wearing someone else's mask. It's this money I'm taking to keep silent. No good can ever come of such a thing. I don't know why I thought I could justify it with the idea that I was being strong again. Perhaps the greatest weakness in our lives is our desire for control. Real strength is not control; it's knowing when to let go.

I leave the dreaming man and go through the witch's files. I turn on his computer and search through everything in there as well. I go through his address book, his bills and letters. He is new to Tokyo, I discover. Has only been here several months, for nearly the same time I've been cleaning his apartment. He's moved from Nagoya. A work transfer. But how did he do it? How did he transport the man dreaming in the next room without being discovered? Or did he cast the spell that traps the man in his dreams here, after he came to Tokyo? But that's not possible. Listening to the dreamer's stories, I know they've known each other for at least a year. As I said, the world is full of more unlikely things than one will ever realize. Be wise, I tell myself. Come on, Ai, what would someone wise do?

I could call the police, but these situations are scary. I don't trust the police and I'm only a cleaning girl. Why should I be believed? What if there's an excuse the witch can offer them? "This is my dead sister's American husband. They were in a car accident. She died. He has no other family. I am taking care of him." As stupid as that sounds, the police would accept it. They'd swallow that lie like an eel in order to avoid any confrontation that might damage someone's reputation. Be wise, Ai, I tell myself again. And that's when I know what it will take for me to be really strong.

I get up and slide the door of the bedroom open, kick off my slippers and step over to the futon, kneel at the dreamer's side. He turns his head toward me and his eyes flash open, as they occasionally do. I've grown used to this now. The first time I scrambled back on my hands and feet like a crab, but after I realized he could see nothing out of those eyes, I calmed down.

"You're still here?" he says. "I thought you'd left again. Won't you touch me?" he says. So I touch his forehead and take his hand in mine. "Won't you kiss me?" he says. So I lean down and kiss him softly on his forehead and both cheeks. "Won't you speak to me, my love?" he says. So I open my mouth, remembering the words of the woman by the creek. You can tell the truth, she told me, if you just open up your mouth and let it out.

"I'm here," I tell him in my bad English. It's been too long since I spoke it and I was never very good anyway. "But I'm not the man who keeps you. I'm Ai. I'm going to help you. I'm going to take you out of here."

His brows furrow and his face looks worried for a moment. "Ai," he says. "That means love, doesn't it?"

I nod. And suddenly tears roll out of my eyes unbidden. That's it, so easy. He's recognized who I am, who I was all along. I'm Ai. I'm love. I just didn't know it.

I lean down once more and kiss his lips as I've been aching to do since I first saw him. When I pull away, he is looking at me with those blue eyes and seeing me for the first time. I've spent these several months watching, listening, getting to know him without him knowing I was even at his side. Now he sees me. Now he raises a hand to his face to feel his cheeks, the stubble on his chin, checking to make sure he's still alive.

"That's right," I tell him. "In your language, my name is love. And I'm going to save you."

As I struggle to help him stand I tell myself, I'm going to save us both.

AND SUCH
SMALL DEER

CHRIS ROBERSON

Letter to Frédéric Lerne, student, c/o University of Paris, Sorbonne, July 15th, 1860

MONSIEUR LERNE, I am writing in regards to your recent correspondence on the inheritance of characteristics from one generation to another. I would like to thank you for your kind and insightful words, and I only wish that my recently published paper had been as well received here at home in England. Sadly, it was not, and I am forced temporarily to look beyond the arena of pure research for employment. Luckily, I have received an offer to practice medicine in the Dutch East Indies, and have only this past week accepted. *Bidui luminosua praecursionis,* in my bad, schoolboy Latin. Brighter days ahead!
    —F.A.M.

* * *

Abraham Van Helsing's Journal
(translated from the Dutch)

1 MAR., 1861. *Belawan*—After a journey of several days from the northern coast of Borneo, past Singapore and through the Strait of Malacca, I arrived this morning at the newly built port of Belawan, in the North Sumatran province of Deli. The region has only recently come under the colonial jurisdiction of my countrymen, so I had hoped to find some relative comfort in my brief stay here. The ship that makes the regular circuit between the Dutch East Indies and India, though, is not due to arrive for another week, and I am finding conditions less hospitable than I might have expected. I wonder now whether I might have been better off waiting in Sarawak for the next ship to England, but to do so would have meant another week in the company of the mad Raja Brooke, and any deprivation is better than that.

Carrying my small amount of luggage with me, nothing more than a valise and a small case, I left the rough docks behind and tried to find an inn in the town. To my disappointment, I found very little of note in the whole of Belawan. The buildings all look as though they've been constructed in the last year; some of them bare wood without stain, paint or varnish, while the roads are newly made tracks of dirt running between. Besides a small port authority building and a warehouse for the storage of goods being sent and received by the dock, the only other structure of note in all of Belawan is a store of sorts. Not very imposing, but needs must when the devil drives.

I entered the store, hoping to find direction to accommodations, and perhaps a bite to eat. The store was ramshackle, bare wooden floors and walls, and roughly hewn shelves piled high with haphazard goods, alcohol, cigars, salt, sugar, some items of clothing, sweets, and the like. Behind the counter was an ancient native man, while in a back corner, a European man in shirtsleeves rolled to his elbows was knelt down, bandaging the foot of a native man beside a broken crate.

Before I'd had the chance to address the man behind the counter, my eyes fell on a package of Dutch chocolates perched on a high shelf. My mouth began immediately to salivate. I'd not seen any confections of that brand since I'd left Amsterdam early the year before, and the mere sight of them caught me in a brief wave of nostalgia. I remembered sharing them with my late wife early in our courtship, or seeing my young son eating them messily on a birthday outing. Whatever the price, I knew I would be willing to pay to recapture those moments, if only for a fleeting instant.

As this is a Dutch colony, I hoped that the few bits of coin from home still rattling in the far reaches of my valise might be considered legal tender in the local economy.

"What is the price?" I asked of the native man behind the counter, motioning to the chocolates on the shelf above his head.

"Fifteen," the man said simply, through tight lips, his face a perpetual scowl.

I scratched my chin.

"Fifteen what, if you don't mind?" I asked.

The ancient man didn't speak, just pointed a calloused finger at a sheet of paper lacquered to the countertop. On it was written, like some Rosetta stone in miniature, a block of text repeated in several languages, one of them my native Dutch. It was a simple statement, informing the reader that this store was only for employees of the Netherlands–Sumatra Company, and that the store didn't accept any currency besides company scrip.

My gaze lingering on the chocolates, I pressed on with business.

"In that case," I asked, "can you tell me if there is an inn in the near vicinity?"

The ancient man looked at me blankly.

"A place where one might hire a room?"

The ancient man took a deep breath through his wide nostrils and shook his head once, side to side.

"No," he said simply.

"Well," I went on, undeterred, "can you tell me if there is a carriage to the nearest town that *does* have an inn?"

Again the long pause, the deep intake of breath, and the single shake of the head.

"No."

I was growing exasperated, not sure whether the native man failed to understand my Dutch and was only shamming responses, or understood and just wished to be unhelpful, but before I could say another word a third party joined the stunted conversation.

The European man who'd been bandaging the native's foot at the rear of the store had looked up on first hearing the discussion between me and the man behind the counter, and finishing his ministrations came forward into the light. He was a powerfully built man in his mid-thirties, with a fine forehead and rather heavy features, with a full, heavy mouth turned down at the corners, giving him an expression of pugnacious resolution. He was well muscled, standing a good six feet in height, with an unkempt mess of dark hair sticking out above his ears, hanging down just below his collar at his neck.

"Van Helsing?" he said, looking at my face intently. Speaking English with a British accent, he added, "Is that you?"

I was startled to be recognized, to say the very least. I had no notion who the man might be. I found in the misty reaches of my memory a dim recollection of the man's face, but nothing else.

"Yes," I said warily. "And whom do I have the pleasure of addressing?"

The man brightened immediately, and came forward, arms outstretched. "Abraham, surely you remember your old friend! Have so many days past since we haunted the halls of Oxford?"

The man seemed overjoyed at our unexpected reunion. For my part, I could barely remember ever having known the man, much less his name. I had vague memories of a lanky, obsessed creature, who was always at the rear of the surgical amphitheater, always asking the strangest questions.

What was his name again? I thought to myself. *Something with an "F" sound...*

I began to form the initial consonant in my mouth, the first hiss of air escaping between my teeth, and the tall man rushed to complete the work for me.

"Francis!" the man said, pounding his chest with a heavy fist and then taking me in his arms in an embrace not at all characteristic of the English. "I knew you'd not have forgotten your bosom chum Francis, even after the years and miles, old Abe."

"I sometimes think the past is a different country," I said, trying to extract myself from his embrace as diplomatically as possible.

"And besides, the wench is dead," the man called Francis answered, leering. "Ah, Abe, remember our days together, studying anatomy and chemistry, dreaming our grand dreams of the future. I had hopes to add a new star to the firmament, my name included in the list of luminaries in the sciences." He breathed a sentimental sigh, but continued before I could respond. "Sadly, I've had to leave the field of pure research behind for the moment, and instead earn a crust of bread in the practice of medicine. I've come to the east to find work, but find that there is little intellectual stimulation to be had, so little, indeed, that I have had to make my own diversions. Still, I'm eager for a receptive audience for my discussions, since so often here my talks fall on deaf ears."

I explained that I, too, had come to the Orient for employment, but found it not to my liking, and was currently in the process of returning home to Europe.

Francis, which is all he is to me still, as I cannot recollect his surname, continued on, talking in an animated fashion, as though we were just rejoining a conversation left dangling the night before, rather than more than a decade since. I have only vague memories of Francis from school, and can't call to mind a single discussion or meal we shared. But as he went on and on, I came to realize that the moment had passed when I could admit to forgetting his name. He remembers me, and assumes I remember him. I have no choice but to continue under the pretense that we are old friends reunited and hope that someone utters his full name in my hearing before too long a span has passed.

"In any event," Francis said, "I'm employed at a nearby plantation, and you simply must come and be my guest."

"Oh, well," I said, playing for time and trying to devise a suitable alternative, "I am of course grateful for the offer, but I don't want to be any bother. If you can just direct me to the nearest inn, I'll be out of your hair."

Francis shook with a braying laughter and clapped me hard on the shoulder with one of his massive hands. He explained that the nearest inn was in Medan, the capital city, fourteen miles away, but that there was no regular carriage service along that route. My only real option was to come with Francis back to the plantation.

Having no choice, I accompanied Francis back to the rustic plantation house, and he showed me to the guest quarters. I've unpacked my valise, and settled in as best as I can. The accommodations are somewhat rough, little more than a rickety chair, a low desk, a hard and narrow bed covered in a thin sheet, and a jug and bowl for washing up. I've heard about the wealth of the Dutch plantations in Java, but these are early days for the expansion of such cultivation into the northern regions of Sumatra, and such successes appear not yet to have followed.

I am invited to dine this evening with the plantation's staff. I hope, at least, to hear at least one Dutch voice among them. I have been in the company of foreigners and mad Englishmen for too long, and could do with some familiar tones.

Letter to Frédéric Lerne, student, c/o University of Paris, Sorbonne, August 30th, 1860

I'VE ONLY JUST arrived in the Dutch East Indies, and have been installed as staff physician at the Netherlands–Sumatra Company's tobacco plantation in Northern Sumatra. The plantation was only started early this year, and is roughly halfway up the road to Medan, capital of the province of Deli. To call it a capital, though, is to slight capitals everywhere. It is a dusty village of a few hundred souls, and nothing more besides. The job is a meager one, but I suppose I am lucky to have it, as it was only family connections that brought me this far. I have a French cousin on my father's side of the family who is in the region working as an overseer for the plantation, which is owned by a Dutch consortium. My cousin is penniless, but styles himself the "Baron de Maupertuis," laying claim to a hereditary title that held no cachet even before the storming of the Bastille, much less after the rousing cries of "*liberté, egalité, et fraternité*" from the proletariat.

My cousin invited me to the plantation to act physician on the staff. As I believe I mentioned in an earlier missive, I have had some difficulty in the London scientific community following the recent publication of my paper, with certain intractable elements of the medical establishment objecting to my arguments on the proper uses of science and medicine. As a result, I was grateful for the opportunity of gainful employment, and especially grateful that I will have the time and space here to continue my researches unmolested.

—F.A.M.

Abraham Van Helsing's Journal

1 MAR. LATER—Since I hoped to hear at least one Dutch voice among the plantation staff, I suppose I should count myself lucky. But Dame Fortune is not overly generous, as there is only one of my countrymen among all those employed here, the balance of them being Frenchmen and more mad Englishmen.

In the drawing room, before the evening meal, Francis introduced me to his cousin, the supervisor of the plantation, the self-styled Baron de Maupertuis. With him was the sole Dutchman of the crew, the accountant, Kasper de Vries, and the accountant's clerk, an Englishman in his early twenties introduced to me only as Culverton, though whether this is his given or surname, I cannot say.

The baron is a large man with a barrel chest, and a somewhat smug, self-important look plastered to his crude features. De Vries is the perfect model of the accountant, thin, wan, with long and precise fingers that seem always to be in motion; behind thick glasses, his liquid eyes seem to take inventory of his surrounding at every moment, calculating values and risks. Culverton, the young man, is small and frail, his shoulders and back twisted like someone who had suffered from rickets in childhood, with an oversized head perched on his uneven shoulders, blond hair already beginning to thin.

They were a strange lot, the baron as loud and boisterous in his way as his cousin Francis was in his; de Vries quiet and calculating; Culverton timid and retiring. Dinner was served, a simple but passable fare, and the subject of the discussion turned to fortunes of the plantation, such as they were, and better days ahead. This entire region has only recently fallen to Dutch control, and as always the businessmen waste little time in exploiting the region's usefulness. That the Dutch foreign offices were so overtaxed as to hire a threadbare

Frenchman with a valueless title as overseer only serves as evidence of the strain the rapid colonial expansion is having on the infrastructure.

During the dessert course, Culverton mentioned rumors he'd heard from one of the household servants. The plantation workers, so the rumor went, were nervous. In the fields by day and in their tarpaper shacks by night, they talk of a foul spirit that haunts the area, preying on the flesh of men. It is supposedly some ancient Sumatran spirit, servitor of the ancient Batak kings, that finds the presence of the Dutch colonial masters to be offensive. The baron joked that if that were true, then they'd have only to feed the spirit de Vries and me, and the rest could work in peace. The laughter, what little laughter followed, was thin and anemic.

Abraham Van Helsing's Journal

2 MAR.—THIS morning I dined again with the plantation staff, and Francis (whose surname no one last night had the courtesy to utter) invited me to come visit his facilities. He explained that the building had been intended for use as a surgery, but that he had devoted a small portion of the space to his researches, continuing the work begun back in England.

I wished I had some suitable excuse, some alternative to a day in this virtual stranger's company, but I could not help but feel gratitude to the man for taking me in off the streets, and so reluctantly I agreed.

On our exit, the baron called after me, his manner blustery.

"*Au revoir,*" he said with a raucous laugh. "Enjoy the House of Pain."

Once we were outside and on our way to the surgical facilities, I asked Francis what his cousin had meant. His expression distracted, he waved a hand as though to dismiss the matter entirely.

"Oh, it is just a name given by the plantation workers to my offices," he said. "They are a rude and unrefined segment of humanity, if ever there were."

We entered the rude building, little more than four walls and a sloped roof, with planks of wood laid directly on the hard-packed dirt for flooring. There was a long, narrow bench along one side, a desk and chair along the back, and an array of surgical equipment hanging from hooks on the walls. Oil lanterns hung from the rafters, which issued tongues of foul black smoke when Francis lit them one by one.

Francis made his way to the desk at the rear and returned holding a sheaf of papers under his arms.

"I've been doing some researches into the uses of blood transfusions, these past months," he explained, growing excited as a child on Christmas morning, "and on the inheritance of characteristics. As every educated man knows, Lamarck has been completed contravened, his notion that organisms pass attributes acquired in life to their offspring revealed for the unadulterated poppycock it patently is. But the rejection of a negative does not necessitate a positive, and we are left with the simple question: how *do* organisms pass inherited traits from one generation to the next?"

"So you're an adherent to Charles Darwin?" I asked, referring to the evolutionary theories published in England only two years ago, which caused some significant controversy among the scientific establishment.

"I agree in principle with Darwin, I suppose," Francis answered with a dismissive wave, "but he is only in essence restating the doctrine first put forth by my own famous forebear, Pierre Louis Moreau de Maupertuis, my grandsire several times removed, who anticipated the evolutionary theories of Darwin by more a century. Why, in his *Système de la nature* he clearly stated—"

A commotion at the door saved me what promised to be a lengthy response to such a simple question, but my escape from the litany came at a heavy price.

A group of men were bustling through the door, carrying between them a wounded man, shrieking in agony. As they arranged their wounded comrade on the narrow bench along the wall, they explained what had happened to Francis in their broken English. The man had gone missing in the night, and when they went out to the tobacco fields in the morning, they found him, mauled by some enormous animal.

The man was in tremendous pain, and as Francis arranged his medical equipment, I stood at the man's head, his hand in mine, doing what I could to comfort him. Francis began to treat his wounds, deep gashes in his abdomen from which viscous, dark blood burbled.

"Relax," I told the man, in as comforting a tone as I could manage. Mustering my best bedside manner, I uttered soothing words, such as "You're in good hands" and "We'll put you to right," and further such imprecations of good will.

Francis, on hearing me, laughed.

"Oh, Abraham, you surprise me. Surely you've come to realize that pain is needless, a residual instinct from man's more animalistic past, and should hold no sway over a rational man."

I was shocked.

"Have some pity, man," I said. "This poor devil is suffering."

"Ah," Francis answered, glancing up from his ministrations, "we are on different platforms. You are a materialist."

"I am not a materialist—," I began hotly.

"In my view, in my view. For it is just this question of pain that parts us. So long as visible or audible pain turns you sick; so long as your own pains drive you; so long as pain underlies your propositions about sin—so long, I tell you, you are an animal, thinking a little less obscurely what an animal feels."

The man screamed, insensate in agony, but Francis remained obdurate, merely shrugging.

"You see," Francis said, "like the beasts of the field."

Without warning, the crying stopped. I laid a finger against the wounded man's wrist, felt the beating of his life fluttering away, and when it was still, tenderly lowered the man's arm onto the bench.

"You've one less beast to worry after, in that case," I told Francis, my face flushed red and my hands tightened into fists at my sides. "He is dead."

"Just like the others," Francis said, annoyed. He wiped his hands clean on a rag, and began to roll down his sleeves.

"Others?" I asked. "What others?"

"Oh," Francis answered, dismissively. "This is not the first, but the sixth to have died of similar wounds in the last week." He shook his head, his expression dark. "Damnably disruptive, I have to say. How I'm expected to get any work done under these conditions, I'm sure I don't know."

I had little patience for Francis at this stage, and while he returned to his notes and papers at his desk, I made my own postmortem examination of the man. My initial suspicions were that a tiger had gotten to him, based on the extent and savagery of the wounds, but on closer examination, I found that the bite marks were not consistent with a tiger attack. There were the impressions of incisors, but they were too closely spaced and shallow to be those of a cat; the majority of the injury resulted from incisors. The man looked more like he'd been gnawed.

Leaving Francis to his solitude, I made my slow way back to the main house and my guest room, rambling near the workers' quarters as I went. I've come to learn that the majority of the plantation's laborers are Chinese, with a mix of Javanese, coastal Malay, Tamils brought over from Ceylon, and native Bataks. They bring with them their religions and superstitions, their work huts by nature a latter-day Babel, but they all agree on one thing: something hunts the night, stalking them.

Letter to Frédéric Lerne, October 1st, 1860

FRÉDÉRIC, I WAS heartened to get your last letter. Your questions are very much in line with my own thinking of the moment. I have begun to suspect that there is in the blood or flesh of the body some element that governs the inheritance of characteristics from one generation to the next. If that be true, then it stands to reason that by transposing these miniscule elements from one body to another (supposing that we can overcome the problems attendant with the host body rejecting the introduction of the foreign material), then one might be able to introduce novel characteristics into the organism.

To be frank, I am lucky to find myself in Sumatra at this juncture, for one reason if no others, and that is down to the abundant variety of fauna ready to hand. There is an abundance of organisms for my experiments—birds, butterflies, buffaloes, deer, mouse deer, orang-utans, and rodents.

Yours, Francis

Abraham Van Helsing's Journal

2 MAR. LATER—Tonight, in the drawing room after the evening meal, I asked whether the baron was

going to intervene in the matter of the attacks, or else appeal to the colonial government for assistance.

"Well," the baron said, absently scratching his ample belly, thinking it through, "I have no desire to involve the Regent of Deli, squatting over in the capital city of Medan. He was only some months ago an independent sovereign, and still ill wears the yoke of the Dutch colonial government. You see? For that matter, I've no interest in attracting the attention of his 'advisor,' the Assistant Resident Max Havelaar."

The baron paused, taking a long draw on his cigar.

"Havelaar is entirely too soft on the natives," he went on, "and no doubt would arrive lobbying the Netherlands-Sumatra Company to reduce productivity by better treatment of the plantation workers, were we to invite him into our midst."

"Yes," de Vries offered, uncharacteristically forthcoming. "Havelaar is one of those who think that the plantations draw too heavily on the labor of their workers, such that their rice crops have materially diminished and famine has been the result. He was previously Assistant Resident in Java and was transferred after conflicts with the colonial authorities there."

"That said," the baron pointed out impatiently, interrupting de Vries as though he were a constant chatterbox, "a hunting party is not a bad idea. How about it?" He motioned to de Vries and Culverton, who sat by the side table. "Will you come along if I mount an expedition?"

"I cannot, sadly," de Vries answered without a hint of regret, "as I'm too busy with my tallies." He paused, and then added with some kindness, "However, Culverton, you may go along if you wish. Your duties this week are light enough that they will not suffer as a result of a few days' inattention."

"That's two, then," the baron said, thumping his chest and pointing his cigar at the young Englishman. "We'll need a doctor along, as well, in the event that someone is injured and needs medical attention. Francis, *ça va?*"

"Well, I suppose, but..." Francis began, then trailed off. His gaze shifted sheepishly around the room. "My researches are in a critical state at the moment, and I don't want to leave them unfinished."

The baron began to sit up straighter in his chair, his face flushing red.

"Francis," he said, his tone strained, "need I remind you that you are being paid to be our staff physician, and not a general researcher. Perhaps if I were to..."

"If I might," I said, holding up a hand apologetically and interrupting. "I'd be happy to take Francis' place on your hunting expedition, if you'd have me."

The baron looked from me, to his cousin, and back, his expression dark, but then relaxed by inches and settled back in his chair.

"Very well," he said. "So we'll be three. *Très bien*. We'll leave tomorrow."

And that, apparently, was an end to the discussion.

I am hardly excited about a few days' march through the jungle, much less with a timid Englishman and a blustering Frenchman, but in the face of another day spent in the company of this foul Francis, I will persevere.

Abraham Van Helsing's Journal

3 MAR.—THIS morning we set out, Baron de Maupertuis, Culverton, and myself, along with half a dozen plantation workers brought along as bearers. The jungle tracks and paths are too narrow for horses, and so we are traveling, as the baron puts it, *à pied*. I am reminded uncomfortably of my journey last month through the wilds of Borneo, lashed by wind and rain, stalked on all sides by fierce creatures. That this morning presented a truly Edenic scene, sunny and bright, the lush greens of the landscape brushed lightly with dew, did much to quell my nascent fears.

Previously, I had seen the tobacco fields only from a distance, but our course to the wilderness beyond took us right through them. As we passed through the rows of plants in their serried ranks, the baron explained that the tobacco grown here is used as cigar wrappers, rather than providing the meat of the cigar itself. The plants this week are in their first flush of grow for the season. The season will last for six months, and then after harvest the fields must be used to grow sugarcane for two and a half years, and then left fallow for two years beyond that. This, then, explains why so much of the land around the plantation is fallow.

At the borderland between the cultivated fields and the forests, we came upon strange tracks, the likes of which none of us had ever seen. They were as long as my foot, with phalanges that flared wider, so that the tracks were fanned out like a rake. The baron in the lead, we followed the tracks, on into the thick virgin forests and up among the low hills.

Near midday, we paused near a swift moving river, just above a coruscating waterfall. Birds wheeled overhead, and a riot of butterflies drifted by like a kaleidoscopic cloud. On the far side of the river, a deer appeared, gently grazing, eying us with disinterested eyes black as midnight pits. I sat watching the deer in quiet contemplate, but Culverton jumped to his feet and raised his rifle, eager to shoot.

"*Un instant!*" the baron shouted, stepping forward and placing his hand on the barrel of the young man's rifle.

"Yes?" Culverton asked, confused and not a little startled.

"Do you want to be the one to swim to the far side and swim back against this current with the corpse of a deer on your back?"

Culverton shook his head, his expression sheepish.

"Besides," the baron went on, "the shot could frighten off better sport, the beast we are after. This is one instance, Englishman, where the proverbial birds in the bush may be worth more to us than that we have already in hand. *C'est vrai?*"

Culverton, cowed, agreed, shouldering his rifle.

We continued on, deeper into the woods, higher into the foothills. From all sides came slight noises, rustling in the forests underground around us. Remembering the forests of Sarawak, I grew increasingly nervous and clutched my rifle tighter, my eyes shifting warily from one side of the forest track to the other.

The baron, watching alongside, read the tension in my expression and attitude, and laughed.

"What is it, my friend?" he asked. "Do you fear the Wild Man of the forests?"

Culverton, following close behind, looked at the baron with eyes wide.

"What is that?" the young Englishman asked.

The baron puffed up, his manner grandiloquent.

"Well," he answered, his laughter barely restrained, "it is a primitive species of man from primeval times that haunts the woods hereabouts."

Culverton shuddered.

"Those are just stories, surely," he said, uneasy.

"No," I interjected, finding myself with little patience for jibes and games, "it is neither mythical, nor man, but rather a species of anthropoid ape called the orang-utan. They are herbivores, Culverton, and quite harmless."

This recitation of scientific fact worked on my nerves almost as a mantra is said to function for the fakirs of the east. To apply a taxonomy to the unknown, to bound the noises beyond the sphere of our senses in categorical boxes, went a great distance towards calming my nerves. It reminded me that, but for minor exceptions, we live in a comprehensible world.

"So it doesn't eat meat?" Culverton asked, not letting go of his own misgivings quite so easily.

"It eats nothing living that is larger than an insect, I shouldn't think," I answered.

"Then Culverton should suit its appetites just fine," the baron said, laughing.

Culverton shrank back, and we continued, keeping our silence.

Tonight, in a clearing, we rest our weary bones by a crackling fire. We've still had no sign of the strange beast that has attacked the men. Even so, the tracks have persisted, and it is clear that whatever our quarry is, it is large and makes frequent pilgrimages from the forest deep, high on the hills, down into the fields, and back again. There is disagreement among the men as to whether there is one or more of the creatures, with some saying there is variation in size of the tracks, and others insisting they are all of the same size. All we've learned is that the animal seems to favor the lowland forests and likes to stay close to rivers and streams.

We have brought bearers along on the trip, a half-dozen plantation workers impressed into service on the journey. Earlier tonight, after we ate our rough meal, Culverton and I sat near one another in quiet contemplation. Culverton, for his part, continually glanced nervously at the far side of the clearing, where the workers sat huddled around another fire. Seeing his suspicious glances, I asked why he was so nervous. After all, weren't these men in the company's employ? What would it profit them to turn their hands against their supervisors?

"Oh," Culverton answered me, his voice low, "there's many a man among them would turn against us in a trice if they only had the sense to twig how bad off they are."

"But, they are paid, surely?" I asked.

Culverton explained that they are, but that few of them ever collect. Given unlimited credit at the company store, whether for liquor, what is euphemistically termed "female service," or tobacco, ironically enough, the workers to a man will spend faster than they earn. And if any do make it to the end of the harvest season with any money in hand, management licenses gambling during this brief intermission, to milk what little more blood they can from the stones. Any man left owing the company money at the end of his contract is obligated to renew for another three years until his debts are made good.

I listened while Culverton explained these practices, and then could contain my reaction no longer.

"It sounds monstrous!" I barked.

"That's as may be," Culverton said, brightening. "But from a management perspective, it's bloody brilliant!"

Excusing myself, I retired to my tent. I've had enough of these madmen, all of them, and wish I could be home in Holland tomorrow.

Abraham Van Helsing's Journal

6 MAR.—SEVERAL days now have passed since the Fourth of March, but the events of that day are still fresh in my thoughts. Were I not a rational man, I would think myself laboring under some sort of curse. First China, then Borneo, now Sumatra—in each instance I find myself hurled against my will into some sea of madness or another, adrift amongst the impossible. That I have survived all these trials so far, I sometimes fear, perhaps only suggests that I am being preserved for even greater tests to come.

On the morning of the fourth, the second day of our expedition, we continued on. The baron had sent one of the bearers ahead in the night to scout the way before us and he had not yet returned. The baron, always anticipating the worst from those in his employ, thought that the man had likely fled, trying to escape his debt to the company. The baron swore that when the bearer was recaptured, as such escapees always were, things would not go well for him.

Had the bearer, in truth, fled his employment and debts, things could have gone no worse for him than they did.

Midmorning, we found the body of the bearer, or rather his remains. A few limbs and most of the abdomen were missing, the rest left covered by the strange side-by-side gnaw marks seen on the other victims. There were tracks all around, the same we'd followed from the edge of the field. We followed them, deeper into the forest, now more cautious, our rifles always at the ready.

We came to a stand of trees ringing a clearing. The trees above, though, were bent over towards one another, creating a sort of naturally occurring arbor, a bower shaded by the domed lattice of trunks and branches overhead. There was a break in the tree line, and tracks leading up to it.

We all readied our weapons and, with the baron in the lead, entered the shady bower. While our eyes adjusted to the darkness, our senses were assaulted with an aroma like the smell of rotten onions, or ammonia.

The area within the arbor was large, with piles of branches and twigs scattered around. In the gloom, we could not see to the far side, with only large shadows lumped on the ground all around us. Which were piles of branches and which something more sinister, though, we couldn't say.

The baron called for a torch to be lit, and one of the bearers rushed in with one. We now stood in a semicircle around the entrance, our backs to the light, our faces to the darkness, with only the flickering light of the torch to guide us.

We didn't have long to wait. One of the dark piles erupted, and a massive figure lurched forward, baleful eyes glittering in the torchlight.

The creature was long and narrow, its head white, a uniform midnight black everywhere else. The long tail was scaly and hairless, and there were black spots on the long face above and below the eyes. On the long, mobile nose was a groove along the underside that ran from the nose's tip to a point between the upper incisors. Its canines were most prominent, two of them pointing downwards, like drawn sabers flashing dully in the dim light.

We fired into the enormous figure, the baron, Culverton, and I all together, which seemed barely to slow it. As it lunged forward, we beat a hasty retreat back into the open air, beyond the natural walls of the arbor, but the beast followed close behind.

In the open air, we started running, back the way we'd come. By this point, it was every man for himself. On and on we ran, we the three Europeans firing behind us as we went, the bearers abandoning their burdens in their flight. One of the bearers still carried a trunk across his shoulders, trying to run, his fellows shouting at him in their native language, calling for him to hurry, or to drop his load, or some such. The beast was on him the next instant, taking him up in its massive jaws, the saber-teeth doing their work, the pair of them ripping into his flesh.

We had a brief respite, then, as the monster busied himself eating the fallen bearer, but we all knew it would continue after them. We had to press on. Our pace not slackening, we rushed on, side by side along the narrow forest tracks.

"What… was… that?" Culverton asked one syllable at a time, ragged and out of breath, feet pounding on the undergrowth.

"It's size is… ludicrous," I answered, as best I could, "but in every other respect… it appeared to be a rat."

"A… rat?" Culverton responded.

"Yes," I answered, "of a type… native… to this region."

"Nonsense," the baron shouted from behind, keeping up his steady pace. "I don't believe it."

"Perhaps," I said, calling over my shoulder, "you'd prefer to take it up with the giant rat?"

The baron kept quiet, and we raced on.

Letter to Frédéric Lerne, December 2nd, 1860

SUCCESS! I HAVE successfully transfused the essential generative elements from one animal to another, and when the target subject bred it produced substantial changes.

I introduced specific traits of the Sumatran elephant (genus *Elephas*, species *maximus*, subspecies *sumatrensis*) into the "moon rat" native to these climes (genus *Echinosorex*, species *gymnura*). The resultant rat specimens are easily twice the size and weight of their parent, with an attendant increase in strength and resilience.

I have chosen the *Echinosorex gymnura* because, unlike other specimens available here, these rodents breed throughout the year, and typically produce at least two litters per year, with two young per litter being typical. I am working to modify the reproductive rate, though, to see if I can speed the process and introduce even greater degrees of improvement.

Yours, Francis

Abraham Van Helsing's Journal

6 MAR. LATER—We raced on, knowing that the monstrous rat might be on us at any moment. We reached the river we'd passed the day before, just above the waterfall, the water cascading down to jagged rocks below.

"We are boxed in," the baron said, leaning over and with his hands on his knees, catching his breath. "We must stand and fight."

Culverton whimpered, summing up nicely my thoughts on our chances of survival facing the giant beast head on.

"No," I countered, recovering my composure. "There is a chance. If we ford the river here and cross to the far side, we'll have the river to act as a barrier between us and the monster."

"But if the rat can't cross this current, what makes you think we can?" The baron snapped.

"Because," I answered simply, "we are men and it is but an animal." I paused, considering the options. "You have strong cord among your supplies?"

"We did," the baron answered hotly. "But it was left somewhere far behind, when the bearers abandoned their duty."

"One didn't," Culverton said, his voice low.

"Yes," I said, "and he paid for his loyalty with his life. Very well, there is another option. We are now eight, and our outstretched arm-span reaches near six feet. The river at this point can't be much more than forty feet across. If we join hands in a human chain and then enter the water further upstream, one at a time, we can use those still on shore as anchors, inching our way to the farther shore."

The others were hesitant, but in the silence that followed my last words we could hear the sound of the monstrous rat crashing through the undergrowth, not far behind. Then, they were willing to try anything.

I was the first to enter the water. Before we'd begun, we all wrapped our firearms in our oilskin jackets and secured them over our shoulders, in the hopes they'd still fire on the far side. My rifle strapped across my shoulders, I entered the water, the baron holding my hand. He had to kick hard to keep from being dragged downstream and over the falls, but with the baron's strength pulling from shore to secure me, I managed to stay in position, my feet just barely touching bottom. I kicked further out as the baron slipped into the cold mountain water, and then the baron moved out as the next bearer in line plunged in, and so on.

I reached the opposite side just as the rat crashed through the trees. The rat paused at the river's edge and then plunged in with its mouth and forepaws, catching the last bearer in line in its teeth. It dragged the screaming man back on shore, dropped him on the ground, and then turned its attention back to the men still in the water. The baron and I were by now on dry land, trying to drag the rest of the men out after us. The baron left me to pull the men in alone and busied himself with unwrapping and loading his gun. The powder, fortunately, was still dry enough to fire, and without preamble he began shooting at the rat.

The rat plunged into the water, following us across the river. It must have been between ten and fifteen feet long, and once its rear legs were in the water, it began to drift downstream. By this point, nearly all of our party were on shore, and with our rifles unencumbered we began to fire and reload, fire and reload, and with every shot that hit home, the rat thrashed with less strength, red streamers of its monster's blood pouring downstream and over the falls.

Just as the rat was about to reach us, it drifted too far downstream and plunged over the falls, crashing into the jagged rocks down below.

When the giant rat had disappeared from view, we all of us collapsed onto the soft loam of the riverbank and breathed deep. It was a long hour before we rose, and longer yet before anyone spoke.

We made our slow way back to the plantation, having to divert miles out of our way to find a bridge across the river. We were bone weary and anxious for a fire and our beds, but we had no desire to try to cross the river in that fashion again, and so crossed the long distance in silence.

We returned to the plantation and relative safety. None of us has ventured out of doors in the days and hours since, the surviving bearers in their quarters, the staff and I in ours.

Letter to Frédéric Lerne, student, c/o University of Paris, Sorbonne, March 7th, 1861

MY MOST RECENT experiments have ended, and perhaps not on quite the note I'd have chosen. However, I have gathered the pertinent data and have to consider the project a resounding success. I am growing tired of island life and am eager to return to England. Well, for all of that, England is still an island, I suppose, isn't it. So I'll just be trading one island for another. But there my experiments will continue, and I will gain the notoriety and acclaim I so richly deserve.

Yours very truly, Francis Arnaud Moreau

Abraham Van Helsing's Journal

8 MAR.—I write now from my stateroom onboard the *Matilda Briggs*, bound for Calcutta on the western coast of India. I'm only too happy to be continuing my homeward journey. And, as glad as I am to be away from the monstrous creature that haunted the Sumatran forest, I'm just as glad to be quit of Francis. I never have recollected his name, though I now remember him more clearly from our school days. I recall him now an awkward and withdrawn youth, who failed to make the connection between his studies of the human body and the individual people who surrounded him at all times, able to obsess in minute detail over the

functioning of some gland or minor bone, but unable to evince the slightest interest or concern in his fellow man, seeing them as little more than animals. Perhaps, then, his decision to practice medicine may, in the long run, be to his credit. Perhaps, forced into constant and close contact with the people around him, he will by turns become more "human" himself.

In my darker moments, though, I wonder. What if the reverse should happen, instead?

THE WIZARD'S COMING

JULIET E. McKENNA

ON THE CUSP between winter and spring, snow-drops shivered beneath thorn bushes swelling with buds in a sheltered nook at the heart of the copse, though the wind slicing through the bare and twisted oak trees was bitterly cold. Gray clouds above threatened the rain that still turned too easily to sleet or snow.

"Another frost-killed bird." A young man with tousled brown hair gloomily nudged the pathetic corpse with a booted toe. "Why don't they just fly away?"

"You're supposed to be looking for firewood." As his older, balding companion kicked at a heap of sodden leaves and bent to retrieve a blackened, rotten branch, a sharp whistle raised both their heads.

"Find some god-cursed fuel before that fire dies!" As the man out on the exposed headland shouted angrily at the two of them, everyone else scattered along the cliff-top grassland halted. Three men were walking horses around, in charge of two or three apiece, each beast saddled and bridled. The foremost, lithe and wiry, hauled on the reins wound around each hand and broke into a run, forcing the reluctant animals to trot beside him.

"Come on." The second man groaned as he gathered up their meager haul of sticks and thorny twigs.

"Elkan, Serde, and Treche have got the horses to warm them," the first man complained.

"Stop your moaning," his companion said wearily.

Both shivered as they left the inadequate shelter of the trees. The man out on the headland huddled into his rough gray cloak and scowled at them as they headed for a shallow hollow in the slope running up to the cliff edge. Two tents were angled to shelter the fire pit from the ceaseless wind.

A man seated cross-legged on the turf was skinning a brace of winter-starved rabbits. "Maewelin's tits," he muttered. "My hands are so cold I can't tell if I'm cutting coney or my fingers."

"There'll be more meat on your fingers." The younger man who'd found the dead bird dumped his burden.

"This is all we gleaned, captain," his bald companion apologized.

"Then bind the faggots tighter so they burn hotter," a tall man ordered curtly. His close-cropped hair as steely as his eyes, his gaze didn't shift from the man isolated out on the headland who was staring out to sea once again. The cold gray waters ran away to the horizon to merge with billows of leaden cloud.

Where the rest wore rough woolens beneath scuffed buff leather and coarse cloaks that could double as blankets, the captain boasted a linen shirt beneath his padded green tunic, scarlet embroidery vivid as blood around the high collar. His cloak was woven from sturdy green wool and lined with brown.

"What about that thicket beyond the track, captain?" The older of the wood-gatherers twisted strips of bark to secure the sticks into a bundle. "I could take an ax to an ash tree."

"Perhaps at dusk. When we know he's not coming today." The captain withdrew his gaze to glower at the youth standing idle. "Hosh, if you're not helping Avayan, relieve Narich."

"It ain't my turn," Hosh protested. "Bair's next."

The stolid, square-faced man continued butchering the rabbits. "Do you want to eat or not?"

"Relieve Narich, Hosh," the captain ordered sternly.

The youth opened his mouth, shut it, and began walking. If he was muttering under his breath, the words were lost as hooves pounded the turf and harness rattled. The men exercising the horses hurried toward the tents, the restive beasts' whinnying initially drowning out the first man's words.

"Unlil whistled us, captain," he repeated, soothing the dappled gray with a stroke on her soft, mottled nose.

"What's he seen?" the captain wondered.

"Not the wizard." Elkan rapidly gathered all the reins thrust toward him by the two others who'd been exercising the horses.

The wind tugged at the captain's mossy cloak as he watched his man breaking cover from the thicket that offered a sentry a clearer view both ways along the track cutting through these coastal pastures. "He can tell us himself."

Every man drew his sword, even Bair with his hands still gory. Up on the headland, Narich did the same. Caught halfway between the tents and the cliff, Hosh dithered, looking this way and that.

"Horsemen, captain." Bair stood beside him, half a head shorter but considerably broader in the shoulder. He pointed with his sword.

A trio of riders appeared as the track rounded an undulation in the cliff-edge pastures. The first horseman lifted a fist in salute. Up on the headland, Narich raised a spyglass, swiftly lowering it to wave his own clenched fist in reply. He began running down the slope, pausing only briefly to berate the hapless Hosh and order him up to the exposed headland.

"It's Corrain," the captain said tersely,

"With Dancal and Ostin," Bair breathed, relieved. "All safe."

Neither he nor any of the rest moved to sheathe their swords until the three riders arrived. Unlil, the sentry, arrived scant moments ahead of the horsemen.

"Gefren—" The foremost rider recollected himself as he halted his mount. He wore finer linen than the others beneath his uniform of gray wool and buff leather. "Captain."

Gefren waved away Corrain's familiarity. "Report."

"Nothing." Corrain glanced at the two riders flanking him for their nods of confirmation. "Not even a peasant grubbing up acorns to feed his pigs."

"Captain!" Hosh's shriek startled everyone. Up on the cliff edge, he was hopping from foot to foot, pointing out toward the distant horizon. "The wizard! The wizard's coming!"

Corrain hauled on his reins to turn his horse toward the sea before Gefren could give any order. "Narich, let me see!" Kicking his mount into a canter, he barely slowed to snatch the spyglass from the man's raised hand. He stood in his stirrups to search the rolling gray sea, pulling the horse up just short of the precipitous drop.

Narich hurried to the tents. "We're packing up, captain?"

Unlil the sentry and the bald man Avayan were already hauling packs and blankets out onto the damp grass. The curious wind tugged at flapping canvas.

"Don't bother striking camp." Gefren watched Corrain intently. "Get ready to ride."

"Hosh, get down here," Narich bellowed.

"It's them," Corrain shouted, cantering down from the headland. "It must be," he said with quieter desperation as he reached them. "Saedrin save us, it must be."

"Are they flying the flag?" demanded Gefren, still stony-faced.

Corrain nodded and gestured toward darker gray skeins of cloud promising an approaching storm. "They must have a mage aboard to be countering those squalls."

"Get your gear together, Hosh." Unlil kicked clods of turf into the fire pit as the youth arrived, puffing hard.

The youth stared at Bair instead, accusing. "You're taking all the meat to fill your own belly?"

"I snared it." Bair swathed the skinned rabbits in a linen rag and scrubbed blood off his hands onto the turf.

"You know what we must do." Gefren looked around his men. Dancal and Ostin, the scouts who'd arrived with Corrain, were already on the verge of departing while Hosh was still struggling to roll up his blankets. Gefren's gaunt face grew grimmer still. "You already know that we've been betrayed. May all the gods watch over you. I pray we'll meet at Lord Halferan's gate."

"Or we'll see each other before Saedrin's door to the Otherworld," Hosh muttered bleakly.

"Forewarned is forearmed—" Corrain rebuked him.

Gefren spoke over him. "Our lives will be well spent if we save our lord and our families with our deaths." He accepted the reins of his own horse from Elkan and mounted swiftly. "Corrain, you can wait and take Hosh with you. Bair, go with Serde instead."

Without a glance for those left behind, the captain kicked the restive bay gelding into a gallop for the track. Avayan, Narich, and Elkan followed close behind. Reaching the pale scar in the grassland, all four men turned their horses to the south.

"We're away." Dancal clicked his tongue and his dun horse obediently pricked up its ears. Ostin rode away beside him, stirrup to stirrup. When they reached the track, they lashed their beasts into a headlong gallop for the north. Bair and Serde followed swiftly, Treche and Unlil scant moments behind them, all heading northward.

That left Corrain, still up on his horse, thin-lipped and tight-faced as he waited for Hosh to finally secure his pack to his saddle.

"You've no call to scowl at me." The youth looked up, sullen. "None of my doing brought you back down the ladder to ride as a common trooper."

"Believe me, I've learned my lesson," Corrain said with a humorless smile. "The next time I get drunk and seduce my lord's steward's wife, I'll make sure the old cuckold is out of town."

THE TRACK CURVED inland to join a lane long hollowed out by the remorseless tread of sheep and cattle. Dancal and Ostin's horses' hooves echoed noisily between the thorny banks. The storm from the sea pursued them, finally breaking over their heads as they left the lane for a wider road cutting between freshly hedged fields. The road was deeply rutted with wagon tracks and edged with intermittent coppices venturing their first pale spring leaves. There was no one to be seen in either woodland or pasture.

The riders didn't pause as cold rain hammered down on their heads. They only slowed leagues later when their horses threatened to stumble from weariness, as ruts dissolved into muddy puddles beneath their hooves.

"We get fresh horses at the next coaching inn." The gray wool of Dancal's cloak, his leather jerkin and the padded tunic beneath were all sodden. "Hire them or steal them, whatever it takes."

"We want two each." Ostin swiped at trickles of rain running down from the knitted cap pulled low to tame his black curls. "So we've remounts to hand."

As Dancal considered this, his horse took the opportunity to slow and halt. "No." He shook his head decisively, urging the unwilling horse onwards with his boot heels. "A horse on a lead rein will slow us, and they won't be fresh when we need new beasts."

"What if we're ten leagues from nowhere when the new horses founder?" Ostin protested.

"I said no." Dancal slapped at his horse's neck, dark mane clinging in ratty tails. He pointed to a crossroads marked by a gibbet and a fingerpost.

"Look, there's the high road. Let's be the first to win Lord Halferan's gratitude."

He used his short blunt spurs to force a reluctant canter from his horse. Ostin slapped a token loop of rein across his own mount's shoulders. The beast strove to catch its stable mate but a substantial gap stretched between them as Dancal reached the high road.

Ostin was wiping at rain trickling into his eyes again when Dancal's horse screamed. The curly headed man gaped as muddy figures scrambled out of deep ditches cut to catch the rain running off the hardened road. His own horse halted, shivering and unnerved.

The first attacker seized Dancal's bridle, gripping either side of the foam-slimed bit. Dancal couldn't reach him with his sword without decapitating his horse.

"Behind you!" Ostin screeched a vain warning as three more men assailed the bay's flanks. Greedy hands grabbed at Dancal, wrenching him from the saddle. He fell amid jostling bodies.

Ostin saw dull steel plain in their upraised fists. He hacked at his horse's muddied ribs with merciless heels, sobbing with fear and frustration. "Shift you bastard—"

He coughed, his words cut short. He frowned at the bloodied head of a broad-bladed arrow protruding from his breast. As he tried to protest, only scarlet foam bubbled from his mouth. The reins slipped from his numbed hands as the weary horse shifted its footing. Ostin fell sideways, helpless. He landed with a splash on the puddled road, gasping a last futile breath.

DUSK WAS FALLING when Bair and Serde reached an inn. They'd taken a road that cut inland rather than following the coast. The rain was long enough past that their clothes were now merely damp instead of soaked, but that still left them vulnerable to the deepening cold. As they rode into the yard, a stable door opened, spilling out a golden glow. Catching the scent of hay and companionship, Bair's horse lifted its head and quickened its pace. Serde's chestnut whickered cheerfully, misty breath glistening in the lamplight.

"We stay close together and close-mouthed," Serde said quietly as he dismounted. "We eat what's offered, get warm at the fire, and go to our bed."

"If someone asks our business?" Bair raised a friendly hand as an ostler appeared in the entrance to the stable.

"We say it's none of theirs." Serde slung his saddlebag over one shoulder.

"I'll get the boy." The ostler hurried across the yard to disappear through the back door of the inn.

"We'll see to our own horses," Serde called after him, irritated.

The only answer was the slam of the solid oak.

"Do you reckon they'll give us a meal in return for these rabbits for their pot?" As Bair slid down from his saddle, he prodded the bundle of linen blotched with darkened crimson. He chuckled. "Do you reckon some scullery maid might spread her legs for them?"

"The only person you're sharing a bed with is me." Serde led his chestnut horse into the stable.

Bair followed him with a gap-toothed grin. "I'll kick you if you snore."

Half a dozen horses were already in the stalls, straw deep around their hocks. Nets of hay were hung and their harness was racked tidily.

"The grooms here know their business." Bair patted a black cob's questioning nose as he relieved his own horse of its burdens in the stall beside it.

"We should ask if they've any horses for hire." Letting his gear fall to the dusty floor, Serde lifted the saddle flap to unbuckle his mount's girth. He bent to brush away mud and sweat crusted on the chestnut's belly.

"You can rest and get your strength back." Bair grinned as he slid the bridle off his horse's ears. The animal lipped his hand in search of some treat.

"Where's that lad we were promised?" Serde straightened up.

A man sitting motionless in the shadow behind the door sprang forward, his short sword menacing. As Serde and Bair swore, each reaching for their own blades, the trap door to the hayloft above flew open. Two men dropped onto a waiting heap of straw, naked steel in their hands.

One stumbled on landing. Serde was on him, his sword cutting a gleaming arc in the lamplight. But a fourth enemy erupted from the empty stall where he'd lurked beneath soiled litter. He caught Serde's descending forearm with one metal-gauntleted hand. Serde's fingers were numbed by the brutal collision and he dropped his blade. The attacker drove the long dagger in his other hand deep into the horseman's belly. They stood, pressed close as lovers. Serde looked into the man's dark eyes, astonishment momentarily outweighing his agony. Then his killer ripped the blade sideways, spilling out Serde's life with his entrails.

Bair had taken a mortal blow. The man hidden behind the door had hacked a deep gash between his neck and shoulder. Bair collapsed to his knees, feebly thrusting his sword at the men who'd dropped from the hayloft. The first attacker knocked his weapon aside with a contemptuous gauntlet and kicked Bair full in the chest with a steel-bound boot. Bair fell backward, his legs twisted painfully beneath his burly body.

The booted man bent to make certain Bair was beyond feeling such discomfort. He looked at the man who'd gutted Serde, raising his brows in silent question. The man was cleaning his blade on the dead horseman's cloak. He nodded in confirmation.

The attackers retrieved their horses from the stalls. Once the booted man had saddled his own black cob, he hung a leather bag of money from the bridle hook before silently leading the killers out into the night.

Within the stable the remaining horses stirred restlessly at the disquieting scent of blood. Dulling slowly, the ruby flow from Bair's neck seeped into the bloodstained linen wrapping the butchered rabbits.

HOSH MOANED BENEATH his blankets. "Cock crow?"

"Go back to sleep," Corrain said quietly.

"Why are you up?" Roused, Hosh fought free of his bedding.

"I'm going on alone." Corrain was by the door to the attic room, already dressed in his creased clothes. Stubble darkened his lean face.

Hosh sat upright, blankets slipping. "We're supposed to stay together. The captain said—" He shivered, his grimy shirt inadequate protection in the dawn chill.

"You can't keep your mouth shut." Corrain leaned against the thin plank door as he pulled a boot on. "Get your own throat cut and see if I care, but you won't take me to face Saedrin alongside you."

"Go kiss a pig's arse." Hosh's youthful face turned ugly with anger. "We're to stay together so my lord knows each man stays honest. Anyway, what did I do?"

"Besides trying to impress that ale-wench with your boasting about being Lord Halferan's trusted envoy?" Corrain queried with acid contempt.

"I was explaining why we're traveling together and why you were insisting we have a room to ourselves." A furious flush rose from Hosh's creased collar. "Half the taproom were guessing you were renting my arse."

"As long as they don't guess our real business, who cares." Corrain paused as he buckled his long boots at the knee. "But can you keep your mouth shut if I leave you behind?" he mused, staring at the boy.

"About the wizard?" Hosh swung his feet out from under the frowsy blankets.

"Apparently not." Grabbing his shoulder, Corrain hauled the youth off the low bed, dumping him on the floor.

"Hey!" Hosh sat on the bare boards, bemused, gooseflesh prickling his naked thighs.

"You've been complaining how tired you are." Corrain plucked Hosh's belt from the heap of breeches and jerkin at the end of the bed. "You can spend a few days here catching up on your rest."

"You want to leave me behind because you're the traitor!" Hosh grabbed for a muddy boot and threw it full at Corrain's head. The lean man dodged easily and the boot thudded against the cracked plaster. Hosh scrambled to his feet. "Now you want to make a run for it, back to your filthy paymaster."

"Say that again and I'll cut out your tongue." Corrain scowled blackly, slipping the tongue of the belt through the buckle to make a noose.

"They'll hunt you." Hosh's voice cracked with terror. "You can't get rid of a body that easily."

He couldn't escape the taller man in the confines of the cramped room. Corrain feigned a grab at Hosh's sword hand. As the youth recoiled, Corrain punched him deftly in the side of the jaw, hard enough to knock him sprawling on his belly on the bed. Before Hosh could gather his wits let alone regain his feet, Corrain was straddling him. He pushed the boy's beardless face into the lumpy mattress.

"I'm leaving you here." He bent down to speak close to Hosh's ear, low and menacing. "You have a choice. Keep your mouth shut, and don't say a word, whatever happens, whatever you're accused of. Then you'll probably live until I come back to get you. Whine like a whipped cur, telling everyone our business and you'll probably get your throat cut. If they don't hang you first just to shut your noise."

"Traitor—" Whatever else the lad tried to say was lost as Corrain pushed his face deeper into the bed.

Holding Hosh immobile with his muscular thighs, the saturnine swordsman clamped his strong long-fingered hands around the boy's pimply neck. Hosh struggled briefly before going utterly limp. Corrain swiftly hooked an arm under his knees to lay him on the bed. He used the lad's own belt to lash his feet together and cut strips from the blanket to fashion a secure gag and to tie his hands. Scowling, Corrain caught up his own saddlebags. As he reached the door, Hosh was beginning to stir, his eyes rolling beneath closed lids.

Corrain cursed between clenched teeth. He strode back and punched Hosh hard on the side of the head. The lad lolled back into unconsciousness and Corrain snatched up Hosh's clothes. Stuffing them into the lad's ungainly leather bag, he slung that over his shoulder with his own gear.

This humble inn had no locks to its doors so Corrain couldn't secure the room. He strode swiftly down the narrow passage and took the winding stair to the hallway two steps at a time. Sticking his head into the kitchen, he found a weary maid yawning as she swept ash from the hearth. He grinned. "Who's Head of the Watch hereabouts, sweetness?"

The girl blinked at him, bewildered. "Master Emmer, the baker."

Corrain fished in his shirt for the purse strung around his neck. "You do me a good turn and there'll be another silver mark to go with this one." He flipped the shiny coin toward her and she snatched it out of the air. "You remember that lad I was traveling with?"

She nodded mutely, wide-eyed.

"He tried to rob me in the night." Corrain shook his head. "I've left him tied up. Fetch this master baker, whenever you've done your chores. I've got my own business to be about but I'll be back to swear out an affidavit against the louse." He favored the girl with another winning smile.

Still confused she half-returned it, clutching her coin, the ash-pan in her other hand.

Corrain disappeared through the door to the stable yard.

* * *

"THE CAPTAIN SAID make haste." Treche looked warily around, his face shadowed by a dusty black hood.

No one was hurrying through this market place, thronged with people. Merchants were selling all manner of wares from trestle tables beneath broad awnings. With the sun turning its face toward noon, most were replenishing their stock, stacking baskets as they emptied them.

"The captain said get the word through." Unlil had swapped his gray uniform cloak for a long green cape. A man carrying freshly baked pies twisted through the crowd and trod on the tattered hem, tearing it further.

Treche lowered the handles of the laden push-cart he was laboriously shoving over the cobbles and blew on his fingers. While the day was agreeably bright, it was still bitterly cold. "You don't think everyone else will already be home?"

Two men peddling trinkets from trays hung around their necks paused just ahead, rearranging their depleted offerings so their displays looked less sparse.

"Maybe so, maybe not." Unlil glowered at a plump townswoman as she barged past him.

"You can explain to my lord's horse-master how you traded two good mounts for a barrow load of pease and a rag-man's cast-offs," Treche muttered. He reached for the pushcart's handles and grunted with pain. "Ah!" Straightening, he knuckled the small of his back.

"I'll take my turn—" Unlil broke off.

As Treche brought his hand forward, they both saw the glistening red bright in the sunlight. Treche's knees gave way and he slumped over the handcart. There was a dull gleam on his faded cloak, the cloth freshly dyed with his blood.

Unlil looked around wildly. No one looked back. Everyone in the crowd was intent on their own affairs. A man jostled him from behind. Unlil turned, fumbling for his sword. Hampered by the voluminous cape, he was too slow. As the heedless jostler went on his way, Unlil looked down to see a stubby knife hilt pinning the green cloth draping his thigh.

He gasped in sudden agony. Crippled by the burning poison, he fell to his knees like Treche. He wrenched the knife out of his leg but never heard the rising shrieks as passers-by suddenly realized there were two dead men in their midst.

"YOU KEEP LOOKING at the door, my lord Halferan." A short man spoke, his gaudy robe of embroidered scarlet velvet like a flame against the dark wooden paneling hiding the lower half of the hall's tall stone walls. Long lancet windows pierced the whitewashed upper expanses, burning with the last glow of sunset. "Are you expecting someone?" As his dark eyes slid toward the entrance, he toyed with his short black beard, slicked to a point with scented oil.

"My people often seek my counsel." Halferan's poise was commendable, apparently relaxed as he sat in his canopied chair. It dominated the dais at the northern end of the hammer-beamed hall.

"They rely on you to defend their interests." The man in the red robe walked along the edge of the dais, disdaining the gray-liveried swordsmen standing around the smoldering hearth just below. "Which means protecting them from the corsairs' raids."

Though Halferan was dressed in finer cloth than his warriors, he wore fighting gear like them, booted and spurred. Such garb flattered his wide shoulders and long, muscular legs. Like most, his hair was an undistinguished middling brown, his complexion faded from summer's deep tan to a winter's pallor.

He looked at the stocky man with undisguised contempt. "My men cut their teeth driving off such curs, Master Scavarin."

Though the men around the hearth growled their agreement, their lord's defiance rang painfully hollow.

The bearded man smiled, quite confident. "But then those teeth are knocked out by corsair fists, which black their eyes besides, and break their bones." As he turned to stroll back across the dais, his unprotected back was impervious to the warriors' lacerating glares.

Distant, away by the double door, men in drab brown sniggered into tankards of ale. Like Scavarin, they were dark of hair and eye, sallow skinned. Only one wasn't drinking, gold rings glinting on his fingers as he watched intently, his hands loose in his lap.

"Even victory leaves wounded men sapping your strength," Scavarin continued with blithe assurance. "How many raids do you successfully drive off? How often do your men arrive too late, to find houses burned and barns ransacked? How many women and children have been ravished or stolen away to be sold into slavery among the Aldabreshi?"

Lascivious guffaws down by the door prompted one of Halferan's men to half draw his sword, the rest stirring with anger.

Halferan gestured and the man rammed the blade back into its scabbard. "Keep your ruffians quiet, Scavarin. Don't imagine I don't know they'll have to account for my people's blood before Saedrin."

"Blood or gold, my lord. Which do you prefer to pay?" Scavarin waved artless hands, a ruby seal ring catching the light of candles lit against the encroaching twilight. "And you promised us safe conduct, my lord. My associates have surrendered their swords. Go back on your word and utter destruction will be visited upon your lands," he hissed with sudden venom.

"What if no one's left alive to tell them how you died?" a voice demanded, anonymous among the warriors.

"They might conclude you betrayed them," Halferan mused. "And took my gold for yourself."

Scavarin stood motionless for an instant before smiling serenely once again. "To business, my lord. My associates, or rather, their masters, undertake to leave your lands alone if you pay a suitable sum—"

"A suitable sum?" Halferan's scorn was caustic. "Will your associates be satisfied with the same amount next year? Or will I be asked for more and still more the following year? You would beggar me."

Scavarin sighed heavily. "I understood on my last visit that this was all agreed in principle. I thought I was bringing my associates to agree a figure acceptable to both parties. Why the delay, my lord?"

"I am reconsidering my decision to accept this thieves' bargain," Halferan said austerely.

Scavarin shook his head sorrowfully. "You don't want your people to welcome spring planting secure in the knowledge that they can raise their crops and husband their livestock and cherish their children in safety?" He looked straight at Halferan. "Winter's storms will soon be over, my lord. The corsairs will sail and your people will suffer. How much greater their anguish will be, when they learn you could have stopped all their torment. Will they thank you for hoarding your gold in your strong room? Because they will find out, my lord." He waved his hand toward the door once again. "We shall make sure word spreads."

"You admit you're as one with these scum." Halferan nodded, contemptuous. "So much for your claim of being an honest broker."

"This isn't about me, my lord. It's about you." Scavarin was unperturbed. He smiled as if suddenly amused. "Or are you delaying in hopes that the wizard will come?"

"I don't know what you mean." Lord Halferan tried to pretend confusion but too many men in the hall froze at the corsair envoy's words.

"Do you honestly believe a wizard's coming will save you?" Scavarin was openly pitying. "Don't deny you've sent begging letters to the mage-halls of Hadrumal, to the Archmage himself. I know you have. Know this, my lord. No mage will ever involve himself in the petty squabbles of Caladhrian lordlings and insignificant coastal raiders. Because that's all we are to the mighty wizards of Hadrumal."

"When I find whoever is passing you information I will hang them to feed the crows," Halferan said tightly.

"Build a big gallows, my lord." Scavarin shrugged. "Many people have doubts about your rule. Concern prompts loose talk." He spread his hands in an obsequious appeal. "Let's concentrate on the issue before us. Agree a sum, pay up and secure peace for your people. Delay, and the price goes up until the black ships come ashore. Mages have no need of gold or land or even a precious daughter's hand in marriage. But we will accept your gold, my lord, and leave your lands in peace." His smile turned cruel. "Your daughters will go virgin to their marriage beds."

"You go too far!" A red flush of fury seared Halferan's cheekbones.

Tense silence held the hall in thrall. The swordsmen around the hearth glowered at the corsairs by the door. The unwelcome guests sat motionless.

The man who wasn't drinking clenched beringed fists.

Scavarin threw up his hands in apparent surrender. "Forgive me, my lord. That was uncouth—"

Outside, a thunderous storm of blows attacked the great entrance.

"My lord—" A man-at-arms threw open the small porter's door cut into the larger one and stuck his head through. He vanished abruptly as a hand wrenched him backward.

"My lord Halferan!" A second man ducked through the low portal, scraping his shoulder. "The wizard's coming!"

"Corrain?" Incredulous, Halferan sprang to his feet.

"Alar, no!"

The corsair with the fists full of rings was instantly on his feet. Ignoring Scavarin, he drew a broad dagger from some concealed sheath to threaten Corrain.

Several of the guards had made for the door as soon as they heard knocking. They broke into a run down the long central aisle, others hard on their heels. None could hope to reach Corrain before the corsair was on him.

The saturnine trooper recoiled from the dagger's murderous down-stroke. The squat blade ripped into the coarse weave of his cloak. Corrain snatched a handful of the cloth and wrapped it around the corsair's dagger and forearm both, punching the raider full in the throat with his other hand. The corsair collapsed, choking and clawing at his neck.

"My lord, our safe conduct—" As Scavarin turned, protesting, he found Halferan's sword point pricking just below the oiled point of his beard.

"Safe conduct on condition you surrendered your blades," Halferan spat. "Seize them!"

Scavarin called out in an unknown tongue. The rest of the corsairs threw down daggers they had belatedly produced, raising empty hands in insolent surrender as the guards reached them.

"My lord." Scavarin swallowed hard and looked down the length of the shining steel. "Your man says a wizard is coming. No mage is here yet. You'd be ill-advised to kill us before you're certain of him. If your man's mistaken, I can still negotiate a new agreement to safeguard your people. If I'm still alive."

"True." Halferan didn't lower his sword. "Take them all to the dungeons. Lock this weasel up apart from the rest of the vermin."

"Have a care, my lord." Scavarin made no move as two warriors scrambled up to the dais to seize his arms. He twisted in the men's grip to look around at Halferan as they hauled him away unresisting. "If I don't send word to my associates out at sea within three days, they'll assume you've killed me and attack regardless."

Halferan ignored him, intent on Corrain as the man hurried down the hall.

As the men dragged Scavarin out through a side door his voice cracked with fear and anger.

"They'll burn your hall to the ground, my lord, and slaughter every living thing within it. Once they've raped everything in skirts—"

The door slammed on Scavarin's threats as Halferan jumped down from the dais to meet the swordsman. "How soon will Gefren get him here?"

"I don't know," Corrain answered apprehensively.

"WHERE IS HE?" Narich backed down the stubby jetty, naked sword in hand. His gaze searched every doorway and alley dividing the shuttered houses huddled beneath the sandstone cliff.

"Where are they?" Hollow-eyed with tiredness, Gefren was intent on the single-masted ship tied up beside the outthrust finger of squared-off stone. On deck, a few sailors were tidying ropes and storm-torn sails in desultory fashion.

"We lost them." Narich didn't sound convinced. "Elkan and Avayan are keeping watch."

As he gestured, the two other men waved back. Elkan was at the end of the row of houses, beside a modest tavern. Avayan was at the top of a path writhing back and forth up the sloping shoulder of land sheltering this fishing village. It was the only way to the top of the cliffs.

"He's here," breathed Gefren.

Narich looked back over his shoulder to see a slight figure walking down the gangplank. Despite the unceasing wind, a cobalt cloak hung down from his shoulders in untroubled folds. Beneath it he wore riding boots and breeches and a long-sleeved midnight-blue jerkin over a creamy linen shirt.

"Master Minelas." Gefren hurried down the jetty. "We're here—"

"From Lord Halferan. I know." The slim wizard was quite composed. "I assume you have a horse for me?"

"Can't you—" Narich hesitated. "Isn't there some magic—"

The wizard turned pale blue eyes on the trooper. "Not to take a mage somewhere he's never been before." He shook his head ruefully, the watery sunlight burnishing his golden hair. "Otherwise I'd have been at your lord's side as soon as I'd read his letter."

"That's a shame," Narich said with feeling.

"We've horses stabled." Gefren gestured toward Elkan, who waved back and vanished into the yard behind the tavern.

Avayan's loud shout from the heights echoed around the cliffs. "Raiders!"

"Corsairs have been hunting us all along the coast." Narich sounded on the verge of despair.

As the three men on the jetty watched, Avayan scrambled down the precipitous path.

"We're betrayed, master mage," Gefren said tightly.

"Indeed." Minelas was untroubled.

Gefren groaned as six horsemen appeared and their steeds began picking cautiously down the steep slope. "Let us go first, master mage. We'll try to cut you a path." He looked toward the tavern as Elkan reappeared, a boy helping him control a handful of saddled and bridled horses. "Narich will stay with you—"

"Your lord asks for wizardry to defend his people against these brutes." Minelas took a pace forward, flexing his long fingers. "Let's make a start here."

The foremost corsair's horse stumbled and whinnied. Its hind hooves slid out from under it and it sat down hard on its black rump, forelegs thrust out forwards to brace itself on the perilous path. Its rider managed to keep his seat to no avail. Neither spurs nor whip could induce the petrified horse to stand, leaving the path blocked.

Gefren was surprised into a bark of laughter. Narich groaned, raising a helpless hand. He had been watching Avayan. The burly man had tried to cut off an angle of the path by sliding down the steep turf. He'd lost his footing and was rolling, helpless to save himself from a bone-shattering fall onto the faceted rocks at the foot of the slope.

Minelas flung up a hand and a swirl of sapphire light halted Avayan's headlong tumble, righting him just before the final drop. The warrior clung to the steep slope, pressing his face into the grass, digging in his fingers and toes. Then he looked cautiously up, first toward the cliff top, then slowly around and down, to stare open-mouthed at the men down on the jetty. Above, the corsairs were still trying to flog the black horse to its feet.

"If they can't get down, we still can't get up." Gefren tried to keep reproach out of his voice.

Minelas didn't respond, the slightest smile tugging at one corner of his full mouth.

One of the other corsair horses whickered, disconcerted. The wind from the sea wound a skein of pale dust around the would-be attackers. Another horse neighed, panicked as the soil beneath its hooves blew away. Now all the animals were seized with the same fear, tossing their heads and scrabbling vainly for a firmer footing.

The rearmost riders tried to turn their horses around, to make for the top of the cliff. As they did so, one swung its muscular rump into another horse, sending it sliding down to fall against the first to stumble. Both riders fell from their saddles. As they tumbled down the slope, they grabbed at each other, at tufts of grass and knife-edged rocks. A slick of blue light appeared, not to save them but to stop them getting any handhold.

On hands and knees, Avayan had been cautiously picking his way across the slope to the comparatively safety of the path. He pressed himself to the grass shuddering as the corsairs slid past him to plummet, screaming, onto the murderous rocks below.

"Saedrin save us," Narich breathed.

Now the topmost edge of the sandstone cliff was crumbling into razor-edged shards. Slings of sapphire magelight whirled around to hurl a lethal rain at the corsairs still struggling with their horses. A screaming man fell head over heels before his falling steed crushed him into bloody silence. Men and animals slipped, stumbled and fell with yells and uncomprehending shrieks of pain. A horse tumbled helplessly, its legs snapping audibly. They all landed hard on the broken rocks, agonized echoes of their final screams lingering for some moments after the last corsair had fallen to his death.

Gefren drew a shaking breath and bowed low to Minelas. "Master mage—"

"Let's be on our way." Entirely indifferent to what he had done, the wizard strode along the jetty toward Elkan and the boy with the horses. The warrior was looking as wide-eyed as the child at the mangled bodies at the foot of the slope.

"Trooper!" Gefren shouted harshly. "Mount up."

Elkan gathered his wits and proffered a set of reins with a shaking hand as Minelas reached him. The wizard sprang competently into the saddle while the fisher-lad fled, ashen-faced.

Narich's dour face cracked in a slow grin as he walked beside Gefren. "Those bastard raiders aren't going to know what's hit them."

"I HAVE BEACONS manned all along the coast and fast horses ready to carry word inland." Lord Halferan was pacing back and forth in front of his canopied chair. Below, the great hall was full of men quietly speculating with suppressed excitement. Halferan's brown eyes grew distant. "As soon as we see the first ships—"

Minelas was seated at a trestle table set up on the dais. He leaned over a wide silver bowl of water tainted with ink. "No."

The mage's single soft word silenced the entire hall.

"What do you mean?" Halferan asked the question for everyone.

"See for yourself, my lord," Minelas invited.

Halferan squared his shoulders and walked over to look into the scrying bowl.

"This spell—" He hesitated.

"Do you recognize this anchorage?" asked Minelas.

"I do." Halferan frowned. He raised his head to look at his expectant warriors. "It's the mouth of the Linney, in the middle of the salt-marshes."

"What do you see?" the wizard prompted.

"Three corsair ships." Halferan rested his hands on the table, peering into the bowl. Blue magelight from the ensorcelled water cast eerie reflections on his face. "A substantial encampment. Timber buildings within a palisade. A sizeable midden and the fen despoiled." He swallowed hard.

"I'd say they've over-wintered there," observed Minelas. "They've a foothold on your land, my lord."

"This summer's raids will be ten times worse if they have a forward base." Halferan slammed his fists on the table. Sapphire light slopped over the bowl's rim to sink into the wood. He snapped his head around to find Gefren waiting patiently at the side of the dais. "Bring that weasel Scavarin up from the dungeon," he snarled. "We'll learn what he knows about this if we have to skin him alive to loosen his tongue."

"No," Minelas said forcefully. "If he suspects you know they're there, he'll send a warning. You know there are traitors in your household."

Bitterness twisted Halferan's wrathful expression. "Can't magic unmask them?"

"No," Minelas said evenly. "But my magic and your men can destroy this nest of vermin. That'll send a message to the other corsairs."

"Telling them to raid our neighbors instead." Halferan said unwillingly.

"Your first duty is to your own," Minelas reminded him. "We can help your neighbors as and when raiding ships come."

"Burning these scum might delay the first raids," ventured Gefren.

"Leave them and they'll launch their own attacks any day," Minelas pointed out. "They needn't fear any late storms out on the open ocean."

"Those salt-marshes run all the way to Lord Ermeth's borders," Halferan said thoughtfully. "We could ask him—"

"No." The wizard was adamant. "We must leave now, with just the men present in this hall. As long as you can swear they're all loyal." He raised a hand and every door glowed with ominous blue light. "Any man you doubt must be locked in a dungeon until we return."

"Every man here is true as Gidestan steel." Gefren was outraged.

Minelas ignored him, intent on Halferan. "If these corsairs get a hint that they're threatened, they'll disappear into the mosses. We must leave at once, and you must hang this envoy you have chained below, and all his men too, so we can't be betrayed after we've left."

"How are we to attack a camp in the middle of these marshes?" Gefren appealed to his lord. "The corsairs will post sentries. They'll know we're coming before we're within three leagues." He risked a fearful glance at the wizard.

Minelas vanished without so much as a hint of magelight. "I can hide your men from corsair eyes." His voice was calm in the empty air. "As long as they haven't had word we're coming." The wizard reappeared, that half-smile lifting the corner of his mouth.

Halferan stared down into the scrying bowl, gnawing at his lower lip. "Very well," he said with sudden decision. He surveyed the men waiting motionless in the hall. "Get your gear and weapons from your barracks and muster in the outer ward. Go nowhere else. No farewells for wives or sweethearts or whores. Do I have your oath?" he demanded harshly.

"Aye, my lord!" The fervent shout shook dust from the high hammer beams.

Minelas nodded, satisfied. "And order that corsair envoy and his men hanged before we leave. Just to be certain."

"Their crimes doubtless deserve death." Halferan waved a dismissive hand as he strode toward a door at the rear of the dais. "See to it, Gefren."

"My lord." The captain bowed obediently.

"I shall want the bay stallion, captain, and a man to see to my needs." Minelas passed a hand over the silver bowl, quenching the sapphire light before following Halferan.

"As you wish, master mage." Gefren regarded the scrying bowl with misgiving before looking down the long hall.

Troopers were shoving at each other in their haste to reach the doors, eager to embark on this campaign against the hated foe. Only a few were hanging back, to let the crush lessen. One was Corrain. He met Gefren's gaze, a frown creasing his forehead. Stifling his own unease, the captain turned abruptly around and went after his lord.

"Do you think he has the stomach for this fight?" Corrain urged his horse to draw level with Gefren's stirrup. He leaned sideways to see past the riders ahead to the blue-cloaked figure riding beside Halferan. The track through the fens had been only just wide enough for two horses.

About half the force rode ahead of their lord and his knot of trusted troopers, the remainder following behind. Travel-stained, horses roughly groomed, every man rode straight-backed and alert, impatience for this battle on every face.

"Do you think this wizard can do all he claims?" Corrain persisted.

"He slaughtered those raiders at the harbor." Gefren looked bleak.

"He saved my life," Avayan said robustly, riding on Corrain's other flank.

Corrain shook his head dubiously. "He wouldn't watch those corsairs hanged. He asked me if they were all dead before he'd join my lord in the outer ward."

"He's no milksop." Narich turned in his saddle to look back at them. "He couldn't handle that stallion if he was."

"True enough." Doubt still shadowed Corrain's eyes.

"How can they not see us?" Hosh was riding behind with Elkan.

"Magic," Elkan said repressively.

"Everyone's plain as day," Hosh persisted. "Where's that blue light he raises his visions with?"

Elkan glared at him. "Shut up or they'll hear us coming regardless."

"Or I'll leave you behind bound and gagged again." Corrain looked back over his shoulder. "I won't come back to get you a second time."

Hosh opened his mouth to laugh until he saw Corrain's expression. He subsided into uncertain silence.

"How far to the corsair camp?" Avayan asked quietly.

"Not far." Gefren looked up at the sun high in an untroubled sky. "That rise where we last camped was the end of the solid ground."

"This is salt marsh." Narich pointed at a tangle of dirty red stems beside a cluster of tall dark green plants with sharp, toothed leaves. "See, samphire and spearweed."

The plants suddenly shimmered as if seen though a heat haze that this spring day couldn't hope for. Azure light flickered on the edge of sight.

"There's your magic," Elkan grinned.

A flash, brighter than lightning, dazzled them, painful in its intensity. Another came, then another, blinding radiance exploding on all sides.

"What—?" Corrain groped for his sword hilt, struggling to force his eyes open.

Narich cried out in startled anguish as an arrow buried itself in his shoulder.

"Corsairs!" Gefren bellowed, standing in his stirrups and drawing his sword.

Corrain ripped his blade from its sheath and flailed wildly around, purple smears blurring his vision. More men yelled as raider arrows bit deep. Fearful horses whinnied and stamped. Corrain's mount tossed its head wildly, ears pressed back flat.

"Help me!" Hosh was unhorsed. He struggled to his knees, flailing wildly at shimmering lights whirling all around.

"Leave the horses!" Gefren dismounted as he shouted the order

"I can't!" Narich could only cling on with his unwounded hand as his horse reared, lashing out with its forefeet.

Elkan was still mounted, slashing his sword at the lights circling Hosh. A glimmer dodged sideways before darting forward to run up his blade and sink into Elkan's hand. He yelled and dropped the weapon. The stink of burned flesh and charred leather floated over the salt scent of the churned mud. Elkan fell and screamed only once as his terrified horse trampled him.

Corrain dropped to the path and let his horse go. He scrubbed at tear-filled eyes with the back of one hand as he brandished his sword blindly.

"Stay at my back and I'll stay at yours." Avayan slid from his saddle and pressed his shoulders to Corrain's. "I can't see," he raged.

With the purple stains in his vision fading to yellow, Corrain glimpsed a figure behind a thicket of stunted buckthorn. "Corsairs!"

As he blinked, the man vanished. Then a different raider stepped out of nowhere to swing a brutal cudgel at his head. Corrain ducked, thrusting a furious, instinctive riposte that bit deep into the raider's forearm. His blade passed straight through the insubstantial wrist, leaving no wound. Corrain blinked again and the man was two paces to the right. His club was coming so fast there was nothing Corrain could do. As the blow landed he went sprawling in the mud.

Feeling emptiness at his back, Avayan whirled around, his sword ripping through the air. A blue spark leaped to the point of the blade. With an ear-splitting crack, the weapon twisted into useless scrap. Avayan dropped dead, his face a rictus of agony. A raw score seared his wrist, disappearing up his sleeve.

"I yield!" Corrain wrapped his arms round his head in abject surrender. "Saedrin save me," he wailed. "I yield!"

All up and down the path Lord Halferan's warriors were being clubbed into submission and dragged away.

"You craven swine." On hands and knees beside Corrain, Hosh was bleeding profusely from a broken nose. Drawing a ragged breath, he spat his contempt full in the older man's face along with a broken tooth.

Corrain rolled over into a low crouch, wiping the blood and spittle awkwardly onto one shoulder. "Learn to roll before a punch lands, boy." There was no panic in his whisper. The club had left the merest graze on his temple. "We can't fight magic so save your strength. They're not out to kill us."

"What do they want?" Hosh quavered.

A raider approached with a handful of jangling chains, grinning. "We want slaves."

"No!" Hosh reared up, bunching his fists.

Corrain deftly tripped him, glaring furiously at the boy. "Don't be a fool!"

"Listen to him." The corsair fastened manacles on Corrain's unresisting wrists before stripping the warrior of dagger and sword belt. "You might live to see tomorrow."

"Where's—?" Hosh yelped. "Narich!"

Corrain saw the wounded man was slumped on his knees, ashen with blood loss. A raider grabbed his hair, hauled his head back and cut his throat.

"We want fit and healthy slaves," sneered the corsair who'd chained them. "Better hope that nose heals cleanly, boy."

Corrain looked swiftly around. A handful of men lay dead close by. The rest he could see had been taken captive. "There's the wizard." As Hosh cowered beside him, whimpering, he indicated Minelas with a jerk of his head.

Some way beyond Gefren, who was kneeling in chains, his chin on his chest, Lord Halferan lay face down in the mire, a corsair's boot on his neck. Minelas stood a few paces away, unsullied, brushing wisps of sapphire mist from his thin hands.

A corsair walked up to him, head and shoulders taller. Massive in black leather and a steel breastplate, gold chains were plaited into his beard. "Well done, my friend."

"You betrayed us." Halferan tried to lift his head, spitting mud. "You bastard."

"I got a better offer," Minelas said conversationally, hunkering down beside him. "When my friend here heard you were looking for a wizard, he made it his business to outbid you."

"He haggles like a fishmonger, this wizard. You should have paid Scavarin and saved yourself this grief." The corsair leader kicked Halferan in the ribs with casual brutality. "And saved me my gold. But I'll make it back selling your men for slaves."

"Make sure you sell them to the most distant domains of the Archipelago," Minelas said sternly. "And cut out their tongues. We want no witnesses."

"You mind your business and I'll mind mine," the giant corsair retorted.

"Why did you ever believe Hadrumal would be your salvation, my lord?" Standing up, Minelas shook his head pityingly. "Most wizards only want peace and quiet to study their books and swap magical theories with tedious mages as blinkered as they are. They'd never be interested in your miserly offer of gold and gratitude. No one ten leagues beyond your borders even cares about your pitiful little fiefdom's fate. Now, me, I want a lot more than a lifetime in dusty libraries to look forward to. I want wine and women and people looking up to me, and enough gold to keep all that coming till I'm old and bald."

"You think this scum will keep paying you?" Halferan twisted in impotent rage.

"He won't have to." Minelas reached inside his jerkin for a blank leaf of parchment. "Because I'll be taking news of your valorous death back to your family along with your death-bed grant of your lands and family into my guardianship." As he spoke, black writing rippled across the creamy surface. "Isn't that your signature, my lord?" He bent to show Halferan the dark flourish at the bottom. "Your rents and revenues should keep me in the luxury to which I wish to become accustomed."

Gefren sprang to his feet, taking everyone by surprise. Gripping the chain linking his manacles in both fists, ready to strangle Minelas, he took two long strides toward the wizard. A bolt of lightning from the empty sky lanced into the top of the guard captain's head. He stood motionless, already dead. A bloody blackened gash ran down the side of his face, the scorched line continuing down his tunic and breeches to one boot burst into a smoking ruin. Falling forward, he landed beside Halferan, his sightless eyes staring into his lord's horrified face.

"You won't get away with this," Halferan raged impotently.

"He will." The corsair captain plunged his long sword into Halferan's back to skewer his heart. "As long as he keeps our little hideaway here safe and secret." He smiled at Minelas with cheerful menace.

The wizard was unmoved. "As long as you send me a modest share in whatever loot you find outside my fiefdom."

The corsairs down the path had dragged off all the other men. Now they came for Corrain and Hosh.

"What are we going to do?" the boy sniveled wretchedly as he was hauled to his feet.

"We stay alive." Corrain set his stubbled jaw while ducking his head in apparent submission. "Until we can escape and come home to see that wizard hanged."

"When did any slave last escape the Aldabreshi." Desolate tears trickled down Hosh's face to mingle with the blood and mucus oozing from his broken nose.

* * *

IT WAS DAWN when the coastal trader's ship sailed up to the stubby jetty. Sailors leaped ashore to secure mooring ropes and fenders. As soon as the gangplank crashed onto the square stones, a young woman in a black cloak walked swiftly down onto the jetty, a battered leather sack slung over one shoulder by its drawstring.

The ship's brawny captain hurried after her. "There's the tavern, my lady. You can rest and take some breakfast—"

"Thank you, but I've no time to waste." Smooth-skinned, with large and luminous hazel eyes and silken auburn hair to offset an otherwise unremarkable face, she turned a smile of surpassing sweetness on the sailor. "Where exactly did these men die?"

"Over there, my lady. At the foot of the cliff." The captain licked dry lips and ran a calloused hand over his grizzled beard. "But there's naught left. They threw the carrion into the other cove."

He made no move to follow as the woman walked away, her soft leather half-boots whispering on the stones. She soon reached the broken rocks in the angle between the sloping ridge running down to the sea and the sheer cliffs.

After walking back and forth a few times, she bent to study a gory patch of scree, old dry blood now veiled with windblown dust. Quite composed, she tucked her black cloak around her long skirts and sat cross-legged on the ground. Despite the strengthening sunlight, she took a candle in a shallow pottery holder from her bag, together with a silver bowl and a small mirror of polished brass. She laid the mirror flat, stood the candle beside it, and kindled a scarlet flame with a snap of her fingers. Finding a small bottle in the bag, she uncorked it and poured clear, viscous oil into the silver bowl. As she selected a piece of bloodstained stone, crimson magic shimmered across the mirror.

"Jilseth? Are you there?" A voice echoed distantly from the swirling radiance.

"I am, Archmage." She dropped the stone shard into the oil. Dark amber light boiled up around it.

"Was it him?" the unseen wizard asked with clipped anger. "What happened?"

Jilseth leaned forward to gaze into the bowl. "Six men died, and their horses. Minelas definitely killed them. They were certainly corsairs."

The distant Archmage's sigh sent ripples across the spell reflected in the mirror. "Doesn't he know he'll never get away with this?"

"He's managing to hide himself from everyone's scrying, element masters and all." Jilseth's smile didn't reach her beautiful eyes. "And I imagine, like everyone else from the Council of Hadrumal down, he considers necromancy a perverted and pointless magic."

"We have more important concerns than that well-worn debate." There was a suggestion of apology in the Archmage's words. "What about this lodestone magic you promised me?"

"Let's see." Jilseth reached into the neck of the modest gray dress she wore beneath her black cloak. She pulled out a metallic black crystal pendant on a silver chain. Lifting it over her head she dangled it above the seething bowl.

Thick wisps of smoke rose from the oil. Jilseth swept her hand through them. Golden glints flowed from her fingers to shape tiny phantasms. The magic made a gruesome shadow play of the deaths of men and beasts falling down the cliff, once, twice and a third time. Then Jilseth brushed them away and the smoke reformed into a single corsair face screaming in silent terror. A third pass of the magewoman's hand destroyed it and all the smoke vanished. The boiling oil subsided into stillness.

"Well?" The brass mirror rang with the Archmage's impatience.

Jilseth ran the chain through her hands before holding the pendant out at arm's length. The lodestone twitched and drifted inland, gradually rising, the silver links following. It only halted when it had drawn the chain out to its fullest extent.

"It'll take me to anywhere Minelas has ever worked magic." Satisfaction warming her smile, Jilseth hung the pendant around her neck once more. "And my other spells will show me exactly what he's done, wherever he's spilt blood."

"Then we can decide how to punish his crimes." The Archmage's voice was flinty.

Jilseth nodded as she drew the oil out of the bowl and back into the bottle in a swirl of amber magic. Licking finger and thumb ready to snuff the candle, she looked intently into the mirror. "I'll find him, Planir, however long it takes."

SHELL GAME

A JOHN JUSTIN MALLORY STORY

MIKE RESNICK

JOHN JUSTIN MALLORY stalked into the office, muttering angrily to himself. He sat down on the chair behind his desk, pulled out a cigarette, glared at it, then broke it in half and tossed it onto the floor.

"I take it you didn't have a good afternoon?" said the pudgy, gray-haired woman seated at the other desk.

"Don't ask," growled Mallory.

"That poor creature lost again, didn't he?" persisted Winnifred Carruthers.

"No, he didn't."

A human-like but definitely feline creature strolled in from the kitchen. "He must have lost. The stars are still moving in their courses."

"When I want the opinion of the office cat, rest assured I'll ask for it," said Mallory.

"I'll be honest with you," said Winnifred. "I thought Flyaway would never win. I mean, my goodness, sixty-one straight losses! You should be overjoyed, John Justin. Why do you look so morose?"

"He didn't win," replied Mallory.

"I thought you just said he didn't lose."

"He didn't run."

"Is the poor beast injured?" asked Winnifred.

"He doesn't run fast enough to hurt himself," said the feline creature.

"Hush, Felina!" said Winnifred. "Don't berate him now that he's injured."

"He's not injured," said Mallory. "He's healthy as... well, as a horse."

"Then I don't understand."

"He broke the damned tote board! It couldn't compute odds of more than a googol to one, so it went on tilt! They shut down the track for the day, and now he's barred from Belmont until they get a new board."

"Is that all?" said Winnifred. "It just means you'll have to bet on some other horse for a while. Who knows? You might even pick a winner."

"Today was the day for him," said Mallory bitterly. "I felt it in my bones. I've been on that damned horse since his first start. He's so overdue to win it makes me sick."

"It makes you poor, too," added Felina helpfully.

"How can a horse with a name like Flyaway lose sixty-one in a row?" continued Mallory.

"Flyaway. It just smacks of class. It's obvious that they've been holding him back, waiting for the right price. And today would have been the day. He opened at eighty-six trillion to one. In a seven-horse field. On a fast track."

He opened a drawer, pulled out what he fondly considered to be the office bottle, though Winnifred didn't drink, and poured himself a shot.

"So," he said, taking a swallow, "did we have any calls today?"

"No," said Winnifred. "It's probably just as well you didn't make any bets. We haven't had a case in almost two weeks."

"We should feel good about that," replied Mallory. "It means all's right with the world and no one needs a detective."

"They may not need a detective, but we need a client. Our bank balance is getting very low, even without your betting on that poor benighted animal."

Felina leaped onto Mallory's desk, then lay down on her stomach. "As long as you're not working, you can skritch between my shoulder blades."

"I'm thinking," said Mallory. "That counts as working."

"Not if no one pays you for it," said Felina. "Remember, I want you to skritch, not scratch."

"I'd ask if there was a difference, but I'm afraid you might tell me."

Suddenly Felina sat up and hissed. "You ruined everything, John Justin!"

"By wondering if there was a difference?"

"By taking so much time. Now you're going to have a client, and you won't have time to skritch me until tonight."

"What makes you think we're about to get a client?" asked Mallory.

"Cat people know things that human people can never know," she replied just as someone knocked at the door.

"Do they know how to get off my desk?" said Mallory as Winnifred got up, walked to the door, and opened it to reveal a small, undernourished man with watery blue eyes, a sparse brown mustache, an ill-fitting suit, and a thick shock of hair that refused to stay combed.

"Well?" he said.

"Well what?" asked Winnifred.

"Will you take my case?"

Mallory and Winnifred exchanged looks.

"Strictly speaking, possibly," replied Mallory. "Why don't you come in and tell us who you are and what your problem is?"

"Yes, I suppose I should do all that first, shouldn't I?" said the man, entering the office. "I'm so upset I'm not thinking clearly."

"Did you try to bet on Flyaway too?" asked Felina.

"Shut up," said Mallory.

"I thought you wanted me to tell you about my problem?" said the man, confused.

"I meant her, not you," said Mallory. "Have a chair."

The man sat down, the muscles in his sallow face twitching nervously.

"My name is John Fitzgerald Kennedy."

"Of the Boston John Fitzgerald Kennedys?" asked Mallory, wondering how long it would take for the ambulance from the Bellevue Asylum to arrive if he called them in the next ten seconds.

"It's not my real name, of course," continued the man. "But for reasons that will become apparent, I cannot tell you who I am."

"Well, it's a nice, unobtrusive alias," said Mallory wryly. "Guaranteed to attract almost no attention at all."

"Do you really think so?" asked the man hopefully. "I was torn between that and Elvis Presley."

"You'd have gone broke on the wardrobe," said Mallory. "Could we get on with the problem, Mr. Kennedy?"

"All right," he agreed. "But first I must ask you a question. What do you know about lamias?"

"I think the lamia is some religious leader in China or Tibet or somewhere, isn't he?"

"No, John Justin," said Winnifred. "It is a creature with a woman's face and breasts, the front legs of a clawed carnivore, the back legs of an antelope, and skin covered with scales like a snake's."

"It sounds very confused," commented Mallory.

"It's also very dangerous," said Winnifred. "It is said that they drink the blood of children." She turned to Kennedy. "But there hasn't been one seen in decades. What do lamias have to do with your problem?"

"The last lamia died two months ago," said Kennedy. "In Libya, which is the ancestral home of the species."

"Okay, the last one died," said Mallory. "So what?"

"It left behind a single fertilized egg," said Kennedy. "An egg that could be worth millions, because once it hatches out, that will be the last lamia ever. Think of the money that can be made putting it on exhibition!"

"My partner has some difficulty thinking of more than two dollars at a time," said Winnifred. "Why don't you proceed with your story?"

"That's almost all of it," said Kennedy. "Except that I paid a confederate fifty thousand dollars to steal it, smuggle it out of Libya, and deliver it to me."

"And he hasn't shown up?" asked Mallory.

"Oh, he showed up. I had it in my hands yesterday." Kennedy seemed closed to tears. "And today I don't. Some dishonorable bastard stole it from my apartment last night!" His face was twitching so rapidly now that it looked like a bad computer game. "Can you imagine the gall of that son of a bitch?"

"Yeah, there ought to be a law against stealing valuable eggs," said Mallory.

"Right!" said Kennedy furiously. "Well, will you take the case?"

"I assume you want us to retrieve the egg?"

"Of course!"

"I suppose we can take a stab at it."

"Don't say stab!" howled Kennedy. "It is as delicate as a dragonfly's wing." He made an effort to calm himself. "Lamia eggs take four months to hatch. If anything happens to it in the next sixty days, it will kill it."

"Okay, so we won't make an omelet," said Mallory. "Just out of curiosity, how did you happen to choose the Mallory & Carruthers Agency?"

"You're the guy who found the unicorn* and that missing reindeer,** and broke up the elephant scam at the track,*** aren't you? I figure you're an animal expert, and an egg is almost an animal."

"About the same way you're almost a Kennedy," said Mallory. He shrugged. "All right. How do we spot this particular egg? Big as an ostrich egg?"

Kennedy shook his head. "No, it's just the size of a regular chicken's egg now. It will grow over the next two months, though it will never be half the size of an ostrich egg."

"I don't want to seem unduly pessimistic, Mr. Kennedy," said Mallory, "but do you know how many eggs there are in Manhattan at this very minute?"

"Oh, you'll be able to spot this one," said Kennedy.

"Please tell me it isn't white."

"It's white, but it has an intricate pattern of red and blue dots, each the size of a nail head, all over it."

"Kind of like a colorful case of the measles."

"If you say so," said Kennedy. "I am prepared to pay you a handsome retainer plus your daily rate, whatever it may be. I'll cover all expenses, and there will be an equally handsome bonus when the egg is returned to me."

"Winnifred, do you want to draw up a pair of contracts?"

"Why bother?" she said. "He's not going to sign his real name anyway."

Mallory shrugged. "I don't know. Maybe we can sue all the other Kennedys if he finks out."

"I am not a fink outer!" said Kennedy angrily. Suddenly he frowned. "A finker out," he amended. He shook his head distractedly. "A—"

"We get the picture," interrupted Mallory. "Just give us the retainer and let us know where we can contact you."

"No!" said Kennedy nervously. "I can't tell you where I live or what my phone number is. You might turn it over to the cops, or sell it to the Libyans. I'll contact you."

"When?"

"When you have the egg, of course."

"How will you know?"

Kennedy frowned. "I haven't thought about that." He closed his eyes for a moment. "All right," he said. "Take out an ad in the *Times* saying that you've got the egg."

"Okay."

Kennedy pulled out a wad of bills, peeled off a goodly number, and laid them on Mallory's desk, then walked to the door. As he reached it, he turned back to the detective. "One more thing."

"What?"

"I'll be using the Kennedy name for the next few days, and we don't want any Libyan agents to know when you've found the egg, so when you run the ad, direct it to the attention of Richard Nixon."

Then he was gone.

"What do you think, John Justin?" asked Winnifred.

"I think maybe eggs aren't the only things that are scrambled," replied Mallory.

MALLORY LEANED BACK in his chair, staring at the Playmate he had taped to the wall, and on which Winnifred had meticulously drawn a bra and panties with a black magic marker. He'd been staring at it for twenty minutes, until Winnifred and Felina both thought he'd fallen asleep with his eyes open.

Suddenly he sat up. Winnifred jumped, startled, and Felina hissed.

"I can't see any way around it," he announced.

"Around the magic marker?" asked Winnifred. "I should certainly hope not."

"Around the case," said Mallory. "We don't have a single lead. All we know is that we're after an egg." He paused. "You know how many places you can hide an egg in Manhattan?"

"I have a horrible feeling I know what you're about to say next," said Winnifred.

"I might as well talk to the guy who's most likely to have stolen it, or at least know where it is."

"But he's the most powerful demon on the East Coast!"

"Who better to ask?" said Mallory.

"I just hate it when you meet with him!" said Winnifred.

"He's a man—well, a demon—of his word," said Mallory.

"Besides, we've been on the same side a couple of times."****

"Those were aberrations," said Winnifred. "Don't forget—he's also threatened to kill you."

"He's promised to kill me," said Mallory. "That's different."

"How?"

"It's less imminent."

"And that makes it all right?" she said.

"Have you got a better idea?" said Mallory. "I'm all ears."

"No, of course I don't have a better idea," said Winnifred irritably. "But you know what I think of him."

"Go out for a sandwich. I'll be through with him by the time you get back."

Winnifred walked to the door. "Come along, Felina."

"I'm not afraid of the Grundy," said Felina, stretching languorously. "I'll stay."

"Loyalty," said Mallory. "I like that in the office cat."

"Oh, I'm not loyal," said Felina. "But if he tears you into little pieces, I want to be here to watch."

"Thanks," said Mallory dryly. "I can't tell you how comforting that is."

"I knew you'd approve," said Felina happily as Winnifred walked out the door.

"All right," said Mallory. "We might as well get this show on the road."

He walked over to the phone, picked it up, and dialed G-R-U-N-D-Y.

There was a clap of thunder, and suddenly a strange being materialized in the middle of the room. He was tall, a few inches over six feet, with two prominent horns protruding from his hairless head. His eyes were a burning yellow, his nose sharp and aquiline, his teeth white and gleaming, his skin a bright red. His shirt and pants were crushed velvet, his cloak satin, his collar and cuffs made of the fur of some white polar animal. He wore gleaming black gloves and boots, and he had two mystic rubies suspended from his neck on a golden chain. When he exhaled, small clouds of vapor emanated from his mouth and nostrils.

"I am getting tired of being summoned by my mortal enemy," said the Grundy, glaring at the detective.

"Well, you never invite me over for drinks," said Mallory. "How else are we going to meet?"

"Spare me your humor, John Justin Mallory," said the demon. "Why am I here?"

"Do you have the egg?"

"Egg?" repeated the Grundy. "What egg?"

"A little man calling himself John F. Kennedy got his hands on a lamia egg, doubtless through totally illegal means," said Mallory. "And of course, someone of even lower moral standing stole it from him. I don't think it was you, if only because you'd derive far more satisfaction taking it from him while he was watching than sneaking into his room and stealing it, but before I start my investigation, I thought I'd ask."

"I don't have it."

"Do you know who has?"

The Grundy shook his head. "No. I wasn't aware it was in the country. It is the last lamia egg in existence, you know."

"Yeah, that's what he said."

"It should be mine."

"Come on, Grundy," said Mallory. "I've been to your castle. You've already got more trinkets and possessions than any twenty men I know. Does owning the egg confer some additional dark power on you?"

"No."

"Then why do you want it?"

"I don't especially want it," answered the Grundy. "I just don't want anyone else to have it."

"Spoken like a true collector," said Mallory. "I don't suppose you'd like to help me find it."

"Helping lesser mortals is not part of my job description," said the Grundy.

"Why don't you try it once? You might enjoy it."

"I know."

"You want to say that again?" said Mallory, surprised.

"You are the only entity, living or dead, who has never lied to me. You are the only human in my domain who is not terrified of me. You have, reluctantly or otherwise, done me some services in the past. I will not help you precisely because I might enjoy it, and if I were to enjoy it, my usefulness would be at an end."

"No insult intended," said Mallory, "but just what the hell do you do that's so useful?"

"I keep explaining in terms I hope you might understand," said the Grundy. "I am a balance point, a fulcrum, against the best and worse tendencies of worlds. Where I find order I create chaos, and where I find chaos, I impose order."

"I've heard this song before," said Mallory. "But I sure as hell don't see how it applies to a missing egg."

"Neither do I," admitted the Grundy, his body suddenly becoming translucent and fading from sight. "And until I do, I think it best that we remain enemies."

And then he was gone.

Felina began licking her forearm noisily, and finally Mallory turned to her.

"You sure you don't want a little mustard and maybe some onions to go with that arm?" he asked sarcastically.

"It's a cheat!" she said unhappily.

"That he wouldn't help me?" said Mallory. "I never really expected him to."

"No," said Felina. "That he didn't tear you into tiny pieces. I might as well have gone out to eat with Winnifred."

"We'd better divide things up," said Winnifred when Mallory told her about his brief meeting with the Grundy. "It's a big city and a very small egg."

"Makes sense," he agreed.

"I have a number of underworld contacts," she continued. "I can start checking with them and see if anyone's been offered the egg or heard of it changing hands."

"Okay, you do that," said Mallory. "I've got an idea of my own."

"Don't leave you-know-who alone in the office."

"She just might come in handy where I'm going," replied Mallory. Felina suddenly lay on her belly and peered under the detective's desk.

"What are you doing?" asked Winnifred curiously.

"Looking for someone called You-Know-Who." She licked her lips. "I hope she's a mouse. I'm hungry."

It took up a square block on the waterfront. Once it had possessed windows, but they'd initially been boarded over, and finally covered with bricks. There was a single door, always guarded, and nobody ever came to the Old Abandoned Warehouse without a reason.

It was nearing midnight when Mallory and Felina approached the warehouse. A drunken man lay face down on the wet pavement, and a goblin suddenly appeared from between two buildings.

"Pretty goblin girls!" it whispered in a sibilant hiss. "Dirt cheap. Pretty goblin girls!"

"Not interested," said Mallory.

"Well, then, pretty goblin boys, if that's more to your taste."

"Buzz off."

"I've got pot, crack, and horse."

"Sounds like a bad rock band," said Mallory. "Go away."

"Wheaties. Cheerios. Tang. Skippy Peanut Butter. Tide. Palmolive."

Mallory stopped and turned to the goblin. "What's with you? I can buy all that stuff at the supermarket."

"Yeah, but it closes at ten. If you want a bottle of ketchup, you have to come to me."

"But I don't want one."

"Okay, half a bottle. Belonged to a little old lady who only used it on Sundays."

"Go away."

"How unfeeling can you be?" demanded the goblin. "I've got to meet my quota for tonight."

"That's not my problem."

"It might be," said the goblin. "If they throw me out of my apartment, I might have to move in with you."

"Why not move in with one of your pretty goblin girls?" said Mallory.

"I can't afford them," said the goblin unhappily. He grimaced. "Besides, they're ugly as sin."

"Somehow I get the feeling you're in the wrong business," said Mallory.

"I know," said the goblin. "I'm studying accountancy at home. *That's* where the excitement lies—creating endless columns of numbers and having them come out exactly right. Girls and drugs and the rest are just until I can get established."

"Good luck to you, and I wish you nothing but success," said Mallory. "Now leave me alone."

"That's your answer?" demanded the goblin. "I pour out my heart to you, I tell you my hopes and my fears, and all you can say is 'Leave me alone'? What kind of unfeeling fiend are you, anyway?"

"The uninterested kind."

"All right for you, buddy," said the goblin petulantly. "You'll never see me again."

It disappeared into the shadows. Mallory began walking toward the Old Abandoned Warehouse again when the goblin jumped out of the shadows again.

"I've decided to forgive you," he said.

"Don't do me any favors," said Mallory, continuing to walk.

The goblin raced ahead of him and then turned and stopped, blocking his way.

"Last chance!" he said. "I've got an almost-Rolex watch for sale cheap."

"I'll bet it almost tells time."

"Fifty-three minutes to the hour," said the goblin. "Think about it! It means you'll only age fifty-three years every six decades."

"And you're going to make columns of figures come out right?" said Mallory with a laugh.

"That's it!" cried the goblin. "I'm not going to stand here and be insulted."

"So go inside," said Mallory. "I'm sure you can find someone to insult you there."

"I'm leaving."

"Promises, promises," said the detective.

"A curse on your second-born!"

"What about my first-born?" asked Mallory, curious in spite of himself.

"I'm putting her to work for me."

"Well, that's one way to make sure she's still a virgin when she gets married," replied Mallory.

"Just wait until I'm an IRS auditor! Then you'll be sorry!" The goblin stalked back into the shadows.

"He was cute," said Felina.

"You have an interesting notion of cute," remarked Mallory.

"Yes," she agreed. "Everything about me is interesting."

"Especially your sense of modesty."

"Is that like my sense of smell?"

"Exactly the same," said Mallory. "Except that your sense of smell works."

He picked up his pace, and a moment later stood about twenty feet from the Old Abandoned Warehouse's front door, which was guarded by two leprechauns and an elf.

"That's close enough, Mac," said one of the leprechauns.

"Right," said the other. "Nobody goes in here who isn't on the list."

"And you ain't on it," added the elf pugnaciously. Suddenly he frowned. "At least I don't think you are."

"What's your name?" demanded the first leprechaun.

"Mallory."

"Sean, is he on it?" said the first leprechaun.

"The name's not familiar," said the leprechaun named Sean.

"So look at the list."

"I thought you had it, Liam," said Sean.

"Me?" replied the first leprechaun. "Do you see any pockets on me?"

"I don't even see any pants on you," said Mallory.

"My alarm clock didn't go off," said Liam defensively. "It was a choice between showing up without my pants or getting my pay docked." He turned to the elf. "How about you, Maury? Do you have a copy of the list?"

"I had one," said Maury unhappily.

"What happened to it?"

"I ate it," said Maury.

"You ate it?" demanded Sean incredulously. "What's the matter with you?"

"I got hungry," answered Maury with a shrug. "Besides, what did I need the list for? I can't read."

"You each had a copy of the list and neither of you brought it?" said Sean. "I'm telling!"

"This has gone on long enough," interrupted Mallory. "Since no one has the list, no one knows for a fact that I'm not on it."

"We're at an impasse," agreed Sean.

"I'd call it a stand-off," put in Liam.

"A Mexican stand-off," added Maury.

"Are any of us Mexicans?" asked Sean.

"Okay, so it's an Irish stand-off," sand Liam.

"I'm not Irish," protested Maury.

"You're green," said Liam.

"It's the pasta I ate for dinner," said Maury, making a face. "Terrible stuff."

"Uh… fellas," said Mallory. "You're missing the point. I have to see your boss."

"No problem, Mallory," said Liam. "My shift is over in another five hours. As soon as I'm off-duty I'll rush home, stopping only for a drink or two along the way. Once there I'll refresh the missus, get into my pants, pick up the list if I can find it— I know where it was three weeks ago, before we painted and redecorated—and I'll come right back as soon as I've had a nap and some breakfast, and if you're on the list, why, you can go right in."

"I've got a better idea," said Mallory.

"Oh?" said Liam. "We're always willing to come to a meeting of the minds. What's your proposition?"

"I'm going in right now, and my friend here"— he gestured to Felina—"will shred anyone who tries to stop me."

"Well, that's an interesting proposal," said Sean, "but of course it's totally unacceptable. Now, if I may make a counter-proposal..."

"My proposal was non-negotiable," said Mallory.

"So is mine," said Sean. "What I suggest is—"

"Felina?" said Mallory, and the catgirl displayed ten long sharp claws and a hungry smile.

"Of course," said Maury quickly, "you have to admit that his proposal has merit."

"And a certain inexorable logic," added Liam.

"To say nothing of a *je ne c'est quoi*," said Maury, backing away.

Felina took a step forward.

"Yeah, there's clearly a mathematical purity to it," agreed Sean, staring at her claws in fascination. "Okay, Mallory, you can enter."

"Thanks," said Mallory. "Cold hard logic does it every time."

"There's one condition," said Sean.

"Oh?"

The leprechaun pointed a shaking finger toward Felina. "Take her with you!"

MALLORY WALKED PAST the dozen huge storerooms until he came to the large, comfortable office at the back of the building. The room was filled with fish tanks, and the walls were covered with paintings of the ocean. Seated at a desk was a huge blue-skinned man in a purple sharkskin suit, light blue shirt, violet tie, and navy blue shoes and socks. He was just under seven feet tall, and weighed in the vicinity of five hundred pounds.

"Mallory!" exclaimed the Prince of Whales. "I haven't seen you since you saved me from my crazed sibling."*****

"It doesn't look too good for a detective to be hobnobbing with the biggest fence in the city," replied Mallory, taking hold of Felina's wrist as she tried to reach into a tank and grab a fish. "Are you doing okay these days?"

"Yes," said the Prince of Whales. "Business is booming."

Felina hissed and tried to twist free. Mallory tightened his grip and paid no further attention to her. "I'm glad to hear that."

Suddenly the Prince of Whales smiled. "Let me guess: you're after a stolen object, and you think I might have it."

"Or if you don't have it yourself, that you know where it is," said Mallory.

"Well, I owe you a favor…"

"That's the favor we want!" said Felina, pointing to a golden fish that was darting around the nearest tank.

Mallory moved to the middle of the room, still holding her wrist firmly.

"Or that one," she said, pointing at a silver fish in the next tank. "Or that one. Or this one. Or those three. Or…"

"Felina, if you'll be quiet and behave yourself, I'll give you a treat just as soon as Mr. Mallory and I are through with our business," said the Prince of Whales.

"Promise?" she asked.

"Yes."

"Okay, I'll be good," she said. "For a while." She smiled a feline smile. "Probably."

"So what is it you're looking for?" asked the Prince of Whales.

"An egg," said Mallory.

"With red and blue dots in a complex pattern?"

"That's the one."

"I've seen it."

"You got it lying around here?" asked Mallory. "I need it."

"I said I've seen it, not that I've got it," responded the Prince of Whales. "Have you ever heard of a gremlin named Gumfinger McGee?"

Mallory shook his head. "I'm drawing a blank."

"That's what anyone he visits draws when they go looking for their valuables."

"And he's got the egg?"

The Prince of Whales nodded. "He brought it by yesterday and tried to sell it to me. I turned him down."

"What was he asking?"

"A quarter of a million."

"It's going to grow up to be the last lamia in the world," noted Mallory. "You could probably have unloaded it for twice that much."

"Someday, maybe," said the Prince of Whales. "But I'd have to hatch it and grow it out first. Do I look like someone who wants to housebreak a vicious little bloodsucker like that?"

"Not really," admitted Mallory.

"So I sent him on his way."

"Do you know where I can find him?"

"There's a run-down hotel at the corner of Sloth and Gluttony," answered the Prince of Whales. "Last I heard, he's got a room there."

"Thanks."

"Does that erase my debt of honor?"

"Yeah, but I'm still going to come by for information from time to time."

"I certainly hope so. But in the future I'll charge you for it."

"Fair enough," said Mallory. He pulled at Felina's wrist. "Come on."

"He promised me a treat!" she said, pulling back.

"So I did," said the Prince of Whales, digging a hand into his pocket. "And here it is—my very favorite." He tossed her the treat.

Felina studied the tannish-brown mess, frowning. "It looks funny," she said. She took a deep breath and wrinkled her nostrils. "And it smells bad."

"I'll have you know that no one in the world can lay their hands on better quality ambergris than this!" said the Prince of Whales with injured dignity. He looked at Mallory. "It's clear that her education has been sadly lacking. Next you'll tell me she has no interest at all in algae."

"She never expressed any," answered Mallory. He tugged at Felina. "Come on. It's time to go."

"I behaved for two whole minutes," she whined, "and this is all I got for it." She tossed the ambergris in the golden fish's tank.

"Cat people are a remarkably unsophisticated race," remarked the Prince of Whales.

"Everybody hates me," complained Felina.

IT WAS CALLED Frank's Flophouse, and it advertised Once-Elegant Rooms For The Newly Destitute. There was also a little needlepoint sign stating that long-time paupers were welcome too. The lobby was threadbare in the truest sense of the word. There wasn't a thread to be seen—no carpet, no rugs, no upholstered furniture. There were three paintings on the wall; each was so poor that thieves had stolen the frames and left the canvases.

Mallory walked up to the registration desk, which was being manned by a thin, ascetic man in a cheap suit, a bow-tie affixed at an awkward angle, and a thick, steel-rimmed pair of glasses. It was only when Mallory was just a few feet away that he saw the man had a third eye, just above the bridge of his nose.

The clerk studied him carefully for a few seconds. "You got a dollar bill, Mac?" he said at last.

"Yeah."

"Then what are you doing here?" demanded the clerk. "You ought to be staying at Modest Maisie's down the block."

"Modest Maisie's?" repeated Mallory.

"You guys are all alike. You take one look at the name, and figure she's talking about herself and not the prices." He leaned forward and lowered his voice confidentially. "She used to be the biggest stripper in town."

"I remember Tempest Storm and Blaze Starr," said Mallory, "but I don't remember any Maisie."

"You never heard of Maisie the Lizard Girl?" said the clerk, clearly surprised. "She used to shed her skin four times a night at the old Rialto."

"Could you eat it?" asked Felina.

"Shut up," said Mallory.

"Just passing the time," said the clerk in hurt tones.

"I meant her, not you."

"All right, so you're not going to Maisie's. Do you want a room with or without?"

"With or without what?"

"Cockroaches. Mice. Rats. Chimeras. Banshees. You name it."

"What I want is some information."

The clerk smiled. "That's gonna cost you a lot more than a room, pal."

"If it comes without all the extras you just named, I'll settle," said Mallory.

"So what do you want to know?"

"You've got a Gumfinger McGee staying here?"

"The gremlin, right," said the clerk. "Watch yourself around him, fella. He could steal the words right out of your mouth."

"Is he in or out right now?"

"Yes."

"Yes, what?" demanded Mallory.

"Yes, he's in or out right now," said the clerk, extending his hand, palm up. Mallory laid a five-dollar bill on it. "That's two months' rent," he noted. "You sure you wouldn't rather have a room here? You'd only have to share it with six drunks, two hoboes, a sex maniac, and three goblins. Fifty cents more and you get bathroom privileges, too."

"Just the information."

"He went out about ten minutes ago."

"What's his room number?"

"No," said the clerk, extending his hand again. "What's on second. Who's on first."

Mallory gave him another five.

"Three-sixty-two."

"Thanks. Come on, Felina."

Mallory headed off to the elevator.

"I could give you something that would save you a world of bother," said the clerk.

"What's that?" said Mallory, stopping and turning back to him.

"It's a piece of advice," said the clerk, his hand out again.

Mallory handed him a third five-dollar bill. "Okay, out with it."

"Don't take the elevator."

"Why not?"

"McGee stole the floor this morning." He shook his head sadly. "I forgot to tell poor Mrs. MacAnanny."

"How's the staircase?"

"It's pretty good, except for the fourth and eleventh stairs," answered the clerk. "That one's on the house."

"You're all heart."

"I know I seem cold and crass and uncaring," said the clerk. "But that's only because I am."

"A lot of people are," said Mallory, "but hardly any of them brag about it."

"Hardly any are that way for a purpose. I'm saving up for a new pair of glasses, one that has lenses for all three eyes."

"I'll bet they teased the hell out of you when you were a kid," said Mallory, not without a touch of sympathy.

"Oh, they did," said the clerk. "It was terrible. It kept on right up to my fourteenth birthday."

"What happened on your fourteenth birthday?"

"My parents bought me braces and cured my overbite."

"Could have been worse," said Mallory. "Could have been pigeon-toed."

"How true," agreed the three-eyed clerk. He rapped his knuckles on the counter. "Knock wood."

The counter started falling apart, and Mallory, followed by Felina, began climbing the stairs as the clerk tried desperately to hold the counter together. When they reached the third floor Felina started purring loudly.

"What is it?" asked Mallory.

"Mice," she said. "Fat little juicy little tasty little mice."

"If you see one in the corridor, you can have it," said Mallory, starting to check the door number in the dim lighting.

"That's not fair!" complained Felina.

"Why not?"

"They're invisible mice."

Mallory cursed under his breath. He'd left his own Manhattan for this one two and a half years ago, and every time he began feeling comfortable and at home, something like this came up and he realized that he wasn't in Kansas—or the New York he had known—any longer.

Felina pounced at an empty spot on the floor, and a moment later was crunching happily on something Mallory was grateful that he couldn't see or hear.

"What's a mortgage?" asked Felina.

"Why?"

"Just before I bit its head off, it asked me to let it go because it had a wife and sixteen kids and a mortgage."

"Compassion isn't your long and strong suit, is it?" said Mallory sardonically.

"Oh, it's all right," answered Felina. "His wife—she's hiding behind that door—told me he hadn't worked in years and was cheating on her with his kids' schoolteacher." She paused thoughtfully. "What's a schoolteacher?"

"Never mind."

"Is it good to eat?"

"Most of the ones I knew were dry and tasteless." Mallory stopped when he came to Room 362. "Here we are. Let me know if anyone's coming while I pick the lock."

He knelt down and pulled out his pocket knife, only to discover that the door didn't have a lock, or even a knob. He pushed it gently, and it swung inward with a creaking noise. Mallory entered the room, followed by Felina.

"Turn on the light," he said.

She looked around. "There isn't any."

"I keep forgetting," he said. "You don't get a lot of amenities for a dime a night."

"What are amenities?"

"You can't eat them," said Mallory.

"You can't?"

"No. Do you still want to know?"

"No."

"Figures." The detective walked over to a dilapidated desk and opened the drawer. He couldn't see the contents, so he pulled a small flashlight out of his pocket.

"Old Gumfinger's been a busy boy," he remarked as the light hit the drawer. He held up some photographs of the Deputy Mayor and studied them. "I've heard of animal husbandry," he continued, "but this is carrying it to extremes. These pictures ought to bring a pretty penny on the blackmail market." He pulled out his lighter, set fire to them, and dumped them in the wastebasket, then continued rummaging through the drawer, but found nothing of interest.

"Okay, the dresser next."

He walked over to the rotting dresser and pulled out the top drawer. "Empty," he said. "No, wait. There's no bottom." He pulled out the next three drawers. All were missing the bottoms. Finally he squatted down and pulled out the bottom drawer. It was filled with socks (not matching), underwear (men's, women's, and something else's), and shirts (all gravy-stained).

He began pulling them out one item at a time. When the drawer was almost empty he moved one last bra (A cup on the left, C on the right, DD in the middle) and found a small box. He picked it up, carried it over to the desk, and opened it to reveal a white egg covered by red and blue dots in an intricate pattern.

"Eureka," he whispered.

"She's not here. I'm Felina."

"Let's go," said Mallory, walking out into the corridor.

Felina followed him, and they were soon at the corner of Sloth and Gluttony, hailing a cab. None stopped, but a few minutes later the detective flagged down a centaur-drawn carriage and headed home with his treasure.

"Let's see it!" said Winnifred excitedly as Mallory put the box on his desk.

He opened the top, and there, on a plush velvet lining, sat the egg, the pattern of red and blue dots looking remarkably like a celestial diagram.

"I guess it didn't matter that my contacts came up empty," she said. "How difficult was it for you to get?"

"Not difficult at all," said Mallory. "Hell, seven hours ago we didn't have a lead, and now we've got the egg." He smiled. "We must be as good as our ads say we are."

"We don't have any ads, John Justin."

"Well, if we could afford ads, we're as good as they'd say we were."

Winnifred studied the egg. "Poor little lamia," she said. "The last of its species, destined to be an exhibit in a sideshow. It's so demeaning."

"Well, we could crack it open and fry the damned thing," said Mallory.

"I'm serious, John Justin. I think it's tragic."

"Winnifred, it eats the blood of children."

"And you eat the flesh of them every time you have veal cutlets."

"Not human children."

"That means a lot more in the Manhattan you left behind than in this one," she pointed out.

"Are you seriously suggesting we return JFK's money and not give him the egg?"

"I'm not suggesting anything," said Winnifred. "I'm just feeling sorry for it."

The egg began shuddering.

"I think it's trying to thank you," said Mallory.

"Don't be silly, John Justin," she said excitedly. "It's hatching!"

"Get a net or something," said Mallory. "We can't have a baby lamia running around the place."

"It won't," said Felina, licking her lips. "I'll see to that."

"You touch it and you're out of here, for keeps!" snapped Mallory.

"Everybody hates me!" said Felina sullenly.

"Not everyone," replied Mallory. "Just the people who know you."

She turned her back to him and began licking a forearm.

"Here it comes!" exclaimed Winnifred. "Get ready, John Justin!"

The shell cracked open—

—and out stepped a bright yellow chick.

"Do baby lamias look like baby chickens?" asked Mallory, grabbing the chick before Felina could reach it.

"Not even a little bit," said Winnifred.

"No wonder it wasn't difficult!" growled Mallory. "The son of a bitch left a ringer for me to find!"

"Let me see," said Winnifred. She picked up a piece of the shell, took it to the kitchen in the next room, ran some warm water over it, and rubbed it gently with a paper towel.

"Well?" asked Mallory as Winnifred returned with the shell.

"Take a look," she said, holding it out.

It was perfectly white.

"So he's still got it," said Mallory. "And there's no way it'll be in that room. Not with a door that doesn't lock."

"Nice birdie," cooed Felina. "Pretty birdie. Fat birdie. Tasty birdie. Slow—"

"I told you not to touch it!" said Mallory, slapping her extended paw.

"You told me not to touch the egg!" sniffed Felina.

"That goes double for the chick."

"Double?" she said, looking around eagerly. "Are there two of them?"

"I think it's time to put the cat out," announced Mallory, getting to his feet.

"I'll behave!" cried Felina.

"Promise?"

"I promise," she said. Then: "You can have half."

"Out!"

Mallory opened the door and waited until Felina left the office. Before he returned to his desk there was a knock at the door.

"Kennedy?" he said, frowning. "How the hell could he have found out so fast."

He opened the door.

"Can I come in now?" said Felina, standing in the doorway.

"Into the kitchen, and stay there."

Felina lowered her face to the chick in Mallory's hand.

"Later," she whispered, and stalked off to the kitchen.

"As I see it, we're still on the job," Mallory told Winnifred. "He didn't pay us to steal a chicken's egg. Check with your contacts and see if any of them know where Gumfinger McGee holes up when he's not at Frank's Flophouse. I'll wait here for your call."

"Right, John Justin."

"And take this with you," he said, shielding the chick from Felina's view with his body and handing it over to her.

"I suppose I'd better," she agreed, shooting a quick glance in Felina's direction.

Mallory spent the next twenty minutes studying the Racing Form, and the ten minutes after that watching an endless replay of the third inning of a 1933 Continental Association minor league game between the Gainesville Geldings and the Ephrata Eunuchs in his magic mirror. The phone rang just as No Nose Mutchnik was punching the second base umpire. Since Mallory knew how it would end—a standing ovation and a three-game suspension for Mutchnik, expensive bridgework for the umpire—he turned away from the mirror and picked up the receiver.

"Yeah?"

"Park Avenue, between Lust and Depravity," said Winnifred's voice. "And I bought a bird cage for the chick."

"Got an address?"

"My contact didn't know, but he says the doorman's got rotting teeth and a tail."

"That'll have to do. I'm on my way."

He hung up the phone and walked to the door.

"I'm coming too!" cried Felina, bounding out of the kitchen.

"Why am I so blessed?" muttered Mallory.

IT WASN'T HARD to find the hotel. It was the Pinochle Tower, built as an answer to the considerably less garish Trump Tower. Mallory couldn't tell if the doorman had rotting teeth, but he was the only one on the block with a tail.

He entered the lobby, walked past all the gilt-painted furniture, the wandering string octet, the endless high tea, and the swimming pool, and approached the desk.

"A room for you and your daughter, sir?" asked the neatly groomed clerk.

"She's not my daughter."

"A room for you and your illicit lover, sir?"

"You got a pair of glasses?" said Mallory.

"Yes, sir, but they don't like us to wear them. It ruins the image."

"Put 'em on."

"If you insist, sir." The clerk reached into a pocket, withdrew his glasses, and donned them. "A room for you and your cat person, sir? I would suggest the sixty-third floor. They're very broad-minded up on the sixty-third."

"I just want to know where Gumfinger McGee is staying."

"It's against our policy to release that information, sir," said the clerk haughtily.

"Okay, give me a room right next to his," said Mallory, slapping a few bills on the counter.

"That will be room four-seven-two-three, sir."

"That's my unlucky number," said Mallory. "Give me one on the other side."

"I can't, sir," said the clerk. "I'm afraid four-seven-one-nine is occupied."

"Well, I tried," said Mallory. "Thanks for your time."

"My pleasure, sir," said the clerk, removing his glasses and replacing them in his pocket. "And good luck with your unconventional romance, sir."

Mallory turned the corner, then asked a bellhop where the elevators were. He was directed to them, and a moment later he and Felina emerged onto the forty-seventh floor.

He walked down the thick carpet, ignoring the murals of nude gods and goddesses chasing each other up and down the walls, and made his way to Room 4721, stopping a few doors short of it.

"Felina," he whispered, "can you giggle like a human girl?"

"It depends."

"On what?"

"On whether you'll feed me and skritch between my shoulder blades."

"You're a walking appetite," he complained. "Okay, I'll feed you as soon as we get home."

"I like chicken."

"You'll take what I give you."

"And what else?"

"I'll scratch your back."

"No," she said. "You have to *skritch* it."

"Whatever," he said. "Now, you're sure you can giggle like a girl?"

"Do you want to hear me?"

"In a minute."

He walked up to 4721 and knocked on the door.

"Who's there?" said a man's voice from the other side.

"Room Service," answered Mallory.

"I didn't order anything."

"It's compliments of the management."

"What is it?" the voice asked suspiciously.

"I can't tell you, but you'll like it."

Mallory nodded to Felina, who began giggling.

"I'll be right there," said the voice.

Mallory waited until the door started opening, then threw his weight against it. Gumfinger McGee went flying into the room, Mallory waited until Felina was inside, and then closed the door behind him.

"Hello, Gumfinger," said Mallory, pulling his gun and training it on the gremlin.

"Who the hell are you?"

"Me? I'm a farmer. I was just shipping my goods to market, and I find that I'm one egg short. I thought you might like to supply it out of the goodness of your heart."

"You go to hell!" snapped McGee.

Mallory, his gun still aimed at McGee, walked to the huge armoire and opened the double doors. He took a quick glance inside, didn't see anything out of the ordinary, and began pulling out each drawer in turn. When he still hadn't come up with the egg, he walked over to the bathroom and peeked in.

"You could just tell me," he said. "We both know I'm going to find it sooner or later."

"Later," said McGee sullenly.

Mallory looked around the room, wondering where the egg could be. Suddenly his attention was captured by one of the nightstand's lamps. All the other lights in the room were on, but the lamp was dark. He knew a place like Pinochle Tower would replace bulbs as quickly as they burned out, so that couldn't be the reason.

Curious, he walked over to the lamp, reached in under the shade, and smiled as his fingers came into contact with a decidedly un-bulblike object.

"Well, what have we here?" he said as he pulled the egg out and held it up.

"You're in deep trouble, buddy," said McGee. "Breaking and entering, threatening a citizen with a gun, and theft. If you'll give me back the egg, I won't press charges."

"I'm surprised you didn't include bringing a cat into a pet-free hotel."

"She's a catgirl," answered McGee. "I don't know if they count."

"There's the phone," said Mallory. "Call the cops. You tell them your story, I'll tell them mine, and we'll see who they believe."

"We don't need any cops," said McGee nervously. "How much is Kennedy paying you? Whatever it is, I'll double it."

"You'll pay me twice as much as he will for returning the egg to Kennedy?" said Mallory. "I call that damned sporting of you."

"Goddammit, you know what I mean!"

"I know what you mean," said Mallory. "The thing is, I don't care what you mean. The catgirl, the egg and I are going to leave now, and you're not going to try to stop us or follow us, because if you do I'll call the cops."

"Then you won't wind up with the egg either."

"I'm being paid to return it, not keep it," said Mallory. "You weren't the brightest one in your class, were you?"

And with that, the three of them—Mallory, Felina, and the egg—left the room and headed back to the office.

WINNIFRED WALKED OUT of the kitchen, rubbing the damp egg with a handkerchief, and returned to the office, where Felina was trying futilely to reach her claws through the bird cage that Winnifred had bought to house the chick.

"It's the real thing, John Justin," she said, handing the egg.

"I knew it was," he said, setting it down gently on a folded towel.

"Are you really going to give it to Kennedy so that it can live its entire life in captivity?"

"He's paying us for it."

"It's not his, John Justin," said Winnifred. "He stole it, or had it stolen, from Libya."

"Look, if he doesn't get it, the Grundy will." Mallory raised his voice. "You've been watching me every step of the way, haven't you?"

The Grundy suddenly materialized inside the office. "Yes, I have," he said as Winnifred shrank away from him and Felina didn't even acknowledge his presence.

"And?"

"I told you before. I will never allow your client to keep the egg."

"Even though you don't want it yourself?"

"I am a captive of my nature, even as you are of yours," said the Grundy.

"I'm getting an idea," said Mallory. "Grundy, if no one else has the egg, you don't care what happens to it, right?"

"Right," said the Grundy. "But of course, someone will have it."

"Somebody will," agreed Mallory. "The occupant."

"What are you talking about?"

"We're sending it back to Libya."

"It will be very lonely once it hatches out," said the Grundy.

"That's better than being as un-lonely as Gumfinger McGee would have made it," replied Mallory.

"You give me your word that McGee will not wind up with it?"

"I do."

"Then our business is concluded," said the Grundy, starting to fade from view.

"Almost."

The Grundy froze in mid-fade. "Explain."

"I'm going to call on you as an expert witness."

"In court? Don't be silly."

"No, not in court. Just be on call."

The Grundy continued vanishing until there was nothing left.

"Winnifred, take the egg to the post office or Mystic Express or some other joint like that, have them pack it carefully with all kinds of padding, and send it to Libya."

"Where in Libya?" she asked. "It's a big country."

"I don't know. They must have a zoo. That seems like the place to start. I trust you; you'll figure out the best place for it."

Winnifred walked over and picked up the egg, then kissed Mallory on the forehead. "Thank you, John Justin. You're not half as tough as you act."

"That's probably why we're not rich," said Mallory wryly as she left the office.

TEN MINUTES LATER Kennedy arrived, wearing a white sequined jumpsuit and carrying a guitar.

"You've changed, Mr. President," said Mallory.

"I got some very strange looks when I told people my name was John Fitzgerald Kennedy, and I decided that my cover had been blown, so I jettisoned it."

"And became Elvis Presley," said Mallory. "Very clever. No one will ever see through this one."

"My feelings precisely," replied Elvis. "Well, did you get it?"

"I got it," said Mallory.

"Where is it?"

Mallory pointed to the chick. "You were the victim of false doctrine."

"What kind of scam is this?" demanded Elvis.

"It's no scam. You were suckered. This chick hatched out of the egg I got from the thief's flophouse." He opened his desk drawer and pulled out the fragments of the shell. "As you can see from these"—he held up two pieces of shell, one white, one dotted—"the pattern was painted on, and my partner had no trouble removing it." He pushed the remaining pieces across the desk. "You're welcome to take these home and rinse them off yourself if you don't believe me."

"Rubbish!" yelled Elvis. "This is a trick and you're keeping the egg for yourself!"

"That's not so."

"Prove it!"

"Grundy!" called Mallory in a loud voice.

The demon instantly appeared. Elvis emitted a little shriek of terror and backed away.

"Grundy, this is John Fitzgerald Presley," said Mallory. "Now, Mr. Presley, I'm sure you will agree that the Grundy is many things good and bad—mostly bad—but one thing he is not is a liar."

"No, he never lies," said Elvis, keeping his distance. "Everyone knows that."

"Grundy, did this chick hatch out of the egg I took from the thief's flophouse?"

"Yes," said the Grundy.

"And is this the shell it hatched out of?"

"Yes."

"One last question. Am I keeping a lamia egg, here or anywhere else?"

"No, you are not."

"Thanks," said Mallory. "You can go back to maiming and pillaging now."

The Grundy vanished.

"Well, Mr. Presley?"

"All right, you were telling the truth," said Presley. "Are you going to report me to the cops?"

"For stealing a chicken's egg?"

"I guess you're right," he said, suddenly relieved. "I hadn't considered it that way." He paused. "You might as well keep the money. You earned it."

"Thank you, Mr. Presley. I believe that concludes our business."

Presley nodded unhappily and walked to the door.

WINNIFRED ARRIVED HALF an hour later.

"It's done," she announced.

"Just as well," said Mallory. "This office has enough pets."

"Speaking of pets," said Winnifred, looking around, "where is Felina?"

"Sulking in the kitchen."

"Why?"

"I wouldn't let her eat the chick."

"I'm never speaking to either of you again," said a sullen voice coming from atop the refrigerator.

"I guess we all have to learn to live with life's little disappointments," said Mallory.

"And I guess I won't have to buy that half-gallon of milk tonight," said Winnifred, raising her voice as well.

"Or the six cans of sardines," added Mallory. "Just as well. I've been saving up for a box of Havana cigars."

Suddenly a feline figure flew through the air and landed on Mallory's lap.

"This is your lucky day, John Justin!" it said. "I forgive you."

"Are you sure?" said Mallory. "You don't want to be too hasty, you know."

"I'm sure," she said, laying face down across his knees and purring noisily. "Now skritch my back."

* — *Stalking the Unicorn*
** — "Post Time in Pink"
*** — "The Blue-Nosed Reindeer"
**** — "Post Time in Pink" and "The Chinese Sandman"
***** — "Card Shark"

THE SONG HER HEART SANG

A STORY OF THERA

STEVEN SAVILE

THE TROUBADOURS SANG their songs, painting the world and its beauty in wonderful colors.

In truth the music did little to mask the twin shadows of doubt and anxiety that hung over a lover's shoulder.

Lukas Meya walked in those shadows, head down, heart on fire. Her name was Lili. He thought about her as he dragged his feet. It ought to have been the greatest feeling in the world, to be lost in love. But it wasn't.

It had been, but that was before the miracle.

Now fear hid between the silences when he was alone, in the moments between heartbeats, in the fragments of time between inhaling and exhaling. That was when it whispered to his soul the thing he had always known: it was all going to end.

The song of their love was fleeting.

To some, Lili's beauty might have been flawed, her eyes milk-white with blindness, but to Lukas she was perfect. Lukas had known in that first moment. She was framed by the window as she leaned out over the street, breathing in every scent Aksandria had to offer. He knew it was love.

He brought gifts, budding flowers, freshly baked pastries, and essences from the perfumery, gifts with scents so strong they came alive in the darkness of her mind's eye. He talked to her, describing everything, every last little detail, drawing the world with words for her—and she laughed, delighting in his turn of phrase and the odd ways he chose to describe things.

Words brought them together; images tore them apart.

He found her lying curled up on the floor, clutching her knees to her chest and sobbing. Her eyes were closed tight and she refused to look at him. Even as he took her face in his hands, he knew. It was all he could manage to kiss her tenderly, once on each upturned eye. She tried to smile as she opened her eyes and he saw that the film of milk had fallen from them.

That was when she saw him for the first time; her expression tore at his heart. He so desperately wanted to see love and devotion but the only emotion in her eyes was fear. Even though some small part of him knew that her fear was caused by the sudden intimacy of the world pressing in all around her, bright and vibrant where it had been an endless winter night, that knowledge couldn't silence the tiny voices of doubt that rose up to remind him he had been a fool to think himself worthy of her beauty. It was always going to end, they crooned, because every beginning has its end, every life succumbs to sweet oblivion, every song trails off in its final note.

She didn't come to the window anymore because she couldn't bear to see.

Lukas had stopped bringing his little fragrant gifts; with her sight returned what need had Lili of a rose or a scrap of silk bearing a single drop of white lotus? They ceased being gateways to the world of possibility, becoming instead the mundane things that they were, a scrap of cloth, the head of a dying blossom.

Worse, they stopped talking.

He couldn't remember the last time he had sat with his back pressed against the wall of Lili's bed chamber describing the patchwork of colors that were the rooftops of Aksandria for her to imagine, the white-washed walls of the minarets that rose to accuse the sky like angry fingers, and the red clay tiles baked beneath the sun's heat, or the ebb and flow of life bustling through the streets, market traders, street hawkers, the rich and the poor. It was as though Lili's learning to see had somehow robbed him of his own sight and made the world so much more subdued, flatter as the color and wonder leached out of it.

And it was all his fault.

He came to Lili full of the miracle he had just witnessed, unable to contain himself: Versara, the

young woman they called the White Rose, had
healed Arden, the shoemaker's son. She had taken
his clubbed foot in her delicate hands and
smoothed the bones beneath the skin. The lad's
screams had been hideous to hear as the bone was
reshaped and set, the heat from Versara's hands
was enough to fuse the bone. With tears still
streaking down his grubby cheeks Arden had run
out of the market square, no hint of the limp he
had been trying to mask for most of his young life.

Lukas had begged the White Rose to visit Lili,
knowing even as he did that there was a chance
that Versara's touch might give Lili her sight. The
irony was that he couldn't see the implications of
the gift, only that it was the greatest gift he could
think to give. He saw soon enough though; he
made himself mundane, just like the scrap of material and the dead flower. What need did Lili have
of his words now that she could see the world for
herself? What wonder could he explain that she
could not see?

She could see his faults now, all of them laid
plain: his too sallow skin, his pocked complexion,
his crooked nose where he had broken it years
before. He couldn't hide any of them behind clever
words and witty banter now, and suddenly they
seemed insurmountable.

The ghost of Versara's touch lingered still on his
cheek, even as her words haunted his sleep. "She
will not be the same, you do understand that, don't
you, sweet Lukas? She will never be the same
again." He had said yes, but how could he have

possibly known the extent to which Lili would change? That his gift would ultimately be a curse?

He remembered the last time he saw Lili, her face wrapped in bandages, too frightened to face the world that had come alive for her.

And that was why Lukas Meya walked in the shadow of love now, grim, determined as he strode through the low ways of Aksandria, out of the safety of the known streets and into the living wilderness that closed in on all sides of the great city, as all great lovers willing to do something stupid to earn his lady's heart. He would be worthy of her love and she would love him, completely and utterly, body and soul. He would give her a gift greater than sight. He would do something that truly embraced the irrational. Love was worth that moment of sheer abandonment, it had to be or it wasn't truly love.

That was his pledge to Lili—and to himself. From it, he devised a scheme; nothing grand, more desperate in truth, but it was a scheme nonetheless.

It didn't matter what it cost him.

Lukas scuffed his feet and looked back over his shoulder. He was alone in the street; the last of the washerwomen had finished scrubbing her stoop and gone inside. He hadn't ventured out of the Marin Gate since the first reports of oddness in the forests had begun to drift through, embellished no doubt with the every new coming and going of the vagabonds who traded in gossip. It did not matter that they were wholly unreliable, nor that they were braggarts and charlatans to a man. Lukas had seen enough with his own two eyes to know that more than a little of what they claimed was true, and that little was more than enough to keep him behind the safety of the city wall.

The gate guard raised an eyebrow at the young man but didn't bar his leaving.

Lukas fancied the air beyond the wall was different, sweeter than the air within the city. It was ludicrous, of course, to think that such purity could be inhaled let alone tasted. But it did; the air tasted of hope. He stopped on the edge of the living forest to look back at the spires of Aksandria. A curious sensation swept over him then. He brushed it off, more determined than ever to pursue his folly, and disappeared into the forest the locals still knew as Chapfallen.

It was an oppressive place, the thickness of the trees stifling all other sounds. Too soon he was alone with his own footfalls, the snap and crack of deadfall beneath his boots, and his ragged breathing.

Lukas leant against the lichen-smeared side of an ancient oak for support. Through the interlaced leaves he saw that the day was aging fast. It was another sign of the lunacy of his plan; no traveler would ever be foolish enough to begin his journey at dusk, yet here he was, pushing on into the gathering dark. Somewhere close by, a stream broke over a weir, the fresh water dancing to its own haunting tune. A few speckles of sunlight filtered through the canopy of leaves scattering gold coins of light across the ground. The wind rose, an angry voice moving through the trees.

Lukas didn't need to imagine moving shadows or lurking horrors. Chapfallen was a place of fairy tales spun to scare children half out of their wits, a few lies to build a legend upon, and a few truths. Within its green heart, the source of all those stories: Sahnglain.

Before the fall the cavernous subterranean complex had served the scholars of Aksandria well, as a library of sorts, but more importantly to Lukas now, as a repository for the more esoteric treasures of antiquity.

Lukas remembered stories of a precious stone his mother called Lahdioli, which loosely translated from the Old Tongue to mean "the song her heart sang". It was said to have both fallen from the sky and been surrendered by the sea, depending on which story you believed—which though impossible had amused young Lukas enough for the tales to stay with him. It was an apt gift for love, when love itself was a song that filled every ounce of his being. She would understand when he gave her the stone, because theirs was a love for the songs. In his head it really was that simple.

A quarter mile into the thickening forest Lukas finally forfeited the safety of the path and ventured deeper into the trees. He scanned the brambles strangling the rows of thick trunks, looking for a break in the tangle, something barely wide enough for him to wriggle through. The branches were like a constant battery of wings against his body, forcing him deeper into the woods, away from the stream, away from the sounds of Aksandria. He caught the thought, knowing that he was still experiencing the world in words, storing them to share later with Lili, the story itself another part of the gift. The earth took on a new hardness beneath his feet. Lukas knelt, scratching away the thin dusting of dirt to reveal the chipped and broken cobbles of a causeway. Lukas raised his eyes from the ground, trying to see through the dense foliage. He was on the right path. The forest might have reclaimed this road for its own, but without doubt he was kneeling on what had once been the Pilgrim's Road.

He snapped off a thin branch and used it to feel out the buried cobbles, working his way slowly forward until Sahnglain rose like a vision before him, its crumbling walls and empty windows half-glimpsed between the climbers and trees. Red stones cried mortar tears, and splinters of broken glass lay half-buried in the black earth. The walls, Lukas saw as he neared, had been scorched with fire but the damage had been done long enough ago for the forest to have grown back hungrily over the blackened stones. A candletree lay in the black soil at his feet, left where it had fallen. Threads of colored wax, red and purple, still clung to its rusted iron stem. Lukas nudged it with his boot. Beneath it, a shard of glass wore the painted face of a dead saint. The place reeked of death gone stale. He turned slowly in a circle, the reality of the sight sinking in; Sahnglain had been sacked and burned, and whatever was worth stealing had almost certainly been spirited out of Chapfallen— the gold and silver of the sacred relics melted down for ingots, the vellum scrolls and books sold off. Superstitious gossip in Aksandria named the place a mausoleum.

Even so, he had to be sure.

He worked his way carefully toward the huge timber door hanging drunkenly on broken hinges across the darkness.

Lukas pushed the door aside and stepped out of the light.

He was not frightened; despite all this wild evil, love was his armor. He smiled, brushing back the creepers, knowing that no ill could befall him because of it. Love was stronger. He thought of Lili, he thought of the song her heart sang, and knew that if they were meant to be together, fate's will would see him through.

If, that little voice of doubt whispered.

And *if* they were not, he thought defiantly, well if they were not he did not want to live.

So either way he had nothing to fear.

The air inside the ruin was older still, and held tightly to the silence of devotions. The candletrees that ought to have lit the way were gone, their sconces empty save for deeper shadows. His footsteps echoed eerily. Bones lined the floor, some greened with moss, others as pearly as pulled teeth. They had been scattered in a series of meaningless patterns, almost as though the plunderers had used them to foretell the future: a jumble of broken ribs within a circle of femurs, a wheel of destiny that promised nothing but death. A fractured skull stood guard over the doorway.

He had no idea where Lili's stone might be.

He moved deeper into the dead building.

A curious luminous lichen clung to the walls, thickening the further he descended until it cast enough light for Lukas to make out phantoms beyond the shadows. Bones, bones, deeper than bones. He moved slowly, his fingers trailing over the wall. The lichen was slick beneath his fingers. It took a long moment for him to realize that it wasn't his blood pulsing through his fingers but the lichen pulsing against them. The fact that it was alive sent a cold shiver the length of his spine. Instinctively, Lukas flinched away from the wall and closed his eyes but the darkness was worse by far than the strange living light.

There were markings carved into the stone. Lukas leaned in close, his fingers tracing out the forms of what appeared to be snakes coiled around spears or long arrows. The symbolism meant nothing to him. Further into the ruined building he found more markings, less like snakes this time, more like bloated wyrms, though the detail on these was so intricate he saw human features carved into their elongated snouts. There was something repulsive about the fusion of man and beast. Lukas pulled his hand away from the wall.

He heard sounds, groans coming from within the stones of Sahnglain itself.

He tried to ignore them, forcing himself to walk on. An elaborately carved bookcase had fallen across the doorway, its books long since gone. Stepping over it Lukas saw that rot had claimed the shelves. His foot caught the edge of one of the pedestal legs; it crumbled to powder and decayed worm. He knelt, taking some of the desiccated flakes in his fingers and rubbing them together. It was difficult to imagine how something as seemingly permanent as wood could decay so utterly without the constant urging of air and time to wear away at it. By rights, sealed away in the subterranean sarcophagus of Sahnglain, the relics ought surely to have been preserved perfectly? He didn't claim to understand, he could only trust that being stone Lili's gift would have endured, like so much else it was fate's will.

Beyond the doorway he found a narrow spiral staircase, the middle of each step worn down by the passage of countless feet. He followed them down through six tight turns, losing his sense of direction as he turned and turned about. The brickwork was different, coarser, the mortar between each slab rough as though finished in a rush. There were more bones scattered across the floor, and four doorways leading off the narrow passage. The passage itself branched off into three forks with more doors. Walking through the first of the doors Lukas stepped into what must once have been a refectory. Long tables lined up, and at one, the collapsed bones of a man who had died where he sat. Lukas turned his back on the bones and tried the next door. Finding nothing, he tried the next two doors before taking the first of the three forks. The floor took a sharp decline as it rounded the corner. A frosted spider's web brushed against Lukas's head and shoulders as he walked through it. Halfway down the passageway the bones of another man were spread out across the thick dust of the floor. Moving closer Lukas saw more strange markings had been scratched out in the dust. The dead man's knucklebones rested in the last of them.

He reached down instinctively, curious, and picked up one of the knots of finger bone.

The cold owned the underground passage. The melancholy sound of the wind blew through the distance. Touching the bone he felt the life and hope of the building being ripped from its body by savage hands. It was a brutal sensation. He didn't know where the thought had come from but he was almost sure it wasn't his own. He looked up at the distant echo of rolling thunder, knowing even as it rumbled that it was rock falling. White roots crawled through the wounds in the ceiling above him, another sign of nature absorbing Sahnglain into its green heart.

A rough-edged splinter from the bone dug into his palm, drawing blood. The features of a pale white face filled his eyes or his mind or both, he couldn't tell. Blood ran from its eyes and nose as its mouth opened on a desperate scream. Almost immediately a surge of nausea welled up from his gut and he felt his legs buckle. He fell, sprawling

over the broken bones. Each point of contact
brought with it another roaring hallucination.
Lukas rolled over onto his back, staring up at the
roots cracking open the ceiling. Amid the dizzi-
ness, he heard the sounds of slaughter. The ghosts
of scholars cried out their pains and begged their
god's mercy, the crackle of flames finally drowning
them all. The assassins had put their torches to
everything that might burn.

He felt the heat come off the horrific scene that
overlaid his sight. It was such a small detail but it
made everything suddenly real.

"No," he said, neither denial nor exclamation,
just a word to echo off the walls.

From the darkness he heard again another death
cry and then there was nothing.

He lay there, gasping, unsure what had happened, too frightened to move for fear of setting
off another vision. Tentatively, he tried to recall
the bloody face but with it came all sorts of other
memories that weren't his. He knew things there
was no earthly reason he should, fragments of wisdom, the words of better men and their failings, he
knew them all. Names rose in his memory, friends
he had never known and had somehow died
beside. And he saw the deaths too: no gentle passing for the scholars of Sahnglain. They were put to
the sword by superstitious men frightened by the
sudden shift in the balance of nature. The scholars
had not even tried to defend themselves. The realization shocked Lukas. They had meekly lowered
their heads and accepted their violent and bloody

fates. The loss of their magic had already been more than they could bear. Lukas knew instinctively that the man whose thoughts he shared already thought of himself as dead. Leaving the flesh was a merciful release for him.

Lukas recoiled from the invasive knowledge that filled his head, scrabbling across the floor. His feet scuffed up the dust, destroying the peculiar patterns the dead man had drawn as his final act of life.

All of these words, all of these images flooded his head, each one too brutal for him to ever share with Lili.

"No, no, no, no," he said, much more forcefully this time. "Get out of my head! Get out of my head, damn you!"

Lukas pressed his back up against the wall, suddenly frightened. Even as his shoulders and scalp came in contact with the cold stone the passageway around him came alive with warm vibrant light and was suffused with color. The ghosts of four scholars, their tonsured heads low, shuffled past. Lukas whimpered as sandaled feet brushed through his outstretched leg. A frisson of raw energy bristled through Lukas's entire body as he broke away from the wall. He scrambled to his feet. It wasn't just that he had seen the ghosts, though that was unnerving enough; he had known them.

He reached out, touching the crumbling wood of the bookcase. The warmth emanating from the wood was unnerving. He heard the angry cackle of flame, the edge of his vision blurring red as fire long since burned out blazed into angry ghost-life. The spines of books blackened and charred, the knowledge trapped within them shriveling as the vellum and bindings burned. He pulled his hand away when the screams started and the dying began again.

Lukas moved to the next door, his trembling hand resting on the tarnished latch, frightened of what new wraith his touch would conjure. As it swung open he saw a gentle man on his knees, head bowed to accept a butcher's blade. As his hand came off the door the ghostly apparition faded. The man's bones were scattered about the floor where he had fallen, a deep cleft carved into the bones of his neck where several hacks had been needed to sever his head. The skull had rolled away and nestled up against the base of the wall.

Lukas gathered it into his hands, the hopelessness of the scholar's demise resonating through the bone. He then fell to his knees, overwhelmed by the grief haunting these old bones but he could not lay them aside. Each one offered some secret glimpse at the life of these men so long dead now, some fragment of knowledge they felt worth preservation, and he soaked it up thanking the fates for delivering him to the dead.

Feeling out the deep scoring at the base of the skull Lukas understood more and more of the strange transformation that was happening to him. The markings in the floor had been a memory glyph, locking life into the bones and the walls and everything else trapped in this dark place lest they be forgotten. His blood had triggered it, bringing them all back. Everything in Sahnglain had a story to tell him. And that simple tactile act offered a connection with Lili that he had never imagined possible; feeling the coarseness of the cracked bone his mind resonated with understanding. He could see, much as she saw before. Sahnglain itself was telling Lukas its story just as he had told his story to Lili. His horror at the vividness of its story was precisely what she must have been feeling right then. Like him she was scared, binding her eyes to shut out the wonder, but she was hungry for it, too.

And with this realization came another, one that left him feeling utterly bereft: the very worst thing he could ever have done was to heal Lili and then abandon her for his idiot's quest to prove his own manhood to a woman who never needed any such proof. He would have laughed at himself if the irony hadn't been so bitter. Instead, Lukas had to fight to maintain a grip on his own thoughts and memories as the lives of the scholars swept over him, drowning out all the sweeter memories he had shared with Lili with their violence. His head reeled with the new knowledge, for not only did he see their deaths and their shades ghosting from room to room, he absorbed everything from their lives, accruing their accumulated knowledge. And hungry for more knowledge, more words, more stories, understanding instinctively that together they meant more power, Lukas scoured the ruin for the remains of the scholars. He held their bones up to his face, absorbing their lives and their stories into him. And as he moved back toward the surface, he stooped to lift the skull standing guard in the center of the doorway. He had a thousand thousand new stories to share with Lili, and a thousand more thoughts and realizations to offer. The world outside Sahnglain would never be the same for Lukas Meya. When he emerged it would be as a new man, the moth free of the chrysalis, able to spread its wings. But like that same moth he was drawn to the metaphorical flame that was the secret of the bones. He was desperate to be more. He whispered a prayer to them, reverently holding it up toward the iridescent light of the lichen. And through it he saw Lili's stone, the Lahdioli, and knew why they called it "the song her heart sang."

A slow smile spread across his face.

It was more than just a pretty stone; the man who had brought it here had called it the "lover's heart," for its rich red surface was marred by a streak of green.

Lukas reached back through his new memories for the Lahdioli and found it, not hidden away in some chest or vault as he would have imagined, but resting on a scholar's desk, a glorified paperweight used to prevent the man's neatly inked out words from blowing away. He focused on the scholar's face, drawing his name out of the dimness of memory: Atynia. A pilgrim to the sanctuary of Sahnglain, Atynia had been a violent man in his life; his friends said that he had a gift for death. His enemies were less circumspect; Atynia the Butcher they called him. That name always rankled with the man; it suggested a lack of finesse. He was skilled, Lukas knew, reliving snatches of battle, the heady rush of the blood and piss of the field, the grunts of death and the reek afterwards. And yet Atynia had turned his back on the violence, laying down his sword in favor of a life of quiet introspection in the anonymity of Sahnglain. None of his brother scholars knew his secret; they accepted him as he presented himself: a man of peace. He kept the Lahdioli with him as a reminder of his life's one great regret, the woman whose love had not been enough to save him from himself. He had always known that someone desperate enough would come seeking the song her heart sang. He had risked the wisdom of Sahnglain on it.

Lukas's feet followed Atynia's memories unerringly, leading him through the labyrinth of Sahnglain to the scribe's scriptorium. He found the desk from his memory. It was neat to the point of obsessiveness; everything lined up and arranged just so, perpendicular to the next thing. The dip pen sat in an inkwell recessed into the desk. The ink around the nib of the man's pen had long since dried but the sheaf of papers remained, the words faded into illegibility. Lukas didn't care. Lili's stone weighed them down.

He let his fingers linger over it, tracing the green streak before picking it up.

It was cold to his touch as he slipped it into his pocket.

Taking one last lingering look around, as much for Atynia and the other dead as for himself, Lukas staggered back through the passageways to the surface and out into the light. The world was everything he had thought it ought to be for a lover—more vibrant, more full of color, more alive. Even the air tasted alive in his mouth, charged with his desperate hunger to suck the marrow out of it. He wanted to *live*.

Following his own path back out of Chapfallen to the Marin Gate was easier than he had imagined it might be; the torches in the windows of the high towers lit the way, creating the illusion of a second midnight sun in the night sky. Lukas walked toward the light. It was a different guard on the gate. He looked mildly annoyed at being disturbed.

Lukas reached into his pocket, his fingers brushing Lili's stone, and palmed a battered tin bit. He pressed the coin into the guard's hand in thanks, recoiling as snatches of the man's miserable life blazed across his vision brought on by the touch: the woman he didn't love, the fresh-faced youth he did, the jealousies of the flesh and the mundane escape duty offered; endless wasted hours all blurred together leaving Lukas physically sick. Whatever Atynia had done to him down there hadn't ended once Lukas returned to the surface. The man looked at him strangely. Lukas couldn't meet his gaze; the knowledge his touch gave went

below the surface and was too invasive, too personal.

The small postern gate closed behind him.

Aksandria slept.

Paraffin-dipped torches burned on street corners, casting fitful shades across the cobbles as the
wind played out its shadow games. Lukas walked
through the shadows. He no longer felt a part of
them. The stories flowing through his veins held
him apart.

He stood on the corner he had stood on so
many times before. Gathering up a handful of
gravel he threw it at the closed window, scattering
it across the streaked glass. He waited. A moment
later the sash opened and he saw Lili.

"Come down!" he called.

"Lukas? Is that you?" and before he could
answer, "What are you doing down there at this
time of night? You'll catch your death!"

"I have something for you," he grinned. He
hadn't even noticed the growing cold. He stuffed
his hands into his pockets. The stone felt alive
against his skin.

"In the morning, silly."

Lukas shook his head, too excited to be turned
away.

"What is it?" Lili asked, blind in the darkness.
She still carried herself as though she couldn't see,
inclining her head slightly as she listened.

"A story! A truly wonderful story."

"Now had you said 'a kiss' I might have come
down."

"Oh, I have one of those, too."

She disappeared from the window only to appear a moment later rushing out of the narrow door set into the wall beneath it. Lukas swept her up into his arms and spun her around, his lips lingering on hers.

Pictures of Lili came in swift succession, memories of happiness and their time together at first, remembered in words almost as vividly as they ever were seen, and then more, glimpses of what they had yet to share, love abloom, the hope of firsts, first loves, first pains shared and overcome. He saw their daughter, Poli, so like her mother in the set of her jaw and her thoughtfulness, and then where he had thought to see Lili's face grow old, settling into its life and owning every crease and line time offered, there was only a sudden shocking silence and she was gone. What ought to have been decades counted in a scant few years.

Lukas buckled beneath the sudden crushing emptiness as the life he had so desperately wanted to live was snatched away from him even before he had truly dared believe it could be his, stunned by its brevity and the great sucking wound Lili's death would leave. He couldn't begin to think how he could cope without her.

Their song really was fleeting, cut short by young death.

His heart ached for the loss of all the things he would never have with Lili. He looked into her beautiful eyes, glad finally that she could see him. He tried to picture what she would have looked like as an old woman and realized that it didn't matter. He kissed her again and as he did his hand closed around the stone in his pocket: Lili's stone.

He listened to the song her heart sang and knew that it was their song.

And he knew a lifetime with Lili, no matter how short, was worth all the pain the remains of a lifetime without her would bring.

He knew, because he had heard its song from beginning to end and it was beautiful.

"What did you have for me?" Lili asked, her smile holding back his tears.

"This." he covered her eyes with his hands and told her.

A MAN FALLS

JAY LAKE

Boys bound to the Mule Kings by tradition and the lash blew softly into the nostrils of the animals penned in the corral behind the smithy circle. The great, low-bottomed carts of the Smith Kings sat in the darkness like so many fire-bellied beasts, each supporting forge and anvil and a sweating man-god drawing form from iron. The Selenite Rings danced among the stars in the sky, a silver river to draw the souls of men from the stony earth to mysteries beyond heaven.

Peleppos loved to watch the smiths at their work, so alien to his own family's traditions. Peleppos's father Antimony was an important man, first among the Law Kings, which meant that Peleppos was an important boy, a Prince of the Law. He would never need to dirty himself with working over a hot fire, but something in the clangor and bustle called him back time and again. He sometimes thought of the heat-red iron as the blood of the Wheeled City—his city, borne in the shadows on carts and wagons to stand every night amid crumbling towers before scattering at dawn's terrible light. And Peleppos would someday be its hero.

Someday soon, he promised himself.

PELEPPOS STOOD AT the day-doors and stared into the smoldering twilight of dawn. Men in green and gray cloaks woven of netting gathered nearby to the quiet clink of equipment and the snap and swish of signaling fingers.

"Still dream of going out with the day-watch?" Willow-lithe, taller than his father, her hair the color of ash, Arnasa was one of his father's key-keepers, an armed agent of Antimony, King of the Law. She had taken an interest in Peleppos since the boy's last nurse had been dismissed some years earlier. Peleppos didn't remember ever having a mother, but Arnasa had gathered him close a time or two when the terrors of the day overwhelmed him.

"I know all the signals," Peleppos boasted, fingers flickering through the sequence *cartwheel burning—two dogs dance—moss by moonlight.* Which meant, roughly, *move quickly, a disturbance is likely, remain quiet and unseen at all costs.*

Arnasa sighed, stroking the hair along Peleppos's cheek. He loved the feel of her fingers, but resented it all the same. After fourteen summers, he didn't want to be touched like a child anymore.

"Hand signs are neither the first nor the last of it, my boy," she said. "Death takes wing under the day star, and every creature with wisdom finds its nest."

"I am silent as a cat," Peleppos said, "and strike quicker than a scorpion. Besides, I am of age."

"It would break your father's heart to lose you to the sun." Arnasa squeezed his shoulder. "Stay inside, stay safe. In his own time, my Prince of the Law will grow to be a King."

Peleppos bowed his head and sidled off, doubling back once Arnasa had left the day-doors and walked deeper into the day-caves of Wheeled City. He retrieved from hiding the cloak he had bought from a begging veteran near the Corn King's Second Market, shouldered his kit bag, strapped on his knife—true iron and long enough for a sword at his age—and followed the day-watch out the doors.

They spread, each to their own station in the glare of rising daylight, Peleppos dawdling behind to draw as little attention as possible. There were always stragglers, he thought, and strangers, men posted to double-duty from some other watch or guild. I am one of them, nothing more. Who would question someone going out?

The only answer he got was the slamming of the day-doors at the cave mouth and the screech of the bar, thicker than his waist, being drawn to seal them shut.

* * *

AT FIRST, THE day was not so bad. The slitted goggles made of paired goat ribs shielded Peleppos's eyes from the hideous glare of daylight. The sun seemed a tangible pressure on his shoulders and head, as if he were spirit-ridden. He practiced the irregular walk, the frequent pauses, the endless searches for concealment that the men and women of the day-watch discussed freely of an evening over roast kid and honeyed wine.

Peleppos had picked a direction he thought wasn't along any of the usual patrol routes. Just west of the main ruins, a line of hills rose in gentle terraces walled by courses of the debris that lay everywhere beneath the soil. Fields of barley and rye grew there to be tended by night. At their top was a series of watchtowers, older than the Wheeled City but younger than the ruins, perhaps from a time before Peleppos's people had lost the day.

Night dwellers don't need watchtowers, he thought. We have nothing to see but our own fires.

"I will find the secret of the daylight hours," he whispered to a chipmunk watching from a rock pile nearby, "and I will free my people. I am the Prince of the Law. The world is mine to rule."

Peleppos struggled onward toward the ridge and the towers, astonished by the heat within his cloak. He was worrying about having sufficient water for the day when a scream sounded behind him, so loud that Peleppos's guts sloshed with a painful rumble of fear.

He dropped and rolled to the left, drawing his iron knife and managing a long scratch on his left forearm in the process. Peleppos came to rest on his back, partly beneath a bush, to see an enormous bird circling above him.

He had seen owls, and nighthawks, and the small songbirds of dusk and dawn, but this bird was bigger than three men, great sweeping wing-feathers taller than he, brown as a walnut, with a pale beak. It settled toward him, enormous talons outspread to rend his flesh.

Peleppos held his knife upward, an iron thorn between him and the bird, hoping to catch one of the great claws, but it slipped sideways faster than he would have thought possible, grasped his legs, and beat for the air with a strange clattering noise, dangling him beneath even as his water bottle fell away to shatter to damp clay fragments on the heat-parched stones below.

Upside-down, cloak streaming beneath him, Peleppos gripped tight to his knife and cried for his father to deliver him.

WHEN THE GREAT bird finally came to land, in a forested glade far from the ruins around the Wheeled City, Peleppos's thighs were burning bands of pain. Whether this was soreness or puncture wounds he did not know, but he lay in the long cool grass and sobbed his fear until he could stifle his tears. The bird hopped away and stared at him, then bent down its neck to allow a small man to dismount from a tiny leather saddle.

A narrow-toed boot of soft leather nudged Peleppos in the side. "Finished your squalling yet?"

Peleppos rolled over, clutching his knife. "I'm not squalling," he shouted. "I was giving thanks for my delivery." The knife wavered in his hand, pointing at the rider.

"We're supposed to kill you," said the rider, "but you're the smallest warrior we've ever seen scuttle from the cracks in the earth, and we were curious. You we could carry away without cutting into halves or thirds."

The great bird rumbled, perhaps a croak of agreement.

Peleppos pulled himself to his feet. "You're pretty small yourself."

It was true. The rider was no taller than Peleppos, but clearly a man, with stubbly whiskers and a lean face that showed the passing of some years, dark tattoos ringing his long-lashed eyes. His size didn't detract from the impression of danger, for the rider had an entire armory of weapons hung about him—arrows and spears and a wooden sword bladed with chipped flint, slung on leather straps over his nearly naked body. A single great feather stuck out above his back.

The rider ignored Peleppos's remark. "What are you doing out of your hole, little earth-boy?"

"I am a prince among my people, and I have come to take back the day."

"Here it is." The rider spread his arms wide. "Fetch it to your caves, then."

As his captor laughed, a shadow passed over Peleppos. He looked up to see a half dozen or more of the giant birds circling overhead, coming

lower and lower into the meadow. He would stand
them all down if he could. He was the prince here,
and the biggest man besides.

PELEPPOS WATCHED ONE of the great birds nestle
into a hollow in the meadow like a rock dove after
a dust bath. The huge animal was as big as the
Smith Kings' carts come to life. He sat in a circle
with seven of the small men, hard-faced as their
flint knives, with muscles like knotted ropes, each
with a feather on his back and facial tattoos in different patterns radiating around their dark
eye-rings. They passed a leather bag of some oily-
smelling liquor around, the drink skipping him,
and told soft-voiced stories in a language he didn't
understand. They reminded him of the day-guard
of the Wheeled City. At that thought, Peleppos let
his fingers flicker through a few hand signs: *owl
leaving nest—first rain falls—New Moons rising.*
Roughly: *I am new here, can we work as one,
something is about to begin.*

One of the men, not his original captor, smiled
a gap-toothed smile and signed back *apples blossom in spring.* In other words: *Something good
will happen.*

Depending, thought Peleppos, on your definition of "good." He stood, squinting in the red light
of pre-dusk. "I have come to you with a purpose."

Gap-tooth kept smiling, fingers flashing as
salmon splash in the falls.

Peleppos was confused. That meant, *we soon
eat,* or *we will find provisions shortly.*

"Night and day have long been divided by terrible dangers."

"Teratornis," said his original captor. He cocked his head toward the great bird glaring at them with baleful yellow eyes. "You fear the teratornis and call them monsters." Gap-tooth's fingers flickered in a hand sign unfamiliar to Peleppos, though he thought it might mean *death from the air.*

"Teratornis," Peleppos repeated. "Your birds rule our day. Our people are frightened."

One or two of the little men laughed, while Gap-tooth worked at the edge of his flint bladed-knife. "Nimravid cats, great-boars, and worse things walk the sunlit world," said Peleppos's captor. "The teratornis masters them all."

"And man masters the teratornis," Peleppos said with a smile. There was a stirring among the little men, dark mutters, and the nearby bird hissed like an enormous snake before falling into a clicking silence.

A man falls, Gap-tooth said with his fingers. Captor said, "You completely fail to understand the day. Night filth, brawling and breeding within the tired spaces of the world. Your people have lost their way. You are no different." He glanced around the clearing at his fellow flyers, then looked back at Peleppos, his eyes glowing in the failing sunlight. "I honor your ignorance with the gift of your freedom. Go home, boy, if you can make the distance in this one night. Tomorrow your life will be forfeit under our sun."

Gap-tooth's grin grew even wider. *A man falls,* he signed, *the river runs to the sea. You will fail, surely fail.*

The knives came out, dull in the dusk, as the fly-ers licked their lips, kissing and whistling at him. Fingers brushing his own iron knife, Peleppos stumbled from the clearing, past the grounded ter-atornis, which glared at him. He expected to hear chuffing breath, feel heat, but it was silent and cold as a stone. The damp, dark forest received him with open arms and claws of bramble and thorn.

HOURS OF SCRAMBLING down slopes, following gullies, slipping through ravines, trying to find his way back to the Wheeled City, had left Peleppos desperately frightened. He was cold and hungry. He climbed atop a stone outcropping to get his bearings.

The New Moons were up, weaving through the Selenite Rings, their red and blue glare set off against the silvery-gray of night's great braid. Judging by their progress, he had less than half the night left—perhaps four more hours at this season.

A steep valley dropped to his right, heading west toward the rumored sea. Peleppos knew that the Gray River which ran through the ruins sur-rounding the Wheeled City eventually led to the ocean, but the distance was far more than a day's journey away. He had never desired to be a long-ranger. Day-guard was dangerous enough, but most long-rangers never came home in the end.

He strained his vision down the valley, across the shadowed hills, looking for some spark, any trace of the fires of the Wheeled City. And he found an orange gleam, flickering too low on the horizon to be one of the New Moons. In fact, it was below the horizon!

Peleppos set a course toward the spark, marking the next rise from which he might hope to see it, and scrambled on.

THE EASTERN SKY glowed ash gray behind Peleppos, the earliest stirrings of night's end, when he tumbled over a rotten cliff edge and slid down a sharp, painful field of scree. There, on the next ridge perhaps a mile distant, were the watchtowers that rose above the Wheeled City. A fire blazed atop one of them. Peleppos picked himself up, ignoring the pains both sharp and dull, and stumbled onward.

Breath pounding in his chest like a Smith King's hammer, he reached the tower as east's pink stain was marbling to orange. Arnasa stood there in the cloak of the day-guard, sword bare in her hand, watching him climb the ridge.

"Are you wiser now?" she asked. These were the most welcome words he had ever heard.

Together they raced down the hill toward the day-gate as the distant screams of the teratornis echoed across the ruins, Arnasa tugging at his wrist to urge him on, cursing his name with every step.

* * *

"YOU HAVE BEEN bound over to Cadmium, King of the Law, for judgment." Cadmium himself was on the Lawbench hearing Peleppos's case, two key-keepers Peleppos barely knew restraining him before the rule of Law. "Your father's name is breached, and he cannot rule fairly."

It was Cadmium who stood the most to gain by any disgrace that Antimony might fall under here, Peleppos realized. His father had been shrewd to set Cadmium in judgment over Peleppos. There would be fewer questions about the outcome later, while the other Law King would be forced to integrity, regardless his personal desires. And Antimony distanced himself from whatever the judgment might be.

The Lawbench was mounted on a wide, low cart which had been pulled by the key-keepers—trials were the only time in the Wheeled City a cart was not pulled by animals, in keeping with the dignity of the Law. The sides of the cart were hung with shackles, tongs, screws, and other implements of Cadmium's Law, which emphasized trial-by-pain. Antimony's cart was hung with books, scales, and quill pens—the implements of logic and reason.

Other than Cadmium's Lawbench, the Law Market was empty this night, property cases and contracts work being put over to the following night in deference to Peleppos's trial. A crowd of spectators shuffled at the edges of the Law Market, standing behind a ring of torches mounted on brass spear-shafts plunged into the earth. Peleppos knew many of the people who'd come to witness his trial.

I was almost eaten by the teratornis riders, he thought. I can escape this, too.

A key-keeper began to bang the drum of testimony, setting a rhythm that would last throughout the trial. "Peleppos, son of Antimony," Cadmium said, leaning forward slightly on his Lawbench. "You are called to stand to account for your crimes."

The two key-keepers pushed Peleppos into the center of the fire-lit circle. As a Prince of the Law, however disgraced, he knew what was expected of him—to testify with dignity and honesty. "I have committed no crime, but only set forth in service of the people of the Wheeled City," Peleppos said proudly, keeping his words in time to the drum in the best style.

Cadmium ignored him. "These are the charges: that you passed the day-doors without leave, that you invited retribution from the monsters of the day, that you endangered a key-keeper of the Wheeled City in her search for you." He drummed his fingers on the low arm of the Lawbench. "You are perhaps lucky that the charges preferred are so few and limited."

There had been a furious council of the Kings over that, Peleppos knew. Had he simply been a smith's boy who wandered out, his master and his Craft-King would have whipped him for a laggard and set him to a period of hard labor within their own guild. As a Prince of the Law, his fate was a public matter.

"How do you answer to these charges?" Cadmium asked.

"I did pass the day-doors without leave," said Peleppos, "but I aver that I am not bound from doing so. I did not invite retribution, but rather guested with the teratornis riders in their lair." At this, the crowd muttered. "Finally, I endangered no one in my absence. Arnasa sought me of her own free will and regard for me." A few spectators cheered this, and the drum rattled a faster pace, a warning against unruliness or contempt.

Cadmium stared at Peleppos, the Law King's yellow robes flickering gold in the torchlight. "Strange," he said slowly, in half time to the drum, "that a prominent son of the Wheeled City should consort with the demons of the day."

"They are rude and curious cannibals," Peleppos said, "not to be trusted. They bar us from our rightful place in sunlight, closing off half the world with their terrible birds. I did not consort, but sought to know their weaknesses." This was it, he thought; time to make a bid as a hero. The flyers were frightening and cruel, but good men with iron weapons could trump their stone-edged swords and hateful-eyed birds. "I aim to raise an army and make war against the bird-riders, to reclaim the daytime for the Wheeled City."

Cadmium began to chuckle as someone in the crowd jeered. The drum banged fast again, but its beat was lost in the catcalls, the shouting and whistling. Peleppos was laughed out of the Law Market, thrown to the crowd by Cadmium's key-keepers, where he was pummeled and kicked until Arnasa and some of the day-guard hustled him away.

"YOU ARE A fool," Arnasa said as she wiped a cut on his face. "Twice a fool and more. Yet perhaps that was best, to make a mockery of the case before some sterner outcome presented itself. I believe Law King Cadmium thought to set you to service among the smiths."

Peleppos sighed, his heart afire with shame and a desire for vengeance on everyone—the bird riders, Cadmium, the people of the Wheeled City. "I was not mocking. Those flyers are our enemies. They oppress us."

"Did they speak our tongue?" Arnasa asked, her voice sharp. Her fingers flickered: *badger knows his kin.*

"Yes."

"And how do you suppose that is, foolish boy, that they should know our tongue?"

"Prisoners," Peleppos said, his voice faltering. "Interrogation…"

Owl flying—hawk flying—sisters stop their fight, her fingers said. *Fire takes the forest—fox and hare running.*

"The nimravid cats and the great-boars, those are our enemies," Peleppos said grudgingly. "The teratornis hunt them."

"While we sit fat and contented in our holes in the ground, sheltered from sharp teeth and sharper appetites." *Scampering mice—the farmer's corn.*

"It's wrong," he insisted, conviction swelling in his heart. "They keep us in our caves and dine on our flesh."

"No doubt," Arnasa said, "but I would not care to hunt a nimravid of my own accord, when there is a man astride a bird that is the terror of the world to do it for me."

"If we fight the same enemies, we should be the same people."

Arnasa's gaze met his, held it a long time, then she smiled. *Briar rose blossoms,* her fingers said. *Moss by moonlight—night always ends.*

Something had finally come to him, Peleppos realized, but he must be thoughtful and silent in carrying events to their inevitable conclusion. Just a few days earlier, he had visions of conquest and glory and making the world safe for the Wheeled City. Now he had no vision, just a desire for something better, for himself and everyone.

His own fingers flickered. *A man falls—night always ends.*

PELEPPOS WAS UNSURPRISED to find his borrowed day-guard cloak and a fresh store of provisions in his little chamber within the caves. He spent some time in thought, wondering how anyone could best a teratornis, before stepping out with his gear. It was nearly night's end, and he aimed to go back to the flyers and open their hearts to the people of the Wheeled City.

His father's key-keepers sat in a circle outside his chamber, passing a wine sack just as the flyers high in their meadow had. Arnasa was not with them.

"Told Solius he was rough with you in the Law Market," said Young Fredo. He flexed his fist, grinning. "Offered a demonstration."

"Thanks," said Peleppos. Then, surprising himself. "I've been a fool. I'm sorry. Now I'm off to find out how much bigger a fool I can be."

Young Fredo's grin vanished. "There's ties that bind the world together, though you might never see them. And remember—things always change. They used to be different, and someday they'll be still more different."

"Someone built the ruins outside when they were new," Peleppos said. "Someone might rebuild them some day."

The key-keepers nodded like so many wise men, then waved him on his way.

ANTIMONY WAITED AT the day-doors, Arnasa at his side. Peleppos walked up, already in his gear, then knelt to his father. "You may have to find another Prince of the Law, sir. There is something I must do."

"You are a boy, not a man, but perhaps this a boy's mission," said his father. "Your hopes are not yet tempered by experience."

"Bring back the day if you can," said Arnasa, "but mostly, bring back yourself."

Peleppos kissed her then, hugged his father, and walked into dawn's gloaming with the day-guard.

* * *

THE SUN WAS hot, more merciless than before, as Peleppos retraced his trail toward the high meadow. No birds screamed in the high air, no talons swept down for him, but he walked as if there were always a knife at his back. His legs still ached, while he questioned his pride and good sense at every step.

What was the point of going to the flyers, those cannibals of the air? It had all seemed so logical back in the caves with Arnasa, that he could find a way to make their peoples one. But the folk of the Wheeled City were as different from the flyers as wolfhounds from rathounds. Likely they could not even have children together. The teratornis had no place within the caves. What did he intend?

"Do one thing before you do the next," Peleppos told the forest. *First bird hunting,* his fingers flickered.

All day he found company only in the cyclic whir of insects. No animals crossed his path, large or small, and even the shade of the deeper woods seemed stifling. Unsure of his exact route, Peleppos headed upward, seeking the glen where he had sat among the flyers.

Late in the day, as the sun sank beneath the western hills, Peleppos crossed a familiar meadow of bear grass when the scream he had been expecting finally came, freezing his heart. He stood tall, refusing to raise a weapon or whirl in panic, not searching for the bird that would find him much faster regardless.

A teratornis swooped so close overhead that Peleppos's hair was snagged, then it landed just before him. One of the flyers dismounted—Gap-tooth, much to Peleppos's disappointment. For some reason he had been expecting Captor. He and Gap-tooth had no common language except the fingertalk.

A man falls, Gap-tooth signed.

Owl flying—hawk flying—sisters stop their fight, Peleppos signed back, sharing his epiphany.

Gap-tooth laughed. *Fox and hare running—owl never sleeps—sisters always fight.*

"We will never be together," Peleppos translated, speaking softly. His fingers flickered. *A man falls—two men stand—sisters stop their fight.*

Gap-tooth's grin blossomed. He reached backward, pulled the great feather from his weapons harness and tossed it on the ground between them. As soon as it left Gap-tooth's hand, the flier collapsed.

Peleppos watched the feather fall to the ground, then stared at the teratornis. The yellow eyes glittered in the setting sun, bird-mad and huge. He reached for the feather, stopped, and squatted on his haunches. His hand hovered just above the giant quill.

The teratornis still glared.

What was this? Certainly not the kinship between their peoples that Arnasa had hinted at. Was the feather an instrument of control? "Breathe, by the New Moons," said Peleppos to the bird. "If you are an animal, breathe."

Waddling forward and lowering its head so that the beak pointed at Peleppos's chest, the teratornis opened its mouth and screamed, the sound so loud at this short distance that Peleppos felt his ears must surely bleed. The air from its gullet had no warmth, no stench, except the smell of wax and metal. Drawing his iron knife, Peleppos charged into that wall of sound and stabbed deep into the teratornis's throat.

It was as though he had unleashed the lightning. His right arm clenched so hard that bones cracked, while blue sparks shot out, like the greatest iron cartwheel in the world rolling over rough granite. The bird's shriek rose in pitch as smoke poured from its throat, while Peleppos danced a twisting, joint-bruising jig not of his own making. There was a large belch, and he fell backward amid a shower of tiny brasswork and gobbets of bird flesh. The skin of his hand was cracked and burned, and Peleppos could not move his right arm.

He looked up at a hissing noise to see Gap-tooth's body shrinking like a twist of leather laid in a fire, skin darkening and fluids running out onto the soil of the meadow. The bird gave one last croak as the flier crumbled to ash, which the wind blew into Peleppos's face.

Peleppos got slowly to his feet in the darkening gloom. He was amazed that nothing more than his arm was broken. His joints felt as if they had been snapped loose and played for music, but he could still use his legs, and his left arm. The iron knife was lodged somewhere in the bird's throat, doubt-less a hot and twisted ruin, and he had no stomach to retrieve it.

He scooped up some of the tiny brasswork, put it in his kit bag, then studied the feather that Gap-tooth had dropped. He decided after a few moments to leave well enough alone.

As he took one last look at the teratornis before walking away, Peleppos saw a ripple in its feathers, just beneath an outstretched wing. He hadn't the strength for another fight, but he wasn't willing to walk away from this final mystery. With his good left hand he parted the feathers, his motions clumsy and slow.

Something definitely squirmed within. Peleppos wondered what new horror or devilment this might be. Nonetheless he kept working his hand beneath the feathers until whatever it was grasped his fingers. With a shriek of fright, Peleppos drew out a tiny child, the very image of Gap-tooth, with brown eyes that seemed in day's last light to be the exact shade of the teratornis's feathers.

What did this mean? Peleppos could find no answers, except that he had come to unite their peoples, and here was a child he could foster home. He was certain it was not truly human, no more than Gap-tooth had been at the end, but a child was a child.

He hefted the baby to the crook of his left arm. It promptly bit into his shoulder. Tired, wounded, stumbling downhill along his own backtrail through the deepening dark, Peleppos wondered how it was that the child's eyes were the very same color as his own.

"A man falls," he whispered to the child, "but night always ends." Behind him the sky filled with the screams of a dozen distant teratornis.

O CARITAS

CONRAD WILLIAMS

MONCK REALIZED HE had been here too long when
he glanced down at his hands to find the knuckles
turned blue. The flyover fled off to the left and
right of him. Everything else was just scenery. An
acid blue sky was crocheted with vapor trails.
There were half a dozen jets up there right now,
scraping the troposphere, edging 600mph while
their inhabitants grazed on plastic trays of trans
fats and overcooked starch. The air shimmered
with particulates. Blue tremors made the surface of
the road uncertain. He stared at his hands, clench-
ing and unclenching them, watching the tendons
crawl beneath the skin. He remembered, when he
was active in this city, that he had suffered from
narcolepsy. He wondered if, now he was back, it
would return too. Then he pulled the scrap of
paper from his pocket and stared at the name.

COLLEEN MALLORY.

He headed east. This section of road between Marylebone and King's Cross had always been busy, as long as he had lived here, as long as he had been aware of the capital. The buildings that muscled against it were scorched with product: advertisements, tags, fliers, exhaust. Monck moved like something set free from a cage. His lungs burned. What passed for fresh air up top seemed much cleaner than anything he had sampled below stairs for the past five years, although he knew this was not the case. The pollution in Beneothan was oil-based, natural; not this chemical cocktail that twinkled in the lungs for a lifetime.

The tiny screws on his sunglasses were weak; he kept having to press his fingers to the frames to ensure they did not fall off. Midwinter, the sun like a torch fuelled by a failing battery was still strong enough to cause whiteout and tears. And he must see; he must not be caught napping.

The city had healed, much better than he had ever imagined it might. Everything seemed sealed, glossy, like scar tissue. The rich had risen. Structured gossamer, the new form of transport among the moneyed, was sailed between buildings hollowed at their summits to receive it. Ground level was becoming ghettoized, a grid of poverty being redrawn in tar and carbon monoxide and soot.

Where is everyone going? Monck thought. The cars ground and bit and squealed around the peeling tarmac, surging along the Euston Road like some Roman army with its shields raised. Fewer people than he remembered were walking, perhaps because of the dangers. As the city grew taller, the light went with it; the depths were gloomy all the time now, lit up only by the ochre stabs of headlights or some reflected glory chicaning down from the heavens. Though he was tempted to stop and stare, Monck kept moving, remembering that he had a job to do.

Despite his years away, and the changes that had occurred, he still loved his city. There was enough of the old face left behind to offer reassurance, comfort even. Occasionally he happened upon ghosts. Bends in the road that he had swept down in a car with a girlfriend. Zones that pricked at him with meaning until he realized that he was standing where a park used to be, where he had read a novel, or eaten a sandwich in the sunshine, or met someone for a chat and an ice cream. The idea of food found a mate in his gut; he was suddenly ravenous. He hurried along a huge street, wishing for some of the old London kebab shops to still be around, but there was nothing but glass and resin and high-tensile steel. There were no doors. No neon. No human buzz. There was no way in.

Skimmers had delivered reports to Beneothan of gangs roaming these streets. There were horror stories connected to the elite in their penthouse acres high in the clouds. They were hiring muscle to rid the streets of old Londoners, the people who had existed here before the cataclysmic earthquake that collapsed forty per cent of the capital. With the streets cleansed, the rich could spread out, move into some of the big piles that sat idle in the suburbs, regain control of the roads and engage with the earth once more, instead of drifting around like chancing spiders. The rich liked their penthouses, but they liked their mobility too. They did not like to feel restricted in any way.

Monck could care less. Silk linings or age-shined viscose; it made no difference to him.

"In here, *quick*." The voice was panic-scarred and frothy with nicotine. Monck spun toward it and saw the gray blade of face sink back into the dark like a shark's fin. Monck remembered when he had teetered on the brink of discovery: his true identity, his connection with the tribe that lived beneath the city, his talent for melting into the scenery. Fear had been behind it all back then; had partially fuelled the epiphanies he experienced. His scare threshold had receded much in the intervening years; when you spent your life scurrying around in true blackness, this twilight, this daylight, was hardly a place for nightmares to exist.

It was Jermyn, one of the Skimmers. He smelled of burnt grease and air fresheners. Monck saw him flaring his nostrils, perhaps in yearning for the underground. "Your shift over soon?" Monck asked him.

"Another twelve hours. My tripes are sweating, being in this shit pit. I'll be glad to be back in the soil."

Monck nodded. "Have you an in for me? Is there anything doing, this area?"

"This used to be Marylebone," he said. "Very swish. Very Swedish, in its day. Over there, where the road bends off the main drag, Homer Street. There was a very good bar on the corner. Over-priced, but good."

"Anything doing?" Monck pressed. "Anyone who'd look good in white?"

"You think I'm here to grade skirt for you? I'm a water-boatman, Monck. Not a matchmaker. I'm here to make sure Beneothan remains beneath. Unsullied."

"I'll cover for you. Last twelve hours of your shift. Go boating up the Fleet with your sweet-heart. I just need a lead."

"You're on," Jermyn snapped. "This arterial road is cut off at the top by what used to be Edg-ware Road. It's grim as graves that way now. There's a possible breach at the mouth of the old tube station. You have to make sure nothing gets in. I've got a few dogs on it at the moment, while I check the other weak point at the corner of Once Upon a Baker Street. Old video shop boarded up and ostensibly sterile. But don't fall for it. There's a storage room underneath. Something's been at the foundations. Anything enters those hotspots means Beneothan is compromised."

"What about below stairs?"

"Facers are working on the inner sanctum as we retreat. Strengthening the important sections to make sure we aren't pierced, weakening others at strategic zones to ensure major kapow should any spelunkers get too warm."

"Do you really sense a threat? Aren't we beyond that now? We're burgeoning. Population's on the rise. Slowly, I admit, but still... I doubt anyone up here even knows about us any more."

"As long as Odessa breathes, there'll be a garrison at the limits. No harm ever came from being cautious."

Monck smiled. "You say that, but you're getting chilblains."

Jermyn touched his hat. "When you're done, you might consider taking a shower before presenting yourself at the alleyways behind what was once Park Lane. The great hotels are all bandaged up like sore fingers, but you'll find what you need inside them. Go tall. Enjoy the view. There's nothing happening below the fifteenth floors."

He was gone, then, as if the shadows had dismantled him. Monck thought he heard something by way of a farewell, but he couldn't work out what it might have been. It sounded too much like *Ivy* for it to be anything like a goodbye.

Monck breathed into a stiff bowl made by his fingers, tried to work some feeling back into them. The light, such as it was, was failing, but still it was too painful to remove his sunglasses. As the dogs were on guard at Edgware Road, he decided to check on the video shop first. His mind filled with confetti, he headed east.

* * *

A DARKNESS IN waiting. A darkness with poise. The air here has not changed in half a decade. It sags like the final breath in a dead man's lungs. A shoal of post lies on the welcome mat. Shelves prop up cinema ghosts. Anime. RomCom. Adult. Faded labels stained with perished Sellotape: *Video Box Sets Half Price. Sopranos Season One Five Pounds!!!* A different kind of shadow where the cash register stood. A corner of the poster carousel taps gently against its mate, spurred on by a draught, the only sound this space has known until the jemmy splits the halves of the entrance and pops it open.

Monck moves into this, knowing this species of dark as if it were something that might be alive, kept in a vivarium. The rods and cones on his retina spring awake: recognition of a friend. He breathes deeply and tastes air that would have been fresh when he too was known to these streets more readily than the tunnels gouged beneath them.

He freezes, his hands behind him, pressed firmly against doors he has closed again. It's as if no change has occurred. Behind him, cut-up voices in the street. A mish-mash of questions, challenges, rejoinders, but he can't apportion them to separate mouths:

one seventy/scalpel/over/get that light close in/twenty/fifteen ccs/incision/clamp that/prep/ black lung/reinflate/city boy, this is a city boy/bleeder

Street code. Gang slang. A patois of the pavement. He struggles to understand it while his eyes take in the denuded stacks. A few discarded DVD jackets lie on the floor. A price gun. A box that once contained deep fried chicken. The darkness deepens in the southwest corner of the room.

Stairs lead down to a tiny staff area: a sink, a chair, a counter. A box of PG Tips and a bowl of fossilized sugar. Fingers of mold wrap around the edges of a mini fridge. On the wall is a calendar from 1998. A stock room behind this contains a single, empty pallet in the far corner. It is cool in this room. There is a padlocked fire door. A staff whiteboard bears the words *Return stock by April 9th* and *Jenny says yes to Jake!!!* and *Someone else get the biscuits this week, please.* Monck moves cautiously to the pallet and toes it aside. Here lies the breach, or one of them. A narrow blue-black throat sinking into another place. Top to bottom. Head to toe. Monck ducks to the edge and breathes. There is a smell of home, but of danger too. This tunnel is being used for something other than access. What was Jermyn playing at? Had he not been inside this building? Did he think, just because the main entrance was sealed, that there were no other crevices? He had lived for long enough in the city's bowels, Monck thought he might have taken on some of the skills of rats by now.

Carefully, with the green stick of chalk he used to indicate areas of danger, he ringed the fissure and scratched a line on the wall above it. He made another mark on the wall outside the shop too, after closing the doors.

Back along the old Crawford Road. He remembered many of the shops along here, and the people who lived in the flats. There had been a chemist with stained glass windows, a Middle Eastern sandwich shop that advertised *FRESHLY SQUIZZED JUICE*. A man with dreadlocks in his beard pushed a shopping trolley filled with televisions and cardboard; he drank chocolate milk from a carton and smelled of turpentine and plaster dust. London was coming back into Monck, reanimating him. He was almost running by the time he reached the Westway again. Ahead, the dilapidated entrance to Edgware Road's Bakerloo line was a riot of broken masonry and lurching, concertina steel. He saw three dogs sitting on the pavement and knew there was something wrong straight away. These were not Beneothan dogs. They were bullets of muscle, all jaw and forward motion: bull mastiffs, bred nasty. They spotted Monck as he was backing away; they tore after him immediately.

Monck hit diamond link and climbed savagely, feeling the snarl of salivating chops at his trouser legs. He swung his leg over and dropped into a basketball court. Painted lines ruptured by tectonic upthrust, the aftershocks of the quake. The mastiffs were trying to chew through the fence and Monck spent a panicked few seconds checking for gaps they might have missed. He ran to the far end of the court and climbed the fence there, then doubled back in a large arc, hoping that he was downwind of the dogs and that their stubborn idiocy would keep them at the fence, waiting for him to return.

Inside the station, he slid over the ticket barriers. The lifts were buckled and powerless. The Beneothan dogs had been strangled, hoisted up on their leashes and left to hang on the exposed strip lighting cables. Monck took the spiral staircase into pitch, his mind thick with foam and bulging eyes. It was as if he could taste the secretions of foreign bodies in the air; feel the heat from their footsteps through the soles of his boots on these cold, stone steps.

These tunnels had not known trains for half a decade. On the southbound platform, Monck found discarded briefcases and handbags, umbrellas and newspapers fluttering in the breezes that funneled through the underground network. How old was this air? It had no way out. It was being constantly recycled, a stale miasma, a memory. Monck stood and listened to its song, trying to detect something more sinister within it. His mind wandered. He thought of his long dead mother, and of his father, of women he had loved: Nuala, Laura. He had to bite hard against a sudden compulsion to cry. You could not live in Beneothan and entertain thoughts of visiting friends and family. It was too dangerous. It was too uniting. This city beneath the capital was insular, jealous, and proud. It was the hypochondriac fearing infection.

From the tracks, a sudden sizzle of intent. A mechanical exhalation. A death rattle snaking its way along the dust-clogged tiles. Monck steeled himself for revelations, but none came. Only half-formed sentences, techno-babble, more of the argot he had eavesdropped at the video shop.

Swab/Clamp/Suture/I need 5 milligrams/

Frustrated by a lack of stimulus, Monck checked the other platform and the staff only zones, before repairing to the spiral staircase. He ascended swiftly, mindful that the mastiffs might return. He chalked lines on the ticket barriers and entrance and left a mark to convey that basic checks had been undertaken, but a more thorough search was needed. How many failed pressure points like this across the city? How many were accidental, unknown? How many had been created by invaders?

The constant burble of traffic on the flyover. The scurry and rush. Where *was* everyone going? Why was anybody still here?

At a Skimmer node—the private park for residents in what was previously Connaught Square—he passed on the details of his search. It was out of his hands now. The Skimmers would contact the Web, at the heart of Beneothan, and sealing maneuvers would be coordinated within twenty-four hours.

"Jermyn," he said, as he was leaving. "Have any of you seen Jermyn?"

Goldhawk and Frith shook their heads. Delancey suggested he might be in one of the midway zones—a central tunnel, platform, or storage unit—catching up on his sleep before his next shift began.

Monck nodded, unable to shake off doubtful feelings. He hurried into what had once been named Stanhope Place and crossed the old Bayswater Road into Hyde Park.

The sudden vastness screamed into him and he felt afraid for the first time in so many years that it was almost crippling. Tired as he had grown of the enameled feel of the new buildings, their brutal aloofness, that claustrophobia was preferable to this. He had forgotten about space. He began to sprint, unable to stop himself, like some newborn animal having found its legs. It was directionless, terrifying, thrilling. He ran until he saw a massive blade separating the park, glittering in the moonlight. He tore off his sunglasses, disoriented. Time was important up here. It was something that could be measured. Underground there was just the work and the sleep and the love. The compression of time up here, the compulsion to follow it, to be dictated to by it, reminded him that all those things he enjoyed now, he had to place into little boxes before. Life had been a series of tasks. Shape, format, rules, laws; all had been imposed on him. Time was all of those constrictions, and more. It ate through your mind from birth. Your first kiss was defined by how long you mashed your lips against someone else's. *We were at it all night long.* How many years did you devote to the company you worked for? How many birthdays? How many anniversaries? The watch. The clock. The time, sponsored by Accurist.

The blade gleamed, clean and long, like an arrowhead that has fallen free of its spear.

Serpentine. He had boated on this with Laura in a year he couldn't begin to give a number. They had drunk cappuccini and watched children chase pigeons. Looking back, you forgot about how time controlled you. You could erase it from the scene, but it was always there, tutting at you, pointing a finger at its own face.

He angled across the park, conscious of how conspicuous he was under this brilliant moon. He saw a fire up ahead, and shadows pass in front of it, running fast. He would have to negotiate the broad drag at the west edge—Park Lane as was—before he could search the Dorchester or the Hilton. There were enough distractions. A family had taken refuge in a black cab; the father was jabbing something like a poker out of a hole in one window, trying to ward off the pack that were trying to get at them. Someone ran through the wall of fire and gave the flames a piggyback. A horde took off after the screaming figure, although it was gone before Monck could discern whether a rescue was taking place.

He hurried across the road, dodging overturned vehicles and grinning cracks in the tarmac. A trio of children was sitting by the entrance to the Dorchester, playing with dice, or teeth, or pebbles. He slipped past their upturned, hollowed faces and into the hotel lobby. He could hear music. There was a signal of some kind, too. It sounded like the pips of a time code, or the indecipherable beats that untangle themselves from surges of static on a shortwave radio.

As with everywhere else, the lifts were no longer functional. He put his head down and trotted up the first seven floors before he had to rest. His breath came ragged and hot, deafening him. He crouched in the corner of the stairwell until his lungs had calmed, and then proceeded more carefully, rattled that he should have made himself vulnerable at the end of his search. At the seventeenth floor, he found corridors festooned with crepe decorations, silver and blue balloons, the mineral hit of champagne. At the other end of the building, as he turned a corner, he glimpsed a blur of white, heard the shush of silk rubbing against itself. Music came from an unknown source: it crackled with the warmth of vinyl. Cat Stevens, *Sitting.*

...if I sleep too long, will I even wake up again...

He pushed a door open and saw a room that could not be there. It contained a pine wardrobe with thin metal handles. Inside, the smell of the wood had been lost to time, and the things that were stored within: magazines and bottles of malt whisky; old sweet tins brimming with photographs; a cardboard box of births and deaths and marriages; a cricket ball; a tin of Kiwi boot polish.

A dressing table against which his mother had died writing a letter. Her perfume. For a moment, in the triptych of mirrors, he thought he saw her. The arm of her bottle-green bathrobe swung clear of the door, stiff enough to contain her. He stepped back, his throat constricting. Those photographs. He could remember them without having to look again. Mostly from when he was a baby, a toddler. For some reason, his father stopped taking pictures once he had grown beyond the age of four. Maybe he was too busy. Maybe his camera had broken; they weren't so easy with money that such luxuries could be replaced. The novelty of children wearing off; but he couldn't believe that. His childhood had been happy, secure, until the seizure that carried off Mum. Cat Stevens was singing about a boy with a moon and star on his head. If he were to move deeper into the room, he might find his father reading a book about hostas, sipping at his Laphroaig.

A cork popped from a bottle.

"Colleen?" he called. He wondered where they had found her, and why they thought she would be a good match for him. Odessa had warned him of the population's mismatch. Seven men for every one woman. Beneothan would die out within a couple of generations if they did not attract more females.

A door paused in the shutting. He hurried toward it. Inside, the hotel room was a riot of decorations. A partially devoured wedding cake stood on a pedestal. The window gave a view of Hyde Park that made Monck feel dizzy. He had to put his hands flat against the wall; he felt his toes try to dig through the soles of his boots into the carpet.

"Don't be afraid," she said. She was sitting on a bed large enough for a small family to share. Her face was slashed shut by shadows.

Monck shot a look at her before his gaze was dragged back to the window.

"Long way up," he said.

"Long way down, too," she said.

Spanish guitars were still playing from the hotel room further down the corridor. Cat Stevens sings Latin. He imagined his dad nodding his head to the handclaps, the insistent pulse of the strings. *Give me time forever, here in my time.*

"Will you come with me?" he asked.

"I've been with you all day," she said. "I'll be with you for as long as it takes."

Monck watched lights coil around the vast body of the park. Occasional fires burned at its perimeter. Gossamer drifted past the window: a man was pouring wine for two female companions while a Spider steered them toward some penthouse or another.

Colleen approached him, but the shadow would not slip from her features. He smelled apples on her, and her breath was spiced with nothing so exotic, or so intoxicating, as fresh air. It was as if she had drawn a lungful of the winter countryside into her and transported it here to pollution's carbon-scorched heart. She plucked the piece of paper from his fingers and a shift occurred in that knot of darkness, a stretching, a settling. She was smiling.

"You need to remind yourself who I am?" she asked.

"This is unorthodox, I know," Monck said.

"Well, I'm here, ready. My big day."

She returned to the bed and sat down, patted the area next to her. He stumbled toward it, certain that his vertigo was going to tilt the room as well as himself, and spill him through the glass. She did not reach for him, nor him her. They sat together like would-be lovers in the presence of a chaperone. His eyes would not grow accustomed to her darkness. But he felt very strongly that he knew her. The way she sat, the way she talked, the way she moved. Her fingers were busy with the paper. She folded it and refolded it. Sometimes it disappeared between her fingers, but then she unfolded, and the square grew. At one point, busy with it again, it fell from her hands. She didn't pick it up.

"We ought to go," he said. "Places like this, they're vulnerable. Easy for street levelers to come up here."

She leaned forward. It was only at the last moment, as her lips found his, that he realized she meant to kiss him. He thought she was about to share some grim secret. Shock reeled around his body.

"Nuala?" he said. But Nuala was dead. She had burned in a graveyard for trains. Everyone from his past died or faded away. He was like a piece from a jigsaw puzzle whose interlocking parts had become torn off.

When he pulled away, the kiss becoming at once too cloying and too insubstantial, the dress was lying on the bed, old and scarred. The walls of the room were peeling, the window starred with concussions from rocks or metal bars, which lay on the floor before it. Red paint had been sprayed around the walls. Outside, Hyde Park was a mass of smoking bodies, a disaster scene trying to be contained with man-sized pieces of charred tarpaulin.

The static in his head resolved itself into a sequence of beeps, of beats. He looked down at his arm and saw his blood's motion, synchronous in the raised bulge of a vein. As if he had just drawn his arm clear of water, he saw it gleam, saw the shift of his face reflected in a glint millimeters wide. He was reminded of the Serpentine, but when he lifted his head to search for the water, everything went gray. He turned, his heart thrashing, and knew he had to get out of the hotel. It was a trap of some sort. Jermyn's shark fin face leered somewhere out there. Monck was on his knees, scrabbling for the door, when his hand brushed against the paper Colleen had been playing with. Its folds seemed unfinished; her name was obscured. Well, part of it. The initial letters of her given and family names were mashed together. As he was cloaked by the strength of his own astonishment, he saw the word: COMA.

A TUBE LEADING from the cannula sunk deep into the meat of his forearm snaked into the soil. Wires turned the shaved mass of his head into a study of fractures. Trying to move, he noticed he was naked. A monitor *beep* measured the strength *beep* of his life and played *beep* along.

Colleen shifted into his line of sight. He knew it was her because of the smell. He wanted to ask her how she managed that, how she could retain the freshness of the surface after so long in the stale belly of the city.

"Are you smiling?" he asked.

"Shh," she said. "Don't speak. I have to give you something."

"What?"

He heard rumbles move over his head from left to right, dull, distant, but onerous. Trickles of soil fell from the ceiling. A large bang from somewhere. The room, and Colleen, shivered in his eyes.

"You shouldn't have woken up."

"What do you mean?"

Other figures crowded around him. He recognized one as Odessa. "Put him under, quick," she said. "Jesus Christ."

He found strength to fight her as she made to release the seal on the anesthetic. He tore the needle from his arm with his teeth and spat it out. He sat up. The others shifted uneasily, moving away, unsure.

Odessa said, her voice softer now, imploring: "Don't leave us. We're nothing if you go."

"What is happening?" he asked.

"We captured you."

"I'm *with* you. There's no need to hold me prisoner."

"We captured your narcoleptic... other. The you that exists when you have an attack, when you sleep."

Monck tensed himself for another rush at him, but everyone was keeping back. He wished they *would* attack him; it was something he could at least try to deal with.

"Why?" he asked, barely able to summon the breath required by the question.

"We needed you up there, but we need you here too."

"Why?" he asked again. He felt he might never be able to say anything but.

"Storage. We're in trouble. We're under attack. We need to keep our functioning males safe. We're building special, sealed hives. We have cryogenic technicians..." Odessa's voice petered out.

"And what about this... other?"

"Reconnaissance. We could read what was happening up Top without needing to imperil ourselves."

Monck rubbed his face. "I remember a ruined hotel. Colleen was there. Hyde Park was burning."

Odessa nodded. "We know. The city is dying. After the quake, well we hoped it would divert attention. But there were breaches. People came looking. There were deaths. No order after a cataclysmic event. No law to speak of. It was required elsewhere. Scum poured in. We were caught napping. People who lost everything in the trauma up Top found succor in the stores we had built down here. We are being routed and reamed. We are retreating so hard we're meeting ourselves coming the other way."

"I have to go."

"No, we're not finished. We need to find the other breaches. We have to repel and seal."

"Get Jermyn to do it. Or one of the other Skimmers."

"Jermyn's dead. They're all dead."

"I have to go. I'm going. I have to see for myself."

"Come back, then. Soon," Odessa said, and then something else, as she moved out into the tunnels.

He was pulling on his clothes, wiping his needle punctures with sterile tissues, when he realized what she had said.

At least one of you.

LONDON WAS LIKE a model for tectonic realignment, for climate change, for urban terrorism, all rolled into one. Fires and gangs roamed, seeking fuel. Monck noticed his lack of shadow, but it was night; what light there was came as a jittery, uncertain thing. He chided himself for allowing himself to be spooked, and chivvied himself along the old Oxford Street, with glances into the vandalized acres of glass and steel that flanked him, where at least his reflection—a pale craquelure—kept pace.

He approached the Dorchester from the rear, feeling strange at the knowledge that this was his first visit to the hotel, despite what his dreaming self had suggested. He felt light, reduced somehow, and wondered how long he had been lying on the bed. His legs were foal-weak.

He entered via a staff door that linked to the kitchens. The refrigerators had been raided. All of the knives and cleavers had been stolen from the hooks above the work surfaces. Dinner orders were still clipped to a carousel. A waiter's bow tie hung limply on the back of a tea box filled with moldering potatoes. He knew that there was no hope for Beneothan. You couldn't put a finger in every hole; blocking it up only increased the pressure elsewhere. London was too big to police. It had accrued breaches for millennia. It was sieve city. It was groaning with collapse.

Monck methodically checked every corridor off the fire escape as he rose. On some levels he was unable to open the doors because of bodies or barricades. At the seventeenth floor he found cold sterility. Any evidence of the party had been cleared away or had existed nowhere other than in the crevices of his sleep-brain. All of the rooms were open. All of the rooms were empty. He found the shadow of what might have been a wedding dress across the counterpane of a neatly made bed but when he pressed his fingers against it, shadow was all it was.

He heard something back down the corridor and turned to see a hand slide out of view, leaving a track of black in the wall that its nails had gouged.

He hurried after the figure, Colleen's name on his lips, gritting his teeth against the feeling of faintness swarming around him. In the stone chasm of the fire escape, he heard hard, fast footsteps ascending. Monck stared at the risers as he pursued, expecting to see craters. Someone crashed through the emergency exit at the top of the hotel. Monck arose into a silent span of stars. Smoke smudged the horizon. London reared away from him, a mandala of fire, a thousand square miles of potential being forged in the flames of creation. It seemed. The truth was more prosaic, more dangerous. Distance did that for you. Whether temporally or physically. It prettified. It defused.

He/Monck said, "Long way up."

Monck/he said, "Long way down, too."

He was sitting on the edge of the world, a figure so utterly dark it was as if it wouldn't be able to sustain itself. It seemed to tremble, on the verge of sucking itself inside out. It felt strange, saying the things that this *narcoshade* was saying; yet it didn't for a second make him feel as though he were being manipulated.

"I'm tired," he/Monck/Monck/he said. "I'm so tired."

There could be no trickery here, no surprise ending. He knew what was coming. So no need to ask the reason they had come up here. No need to ask what kind of future they might share. No more why. No more who. No more where. No more when. The how of it was the easiest part. Monck/he reached out his arms and began to run. Like a mirror made of oil, he/Monck opened up for an embrace. It lasted for as long as it took Monck to wonder if they would create one impact mark on the road, or two.

LT. PRIVET'S LOVE SONG

SCOTT THOMAS

LT. PRIVET HAD heard tell that there was love magic to be found in the old part of the city, high above the sea, up a perilous set of stairs that innumerable feet and centuries of salty rain had worn to a slippery gray. There, overlooking the waves, the houses were tall and weathered, with steep-pitched roofs and faded paint. The streets were narrow for the nearness of the buildings and there was something about the air that was both damp and comforting, a certain ghost for the nose that told of close-knit generations and the danger that was never far when people settled near an ocean.

A fine drizzle was coming in off the Gantic when Privet stopped to catch his breath. Not even halfway up and he was winded. The stairs rose in a dizzying line before him, to a horizon of shadowy structures. There were no banisters to grab onto and the crudely cut slabs of granite were slick beneath his feet. Only love, or something along those lines, could have made the young man consider venturing further.

He thought of the innkeeper's daughter in New Crown below, her pale round face, her great green eyes, her hair a fluid mystery of nocturnal shades. He thought of her laugh and the soft scallop-colored breasts that leaned to gravity when she bent to place food on the tables. Suddenly he was moving again, up and up and up the ancient stairs, until at last, he reached the top.

It was true what they said about the old half of the city—it might as well have been an altogether different world from the more recent colony below. The architectural styles had been outmoded for more than two centuries, the houses high and thin with tapered windows. While simple in frame, the structures bore embellishing details that featured graceful curves and delicate patterns.

Privet stood and collected himself. He was young, as mentioned, and handsome enough, with warm brown eyes looking out from under his officer's helmet. His uniform reflected the recent increase in trade with the North Islands, for the lightweight breastplate beneath his dark green jacket was the shimmering blue of imported "sea steel." His breeches, boots, and the scabbard containing his new blue sword, were black, but not quite so dark as the hair on the innkeeper's daughter.

The man set to looking for a brick-colored house with a wreath of brittlethorn on the door.

The dwellings were tired things and Lt. Privet saw more scrawny dogs than people. Those upright creatures that were about were cloaked against the weather and, characteristically reticent, peeked rather than stared at the stranger. Slick cobbled veins wove between the houses, taking him through a maze of shadows, until he found the place he sought. It was modest in its anemic paint, two and a half stories tall with thin windows and a projecting entry arch bearing worn carvings like webs and tusks. A big tangled wreath of thorny vines was nailed to the batten door. Privet straightened, despite his aching legs and back, and knocked.

Two old women greeted the lieutenant when the door was opened. They were the Deerfield Sisters... twins, as were the majority of folks in Old Crown. The women, Privet soon found, spoke each word simultaneously, as though two mouths shared a single mind.

"Yes?" they said.

Privet removed his helmet, which was like a bowl with lamb chop sideburns, and held it under his arm. His hair was auburn, swept back over his ears and tied in a neat little tail.

"Good afternoon, ladies. I am Lieutenant Privet of the frigate *North Swan*, on her way to Westheath and anchored for repairs in the port below."

The women were pretty old things, gray-haired, gray-dressed, and leaning forward with great interest. They shared a blush at the sight of the sharp-looking military man.

"Ohhh," they cooed, "please come in, lieutenant."

It was dim and comfy inside and a nice fire heated the parlor against the day. The place smelled of bergamot and old linens.

"Tea?" the sisters asked, seating Privet in the best chair.

"Thank you," the man said, smiling.

Once tea and jam cakes were on hand, the officer got down to business.

"It is told in the town below that you gentlewomen have a singular mastery in the ways of love magic."

The women, seated side by side on a settle, smiled and giggled, "Is *that* what they say?"

"Indeed. And so I have come to ask your help with a certain matter…"

Privet went on to describe the troubles his navy ship had encountered while traveling up the coast from Hemmings Port. The craft shook as if it had taken a cannonball, and a hole appropriate to such an attack was suffered on the starboard side, yet no firing was heard and no source of an attack was to be seen. In fact, no remains of a projectile were found in the damaged section of the craft. Thus, the *North Swan* had been under restoration for a number of days, during which time Privet and others from his crew had frequented the Salty Hag, an inn not far from the docks.

"I have fallen in love with the innkeeper's daughter. She is a flower in a field of weeds, the most fetching lass I have seen in my days. I will not leave to sea without her hand."

The sisters, delighted by the man's profession of affection, looked to each other and smiled before addressing their guest.

"We would be happy to help you win the heart of this woman, Lieutenant Privet."

And so the man sat in the humble little parlor while the twins clattered about in the near kitchen. They might as well have been preparing a great meal for all the noise, and the smells that followed reminded him of exotic spices he had encountered in his years traveling the sea to distant lands. The old women even hummed in unison. Their light and pleasing voices floated in to where the man sat sipping his tea.

The lieutenant was not one, generally speaking, to turn to magic, having witnessed a tragic misfortune when he was quite young. Two half-grown neighbor girls in his home village, intent on seeing visions of their future husbands, had concocted an oracular brew and filled a wooden washtub with it. In order to witness apparitions of their future loves, it was required that each girl submerge her head under the liquid for ten seconds. But magic was a fickle thing, and the hasty twins, rather than take turns with the head dunking, poked under in the same instant. The magic found this disagreeable, for some inexplicable reason, and when the sisters withdrew from the tub, their faces were obscured by a thick connecting tube of tissue as long as a man's forearm, a bridge linking their heads together. All that remained of their features was a single misplaced eye, set off at one side of the anomaly, the dark pupil flittering like a fly under glass. With their faces sealed within this fleshy mass, the girls were incapable of breathing, and fell to the ground, where they writhed, conjoined, until dead. From that point on, Privet had avoided magic whenever possible.

At length the sisters glided in from the kitchen, beaming, one holding a small bottle in her hand. The young officer felt a chill down his spine. He took the jar and held it up to view, but the contents were obscured by the green of the glass.

"Just a sprinkle will do," the Deerfield Sisters cautioned in unison.

Privet stood up and asked what the women wanted for compensation, and, unassuming creatures that they were, they told him to part with whatever petty amount he saw fit. Privet gave them a handsome fifty-moth piece and their eyes bulged.

"Thank you, lieutenant," they sang, "you are indeed a generous man."

It was not long before dark, and Privet still had the long climb down those terrible steps to look forward to. He put on his helmet, bid goodbye to the ladies, and stepped out into the drizzle. From that vantage point, high in Old Crown, he could see the roofs of the contemporary buildings below, and the jagged rocks that stabbed out above them and the silvery Gantic Ocean. His wounded warship was anchored down there, and from this height it appeared to be no more than a toy.

* * *

THE SALTY HAG was host to a good crowd that night, with nearly every table full. Crewmen from the *North Swan* accounted for much of the patronage, and they were welcomed warmly by the proprietor and the local folk who frequented the establishment. Lt. Privet was there with the rest, seated in a corner under low beams, with the sound of a fiddler competing against the many loud voices. He drank from a mug of chestnut-colored squall, while watching the innkeeper's daughter, Hazel, as she tended tables. With so many customers on hand, the lovely young woman relied on the assistance of another serving maid, a redheaded little thing with a cinnamon constellation of freckles.

Unfortunately for Privet, he had wound up on the wrong side of the tavern room, the half *not* being tended by Hazel. He would have to wait for another night to try out the mixture that the Deer-field Sisters had supplied him with. Even so, he enjoyed watching her as she moved about, her dark hair whipping, her dark eyes smiling. She was lovely in a long plum-colored skirt that rippled about her legs like a fluid, and her pale scoop-necked blouse more than hinted at her feminine charms. All the other sailors watched her too, and wanted her, but Lt. Privet grinned a secret grin, knowing that she would soon belong to him.

"Lieutenant..." A man's voice intruded upon Privet's reverie.

He looked up and saw the uniformed Captain Moorsparrow of the fighting class *Swift Cannon*.

He was accompanied by a well-dressed, attractive, middle-aged woman with piled amber hair.

Privet was quick to his feet, quick to salute.

"Sir," he said.

"Might we join you, good fellow?" The handsome older officer asked.

"Of course. Please." Privet was confounded by the appearance of this man. He'd had no idea that the venerable *Swift Cannon* was in the vicinity.

The captain and his wife sat down at the small round table. The officer was bearded, his straw hair tied back in a tight knot. A gleaming blue breastplate with silver inlays of stylized sharks was visible between the dark green halves of his dress coat. The elegant Mrs. Moorsparrow looked out of place there in the simple tavern, adorned as she was in pearls and lace and the fine white material of her dress.

"Well, what's good to drink?" the senior officer asked with a smile.

"The squall is fine. It's all I've tried, truth be told," Privet replied.

"I should like some wine," the Mrs. said dryly.

Lt. Privet, less tactful than usual on account of drink, was quick to ask what it was that brought the respected naval officer to New Crown.

"We were transporting Prince Fenny up to Drumford for the wedding of the Duke when we came under fire," Moorsparrow explained, his manner turning serious. "A ball, or *something* clipped our mainmast and took two of my men with it."

Privet sat forward and nearly spilt what was left of his squall. "Heavens!"

"Queer thing it was. We heard no shot, we saw no smoke, but the lookout spotted a red sloop—red, of all colors—headed off northwest. While I was dead set on seeing the prince safely ashore, *he* insisted we give chase. Thus, we pursued the thing for two days, only glimpsing it here and there, as if it were a ghost. Got as far as this dismal rock and lost her entirely in the fog."

The captain's wife sighed. "We had a horrid time of it, winding about those silly little islands off Nellyhaunt... and *such waves!*"

"Sounds dreadful," Privet sympathized.

The captain studied the younger man. "I hear tell your ship has endured an attack not dissimilar to mine."

"Quite the same," Privet noted. "No noise from a cannon, no smoke. We never even saw what it was fired upon us. What of the prince, captain, would he be on board still?"

"We've secreted him away on shore tonight; better that, than leave him vulnerable on the *Swift Cannon*, should this mystery craft return in the night."

"Ah, yes, a wise precaution." Privet thought for a moment, then asked, "Tell, is the King not better?"

The expressions on the faces of his company answered Privet's question. Even the chilly blue eyes of the captain's wife showed a flicker of concern. King Aven and his twin, Alder, had both fallen ill several months back when spring blooms were on the boughs. Alder, the elder of the twins by a matter of minutes, had passed away as the haying season was coming to an end, and now the remaining brother appeared to be failing.

"He seems no better," Moorsparrow noted with ominous restraint.

"And the healers know not what ails him still?" The captain shook his head.

"*I* think they were poisoned," Mrs. Moorsparrow said directly.

The man hushed his wife and fished a small clay pipe out of his waist-length jacket. He filled the bowl with a pale powder blend comprised of the finest ground moths' wings and tamped it down with a pinkie. Meanwhile, the red-haired serving lass had made her way over and occupied the captain and his wife long enough to allow Privet a good long look at the winsome Hazel. *She* was moving buoyantly through the crowded tables on the other side of the room, her skirt a plum-colored breeze, her hair a shifting banner of night, as her smile—which turned to meet his—grabbed him by the heart and shook it like a dog's toy.

SEEN IN DAYLIGHT, the *Swift Cannon* did not appear as swift as its name implied. It was a massive hundred-gun, three-masted warship, and one might have imagined a number of smaller, quicker vessels overtaking a lumbering craft of the kind were it not for its impressive firepower. The ship was the best that the royal navy had to offer and many a skull beneath the sea could sing its terrible praises.

It was a majestic vessel to be sure, and handsome in spite of its bulkiness, the greater part of the sides a honeyed color, the lower third black all down to the keel; green and gold neatly defined the trim. The docks of the port looked frail and skeletal with this ship anchored there, dwarfing the smaller merchant transports and the frigate, *North Swan*.

There was fog out on the open water and the sky was gray, although a silvery sun could be glimpsed above the high cliffs, over the precipitous buildings of Old Crown. Lt. Privet stood at the base of the incline, where the long stone staircase met flat earth before making its steep ascent. He was looking down the shore to where Prince Fenny, a young man dressed in a fine russet coat and black breeches, was tossing bits of bread to sea moths. Privet walked over to join him and nodded at the two musket-toting guards that hovered nearby.

"Good morning, sir," Privet said, and saluted.

"Lieutenant."

Fenny had mild, clean-shaven features and his blond hair was pulled back into a tail that hung past his shoulders.

"I see you've some friends," Privet said, nodding toward the moths.

"Lovely, aren't they?"

The moths were the size and color of pewter dining plates.

"Yes," the lieutenant realized, "I suppose they are."

Fenny, like his father, exuded benevolence. How sad, the naval officer thought, that the patriarch was failing. At least there was some comfort in knowing that the king's twin sons would be sharing the crown, for together they embodied what made the man so effective and endearing. Fenny was conscientious, blessed with his father's compassion, while Treadson—presently off on an ambassadorial mission in the enigmatic North Islands—had inherited King Aven's savvy and assertiveness.

Observing the gentleness that Fenny extended, even to simple scavenging insects, Privet found it entirely understandable why a mighty warship had been appointed to transport the fellow to a wedding. He was a worthy heir, and with an increase in pirate activity as of late, the kingdom might have been reckless to trust Fenny's well-being to anything less.

The prince moved nearer to the surf, out where the partly submerged boulders were slathered in drippy tendrils of seaweed. He leaned forward to toss some breadcrumbs to one of the moths, which, not as quick as the rest, hadn't been able to grab any. The young man nearly slipped off the granite projection on which he was balanced. Lt. Privet's heart flinched and his body tensed, ready to spring out onto the stones to save the prince, but Fenny regained his balance and turned to smile. For a moment, Privet had felt that the whole of the kingdom, and not just that one young man, had been endangered.

THE REPAIRS TO the *North Swan* were coming along nicely, though the ship was still some days from returning to duty patrolling the western coast for pirates. This gave Lt. Privet more time to prepare... He asked the cook, who was handy with scissors, to trim his hair, and he saw to it that one of the cabin boys ironed his uniform and polished his breastplate. He did, however, shine his own boots, idiosyncratically trusting no other to do as good a job of it as he.

The cook was a stout balding man with a full white beard and a laugh like a seal's bark. He stood in the lieutenant's cabin holding a small green bottle up to the fading light of the porthole.

"A love spell, eh? I wonder what might be in it?" Holdren the cook said.

Privet was busy knotting a lacy white tie around his neck; the ends, which resembled moth wings, hung down against the blue of his chest plate. He grinned and shrugged.

The older fellow put the bottle down and wagged his head. "Love," he grumbled, "makes a man more dizzy than does a wild sea."

"Worse things to be than dizzy," Privet returned lightheartedly.

"And a *woman*..." Holdren said with a scowl, "is what a man agonizes over *not* having when he has none and then is agonized *by* once he does."

"Why, that's rather bleak," Privet said, pleased with the way his tie looked in the looking glass on the wall.

"I'll take the sea," the cook said. He looked out the round window, and added, "no less mysterious, and no less dangerous, but a might more quiet."

Privet turned and headed for the door, clapping his friend on the arm as he passed. "Wish me luck!"

NEW CROWN WAS pretty in the soft pinkish light that preceded the dusk. The round brick houses, with greenish fern-stone shingles on their conical roofs, looked homey and inviting. Lt. Privet walked from the docks, dapper in his uniform, with his sword at his side. His boots made a confident sound on the cobbles, the texture of which was accentuated by the slanted light. He gazed back at the pier, at his ship, and the larger *Swift Cannon*, which was staying on to protect the damaged vessel until the repairs were finished. Both were silhouetted against the western sky.

With one hand on the handle of his sword and the other in a pocket, holding a small glass bottle, Lt. Privet arrived at the Salty Hag. The wooden sign was squeaking on its chains as a cool breeze came in from the sea. The sign depicted a crone's severed head dangling upside down. The terrible visage sported actual hair, pale lengths taken from horses' tails. The hair moved in the air like wrack in rhythmic surf.

This structure, and nearby establishments such as the blacksmith's shop and a bakery, were rectangular in shape, unlike the many cylindrical houses of New Crown. All the buildings were brick of course, and an end wall of the tavern supported a leafy mesh of ghost eye, a vine which at this time of year bore small bluish berries that glowed when it rained. Laughter and the warm luminescence of candlelight greeted Privet as he entered through the main door.

A good crowd, Privet noted, standing in the little foyer, peering into the taproom. That was to be expected, with two military ships anchored in the harbor. The crews took turns alternately manning their vessels and visiting the town, which had little more to offer than this particular place. The lieutenant looked from one side of the room to the other until he saw *her*.

Hazel floated through the tables in a long fluid skirt the color of heather blossoms. She was lovely with her pale round face, her great green eyes, her hair a fluid mystery of nocturnal shades. Her loose white blouse had voluminous sleeves and a scooped neck that allowed generous breasts to follow gravity's sway.

A warm weight flooded Privet's head at the sight of her and he thought to himself… *Worse things to be than dizzy*.

Once again the innkeeper's daughter was sharing her duties with the little red-haired lass, and while all of the tables on Hazel's side of the room were occupied, Privet was not discouraged. He walked straight to a table where some of his crew-mates were seated and, rather than exert rank and demand that they move, offered each of the men a silvery twenty-moth piece. The men, while a bit bemused, gratefully relocated and the grinning Lt. Privet sat down alone.

Hardly a moment had passed when the officer looked up to see Hazel coming toward him, ethereally soft in the pipe smoke and candle glow. She was smiling at him. Privet, who up until that moment had been steeled and deter-mined, suddenly felt as if she could see the little bottle right through his pocket. He tried to return her smile, but his eyes were filled with apprehension.

"Evening, sir," Hazel said in her pretty voice. "What will you be havin'?"

Privet forgot to breathe, forgot how to speak.

"Sir?"

Privet straightened, cleared his throat and man-aged a word, "Squall."

Hazel repeated the word then spun to head for the bar, glancing over her shoulder and holding his eye for a moment.

The lieutenant wondered if the spell, while still contained in its bottle, could already be having an effect on the young woman. Such a look she had given him just then! She held his gaze even longer when she returned with his drink, flicking her dark hair back, leaning so close that he could practical-ly feel the heat of her bosom.

"Here you go, sir," she said.

"Thank you, miss," Privet said, and he gave her a coppery ten-moth.

"How very kind of you, sir," Hazel said, taking the coin—a handsome overpayment—and curtsying.

Left to himself, Privet got about his plan. He slipped the little bottle from his pocket and eased out the cork. Inconspicuously, he angled the vessel to tap a pinch of the contents into his dark squall. *"Just a sprinkle will do,"* the Deerfield Sisters had told him.

Right at that moment a drunken fisherman came staggering along. He was towering and loutish, with a wild red beard that obscured his body from chin to sternum. The man bumped the edge of Privet's table and the bottle of mysterious powder jarred, emptying into the drink.

"Farts!" Privet cursed.

The oaf stumbled away and Privet quickly tucked the empty bottle back into his pocket. For a brief moment he considered taking the liquid out and pouring it in the street, not knowing what it might do if taken in such quantity. Employing magic had been against his better judgment, after all. But when he looked and saw Hazel moving here and there with her dark hair and her green eyes, he found himself rooted to his seat. He would go forward with his plan. Now all he need do was hail the young woman, complain about the quality of his squall, and ask that she taste it (so, as far as the ruse went, he might prove to her that it was not worthy to serve). He was waiting for Hazel to move back toward his table when…

"Good evening, lieutenant." It was a man's voice.

Privet looked up to see a handsome bearded fellow in the dark green coat of a naval officer. The man's frilly necktie spilt over a sky blue breastplate with silver shark inlays.

"Oh, um, good evening, Captain Moorsparrow."

The refined Mrs. Moorsparrow was there as well, dressed as if she were attending a grand ball rather than visiting a port town tavern. Privet stood to salute the man and bow to the lady. When the captain asked if they might join him, the lieutenant gritted his teeth.

"Why, please do. I should be glad for the company," Privet lied.

The lieutenant felt his face frozen in a smile, felt his head nodding, heard his own voice saying casual nothings, all while desperation trembled through his innards. Hardly a second passed that he wasn't glancing at the enigmatic dark of the liquid in his mug, or turning here or there to glimpse the innkeeper's daughter, who had yet to come by to take an order from the man's guests.

Only once did Privet perk his ears with interest to something that Captain Moorsparrow said, that being when it was mentioned that locals on a fishing boat had briefly caught sight of a strange red vessel out by the Kellingrey Shoals. Privet would have pursued the topic further were it not for Mrs. Moorsparrow and her annoying cough.

She had been sitting there like a portrait in her pearls and lace and fine cream-colored dress, nibbling a handful of ghost eye berries she'd picked off the vines growing on the outside of the tavern, when one of the things got stuck in her throat and set her hacking. Her ordinarily composed face became a red grimace and she shook so hard that her neat pile of amber hair began to unravel. Impulsively, she grabbed Privet's mug of squall and brought it to her lips, gulping half of it down before the lieutenant could even cry, *"No!"*

The drink relieved the woman of her blockage. She put the mug down and sat back, sighing. Captain Moorsparrow, who looked rather embarrassed by the commotion, turned to his wife and growled out of one side of his mouth.

"Are you quite well, my dear?"

Mrs. Moorsparrow did not respond. She was staring across the table at the lieutenant.

"I say, dear, are you in fact well?" her husband persisted.

Privet grabbed the mug and looked in it to see how much of the potation was left. There was not much to see. He flicked his eyes back to the captain's wife, and saw her icy countenance melt away. Her eyes, still fastened on him, were feral with desire and her parted lips seemed to plump around her teeth as she shoved her chair back and got to her feet.

"Well," Privet said, pushing his own chair away from the table, "I best be getting back to—"

Mrs. Moorsparrow launched herself upon Lt. Privet, clamping her mouth over his before he could get another word out. She kissed him with fervor, moaning, hands like a vice squeezing the stunned man's face. The captain, bellowing curses, sprang up, sending his chair toppling, and rushed to drag his wife off of Privet.

"What, are you mad?"

Mrs. Moorsparrow struggled to get free of her spouse, thrashing, reaching her arms out to the other man. The room had fallen silent—but for the woman's beastly growling—and the captain, seeing some of his crew in the bewildered crowd, called for assistance.

"Get her to the ship!"

The two men who came forward looked hesitant to be involved in the matter, but responded dutifully. They took the woman by the arms and dragged her through the barroom. As she disappeared out the door, she could be heard calling, "I love you! I love you, Lieutenant Privet!"

Privet, meanwhile, rose from his seat and faced the enraged husband. "Terribly sorry, captain…"

"Sorry! What's all this, Privet?" The older man was gripping the handle of his short-sword.

"There was a love spell in my squall, sir, but not meant for Mrs. Moorsparrow. I swear it was intended for another."

"You lie," the captain snarled. "You've wanted my wife from first you set eyes upon her!"

"Not so, sir, honestly!"

The thin blue length of the captain's sword hissed free of its scabbard. He slapped the side of the blade down on the table, pointing the tip at the lieutenant.

"I call you to duel, Privet. Disgrace me this way, will you? You, sir, are a swine, fixing to steal a decent woman from her husband. And from a fellow officer, at that! I'll see you dead."

Privet tried to explain, but the captain marched briskly from the room, leaving him there in a hazy sea of gaping faces. He felt numb just standing alone in the middle of the room, and when he noticed Hazel gawking with the rest, he wished that he could vanish into the smoky air.

IT WAS THE afternoon following the unfortunate incident at the Salty Hag, and much had transpired in a relatively short time. First off, Privet had rushed to the captain's quarters, upon returning to the ship the night before, to explain the particulars to his commanding officer (before the man heard twisted versions of the facts from lesser sources). Captain Langham appreciated Privet's straightforwardness and believed that the man had no intention of beguiling Moorsparrow's wife. Still, he thought it best not to interfere, not wishing to chance the potentially uncomfortable politics of opposing an officer of like rank, especially when that officer was the commandant of the greatest vessel in the fleet. While secretly disappointed, Privet knew that it was a rational stance to take, all the more so for the presence of the prince. It would hardly have made a good impression on the royal heir if two of his captains were at each other's throats in a time of danger, when an unknown enemy might be lurking out in the fog.

Following the meeting with the captain, Privet retired to his cabin. He slept little, and in the morning climbed the many stone steps to Old Crown, where he again paid visit to the Deerfield Sisters. He explained his predicament, and asked if they might come with him to speak with Captain Moorsparrow, to substantiate his story (how he truly had planned to win the love of Hazel, the tavern keeper's daughter). He offered them a handsome sum for their testimony, but the old women declined.

"But why?" Privet asked.

The sisters looked to one another, then back at the lieutenant, and said, "The stairs..."

"*The stairs?*"

"Yes," they sang, "we're dreadfully afraid of heights."

The women offered to create a spell potion that, if administered to the captain, would alter the man's disposition toward Privet—a sort of magically induced benevolence. The lieutenant thanked them for the offer, but explained that there would not be an opportunity to get the stuff into the man, who was back on board the *Swift Cannon*. He hardly imagined the captain would accept a drink from him in the midst of a duel.

Privet wondered then if the women might pen a letter to Moorsparrow, something that would bolster his argument, but the sisters could neither read nor write.

And so, with no further recourse, Privet returned to his ship off New Crown and solicited his friend, the coxswain Mill Burnshire, to be his "tender." A position of honor, so far as dueling tradition went, this put it to Burnshire to make certain arrangements. He gathered a duel party... a young woman to mourn (if need be), a healer, and a "mercy man" to step in and kill his fellow, if Privet should end up wounded and suffering. This was done efficiently enough, and soon there was nothing left for Privet to do but practice.

Up on the sunny short deck of the *North Swan*, the lieutenant was going through his moves, thrusting and swiping at the cool ocean air. He had the grace of a dancer, and his blade moved with such speed that at times the coxswain Burnshire, who observed from a safe distance, could make out little more than a blue blur.

Burnshire, with his raptor nose, and hair like wild silver shrubbery, applauded his friend.

"Impressive, lieutenant, if I must say," Mill noted.

Having completed his exercises, the officer sheathed his weapon and walked over to Burnshire. The older man clapped Privet on the back.

"You are a brilliant swordsman, I'll give you that, Privet. But I wonder you didn't choose pistols."

The choice of weapon, as signified in the formal written challenge that had been delivered by a courier of Captain Moorsparrow, had been left up to Lt. Privet.

"*Pistols?* I heard tell that Captain Moorsparrow is an expert shot with a pistol."

Burnshire chuckled. "Moorsparrow, a good shot? He'd not hit the side of his ship were he ten foot from it. No, no, good fellow, Moorsparrow is a swordsman. The finest swordsman in the King's good fleet."

Privet, who *was* a keen shot with a flintlock, wagged his head and groaned.

CAPTAIN MOORSPARROW AROSE early on the morning of the duel. His wife—who was still under the care of the ship's healer and only starting to shake off the effects of the love spell—was asleep, and so he moved quietly about their cabin, putting on his uniform and chest plate. Satisfied with his reflection in the looking glass, Moorsparrow took his violin case from a cabinet in the wall and started out of the room. His scabbard bumped the doorframe as he was leaving and the woman on the bed, disturbed by the sound, muttered, *"Privet..."* The captain cursed to himself and locked the cabin door from the outside before climbing above deck.

Though the sun had yet to rise above the cliffs and houses of Old Crown, the sky's tawny haze told the captain that the day would not be bright even when the orb cleared the horizon. Still, it was as lovely a morning as he had ever witnessed. Alone but for lookouts and guards, the man stood on the stern, took out his violin, and played the mournful "Crossing at Wintbridge" to the inexplicable pewter sea. He played the tune twice, then once again, in case this was the last time he would have a chance to.

There was little activity on the opposite side of the pier, aboard the frigate *North Swan*, which was anchored in the shadow of the dwarfing *Swift Cannon*. Sentries minded their posts and lookouts monitored the dusky sea, where a slash of expanding fog haunted the horizon. Below deck in his cabin, the sleepless Lt. Privet sat penning farewell letters. He wrote to his mother back in Hemmings Port and his sister in Upper Noonbury and his favorite cousin down in Blackbirch. He even, for a moment, considered writing a wistful proclamation of love to leave for the tavern keeper's daughter.

That sad business done, the man paced in his chamber as daylight strengthened; he could hear movement here and there in other parts of the ship, and eventually there came a knock at his door. It was Mill Burnshire and the cook, Holdren (who had brought a breakfast of sausage and potato pie). Burnshire took possession of the departure missives, promising to deliver them if need be. Privet hardly sampled the food, even though sausage pie was his favorite choice for breakfast. It was time to dress.

The officer was sharp in his uniform, with his black tricorn, the double-breasted coat left open to reveal the chest plate, the frothy lace of his necktie overlapping pale blue metal. He had shined his boots so well that it looked as if the lower halves of his legs had been dipped in a starry night.

He had spoken little, and remained silent all the way over to the neighboring *Swift Cannon*, where the duel was to be fought. It was the prince who had suggested holding it on one of the vessels, not wishing to incite a morbid fuss among the locals. Better this business between officers be treated in a decorous manner, he thought. A coin had been tossed to decide which of the two ships was to host the combat.

The morning air was cool. Gulls circled beneath a drab sky and the sea had a deathly color, darker than the clouds, though distant fog was edging closer and closer to the shore. There was light enough for the masts and rigging to cast web-like shadows across the raised rear deck where three small groups of people were gathered.

Mill Burnshire walked ahead; he and the lieutenant bowed politely as they passed the duel party of the opposition. Captain Moorsparrow stood tall with hands behind his back, handsome in his woodsy green uniform, the bicorn hat worn crossways on the head, his sword at his side. He looked all the more dangerous for the contained defiance in his eyes, unwavering as he nodded his head ever so slightly to the men. Privet could have sworn that Moorsparrow smirked.

Next the coxswain and the lieutenant passed Prince Fenny and two armed guards. The young heir acknowledged the fellows from the *North Swan* with a tip of his hat and remorseful eyes. One of the wardens gave Privet a pitying look.

The third group consisted of the duel party that Burnshire had assembled. There was the tall gaunt healer from the *Swan*, Polton Juniper, holding an ominous leather satchel filled with bandages, herbs, and amputation tools. Next to him stood the "mercy man," whose identity was hidden behind the impassive black features of a metal mask. This fellow—likely a crewman from the lieutenant's own ship—was authorized to intercede with his flintlock pistol and put an end to Privet, should the duelist find himself in an irreparable state. The last of the three was a young woman in mourning black, her long dress and veil shifting as a breeze whispered in from the Gantic. It was her duty to weep and pray, and sprinkle dead spiders over his eyes, if conditions required. Privet wondered if it were his lovely Hazel behind that veil, but the wind flicked aside her concealment and he saw that it was not. A simple local girl he had never set eyes on. Better a stranger mourn than no woman at all, he thought.

Agents of the duelists, the two tenders met at the center of the raised deck and spoke quietly. Moorsparrow's representative was Lt. Barrow, a bulky little fellow with a peg leg. Violence could be avoided if Privet were willing to pay a hefty sum to his challenger, or if he were willing to throw down his sword and beg for mercy. Burnshire informed Barrow that Privet was prepared to do neither, so the tenders stepped aside and signaled for the duelists to take their positions.

Moorsparrow removed his hat, handed it to Barrow, smoothed back his straw-colored hair, then strode to the center of the deck and stopped. An arm's length of air separated the men. Privet waited for the order to come, swallowing until his throat went dry, his eyes flicking toward the slightest suggestion of motion… a gull's shadow passing over the planks, a line of rope wavering in the breeze, the flutter of his opponent's cravat.

"Swords!" the tenders called at last.

Moorsparrow's weapon hissed as he drew it from his scabbard. It was handsome with its straight thirty-inch blade of double-edged blue steel. The grip was stag's horn with a knuckle bow curving from the shaft to the pommel, which in this case was a gold skull screwed into the hollow handle, entombing a human tooth. A good luck charm of sorts, the molar was a trophy taken from the first man that Moorsparrow had slain in a sword fight.

Privet unsheathed his weapon as well, and while it too had a thin blue blade, it was less showy than his opponent's. The grip was wood, the cross guard and ball-finial simple and silver.

The men touched blades in a metallic kiss, then each took several steps back, their eyes intense and locked. They waited for the final word, legs slightly bent, backs straight, swords held out straight as if dowsing for each other's blood. The order came at last, dulled by the drumming inside ears.

"Engage!"

Privet saw nothing but a blur of dark green and a whipping blue streak as Moorsparrow sprang and thrust. The tip of the captain's sword made a terrible scraping noise as it carved a line across his chest plate—the sound caused the onlookers to cringe. A small piece of the lieutenant's tie was sliced off and fluttered like a moth. The man found himself stumbling back, slashing blindly at the charging foe. Swords clanked and rang and made swift whispers in the air.

Somehow Privet avoided taking another hit, though it was apparent that the captain was now focusing his attack above the chest plate, his swooshing blade so close that the lieutenant felt a breeze on his face. Another swipe sent Privet's hat spinning through the air.

Regaining his balance, Privet ducked into a defensive stance, nearly crouching, as Moorsparrow continued with his bold and relentless assault. Privet ducked and stabbed, the tip of his blade glancing off the lower half of the other's chest plate. Alarmed, the captain pranced back and remained still, poised cat-like with his sword out held. His eyes were a menacing squint.

Though the morning was chill, Privet felt waves of heat rushing though his head, and his heart was bouncing against the inside of his chest plate. It seemed Moorsparrow was baiting him to make an advance, but Privet took advantage of this momentary peace and tried to catch his breath. The day was no brighter, but there were still faint shadows, and Privet dropped his eyes to the deck to note the angle of his own as he turned his back to the captain.

Moorsparrow's shadow preceded him, keying Privet to spin and meet the sudden dash. Blue streaks flashed in the air—the lieutenant's tactic failing as his jab was deflected with a parrying stroke. Snarling, his coat fluttering behind, Captain Moorsparrow slashed a spitting wound down the side of Privet's sword arm. The younger man winced and nearly dropped his weapon. He swiped back in time to thwart another hit and danced sideways, pursued by a flurry of strikes. He dodged some of these, repelled others, but was not quick enough for the master swordsman Moorsparrow. A quick lunge pierced Privet in the cheek. The initial impact felt like a punch, then came searing pain and he saw red crickets leaping away from his face.

"Oh, dear!" the prince gasped, watching from a safe distance.

Privet staggered backward, flailing his steel from side to side. Graceful and composed, Moorsparrow glided forward, and with a flick of his blade swatted Privet's sword free of the bloody hand that held it. The weapon rolled, clattering across the wide boards of the deck. The lieutenant stood stunned and dripping, not daring to turn his head long enough to see how close his sword was. Moorsparrow grinned coldly and took a step closer, raising his blade to the level of the lesser officer's eyes.

"Farewell, lieutenant," the captain murmured.

A soft hiss came on the air, just before a great invisible fist punched the side of the *Swift Cannon*. Privet toppled onto his back and his opponent slid sideways, as if the deck were ice. The ship rocked so violently that those witnessing the duel were tossed. The women screamed and the men bellowed and before the ship could steady itself, another impact blew a hole in the hull.

Moorsparrow waved his sword in the air, "We're under fire!" he called. He shouted orders to his crew, suddenly unmindful of the wounded Lt. Privet.

"A red sloop," the lookout called down, pointing into the fog, which by now had closed the distance between horizon and shore.

The prince was clinging to the railing and staring out into the thick haze. His guards pulled him away and were urging him toward the aft hatchway when a boulder of wind came soaring and shattered one of the armed men. The prince was pummeled by red spray and sharp bits of broken chest plate. The surviving warden tugged the young prince down as another swoosh of air flew over the deck.

Privet pulled himself up and squinted into the mist. He glimpsed the red sloop for a second— like a wound opening in the fog—and then it was gone. He noticed the ruined guard's musket lying on the deck and picked it up, taking aim. When the sloop reappeared it was much closer, so close that he could see figures standing on the deck, figures in long black cloaks. Then, like a ghost, it vanished.

The *Swift Cannon* began to shake again, but this time it was from the firing 42-pounders on board and not the invisible projectiles from the attacking craft. Portside cannons were roaring, coughing great clouds that blurred into the fog. Plumes of water shot up out of the Gantic where the "round shot" hit.

By now the crew of the neighboring *North Swan* was aware of the situation, and men were running to their posts. There was nothing for them to do, however, for Moorsparrow's great warship stood between them and the mystery vessel.

Despite his pain and the dizzying mist in his head, Lt. Privet held to his spot atop the high rear deck, sighting along the barrel of the dead guard's musket. He thought that he saw a red blur in the fog, and then again, even closer. He clicked back the cock and waited until he could get a clearer view, which, eventually, he did.

The sloop was red, sails and all, and the bald women in their long black cloaks stood out starkly against the crimson of their vessel and the pale smoky air. There were round wooden barrels between them, and the women were plucking things out of them—skulls it seemed, though at such a distance it was hard to be sure—and holding them above their heads. Privet saw one of the women hurl a round object his way. His finger found the trigger.

The musket kicked and clapped and the woman, struck by the ball, spun back and fell as the red ship slipped from sight once more. The skull faded also, as it became a ferocious ball of wind that blasted into a gunport beneath where Privet was standing. The *Swift Cannon* shuddered.

The impacts now came in a flurry—it felt as if a giant were kicking the side of the craft. Ragged craters were blown into the gundecks, where agonized cries could be heard. The ship was being destroyed.

"Privet!"

The lieutenant turned and saw Captain Moorsparrow standing with a pistol in his hand. The captain cringed as another explosion shook the ship.

"The prince! Where is the prince? We need to move him off the ship before she goes under."

"He's below," Privet said, pointing to the hatchway where the guard had taken the heir.

"Blast!" Moorsparrow cursed. He rushed off into the pungent cannon smoke that the breeze had blown back over the deck.

The air hissed and a mighty force slammed into the side of the ship just feet away from where Privet was standing. The railing snapped and boards flew and the man was knocked flat back. His vision went dark momentarily, and his ears were ringing when he found himself lying there, looking up at the sky.

"Strange…" he muttered.

Gazing into the blurry air, the young officer noticed small gray objects overhead. They were above the masts, and hardly bigger than dining plates from what he could tell. Winged creatures, Privet concluded, moths the color of pewter, and they were carrying small white sacks, and flying over the *Swift Cannon*, down into the mist where the red sloop hid.

The aft hatch banged open and Moorsparrow came up, pistol first, followed by Prince Fenny and his guard. One of the unseen meteors whistled by and everyone on deck hunched down for a moment. The skull-wind missed, however, and while the men waited for more, none came. At length the captain called for his gun crews to cease firing. It grew still and quiet.

Women's voices came floating through the mist, through the gun smoke, as the red sloop floated out of the vapor and hovered off the portside of the towering warship. The bald women in dark cloaks were calling over to the *Swift Cannon*. Captain Moorsparrow hurried to the side of his crippled vessel and aimed his pistol down at one of them.

"Die, you wench!" he called.

"Wait," Prince Fenny said, grabbing the officer's arm, "Listen…"

The red sloop was now clearly visible and drifting closer, the large grayish moths lighting on the ropes and watching impassively with eyes like juniper berries. The words of the women could be distinguished, the same words repeating like a chant…

"We love you! We love you! We love you!"

Fenny recognized one of the people on the mystery craft, but this individual was not a bald woman, though he too wore the long black cloak. It was a clean-shaven young man with boyish features and blond hair pulled back into a tail that hung past his shoulders. It was his twin brother,

Prince Treadson, and he was chanting along with the rest.

A FINE DRIZZLE blew off the Gantic into Old Crown, but Privet was comfy and dry, sitting in the humble parlor of the pretty old Deerfield Sisters. A nice fire heated the room and the place smelled of bergamot and old linens.

"Tea?" the sisters asked.

"Thank you," the man said, smiling.

Once tea and jam cakes were on hand, the sisters, who always spoke in unison, sat down with their guest.

"What a terrible man, that Prince Treadson," they chimed.

"Indeed," Privet said. "Seems he'd been thrown together a bit too closely with those folks of the North Islands. Ahh, but he's always been a hungry one, and with Fenny dead he'd be the singular heir. *That* was his intent in attacking the ships, it would seem."

"Strange magic those women of the North Isles have," the sisters said, "and not so nice as the kind we're like to cast. A shame he got in with that lot, but what a dreadful man to want to do away with his very twin."

"Well," Privet said, "he'd have made to kill poor Fenny whether he was in with them or not, I should think. Some claim he even poisoned the kings."

The afternoon moved along slowly, the wind freckling rain on the windows, good oak logs keeping a steady blaze in the firebox. There was more tea and more talk.

"What of the moths and the spell?" Privet asked at length.

"It was your doing, in a sense," the old women said.

"*My* doing? Do tell."

"Well, when you paid visit and asked us to act on your behalf, after that dreadful business with the love spell and the captain's wife, oh, didn't we feel just awful? And we so wanted to prevent that nasty duel."

"Hm, yes." Privet absently touched his bandaged cheek.

"But we knew you'd not be able to pour a drink of love potion in the fellow, and so we got thinking. Perhaps there was another way to get a spell to an intended person."

Privet sipped his tea and nodded.

"Powder," they said together. "We thought to try a love spell as a powder. We'd never done such a thing, you know; our love spells were in liquid form always."

"Yes, I recall."

The women sat forward, enthusiastic, eyes gleaming in the hearth-light. "We weren't even certain it would work, we must admit, but we meant it for you, initially. Unfortunately we weren't quite ready with it in time to stop the duel, but thank the gods we had it in time to put an end to that dreadful ship battle."

The carrier moths had dropped small sacks of powdered love potion onto the deck of the red sloop. The bursting clouds of dust had indeed delivered the spell to those on board.

"So," the Deerfields asked, "what becomes of the princes now?"

Privet said, "Well, that rotter Treadson is in dungeon at Castle Wickheath and is like to hang. Fenny will be king when his father's time comes, and a fine king he will make, I believe."

"And you, lieutenant?"

"I'll be at New Crown for some time. They've ordered my ship to stand guard for the *Swift Cannon* while she's under repair. As for Captain Moorsparrow, he has now accepted that the spell his wife drank down was not in fact intended for her. He's apologized heartily, and now can't seem to do enough for me. Perhaps one day we shall even sail together."

"How nice. Then we'll see you again?"

"Yes, I believe you may."

Evening was closing in when the young officer set out to leave. It was still damp and the long line of gray steps heading to the newer half of the city were slick and precarious. The sisters, hunched under a single umbrella, had insisted on escorting him there, though, fearful of heights, they did not venture too near the cliff edge.

"Well," Privet said, "I'm off to the inn. There's something I need say to a certain young woman there."

One of the sisters grinned and produced a small bottle of love potion from under her shawl. She held it out.

"Thank you, but no. I think I'd rather take my chances."

Privet smiled, tipped his tricorn and started down the long, precipitous ribbon of stairs.

CHINANDEGA

Lucius Shepard

Have you never been to Chinandega, my friend? It is no place for tourists.

AT SUNRISE A third-class bus from the capital wheezes and grinds across the coastal plain, the passengers packed so tightly they might be chained together in the darkened interior. The driver hunches over the wheel as though bound to some grim purpose. There are no empty seats so the fare collector stands with back braced against the windshield, holding hard to a stainless steel grip, enduring jolts and sideways lurches, his weary face cast in chiaroscuro as he looks into the east toward three volcanoes limned against the reddening sky. Stars in the west still shine in ancient configuration above the Gulf of Fonseca.

Waking amidst the staleness of sleeping bodies and the smell of diesel, Alvaro Miguez cannot feel his foot and bends to rub it, pushing a drooping wing of black hair from his eyes. A copper-and-roses complexion bespeaks his Mayan blood. His head is large, and his prominent features register emotion slowly if at all. His hands, too, are large, but his frame is compact and this lends him a dwarfish aspect. Straightening, he's startled to discover the seat beside him, empty when he fell asleep, occupied by a gaunt old farmer with an apocalyptic eye, clouded like an embryo and crossed by a machete scar that notches both cheek and brow. His jeans are creased, his plaid shirt buttoned at the wrists. He tips his straw hat to Alvaro, bids him good morning, and asks where he's going.

Chinandega, says Alvaro.

And what will you do there?

I'm on vacation.

The farmer looks askance at him. Have you never been to Chinandega? Unless you have relatives there, or some pressing errand, you would do well to take your holiday elsewhere. The heat is infernal, better suited to tarantulas than men. Half the town remains in ruins from the earthquake in 'seventy-two, and drunken sailors overrun the other half. The whores outnumber the cockroaches and are equally as vile. It is no place for tourists, my friend. A town without a soul.

Alvaro, who studies literature at the university, recognizes that the farmer is an old-fashioned sort and speaks from a Catholic perspective; but nettled by the implication that he is a tourist in his own country, he replies that he does not expect to stay in the city—he plans to find transportation to El Cardon, the island where Ruben Dario wrote a number of his most famous poems. If he intends this comment to demonstrate his intellectual superiority (and perhaps he does, for Alvaro, though not snobbish by nature, has a temper), it has a minimal effect. The old man nods, tips his hat down over his eyes and goes to sleep. An hour or so later, the bus pulls up beside a freshly tilled field and, without a fare-thee-well, the farmer climbs down and strides off along the rows. The field extends to the horizon and Alvaro can see no sign of habitation, not a shed or a shack or even a clump of trees that might shelter a *casita*. It's as if the old man's destination is an infinity of black dirt and pale cloudless blue, as if he has been produced from that medium solely for the purpose of issuing his warning.

HE TOOK BREAKFAST at a restaurant frequented by railway workers, a place of blue-and-white painted boards isolated in a landscape of cinders and weeds, close to the tracks of the *Ferrocaril Pacifico* that crossed the western edge of the city center. After eating, he walked among the tables, showing his sister's picture to the other diners. The photograph was of a pretty fourteen year-old whose looks were more *mestiza* than pure Mayan, and he told the men she was a year older now than portrayed and likely had exchanged her schoolgirl uniform for a more provocative costume.

She is a whore? The man who asked this question was middle-aged, grizzled, fat, and covered with soot, having just come off-shift at the railyard.

So I have heard, said Alvaro.

Well, if she's whored for a year, she's had more dicks in her than there are hairs on a goat, said the man, making sure everyone in the restaurant could hear him. She probably looks like a goat by now.

The other men laughed and, encouraged by this response, the fat man said, Are you sure she is your sister? It appears to me that your mother was shot by two different pistols.

Laughter trailed Alvaro out the door, his cheeks burning with anger and shame.

Though not yet nine o'clock, it was already hot. He removed his shirt, knotting it about his waist, and went along a wide treeless street, Calle del Pacifico, lined with cantinas, shops, restaurants, and hotels whose rooms rented by the hour. Mostly buildings of one or two stories, concrete block done in pastel shades of pink, tan, blue, with lifeless neon signs: they bore on their walls false promises of what lay within: shiny billiard balls and green felt tables adorned a pool hall with warped cues and tattered tables worn to a mossy hue; quarter notes cavorted among bubbles rising from champagne glasses that were tilted at angles suggestive of merriment, decorating the façade of a cantina that had never known the pop of a cork. Many of the businesses had been open since seven, some never closed, but others were just opening, men spraying the sidewalks to wash away the night's debris and rolling up their several corrugated iron doors with a horrid rattling like a portcullis being raised. Vendors squatted curbside, offering cigarettes and sandwiches, displaying cheap jewelry and T-shirts and toys on spread blankets. A few cars jounced over the potholed asphalt and scooters zipped past, making sounds that seemed the amplified buzzing of the flies fussing over a dead cat in the gutter. Greater sounds came from the sky, faint metallic shrieks and drones that formed an umbrella of industrial noise over the town—Alvaro imagined they derived from the container port at Corinto, though it lay miles away.

As he ranged the street, showing his photograph to whoever would look, the sun climbed toward meridian, leaching vitality and color from the scene, appearing to shed a ghastly white pall, almost palpable, as if a gauze winding sheet had been prematurely wrapped about his eyes. Heat pressed in on him, like the heat from a burning forest. The thought of his sister in that heat, among these men, in a windowless back room on an iron bed with stained sheets, it never left him. At the end of the street stood an old frame hotel of forbidding aspect, like a castle without turrets: the Hotel Circo del Mar, three stories of dark green boards with a peaked roof and windows glazed with dazzling reflection that give no evidence of the interior, its entrance guarded by a burly man with a bandito mustache and a holstered pistol.

Alvaro showed him the photograph and asked if he had seen his sister. Her name, he said, is Palmira Miguez. The man told him to fuck off.

That afternoon, he bought a *bocadillo* from a vendor and sat in the doorway of a closed cantina, the only shade available. A starving yellow dog stared hopefully at him from the curb, until Alvaro shied a pebble at it. The stringy meat of the sandwich expanded in his mouth, and he thought that the dog, which had not gone far, sniffing at rubbish in the gutter, may have been attracted by the intoxicating odor of an ex-brother-in-misery. A ragged boy sat beside him in the doorway and, his face arranged into piteous lines, held out his hand and muttered, I am hungry, Senor. Give me a cordoba. My belly aches. Five centavos for bread, *por favor.* Alvaro told him to beat it, but the boy persisted and finally Alvaro broke off a corner of the sandwich and gave it to him. The boy looked disappointed, but popped the fragment into his mouth. He chewed for a while, appearing to assess Alvaro, and then said, Do you wish to buy drugs, Senor? Marijuana? Heroin? Cocaine? I can take you.

I am searching for my sister. Alvaro let him see the photograph.

The boy reacted excitedly. I have seen this girl, Senor. Perhaps I can assist in your search.

Bullshit, said Alvaro.

No, I have seen her! May Dona Bisalia take me if I have not. Where she sleeps, I do not know. But I have seen her... on this very street.

Alvaro examined the boy's face. You're lying.

The boy shrugged. As you wish. But I can guide you to a man who can tell you where she is.

Who is this man?

The Recluse.

Now you're fucking with me.

No, Senor! I am not. Everyone knows of the Recluse, and he knows everyone. He lives in Colonia San Jeronimo. It is very far, but I will take you there for three cordobas. You will not regret it, I promise you.

They negotiated a price of two cordobas, to be paid after the boy had discharged his duty, and started off in the direction of the container port. Colonia San Jeronimo was, indeed, very far. As they trudged over dirt roads, past garbage dumps and through disastrous slums, Alvaro chastised himself for allowing the boy to hustle him. At last they came to a shack with a rusting tin roof in the midst of a patch of cocoa-colored earth, set well apart from others like it. Alvaro knocked and a man's voice said from within, Who is it?

Alvaro Miguez, from the capital. I wish to speak to the Recluse. I am looking for my sister.

After a silence the man said, You may enter.

The boy snatched the money from Alvaro's hand and ran off. Alvaro shook his head. What an idiot he had been.

The gloomy interior of the shack was as expected, though its owner was not. Sacks of flour, beans, and rice hung from the rafters. A bicycle rested in one corner; in another, a small charcoal

stove and some pots and pans. Magazines and
shoes, heaps of clothing, piles of notebooks, and
an assortment of tools littered a packed dirt floor.
Wearing a pair of shorts, the Recluse reclined in a
red-and-blue hemp hammock strung at the center
of the room. He was not the ancient of days that
Alvaro had presumed. In his late twenties, pale
and handsome as a pop star, with long hair hanging over his shoulders: he gazed languidly at
Alvaro and indicated that he should have a seat on
a nearby stool. The tattoo of an antique box camera, realistically achieved, on his left arm and a
gold piercing beneath his lower lip were his only
visible adornments.

Do you have a picture? he asked.

Alvaro handed him the photograph. The
Recluse angled it so that it caught the light from a
rear window. After considerable study, he said,
Her name is Palmira, is it not?

Surprised by this, Alvaro said, You know her?

I have seen her.

Where is she? Can you tell me?

First there is the matter of payment. How much
money do you have?

If I am frugal, enough for a week.

What did you pay the boy?

Again surprised, Alvaro asked how he knew
about the boy, and the Recluse said, He ran past
my window. How much?

Two cordobas.

The Recluse made a disapproving sound. You
should have paid no more than one. Give me

thirty cordobas and you will not need to stay a week.

Reluctantly, Alvaro passed him the money.

Your sister is with Dona Bisalia, the Queen of the Whores, said the Recluse. Or so she is called.

Alvaro recalled that the boy had made mention of Dona Bisalia and informed the Recluse of this fact.

Because she is an exotic, people invest her with the powers of a witch… or a goddess, said the Recluse. I tend to believe she is neither.

Surely you *know* she can be neither?

Death and the mystery of death are the only certainties. Dona Bisalia is not without power. In the mystical order, she stands between the seven and the nine. The Recluse reached down blindly to the floor, groped for and retrieved a pack of cigarettes. You can find your sister at the Circo del Mar, but you must wait three days. The Queen is hosting a private party for a group of government officials and fruit company executives, and the hotel is closed to all but the invited.

And my sister will be there?

Your sister is a favorite of the house. She commands the highest prices. It is nearly inconceivable that she will not be there. But it may be possible to approach her when she is outside the hotel. Sometimes she takes a promenade in the early afternoon, during the siesta. There is an arcade two blocks down from the hotel—Juegos Galaxia. She enjoys playing the racing games when few customers are about.

A car engine turned over outside, but faltered; someone cursed in frustration.

How do you know these things? asked Alvaro. You are called a recluse, yet I cannot imagine you acquired this information without leaving your house.

To be reclusive demands isolation, this is true; but isolation need not be a matter of geography. The Recluse lit a cigarette and directed his smoke toward the window. I realized early on that I was cut out for an idle life. I cast about for a profession that would allow me to indulge my disposition, but found none that met my requirements. And then it struck me that people were always asking questions and that they would pay to have them answered. Since I had no intention of relocating, I began gathering information about Chinandega.

The car engine fired up again, rumbled to life, and then died. Several people began shouting at once.

The Calle del Pacifico was the perfect conduit, said the Recluse. Everyone in town had reason to go there. I wandered up and down the street, mainly at night, when it was most alive, and I listened, I watched. I spoke to no one, interacted with no one—I merely observed. In the midst of revelry and strife, pleasure and pain, I remained distant. Before the year was out people began coming to me, asking if I had seen this person or that, or if I knew where the cocaine dealer with the little black dog had gone. I have performed this service for thirteen years. The longer I performed it, the more expert I grew in interpreting information, in understanding the principles of connectivity. My thoughts became less thoughts than meditations upon the world's facticity. I know so much about the Calle del Pacifico, I am able to anticipate events from changes in the patterns of information. Indeed, thanks to this gift I have learned the answers to larger, albeit trivial questions. I can tell you, for instance, when the world will end and how it will transpire. I am always...

You know the exact date? Or do you mean something imprecise like, let us say, sometime during the next century?

I know the precise hour and minute, the Recluse said, irritated by the interruption. May I continue?

Yes, of course.

I'm always cataloguing information, the Recluse went on. Always excising inessential and outdated details. As a result I have very little interior life relating to my personal concerns. So you see, I am more of a recluse than a hermit in his cave. And my ambition has been satisfied. Many people pay me considerably greater sums than thirty cordobas, thus enabling me to live idly.

What of friends? Alvaro asked. And women? Do you not feel the lack of them?

Friends! The Recluse seemed to ridicule the idea, passing it off with a laugh and a dismissive wave. As for women, they, too, have a need for information. Occasionally I permit them to pay in a currency other than cordobas.

You say you can anticipate events. What do you anticipate, if anything, for me?

The Recluse flipped his cigarette out the window. I will not disturb the order by telling you what may or may not happen. It is enough to know that you will find your sister.

Well, then, said Alvaro, seeking some way to validate the Recluse's information. Tell me when the world will end. Surely my knowing that will change nothing.

It is a peculiarity of men that they tend to place a value on information in inverse proportion to its relevance, said the Recluse. This seems strange to me, but it is a rule I am, out of financial necessity, compelled to obey. For the answer to that question, you must pay a thousand cordobas.

AT DUSK THE Calle del Pacifico woke from its day-long lethargy. The crowds thickened; the vendors became aggressive, shouting the virtues of their wares, setting up grills on the street, these small fires adding to the suffocating heat, and soon the smells of barbecued meat and frying dough mixed with the vague industrial odor of the town; the neon signs were switched on, girdling each block with an embroidery of glowing words, with lime green parrots, purple sombreros, indigo cats, a winking, glittering bestiary, and, as the stars materialized, the sky yielded its dominion to the greater magnitudes of the street below, growing unimportant, an afterthought like a black cloth dropped over a child's model railroad. Walking in groups, sailors from China, from Poland, from Cuba and Angola and America, added their voices to the rubric of music from the bars, pop laments and *punta,* salsa, reggae, and rock. Seething from doorways, the whores of Chinandega pounced on them, tugged at their elbows, fondled their genitals, sleek young girls and fat *mamacitas* and dried-out addicts, their breasts overflowing tube tops and halters, their asses sculpted by mini-skirts and hot pants, peroxide blondes and natural brunettes, black girls from Bluefields and Corn Island, sallow girls from Grenada and Jinotega, all cajoling and demanding and laughing shrilly. A drab infestation that marginally corrupted the general hilarity, beggars shuffled and limped and crawled about the edges of the crowd: shrunken widows in black shawls; abandoned mothers with infants-in-arms; mutilated victims of the Dole Corporation, some missing a hand, some an arm or a leg, but most suffering from the kidney disease that afflicted cane workers and banana workers alike, turning their skins saffron and causing them to piss blood when they could piss at all, barely able to stand, their black stares tunneled inward, empty of vitality, so enfeebled that when they murmured their entreaties you heard only a faint sibilance like the speech of dead men, a few last words extracted by dint of magic from desiccated lungs and bloated tongues, offering inaudible cautions as to what lay beyond the borders of life.

Alvaro had witnessed such scenes in the capital, yet despite its chaos, he sensed that this one possessed a hint of ritual, of organization, and, as he skirted the crowd, passing a clump of young men with cruel mask-like faces and lava flows of black hair and sharply drawn eyebrows and scythe-like mustaches, smoking in the doorway of a shop, he saw that eight or nine smiling men were gently urging people back, creating an aisle down the center of the street that allowed the passage of a yellow-skinned woman with masses of black curls and swelling breasts, a magnificent woman in the full bloom of maturity, clad in a black bustier, high heels and a diaphanous nightgown worked with black lace. She, too, smiled and her smile broadened whenever she stopped to address someone, before proceeding onward in the direction of the Circo del Mar. Behind her came six... no, seven men of grim mien and erect carriage, whose eyes shifted to the left and right as if seeking out a threat.

As the woman drew near, Alvaro pushed to the front of the crowd, the better to see her, for he knew the woman must be Dona Bisalia. She paused to exchange words with a whore not far away, and the whore inclined her head as if receiving a blessing. The lace pattern on her nightgown was composed of interlocking scorpions and the material of her bustier was worked all over with a design of satin faces that appeared to change expression as the light shifted across them. A gold choker with a green stone, the green of the Circo del Mar, encircled her throat. She moved on from the whore and, to Alvaro's surprise, stopped in front of him, engaging him with a steady look and eyes as shiny and depthless as chitin.

What is your name, boy? she asked in a deep yet feminine voice, and touched his naked chest with a tapered black fingernail (or perhaps it was dark green, for he realized now her bustier and robe were of that color).

He told her his name. She repeated it and then asked, Do you know me?

He intended to respond in the negative, yet he felt thickheaded and all he could manage was a nod. Though she stood eye to eye with him, he had a sense that he was in the presence of a giantess, that she was in actuality immense and her apparent normalcy was a disguise, or else this was the way men saw her, their senses incapable of grasping her true dimensions. She continued to talk, chatting about the possibility of rain, about this and that, the sort of things a politician might say to charm a voter, and he came to think her voice was produced by a system of pipes connected to a great organ miles away, and that he heard only its faint resonance. One of the nine who had preceded her staggered sideways, as if overcome by fatigue, then slumped to the pavement and lay still. No one came to his aid and, although she noticed the fallen man's plight, Dona Bisalia did not appear to be in the least perturbed.

You must come to see me, she said to Alvaro, a pronouncement that had less the ring of an invitation than of a statement of simple fact, and walked on toward the Circo del Mar, whose windows blazed with many-colored lights.

The crowd closed in behind her, hiding the body from view, and Alvaro, dismayed by the man's apparent death, by the indifference shown by those in the vicinity, and equally dismayed by his reaction to Dona Bisalia, wandered onto a side street, where it was darker and comparatively quiet, hoping to sort out his impressions. On a corner, under a streetlamp, some kids, five or six of them, were sniffing glue from paper sacks with wet bottoms, and he noticed that one was the boy who had guided him to the home of the Recluse. He waved, but the boy, though staring straight at him, gave no sign of recognition. His face had acquired a sullen aspect and he and his fellows, who all wore the same expression, the same ragged clothing, shuffled aimlessly and bumped shoulders and stumbled beneath the lamppost, like a troop of imps separated from a larger force, cut off from the vigor and direction of their master's will.

HE SPENT THE night in La Gatita Blanca, a brothel that also served as a hotel, in a room that smelled of stale joy, windowless, with a standing floor lamp that shed a bilious light and walls of unfinished stone and a round bed fitted with a plastic sheet. It had a mirrored ceiling, but the mirror was so befogged and bespeckled that all he saw standing beneath was a rough caricature of his face—he imagined that the act of love would show as an indefinite thrashing, more disturbing than arousing. The plastic sheet felt greasy to his touch. He sat in a wooden chair against the back wall and thought about Dona Bisalia; but the whores refused to leave him in peace, tapping on the door and whispering temptations through the thin plyboard. Eventually they stopped, but after an interval of a half-hour there came a knock and a girlish voice said, May I have a moment of your time, senor? This approach was so direct and child-like, he opened the door and found a young *mestiza* standing in the corridor, wearing a white cotton shift that reminded him of Palmira's nightdresses. She asked if she could talk with him, saying that the malediction was upon her and thus she could not work, and further that she was lonely. Would he mind if she kept him company for a while?

He admitted her and she perched on the edge of the bed in the dungeon-like room, sitting with her hands between her knees. She looked no older than Palmira, resembling her somewhat, and had about her a playful air that further reminded him of his sister. Her name was Adalina and she hailed from the neighboring town of Chichigalpa. The death of her father from the kidney disease had forced her to become a whore. He felt at ease with her and talked of Palmira, saying that he intended to remove her from the Circo del Mar and bring her home.

Adalina's mouth tightened and then she said, Perhaps she had a reason for choosing this life.

We are not wealthy, said Alvaro. Yet there is always enough food, enough money for clothing and schoolbooks. What other reason could she have had aside from desperation?

There may have been trouble at home.

Alvaro denied this vehemently.

You seem defensive, she said teasingly. Did she catch you staring at her *tetas*?

If you're going to talk like that, get out!

Calm down! I was making a joke. Once she had succeeded in placating him, she said, You will have to ask her why she ran away, but I can tell you this much: Dona Bisalia will never permit her to leave.

Who is this Dona Bisalia that people are in such awe of her.

Cocaine dealers have their saint; whores have their queen. It's as simple as that.

She is the queen of *all* whores?

All? I cannot say. But her influence is wide. Men come from America, from Chile and Argentina, to speak with her. She has great wisdom. From her window, it is said that one can see the floor of heaven.

Once you scratched the surface of how people felt about Dona Bisalia, Alvaro thought, the oil of superstition came welling up.

She stands between the seven and the nine, Adalina said. She...

Does that refer to the nine men who led her down the Calle del Pacifico last night? The seven who came behind?

She shrugged. It's just something I've heard.

What else have you heard?

Adalina gave the matter some thought and said, That a man can die from standing too near her, yet in her embrace he can be reborn.

Alvaro cast his mind back to the weary manner of the man's collapse on the Calle del Pacifico, and remembered how drained and unsteady he had felt when she spoke to him, as if affected by some radiation emitted by her flesh. He questioned Adalina further, but she grew petulant, saying that people talked constantly of Dona Bisalia—how could she be expected to retain it all? She coaxed him to join her on the bed, to get some rest, assuring him that the sheet was clean, and Alvaro, overcome by stress and fatigue, surrendered to temptation and lay beside her, thinking they might find innocent solace in each other's arms. Looking up at the mirror, he saw his reflection with relative clarity, but of Adalina he saw patches of her white shift— clouds of grime and discoloration obscured the remainder of her image and this seemed to devalue the notion of innocence. After a minute or two she began to caress his chest and stomach, and offered to gratify him orally for ten cordobas. He gave her five and evicted her from the room. She stood in the corridor, complaining loudly that he had cheated her and that he had taken up more than ten cordobas of her time; but as she walked away he heard her telling another whore how the fool in Room Nine had paid five cordobas for nothing.

* * *

JUEGOS GALAXIA CONTAINED three rows of video games, with a cashier's counter at the rear and posters of movie villains and rock stars affixed to the walls. After satisfying himself that Palmira was not inside (there were barely a handful of customers firing chain guns and energy bolts at a variety of monsters), Alvaro went outside to wait. Because it was Sunday, the street was almost deserted. Beggars drowsed in the doorways and a drunk staggered zombie-like along the opposite side of the street, seeking shelter from the dynamited white glare of the sun. A bearded man sat in the gutter, repeatedly touching the blood that matted his temple, disturbing the flies gathered about the wound, and singing brokenly to himself. It seemed a place from which the tide had retreated, leaving behind this debris. Half a block from the arcade, a middle-aged woman in a thin dress, its pattern effaced by repeated launderings, paced agitatedly in front of a doorway, accosting strollers and shrieking at passing cars. Another drunk, thought Alvaro. Yet rarely did you see a woman make such a public display. Curious, he moved closer. Huddled in the doorway behind the woman was a dead man. His eyes were open, but had begun to glaze, and a grayish pallor suffused his saffron-colored skin. Apparently he had been set there to beg the previous evening and had succumbed to the kidney disease during the night. When the woman noticed Alvaro, she ran at him and clutched his shirt and begged him to help move her husband's body. Her worn face was contorted in anguish, her hands patting and clawing at his chest.

I cannot, he said. I have an appointment. But I will call the authorities to help you.

The woman seemed only to have heard *I cannot*. Wild-eyed, she cursed Alvaro and spat at him, calling him a coward and the son of a whore, and she continued reviling him as he backed toward Juegos Galaxia, calling upon God to punish him. Once inside the arcade he approached the cashier and asked him to make the call. The cashier, who was of the same approximate age of Alvaro, said it was none of his business; but Alvaro, shaken by the woman's ferocity and the sight of her husband in the awkward rectitude of death, gave him money and the cashier relented.

Chinandega, Alvaro told himself, was all that the farmer on the bus had said it would be: hot and vile and soulless. He took a seat in front of a shooter game and for the next half-hour tried to smooth out the tumble of his angry thoughts by slaying demons that were turned into yellowish ooze when struck by a sufficiency of bullets. He looked away from the screen now and again, checking the entrance, and came to realize that a woman seated at a game closer to the street bore a resemblance to his sister in coloration and carriage. She wore skintight pink jeans and an off-the-shoulder blouse. Gold bracelets encircled her wrists and dark curls frosted with blond highlights framed her face. Her lips were sketched in carmine and she had on so much eye shadow that from a distance her eyes appeared to have been replaced by deep pits. She looked to be nineteen or twenty, but as he came toward her he saw more youthful and familiar lines emerge from the shell of makeup.

Palmira? he said, still not convinced that this slut could be his sister.

She glanced up sharply and her face hardened. She returned her attention to the roaring, tire-squealing game, maneuvering a red bullet-shaped car between two others and taking the lead in the race. He was tempted to drag her into the bath-room and scrub her face until her natural beauty was restored.

Palmira, he said again and, when she gave no response, he put his hand on the steering wheel, sending the red car flipping end-over-end into the infield, where it burned with unnaturally steady digital flames.

Cono! Palmira said, and pricked the back of his hand with a fingernail, drawing a drop of blood.

That's what you have to say to me? Alvaro asked. After a year?

Don't exaggerate! It hasn't been a year.

All right. Eleven months.

It's closer to ten.

If he hadn't been so furious, Alvaro might have been amused at how quickly they had dropped back into a pattern of childish bickering. Fine, he said. Whatever. Is that all you have to say after leaving without a word? Mama and Papa...

What should I have told them? That I was running away? That would have been self-defeating.

She looked pleased with herself, as if the concept of self-defeat were something she had only recently mastered. He caught her by the arm and tried to pull her to her feet, but she clung to the seat and said, What are you doing?

Taking you home.

She shook him off. I go where I please, nowhere else. I am one of Dona Bisalia's girls.

So you want to be a whore? You sound as if you are proud of it.

And why not? I love to fuck. Men like me. A good whore is the remedy for the illness of marriage. Just ask Papa. Do you still believe he spends his Friday evenings in church? He's on his knees, all right. Licking some whore's *pipote*.

Though Palmira had always been a rebellious girl, Alvaro was shocked to hear her talk in this manner. He tried another tack. Mama thinks you are dead, he said.

Well, now you can tell her I am alive, she said pertly. I am not Mama. I have no wish to make a respectable marriage to a man I do not love and live like a mouse in his shadow. That was my future if I stayed. It's different for you. You are a good scholar. I only had two choices… and I have chosen.

What is your future now? Is it any better than the one you would have had at home?

Who can say? Whatever it may be, it is not Mama's. Dona Bisalia is my mother now.

Alvaro felt like slapping her. How can you say such a thing? Have you forgotten the woman who gave you life... who nurtured you?

Mama may have nurtured me, but it is Dona Bisalia who has given me life. Soon she will rise to her true estate and I will share in it. She picked up her purse, snapped it shut, and her distant, reverent tone grew terse. Anyway, what do you care? We were never close.

That's a lie. Who walked you to school each day? Who walked you home at night?

Palmira seemed about to say something, but she bit back the words and stood. I have to go.

Alvaro followed her as she went toward the dark green fortress of the Circo del Mar, trying to think of some logic or persuasive truth that would move her; but he was at a loss for words. He had expected Palmira to be grateful for his intercession or, if not grateful, sympathetic and glad to see him. He could not have predicted her utter disdain for what he had to say. He began telling her about her friends, how they were faring, seeking to awaken nostalgia, but though she expressed mild interest, her step did not falter and, on reaching the corner across from the brothel, she kissed him on the cheek and wished him a safe trip back to the capital.

I want to talk more, he said. Tomorrow. Can you meet me tomorrow?

So you can argue with me? What's the point?

I am your brother! Despite what you say, I have missed you. I haven't seen you for a year.

Ten months.

I have missed you, Palmira, he repeated. Can't you spare an hour to take a cup of coffee with me?

She hesitated and then said, If you promise not to argue, I will meet you at noon in the arcade.

He promised, she kissed him again and walked briskly off. Two men guarded the entrance of the brothel and, as she passed between them and ascended the stairs, she exaggerated the swing of her hips, causing one of the men to shake his hand loosely in a gesture of lascivious appreciation and share a laugh with the other.

ALVARO WAS ANGRY with himself for not having been more forceful, although he blamed Palmira's shallowness and self-absorption for sapping his aggression. After months of searching for her, their reunion had been anticlimactic—he might have come back from the corner store for all the enthusiasm she had displayed on seeing him again. His face grew hot and numb, as if he were a jilted lover. He should have dragged her from the arcade, he told himself. He should have locked her away in a hotel until it was time for the bus to leave.

He walked up and down the Calle del Pacifico, half-inclined to leave her to fate, yet determined to make some effort, however futile, on her behalf. As evening approached, frustrated, he bought a Coca Cola and a bottle of cheap rum, and wandered into the waste that lay behind the Circo del Mar, a tract of weedy, broken ground littered with

paper trash and flattened cans, patrolled by pariah
dogs who looked at him anxiously, and sat on a
hummock of dried mud, mixing rum and Coke in
his mouth, staring at the rear of the brothel as if its
hulking shape and green boards were a puzzle he
had been challenged to rearrange in a more comprehensible way. Lace curtains fluttered in the
windows on the second floor; heavy yellow drapes
were drawn across a high, narrow window on the
third. Now and again, a blocky young man with a
Mayan complexion, wearing a baseball cap and a
white apron over his clothes, emerged from the
back door carrying a garbage bag, which he
deposited in a bin. After each of his appearances
the pariah dogs would come to sniff the ground
near the bin, hopeful of fallen scraps, and seagulls,
strayed inland from the port, would swoop down
to reconnoiter before resuming their aimless aeri-
als above the town.

Drunkenness overcame Alvaro at dusk and he
slept for a couple of hours, curled up on the
ground, using his shirt for a pillow. He woke with
a throbbing headache and a sore back, and with
the notion planted firmly in mind that he should
make a bold effort to rescue his sister that very
night. He told himself that such a precipitous
action would likely get him beaten or killed—if he
tried to force her, she would cry out or find some
other means of raising an alarm that would bring
men with guns. And yet the idea was irresistible. It
was as if a spirit had visited his dreams and lodged
a message in the front of his brain, urging him to

flee Chinandega before its poisonous heat could steal his will. He staggered to his feet, gazed dumbly at the patternless scatter of pinprick stars showing through a thin cloud cover, and picked his way across the waste to the side of the trash bin, stopping once to pick up a loose board. He squatted in the shadow of the bin, his thoughts reduced to a fretful static, listening to the romantic ballads issuing muddily from the brothel. When the kitchen door banged open, he went on the alert and, when the bin was flung open, he jumped up, startling the man with his load of garbage, and whacked him on the back of his head with the board, dropping him to his knees. A second blow and the man fell forward onto his face. Alvaro bound and gagged him, wedged his limp body behind the bin. He put on the man's apron and baseball cap, jamming it down onto his ears, and, without pausing to reconsider his decision, he pushed into the harsh lights and bustle of the kitchen of the Circo del Mar.

Ignoring shouts that might or might not have been directed at him, Alvaro kept his head down, slipping a steak knife into his pocket as he passed a warming table, and made for an inner door. The door opened onto a corridor that led away to the interior of the brothel. He took the first turning and ascended a stairway to the second floor, where another corridor lay before him—a wide passage carpeted in dark green, with wall lamps shedding a soft light and recessed doors and shimmering, sea-green wallpaper bearing a sparse design of tridents and conch shells and seahorses. The hubbub of the floor below was muted, the air laced with perfume. Made uneasy by the quiet, he started along the corridor, hunting for a place in which he could shelter and take stock. Between rooms were niches in which fleshy, broad-leaved plants in brass urns were set and, on hearing a door open, a man speaking in American English and then a woman's voice, also in English, but with a Spanish accent, Alvaro sprang into the nearest niche, pressing back among the pliant stalks and greenery. There was insufficient space behind the plant to crouch, so he stood peering through the leaves as the man, a thickset sort with bushy gray hair and white sideburns, stepped from a room just down the hall and stood adjusting his belt beneath the overhang of his belly. He patted his sides in apparent satisfaction and strode off toward the stairs. Alvaro went to the door from which the man had emerged. He put an ear to it and listened, then turned the knob and slipped inside. The room, which echoed the color scheme of the corridor, a blending of softly lit greens, was unoccupied, but he heard water running behind a door to the left of the rumpled bed. He took a position beside the door and waited for the woman to be done with her ablutions, his eyes ranging over the furnishings. After a minute or so, the door to the bathroom opened and a pale, dark-haired girl no older than he, wearing a loosely belted robe of emerald silk, came forth. He caught her from behind, muffling her cry with his hand, and showed her the knife and cautioned her to be quiet. She signaled with her eyes that she would comply and he allowed her to sit on the bed, where she began brushing her hair with a jade-handled brush that she took from a bedside table, appearing unconcerned with him.

He asked if she knew where Palmira was and, with an annoyed expression, she said, Why do so many men ask for Palmira? Am I not more beautiful?

She let the robe slip from her shoulders, continuing to brush her hair. Though entranced by her, Alvaro asked again where Palmira was and the girl said, On the third floor, of course. I'll take you if you like.

Don't think you can trick me, he said. If you are tempted to give me away, remember I have the knife.

The girl laughed, a chilly, bright sound, like two ice cubes dropped into a glass one after the other. Do you believe Dona Bisalia is unaware of your presence? She knows you are here. She knows everything about you, whoever you are.

She stood, the robe puddling at her feet, and struck a seductive pose. Her secret hair had been trimmed into a complicated shape, one from which he averted his eyes before he could discern its exact outlines.

I am Josefina, she said. Stay with me and I'll make you forget that skinny bitch Palmira.

I doubt that.

Josefina affected injured pride, but he could tell she was merely playing with him.

Tell me about Dona Bisalia, he said. How can she know anything about me?

She is Babylon's daughter, born of the union between the stars of commerce and pleasure. Josefina winked at him. You know. It's the same old story. You've heard it a hundred times.

Be serious! I'm trying to understand her.

Serious? Very well. Josefina pitched her voice into a spooky whisper. She has been ordained by the light of certain stars to rule over the lower depths.

Stop fucking around, okay?

She is a woman like any other, but soon she will ascend to her true estate. Josefina walked to the door, paused with her hand on the knob, and smiled at him. It could happen at any second. You'd better hurry.

As he followed her up the stairs, he began to be afraid not of being caught, but of the unknown, of Dona Bisalia, his rational outlook giving way before his superstitious nature. At the top of the stairs was a closed door and, as Josefina made to open it, he caught her wrist and said, Keep close to me. Pretend we are together.

We are together, she said drily. But if you think I can protect you, I cannot.

Let me be the judge of that.

She patted his cheek. Don't be afraid. You are lost already, but it is good to be lost, to be free of one's past.

He tucked the knife under his shirt. You may be free of the past, but I am not. Palmira is my sister.

Oh! And you have come to rescue her, I suppose. Again she laughed. Had I the time, I would tell you a story about such a rescue. But you'll know the truth soon enough.

Men standing in groups, smoking and laughing and talking together, populated the corridor beyond the door. American men in casual dress, Latin men in sport coats and suits—they gazed incuriously at Alvaro as he passed, gripping Josefina's arm, and several greeted her and patted her on the ass. He thought he recognized some of them from the newspapers. They were anonymous, well-groomed men of the type who gathered at the elbows of public figures in photographs captioned by the announcement of a new trade agreement or a leasing of mineral rights. They were the powers behind the throne, the corporate functionaries, architects of political betrayal, princes of bureaucracy, defilers of the public trust, dispensers of the kidney disease, liars, thieves, and murderers with summer places in Cozumel and Cancun. Alvaro knew people at the university who would sacrifice a great deal (or would claim as much) for an opportunity to be armed and at close quarters with such men; but his personal concerns dulled his revolutionary sensibility and he was more aware of them as potential threats to his safety than as political adversaries.

This corridor was truncated, scarcely half the length of the one on the second floor, terminating in dark green double doors; both it and the rooms along it (twice the size of the rooms below) were papered in shiny gold foil that was worked with a design too small to make out, their entrances unencumbered by doors or curtains, furnished with yellow sofas and chairs and deep pile rugs upon which men and women were having sex, singly and in groups. Alvaro could hear grunts and cries of delight over the conversational murmur, but nowhere did he spot his sister. There were too many people in the rooms and some wore masks, making identification even more difficult. He asked Josefina to help him and she told him he would find Palmira beyond the green doors at the end of the corridor.

When they entered the room (furnished like the others, yet much larger, filled with a babble of voices and an insistent electronic music), they became separated almost at once, forced apart by the densely packed crowd around the door. Alvaro, certain that Josefina would betray him, tried to hide in the press along the walls, edging along, drawing the occasional stare, but generally going unnoticed in the hubbub. He eased behind a sofa and, between shoulders, caught sight of a girl who might have been Palmira, bent over a chair, her head down as a bearded man took her from behind; but when he pushed close, calling to her, she brushed the hair from her eyes and, shaken by the man's fierce thrusts, looked at Alvaro stuporously, proving to be older and thinner and coarser of feature than his sister. He retreated, bumping into people, wedging past them, until he reached the security of a corner and stood with his back against the wall, his heart jumping in his chest, alarmed by everything, by the milling crowd, the pulsing music, the yellowness of the room, the naked bodies splayed on couches and the men looking on, the gold foil wallpaper... The design it bore was varied yet of a pattern. Close at hand was the image of seven tiny Guanacaste trees juxtaposed with nine oranges, and higher up were seven dogs and nine crosses, seven birds and nine roses, seven children and nine rakes. Always there were seven of one object and nine of the other. He could not grasp the significance of this, yet knew that it must be significant. Moving deeper into the room, he spotted the Recluse in a small open area, his handsome features composed and watchful, and he had a glimpse of Josefina being fondled by a group of men. He came abreast of three men who were engaged in an intense discussion, standing by an unoccupied sofa, and realized to his astonishment that they were debating aspects of the poetry of Ruben Dario. Here, he thought, was a conversation in which he could hide, blending in with these professorial types (all of them wore shabby suits and beards salted with gray, smoking pipes and cigarettes, dribbling ashes whenever they gestured) until he was able to get his bearings. Their concern seemed to be whether or not Dario's *Songs Of Life And Hope* had announced the modern era or if they were the last mutterings of the neoclassical period dressed in new clothing.

Gentleman, Alvaro said, inserting himself into their circle. Dario's impact is clear. He shrugged off the decaying mantle of the neoclassical and adopted new poetic themes.

He paused, summoning lines from memory, and quoted the following lines from *To Roosevelt*:

You think that life is fire,
That eruption is progress,
That wherever you shoot
You hit the future...

Even the syntax was new, said Alvaro. Without Dario, there would be no Paz, no Lorca, no Neruda.

The poem is political, a populist slogan, and thus constitutes an aberration, offered a lanky man with a prominent Adam's apple. Within this same volume, Dario provides us with a text—a major text—that embraces anew the structures of the past. I am speaking, of course, of *The Optimist's Salutation*.

Surely you realize that the antiquated language of the poem is an irony? said Alvaro.

The discussion grew heated and Alvaro lost track to some extent of his purpose for invading the Circo del Mar, though each time a woman passed by the sofa, he looked to see if she was Palmira. He began to hear a ragged unanimity in the voices of the crowd, as if some of them were repeating the same words. This rattled him, but he fixed his mind on the argument, assuming that some ritual—a drinking contest, perhaps—encouraged them to speak in chorus. As he attempted to refute a point by quoting from *The Optimist's Salutation,* quoting the lines, Abominate mouths that foretell only misfortune/abominate eyes that see only ill-fated Zodiacs, he heard the crowd uttering the lines along with him and broke off, knowing that his presence had been discovered.

The crowd finished the quote, hundreds of voices sounding the lines:

…abominate hands that stone the illustrious ruins,
or that wield the firebrand or suicidal dagger.

The music ceased, and the professorial men, the government officials, the whores, the Americans—they fell silent and began to move back against the walls, assisted in this by nine men of pleasant manner, who shooed people to one side or another. Alvaro found himself looking along the avenue that was created at Dona Bisalia. She was enthroned in a yellow easy chair, and she wore a dark green latex cocktail dress that cinched her waist and pushed up her breasts. Her black curls gleamed as if fashioned of polished obsidian. At her back, in casual array, stood seven solemn and unsmiling men, and behind them was a high window partly concealed by yellow drapes. She beckoned to Alvaro and, having no choice—the crowd at his rear was packed in solidly, making escape impossible—he walked toward her, stopping a few feet away.

My sister, he said. Where is she?

You have no sister, said Dona Bisalia.

Alvaro nudged the knife beneath his shirt with the back of his hand. Palmira! he shouted.

Oh! So it is Palmira you wish to see. Dona Bisalia mocked him with her smile. Why didn't you say so?

Palmira stepped forth from the crowd, naked except for a necklace with a green stone, her body agleam with oil. At her side stood a short, muscular man with skin of a ruddy copper hue, a mask in the form of a snarling mastiff covered his head. He was also naked and in a state of tumescence.

Are they not beautiful? Dona Bisalia came to her feet, a movement that captured Alvaro's attention, and posed with her hands on hips, her voluptuous figure tortured into the shape of an eight by the green latex. Yet their beauty is not that of brother and sister, she said. No more than would be the case if you were at her side. She is not your sister, but the child of your father's favorite whore, Expectacion. She told your father the infant was his.

That's a lie, Alvaro said weakly, his eyes returning to Palmira—he had not known she was so womanly.

Whores lie, said Dona Bisalia. It's true. And Expectacion lied. She saw in your father a fool who would take a nuisance off her hands. Blood knows blood, Alvaro. If she were your sister, could you look at her as you are now?

Turning to the man beside her, Palmira removed his mask; as she lifted it from his head, he misted away as though he had never been, vanishing before Alvaro could register his features. The crowd seethed. Palmira approached to within a foot of Alvaro, her expression empty of emotion, and held out the mask.

The man's disappearance did not affect Alvaro—he had seen more spectacular tricks at country carnivals. He stared at the slim perfection of Palmira's body and the blank indifference of her face, half-wanting to believe she was not his sister, yet refusing to take the mask. Dona Bisalia stepped up beside him and slipped her arm through his elbow. The pressure of her breast against his arm seemed to drain him of strength and will.

Will you not entertain us? No? Dona Bisalia gave a dusty laugh. Come with me, then. I have something to show you.

One of the seven unsmiling men sprang to the window behind the easy chair and drew back the drapes that concealed it. As Dona Bisalia guided him to the window, Alvaro cut his eyes toward her. She had, he thought, the simplified beauty of statuary, the statue of a sexual goddess carved from yellow stone, with breasts and hips like sculptural principles, and black eyes like cabochons; yet there was nothing sexual about her, no hint of warmth or humanity. Her smile did not develop, but shifted into place, as if it were an artifact she summoned up whenever necessary, and the perfume that clung to her was a coarse, heady odor like incense. She instructed him to look out the window, which he did briefly, seeing nothing other than the waste that lay behind the brothel. Suddenly timid, overwhelmed by her closeness, he asked what he was supposed to see, and she said, The world... of which the Circo del Mar is not truly a part. You must look deeply or else your journey will have been for nothing.

The darkness appeared to ripple and bits of phosphorescent life bobbed about in the air, as if the night were an ocean beneath which the brothel was submerged... and then he realized that what he had mistaken for phosphorescent glints were the scattered lights of Colonia San Jeronimo. He rubbed his eyes, trying to rid himself of the rippling effect, and when he looked again he found that he was peering in the window of a house, a shack, a foul nest built of canted boards inhabited by two creatures that might have been the fantasy of a medieval artist: an emaciated man and woman, grotesquely malformed, scarcely more than skeletons dressed in rags of flesh and flaps of pallid gray skin, their shoulder blades so pronounced that they resembled stubby wings. They crawled into their matrimonial hammock, croaking love noises and mauling one another, exhausted tides of emotion filming across their faces like washes of scum, their feelings as easy to read as the intent of spiders. He tried to look beneath the surface, to see behind their lives as Dona Bisalia had told him to do, but—though he came to recognize that the window was a lens through which he could view every quarter of the town (and perhaps afforded a wider view than that)—there was no greater depth to perceive, no roots twisting down beneath the houses that tapped into a black reservoir, no snickering demons perched atop the roofs and manipulating those within, no apparent cause for their grotesquerie. Monstrosities populated every house in the colonia, and he knew to his soul that what he saw from the window of the Circo del Mar was literal and real, shorn of all illusory beauty and grace. Each new thing he saw was a blow that weakened one or another of his fundamental assumptions, that abolished some rule of order, and forced on him an unvarnished view of the world. Along the Calle del Pacifico, whores with leech-like mouths and sagging bodies hustled big-bellied American swine, and broken-down old men with goiters the size of pineapples and old women with hairs sprouting from their skin cancers sheltered in the shadowed doorways of unlit shops, their faces seamed with bad life, with ugly hungers, with brutish contempt and blue-movie dreams, the faces of hawk-rats and bat-roaches and scorpion-dogs, and in the more prosperous sectors of the town, wife-beaters and child abusers and priests with their fatty self-absorption and their penchant for sodomy and their love of guava jelly, the average meat nobodies of a dying age stared into nowhere with lechery and avarice. They breathed in brown gas, breathed it out as sulfur; their bones were petrified shit, their hearts were empty leather sacs, their minds were stinging vibrations; pink insects were glued to their groins, and their screams were all the music there ever was; they had larval visions of huge wallowing and gulpings, earthquake moans and enormous torsions of suety flesh. Life had betrayed them... or rather betrayal was the medium of their lives. They fed on the dung of lies, flies orbiting the garbage of illusion. They clung to nothing, squeezing sticky handfuls of nothing hard in hopes that their grip would transform it into a bright something that they could sell themselves, that would provide them with a reason to continue.

Alvaro had always believed that the world was a wasteland and evil, but seeing things in this hard, sudden light toppled the tissue-paper castles of philosophy behind which he had been hiding, banished them beyond recall and unhinged him to such a degree that a powerful hatred of life was bred in him. When he turned from the window and saw grotesques of a kind with which he was familiar, sleek women and well-dressed men, and realized that the illusion of beauty was somehow sustained within the Circo del Mar—this deceit so inflamed him, he could no longer contain his rage and despair. Letting out a yell, he drew the knife from his waist and slashed at the air.

You see, said Dona Bisalia. Here you have found refuge from the world. Here you are free to please yourself however you will.

She made a gesture and the man who had opened the drapes now hurried to close them.

There, she said. You need never look at it again. Now Palmira can be yours. I think she likes you.

She has always liked you, and you her. Now you can express yourself fully one to the other.

She moved closer to him and, though she was draped in firm yellow flesh and a dress of dark green latex, he knew the hateful thing she was; he felt her vile, venereal heat on his skin and understood the release she offered.

You can be my kitchen boy, she said, and smiled broadly. I believe I have need of a new one.

She moved closer yet, the points of her nipples grazing his chest, and just that touch, that slight stimulus, triggered his rage. He stabbed down with the knife, yet he lacked a murderer's conviction—the blade bit into her flesh an inch or two. Dona Bisalia yielded a soft feminine moan, a breathy exclamation of pleasure, and that moan seemed to be echoed throughout the house, as if every woman in the Circo del Mar had experienced a sweet pang. All the whores within sight stood with eyes closed and lips parted, mirroring Dona Bisalia's stance. Blood welled from the slope of her breast. She clutched Alvaro's knife-hand and placed the tip of the blade against the wound he had made.

Strike deeper, she said rapturously.

When he did not respond, she spat into his face, thick spittle that hung from his nose and chin, and when that did not move him to act, she struck him and said that he was not a man. Without knowing why, for his rage had fled, supplanted by a bleak, uncaring emotion, Alvaro pushed the knife home.

A second moan issued from Dona Bisalia's lips and from every portion of the house, louder and longer than the first, a finishing cry, a gush of sound that might have signaled lust well spent. For an instant she appeared to ripple and billow, as if he had penetrated illusion, and he thought that the image of the yellow room and the crowd might be sucked into the rent he had carved in her breast, leaving behind a nightmarish environment populated by sub-humans; but she collapsed on the floor with a meaty thump, looking more vivacious in death than she had in life, with black curls partly obscuring her face and her legs akimbo and the rivulet of blood running down across her skin to pool on the golden carpet.

Alvaro expected to be borne under by an angry mob, but—following a momentary silence—the crowd erupted with shouts of joy and delirium. She has ascended, they cried. She has claimed her estate. The seven and the nine mingled, shaking hands with one another. It seemed that the punishment for murder committed in the Circo del Mar was to be smothered in congratulations. Men came to clap Alvaro on the shoulder and embrace him, women to kiss him on the mouth and cheek. Confused, he shoved them aside, but they lifted him to their shoulders and carried him aloft, all the while exclaiming a shrill, nonsensical litany. She has ascended! She stands between the seven and the nine! He understood none of it, but was infected by their merriment and soon he raised his arms in triumph, joining the celebration, happy that no blame was attached to his crime.

At length Dona Bisalia's body was borne away, and thereafter the room emptied swiftly, everyone going off to their separate revels, leaving Alvaro and Palmira alone in that vast yellow space. She walked up to him and wordlessly offered him the mask worn by the man who disappeared. Alvaro did not know what to say to her or, for that matter, what he would say to anyone, so he took it and turned the thing over in his hand, pretending to examine its snarling, toothy mouth and alert ears, sticking his fingers through the eyeholes.

Put it on, Palmira said.

He hesitated.

No one will disturb us, she said. Go ahead. Put it on.

Why did you run away? he asked.

You know why. I wanted you, and I knew you wanted me, though you would never admit to it. Imagine if you had. We would have become lovers and then the situation would have been even more intolerable.

He started to deny it, but could not. What happened here tonight? Dona Bisalia... I don't understand.

It's not important that you understand. I don't understand. No one does, really. Now put on the mask. It will make things easier.

She reclined on a sofa, positioning herself so as to give him a full display. He pulled the mask over his head. It was hot and smelled of sweat and fit snuggly to his ears, making his breathing sound like a beast pausing open-mouthed over its prey. The tiny eyeholes limited his view. He could see her belly or her breasts or her thighs, but not the entirety of her body. When he lifted his gaze, he noticed there was a pulse in her throat, and her face, ardent and flushed, the mouth distorted by a mature passion, did not resemble his sister's at all.

WHORES LIE.

All men being whores, for Dona Bisalia to have made this statement, one that implied a distinction, was, Alvaro thinks, unnecessary. He wonders if she intended the words to be self-referential, if she lied when she told him Palmira was not his sister. It matters little now, yet nonetheless he wonders. He sports with other women of the brothel, but Palmira is by far his favorite and their hours together are his sole treasure. Their affection is thin, as are all affections, but the sex is good and suffices to sustain it.

Sometimes they walk hand-in-hand down to Juegos Galaxia and play the racing games. Alvaro keeps his eyes lowered, not wanting to see things as they are, though he is aware that the illusion he has accepted is a strong one, made even stronger by the ascendancy and death of Dona Bisalia, and he will likely see nothing out of the ordinary. It has been explained to him that he and Palmira and the seven and the nine were part of a design that permitted Dona Bisalia to assume her place among the gods, and it has been pointed out that a new constellation hangs above the Gulf of Fonseca, one shaped roughly like an eight or an hourglass—this is proof, it's said, that she watches over the folk of the Circo del Mar and guarantees their continued well-being. But the explanations are words, merely, and there are so many stars above the Gulf of Fonseca that one could arrange them into any shape. On occasion he sees her taking a promenade along the Calle del Pacifico, standing between the seven and the nine, and chatting with bystanders. On other occasions she strolls through the corridors of the brothel. In both instances, the wound on her breast is plainly visible, still bleeding. Alvaro is not entirely free of guilt where she is concerned and it is possible that these apparitions are a kind of self-punishment. None of their *proofs* are persuasive, yet he cannot discount the idea of her divinity. It is simply unimportant.

He works in the kitchen of the brothel and sometimes it seems that he has always worked there. The former kitchen boy, whom he struck with a board, has disappeared as completely as the man in the mask. Since both men were stocky and of Mayan blood, like him, and as he never saw their faces, he suspects that they were doubles fashioned of illusory stuff and served some unfathomable purpose; but he is not in the least curious about them. Curiosity is no longer a function of his personality. He no longer cares about literature or politics. He no longer wishes to embrace life's complexity, its cruel simplicity having been confirmed to his satisfaction. He goes through the days ploddingly, carrying trash to the bin out back, scraping off dishes, mopping floors, and taking pleasure wherever he can find it, inspired to this dogged continuance by a single goal.

Money is not difficult to come by at the Circo del Mar and Alvaro does not have to spend much. His meals and a place to sleep are provided, drink is plentiful, and Palmira sees to his other needs. Now and then he buys her a present, a cheap trinket, a CD—she requires no more—but otherwise he saves his tips, the change he finds on floors and in ashtrays, and the banknotes that the whores slip him in return for favors. Someday soon he will walk deep into Colonia San Jeronimo and hand the Recluse a thousand cordobas and then, not with dread, as one might expect, but with eager anticipation (this being the one remaining thing that he is curious about), he will ask to be told the precise hour and minute at which the world will end.

QUASHIE TRAPP BLACKLIGHT

STEVEN ERIKSON

IT BEGAN WITH a hurricane. June, 1789. Rolling over Jamaica with shrieking valkyries riding its winds and raven-haired banshees rollicking in the black clouds. In the narrow, crooked streets of Kingston men had their wigs, and, in some instances, their hair, snatched from their heads. Women whose billowing basket dresses had caught the wind raced back and forth in the air over the town, caterwauling like witches.

Oblivious to the chaos beyond the shuttered windows, Red the Whore and Mowbry the Irishman thrashed about in bed on the second floor of Red's Palace of Delight and Assorted Condiments. White linen sheets twisting and stretching around them, they tossed themselves about in the waves of their lust. Every now and then one of them popped up to gulp much-needed oxygen and pull a hair or whisker from a poked-out tongue.

Despite the establishment's long name, the building was rather small, with a single cramped sitting room on the ground floor almost entirely filled by a brass bathtub, and on the next level the lone bedroom with the bed touching three of the four walls.

Mowbry, who had been press-ganged out of Bristol to serve on the *HMS Piety* for five long years before the slaver turned pirate and then foundered off the coast of Isla Mujeres, was now a free man. Washed ashore at the foot of a cliff that had a Mayan temple on it, he was taken in by a gaggle of young Mayan virgins who, after they'd plied him with intense life-sustaining ministrations, all flung themselves off the cliff cursing some Mayan god named Joseph Campbell all the way down to their gory, bone-snapping, skull-crushing entirely un-celebratory deaths.

He'd been a free man for precisely one month since leaving Isla Mujeres, hauling up in Kingston via a crazed Port-au-Prince (and that was another tale, aye), whereupon he now dived for conch to pay for Red's upkeep while dreaming of marriage and Red tottering about under a twirling parasol a thousand months pregnant with wee Mowbry and maybe Mowbriana, and life all settling out in the blessed buccaneering anarchy of the Caribbean.

Red the Whore, on the other hand, had fetched up on this miserable island as the handmaiden of the governor's wife who turned out to be a wanton vixen who begat with biblical profligacy a whole score of squalling brats, none of whom was lighter-skinned than a cured tobacco leaf; while her preening all-too-effete husband lollygagged with young baby-faced subalterns, playing Jacks late into the night and peg'a'port besides. A mutually pleasing arrangement, no doubt, but one Red had no interest in being part of, given her new-found ambition to set out on her own, opening a business establishment and maybe making enough to pay for a big bathtub. Ironic, then, that her eventual profession set her in direct competition with the governor's wife. But at least she'd paid outright for her bathtub.

By the by, waddling around knocked to the nines was Red's vision of hell.

As yet, Red and Mowbry were a little scant on the old heart to heart gabs, and it was indeed the season for hurricanes.

At this moment, however, the source of the building's shake was, had they taken a moment to consider it, wholly problematic. They paid little attention to the rattling rafters and groaning floor-boards. They were deaf to the wailing wind and clattering shutters. And, as to the sudden weight-lessness that lifted their bodies from the bed in the precise moment of ineffable if mutually misunder-stood ecstasy, well, that had been the whole idea all along, a guinea a poke notwithstanding.

Perhaps it was but a moment later, or it may well have been hours lost in the timeless trance that follows such rampant endeavors, but they came back to earth with a loud crash that shook the whole house.

Red was the first to notice the ominous silence and the glare of bright sunlight streaming through the shutters. She sat up and looked round.

"Hey, Mowbry."

"What?" The Irishman pulled the sheets from his face, pushed his fingers into his mouth and withdrew a black hair seventeen inches long. He studied it bemusedly, adding a sidelong glance at Red and her wild, tousled mane of, well, red hair.

Red scowled. "Something's wrong."

"I'll say," Mowbry agreed, back squinting at the strand of hair.

Red crawled across the bed to the window. She opened the shutters and leaned out.

The wreckage of a small town surrounded her Palace, and it wasn't Kingston. A muddy creek wended down into a milky lagoon off to the left, and a storm-battered jungle more or less came right to the town's edge on all sides that she could see. In a large tree behind the ruined shacks opposite, three howler monkeys squatted on branches, watching her and watching maybe something else, something directly beneath the window. Red leaned out further and looked straight down.

A pink cat, pink because it was hairless. The ugly wrinkled creature was staring up at her.

Red's scowl deepened. Leaning back, she closed the shutters, sat back on the bed and glared at Mowbry.

"Get dressed," she told him. "You're hurtin' my eyes." She rose, threw on her thrice-owned kimono and went downstairs. Everything in the room, she saw, was intact. Walking up to the bathtub, she caressed its polished fixtures. "It's okay, Beauty," she whispered. "You and me, we'll get outa this alive, and that's a promise."

Mowbry was standing halfway down the steep stairs, observing all this, admittedly bemused. "I got this bad feeling," he said as he knotted the rope he used for a belt for his faded navy blue trousers. "The air smells... funny."

Red crossed her arms. "That damned storm," she said. "Plucked us up and plunked us down." She flung her arms out and snapped her fingers. "Just like that!"

Mowbry went to the door, opened it and looked outside. "Where?"

Red came to his side. "Now that's the question, innit? Haulover Creek." The cat stood in the street in front of them and Red pointed at it. "I recognize her, and who wouldn't with what brought her here. That's Ducat, the factor's pet. The factor, Mowbry, in British Honduras. That storm threw us right onto the mainland!"

Mowbry stepped into the street. "That ain't right."

"It's only the start of what ain't right. Let's go see if we can find somebody."

Ducat followed them as they wandered through the littered streets. The hurricane had trampled most of the houses, including the factor's rather larger, more elaborate residence. But there wasn't a soul about, living or dead. They found a glass slipper, a few tattered pieces of cloth, and the factor's white powdered wig.

"Don't think anyone was here when the storm hit," Mowbry said as they walked past the edge of the town and down to the beach.

A quarter-mile offshore was the reef, and on the reef, they saw, sat two wrecks that had, by the rubbish on the water, been delivered by the same hurricane as plucked and plunked Red's Palace. One of the tattered wrecks was a Spanish galleon and the other an English slaver.

Upon seeing the galleon Red's eyes caught fire. "Look at that!" She clutched Mowbry's arm. "Aztec gold! Just sittin' out there!"

The Irishman grunted, studying the beach. "Don't see no boats, no way t'get out there, Red."

"Aztec gold! I'm telling ya, Mowbry. An' it's all ours!"

At that moment a loud boom erupted from the slaver ship, startling gulls from the spine-backed reef, sending monkeys in the forest screaming.

The hull bulged outward. Wood splintered, then burst as dowels shot out like champagne corks. The planks sailed into the air, striking the water with slaps that echoed in the sudden silence that followed.

Mowbry and Red stared.

A giant gray shape appeared in the jagged hole, swaying to the right and swaying to the left. It shouldered its way through.

"Fancy that," Mowbry said. "An elephant. And it's walking on water."

Red licked her lips. "I heard them beasts was strange."

But that was not all that astonished Mowbry and Red, oh no. A black man rode the animal's shoulders, and with a kick he guided his charge forward. Though the pachyderm's walk was a lumbering gait, its big flat feet barely brushed the waves.

Red sniffed. "One of them things sure could trample a body."

Tugging on his nose, Mowbry nodded.

They backed up the beach.

Ducat had gone down to the water's edge with the elephant's appearance, and now stood transfixed, tail twitching, as the rider and his mount approached. They came to within a dozen feet of shore, looming over the scrawny hairless cat, and then halted. The rider leaned forward with his forearms on the elephant's bristly head, and calmly studied Red and Mowbry.

"Met a man, once," Red muttered. "By the name of Toussaint Louverture."

Mowbry, who had seen the ex-slave in Port-au-Prince, nodded again. Aye, the same fire, the same power. Clearing his throat, the Irishman stepped forward. "Hallo," he called out.

The man smiled and kicked the elephant's flanks. The beast strode ashore.

Ducat scrambled to one side and resumed her fixed stare on the intruders.

The man's smile broadened, revealing a startling white row of possibly filed teeth. "I am the last of the Bhudo priests," he said in a deep, cavernous voice. He swung one leg over and dropped lightly to the sand, then leaned against the elephant's front leg and crossed his arms. "Greatest child of Africa am I! My name is Thomas Goff, and I am your savior."

THE UNIVERSE OF the cat is Newtonian, its outlook Aristotelian. Since the days of ancient Egypt *Felix domesticus* was well aware that corporeal reality is, in fact, all there is. When one died its fellows humored their human companions by permitting its mummification. They knew it wasn't going anywhere.

With this notion of pristine cause and effect governing their lives, the domestic cat prospered, despite its refusal to beggar itself as did that most shameful creature, the dog.

Ducat had noticed in passing that none of the settlement's dogs had survived the hurricane. She considered this fortuitous and wholly just. Unhampered now by their frenzied pursuits, Ducat was certain that her hair would grow back. And, she knew, when hair reaches a specific density per square inch it ceases being hair and becomes fur. For Ducat, then, the equation was a simple one: Ducat minus dogs equals fur.

The sudden appearance of Red's Palace of Delight and its two ugly inhabitants had been rather unsettling for Ducat, yet hardly miraculous.

But it was the arrival of the elephant that shattered Ducat's comfortably predictable, albeit occasionally miserable world. Her stand against the monstrosity's approach had not been one of courage, but of intense concentration. Ducat had willed upon herself, in the time-honored feline fashion, rapt disbelief. Much to the cat's chagrin, this effort on her part had not withered the elephant and its rider into non-existence. Rather, Ducat had come close to being trampled.

For the true Aristotelian, however, the perception of what constitutes reality is cumulative and experiential. When it became evident that the elephant and its rider did indeed exist, blasé acceptance followed. She was now free to deal with it as she dealt with the rest of reality that had nothing to do with sustenance or vanity: ignore it.

As soon as the man dismounted and voiced his rather pathetic proclamation, Ducat whirled to present a stiff tail to him, then blithely padded away, leaving the two strangers to sort the mess. After all, she had more important things on her mind; things that required all of her concentration. Leaving the beach, Ducat headed into what was left of the settlement in search of privacy.

The growing of hair, one follicle at a time, was a difficult business, Ducat knew. Difficult, even for the vast mental powers of *Felix domesticus*, student of Newton, Aristotle, and Cleopatra.

IT IS THE nature of tarantulas to sit around for long periods of time conveying the appearance of doing nothing in particular. This, of course, is an illusion. One such tarantula, Agent Six Gee Eff, had been assigned by Arachnid Central to spy on the inhabitants of the Haulover Creek settlement.

Arachnid Central had been tracking the history of humans in this part of the world for some time now, for reasons known only to Director Scorpion and integral to his great plan, The Sting. In the briefings such as Agent Six Gee Eff had attended, the story of humanity went like this:

Around twenty thousand years ago a bunch of people came down from the north and settled in the Yucatan. The entire peninsula is founded on limestone bedrock (hence its ideal environment for Arachnid Central HQ, at least when The God Who Stamps Down wasn't flinging comets), but it took the humans about eighteen thousand years to realize that they could use that limestone to build things taller and more lasting than themselves (thus introducing a plethora of new hidey-holes for eight-legged spies!). Naturally, they went overboard with their newfound playing blocks and, eventually, from this came the Mayan Empire, with all its pyramids, tombs, plazas, ball courts, and temples and stuff.

You may recall, back when you were just a little spiderling clinging to your mother's thorax, hearing all the tales about these Mayans. Bloody sacrifices and all that. So you know that they weren't no angels. Still, it took just a puff of Spanish wind to bring all the blocks tumbling down. True, Six Gee Eff, over-farming and drought didn't help matters, but let's keep things simple, shall we?

The conquistadores, then, chased them everywhere, and that brings us to this present assignment, sub-operation twenty-one of The Sting. One of the Mayan ruling classes, a family called the Itza Brothers, snuck into nominally British territory just a few months back. Now, these are bad people, just naturally bad, and in a bad mood these days since they don't have any peasant farmers to sacrifice by the thousands.

So here come the Itza Brothers, all eight of them, and they've got one of their gods with them, the feathered serpent one, named Quetzalcoatl. The conquistadores are out of their hair now, so they're into flexing their muscles again. And who's going to stop them in British Honduras? They're lording it over the local Indians, and now they've taken over the English logging settlements, rounding up all the escaped slaves and down-and-out pirates and putting them to work building pyramids.

Your mission, Agent Six Gee Eff, is information-gathering in nature. For our files, to keep us apprised of the situation. Head to Haulover Creek, since that's the English capital. See what's going on.

Agent Six Gee Eff, therefore, had been witness to the whole thing. The Itza Brothers showed up last week with an army of their god's mortal servants—fer-de-lances—and promptly enslaved everyone, using the snakes in place of ankle shackles. Then, just before the hurricane struck, they marched everyone into the jungle.

Agent Six Gee Eff made his report to Arachnid Central through the usual Spidermite Network, then awaited further instructions. With the arrival of first the Palace and then the man and the elephant, he amended his report and was told that he should stick to the newcomers.

The tarantula had a week earlier taken position on the roof of the factor's outhouse and had found no reason to move until the hurricane. During the storm he hid beneath the factor's powdered wig, which he found on the floor of the man's office. Although the house subsequently blew away, the wig remained.

As soon as he received his new orders, Agent Six Gee Eff attempted to leave the dark confines of his sanctuary, and immediately discovered that entering a dry wig was much easier than leaving a rain-soaked one. Realizing that he was trapped, he ceased his efforts and became immobile once again.

With his X-ray vision Agent Six Gee Eff had no difficulty following the activities of the newcomers. As long as they didn't go anywhere he could settle into his tiny world and think profound thoughts.

He was thinking profound thoughts when his tiny world was invaded by an apparition from hell, and life for Agent Six Gee Eff became a nightmare struggle against imminent death.

FOR THE ELEPHANT it had been a helluva swim. His present adventure had begun on the Kalahari basin, when he became the target of a rather stubborn !Kung bushman whose only purpose in life, it seemed, involved creeping under the elephant and poking a spear into his vitals.

Distantly related to the pig, the elephant shared its natural and fully justified aversion to being skewered. Unlike the average pig, however, the elephant possessed some options. For one, he could run faster than a human. And, upon divining the bushman's intent, run he did, across the breadth of the basin, up the western escarpment, across endless miles of savanna, through rancid swamps and mountainous rainforests, eventually to the coast.

Still the lone bushman pursued, jogging in his usual crouched fashion, spear held low in one hand, leafy branch clutched in the other. The elephant had no idea concerning the ultimate function of the leafy branch, but it worried him nonetheless. He had been sufficiently worried, in fact, to take to the water in the hopes of confounding his pursuer.

By the time the elephant had reached the Azores, he knew he was in trouble. Behind him he could see that bushman's little head bobbing in the waves.

Then, just east of Jamaica, a miracle! In the guise of a ferocious storm. In the midst of the tumult the elephant shook the bushman. For six days and six nights he was tossed about by mammoth waves in the throes of trumpeting winds, and at dawn on the seventh day a particularly gigantic wave lifted him high then deposited him on the deck of a wooden ship.

He stood in a daze, wobbling, wondering if anyone had noticed his arrival, when he heard a voice
at his left ear and felt a hand pat his shoulder.

"Welcome," the voice murmured. "I have stolen
this ship from the English. This storm is my shep-
herd, friend, for I am Thomas Goff, the last of the
Bhudo priests."

Although Thomas Goff spoke a rare dialect of
Bhundi, the elephant had no difficulty understanding
him. Like all elephants, he understood humans perfectly, even Finns. He felt no need to communicate in
kind, however. With humans he was content to bel-
low and scream wordlessly, since that seemed to
freeze them in their tracks long enough for him to
trample them with his big, flat feet.

But the man who stood beside him now was not
one to be trampled lightly. The elephant sensed a
force about this man, a power at once comforting
and terrible. Quivering, the elephant listened
attentively as the man resumed speaking.

"The !Kung is still looking for you. We must
hide your presence, my friend." Thomas Goff
pointed at the hold hatch. "In there."

The elephant considered the hatch with one eye
(the right eye). Surely, he concluded after some
thought, the bushman would never think to look
down there. Still, he was dubious. The hatch, after
all, was a mere five feet by six.

"I know what you're thinking, friend," Thomas Goff
said. "But don't worry. Look," he held up his hand,
showing the elephant a small jar. "I have some grease."

* * *

MOWBRY WAS IN a conundrum. Long before getting press-ganged in Bristol, he had spent most of his life on the high seas, a free man, occasional pirate, trader, and even fisherman (Gor that was an awful business). He had sailed with gold-buttoned admirals and with one-eyed pirates with parrots on their shoulders. He had taken orders, aye, from pompous lubbers with fancy titles and from men whose faith in luck had cost them arms, legs, and a whole variety of organs—from men who hawed "sirrah!" at the end of interminably long sentences, and from men whose entire vocabulary consisted of the word "aaargh!"

He took the world as it was, with rolled-up sleeves and a brusque nod of his shaggy head. If there was one thing in the world he hated most, it was conundrums.

And this one, now, was brutal. He was madly in love with Red, see, but this here Tommy Goff—on some mission to free the people of British Honduras from some tyrannical god whose name Mowbry couldn't pronounce—this here Tommy Goff, he was offering Mowbry a ride on an elephant.

And so he walked aimlessly down the wreckage-strewn high street. He raised his right hand, looked at it. "My love for Red," he said. Then he raised his left hand and studied it. "A ride on an elephant." It was an either/or proposition. He weighed the choices every way he could think of, yet no matter what it always came out the same. The elephant hand was heavier.

Disconsolate, he wandered through the town.

"Psssst."

Mowbry stopped, looked round.

"Pssssst."

The sound came from an outhouse that had, miraculously, survived not only the storm but also years of overuse.

"Who's in there?" Mowbry demanded, walking toward it.

The door flew open. Inside, Red was drawing tight her kimono. "All right, I'm done already! Geez, a lady needs time, y'know!" She stepped out. "Go ahead, then, wave that willy around like a portable fountain o' youth. Just close the door!"

"Don't need to," Mowbry said. "I just heard... well, I just heard something, that's all."

Shaking her head, Red took him by the arm and they walked on down the street. "That Goff character," she whispered, glancing round, "he left yet?"

"No. He went into some kind of trance, I think."

"Ferget him," she said. "Aztec gold, Mowbry! And I figured a way t'get it. Only I need your help."

They stopped when they noticed the factor's wig, which was lying in front of them, moving slightly. An exchanged glance, then Mowbry tiptoed forward, bent down, and snatched up the wig.

Ducat, a tarantula positioned like a hat on her head, leapt into the air, her private world of concentration and willpower suddenly shattered.

Hissing, spitting, and snarling, she bounced round on stiff legs, tail lashing.

Mowbry jumped back, dropping the wig.

Red cursed. "That damned 'airless cat, again!" She aimed a kick at Ducat, who dodged at the last moment and scampered away, the spider still clinging to the space between her ears. "Wants hair so bad she's taken t'wearing wigs!"

"And spiders," Mowbry said. "Poor thing."

"Poor thing nothing," Red retorted. "I know all about cats, Mowbry, cause I'm a woman, see? There ain't nothing poor about 'em. Now dogs, Mowbry, dogs is the poor ones. You ever see a toy French poodle?" She shook her head. "Sorriest sight ye'd ever see. Even the rats laugh at 'em, and they're from Norway! Since when did anyone from Norway laugh at a Frenchie, Mowbry? Answer me that!"

"I ain't no good on history," Mowbry mumbled, discomfited by Red's evidently prodigious education.

"History!" Red began twisting his arm as they walked. "I'll tell ya about history, Mowbry! Dogs in history, now that's a story! You can tell every time the world's gone bad cause people start kickin' dogs. The connection's clear as day! World goes bad, people kick dogs. And I'll tell you something else. It ain't no dog's fault the world goes bad, cause if you start looking round real careful like, you'll see who's doing the laughin'."

"Who?"

"Cats," she replied. "That's who, and don't you ferget it!"

They arrived back at the Palace and Red led Mowbry inside. "Here's my plan," she said. "Ye help me, Mowbry, and we go fifty-fifty, right?" Walking over to stand beside the bathtub, she reached down and patted its side. "We take Beauty here down to the beach, then jus paddle her out t'the wreck. Easy as that!"

"That thing must weight forty stone," Mowbry said.

"That's right, now give me a hand!"

AT THE JUNGLE'S edge where it came closest to the beach, a pair of beady black eyes peered between the fronds of a fern. The object of its attention was the impressive specimen of *Loxodonta africana*, more commonly known as the African elephant, that stood in swaying bliss beside a man who seemed to be sleeping.

The beady black eyes were set in a head and the head set on a body and in one hand was a spear and in the other a skeletal branch that had once been leafy. The !Kung watched, as he had been watching all morning, waiting for his chance, waiting for the perfect moment to bring his long hunt to a satisfactory conclusion.

He wondered, not for the first time, if he wasn't being too stubborn about the whole thing. After all, carrying the elephant back to his band in the Kalahari would take months. Of course, he had come all this way, it wouldn't make bushman sense to abandon the quarry now. Still, he had to admire the pachyderm's aversion to being skewered.

He heard voices, then saw the white man and woman heading down to the beach. On the man's shoulders was a giant oblong bronze cooking pot (into which an elephant might fit, with a little grease). The !Kung hunter stiffened in sudden alarm. They were going to cook the elephant! His elephant! This was terrible! But wait, they had walked past the beast, were now heading down to the water, and now they were arguing, the woman pointing out to sea and the man pointing at the elephant. Finally, the woman, with much grunting and cursing, pushed the pot out into the water, then climbed in. The man made a move to help her but she waved him off. She laid down in the pot with her arms draped over the sides, then began paddling out to sea.

All very mysterious. Now, if only the two men would leave as well, he could finish his hunt.

His mouth watered at the thought of *Loxodonta africana* soup.

AGENT SIX GEE Eff had never known the wonder of rapid transit before. He gloried in the experience, especially its seeming randomness, as the excruciatingly ugly creature he rode padded this way and that, sniffed this and that, stared fixedly at this and that. When the circumlocution of the cat's intent resolved at last to the powdered wig, Agent Six Gee Eff's spirits sank. Sure enough, they returned to the tiny world where a man's head used to be, and cramped and musty it was. Sighing, the tarantula resumed his deep thinking on the processes of universal harmony within the woven net of his existence.

DUCAT HAD NEVER known such excitement, though she knew that to display it would be to sacrifice the immortal dignity of her kind. Still... success at last! Upon crawling under the wig and settling into this exercise of paramount importance, she had felt— yes!—the first tinglings of activity near her tail. Then it had marched—yes, marched!—the springing reju- venation coming with ordered precision so that she could feel each one, up her spine, to find its thickest and most meaningful expression on her head, between her ears on that pink, wrinkled map of frowning concentration.

She was so excited, so proud, that she wanted to show someone—but someone who would under- stand, someone who would clap their hands in delight and subsequently lavish her with the atten- tion and fame she most assuredly deserved—in other words, there was no point in showing her success to strangers, for how could they ever understand the sheer glory of it?

No, she concluded, there was only one person who would understand. The factor. Of course he had been taken away with the rest of them by the Itza Broth- ers, but she knew she'd have no difficulty finding them, for her kind was skilled at such things.

It was settled, then—she would go to the factor.

MOWBRY STOOD ON the beach waiting for Tommy Goff to rise up from his trance. The Irishman was depressed. He'd been dubious about that bathtub, but Red had set her mind on it, and there'd been no shaking her.

She had been halfway to the galleon when the worst happened—the tub caught a current on the departing tide, and though her hands paddled furiously she was past the wrecks and out through the cut into open sea in minutes.

The last Mowbry had seen of his beloved was as a tiny speck, carried away by the Atlantic Gulf Stream on a nor'-by-northeast heading at an even four knots.

THE ELEPHANT'S RIGHT eye first caught the movement. Curious, he tracked the small powdered wig as it marched toward the jungle on four pink legs. Like all elephants, he had stomped on almost every form of life that had walked or crawled on the earth at one time or another, but this one was something new.

How would it look, he wondered, once stomped? This was the eternal question among elephants and the source of most of their daily stomping activities. Would it spread out evenly in all directions? Or would it squirt out one side? He had to know. He just had to.

At that very moment Tommy Goff jumped to his feet, waving Mowbry over. "We go now," he announced.

"Did your trance tell you where they've been taken, then?"

"What trance?" Tommy Goff pointed at the wig approaching the jungle's edge. "We follow that."

The elephant, delighted at this conjoining of desires, eagerly used his trunk to lift both men to his shoulders. The white man didn't take this very well, sputtering and flailing about, but that didn't surprise the elephant—he never could understand Irishmen in just about anything they did as it was.

The elephant hurried forward, close on the trail of the wig-creature.

THE ITZA BROTHERS could never tell each other apart. Not that it mattered much. They were all of one mind. And this one mind had a singular desire, for the moment at least, and that was to build a pyramid dedicated to themselves. Of course they would have it adorned with little carvings of their serpent god, just to keep the snakes happy.

And so, toward completing the task of building a pyramid they had gathered all the inhabitants of British Honduras to the site they had chosen deep in the jungle just this side of Spanish-held territory. Then, with the help of the fer-de-lances, the Itza Brothers set their new slaves to work, clearing the forest, carving the massive limestone blocks from the bedrock.

Meanwhile, when they weren't kicking dogs, they sat on the veranda in front of their hut, drinking margarita moonshine and whittling small votive figurines that would one day be worth thirteen dollars and ninety-five cents each (they weren't very good).

"How far we have fallen," they said in unison, then nodded agreement.

In truth, conversations were rather boring, since everyone spoke at once and they all said the same thing, but what else was there to do?

(WHY AM I always so hopeful? the !Kung wondered as he padded along in the elephant's wake. Why am I so grim—you'd think I was some kind of reaper or something, a sower of death and destruction. I'm just hungry, dammit. Get off my back.)

(RIDING AN ELEPHANT'S not all it's cracked up to be, Mowbry reflected morosely as yet another tree branch whipped across his face. Mind you, that bathtub would be damned crowded for a transatlantic voyage, wouldn't it?

Yum, wouldn't it just.)

(A PROFOUND THOUGHT came to the elephant suddenly as he envisioned stomping on the wig-creature. A small step for elephantkind, a giant leap for the satisfaction of... uhm, curiosity. Was that right? A small step for elephants, a giant leap for elephantkind, no, a small stomp to satisfy an elephant's craving. Well, whatever, the moment would be momentous, that's for sure.)

(AGENT SIX GEE Eff made a quick report, encoding it on one of the hairs on his abdomen, to be cast off with a flick of his back leg at the appropriate moment.

* * *

> *Office memo:*
> *To Arachnid Control*
> *From: Agent Six Gee Eff*
> *For consideration: the training and domestica-*
> *tion of animated hair for purposes of*
> *clandestine transportation.*
> *Recommendation: introduce human hairstyles*
> *most conducive to spider occupation, said intro-*
> *duction to be done subtly and over an extended*
> *period of time so as to not make anyone suspi-*
> *cious. Suggest bouffants, Midwestern*
> *blonde-bumpers, Mohawks, spikes, multicol-*
> *ored tinting, etc.)*

ON THEIR VERANDA, the Itza Brothers all looked up at the appearance of, first, a four-legged wig; second, two men riding an elephant; and third, a little man with a spear in one hand and a leafless branch in the other.

The nearby slaves voiced a victorious roar that was quickly silenced when the fer-de-lances constricted their ankle-holds and hissed in warning. Nonetheless, all work on the pyramid stopped, and this annoyed the Itza Brothers immensely, so much so that they actually left their chairs and descended the steps to face the intruders, such physical activity leaving them direly winded.

The elephant strode into the clearing, then halted at Tommy Goff's command. Both men climbed down.

Tommy Goff addressed the slaves with arms outstretched. "I have answered your prayers!" he proclaimed. "I have come to free you from slavery and invite you into a life of cold-blooded mayhem, wanton butchery, wanton whoring, and tremendous hangovers on the high seas as pirates and privateers and revolutionaries!"

The Itza Brothers exchanged glances. This particular act, that of exchanging glances, involved immense effort and resulted in five minutes of absolute confusion, as it entailed a grand total of 448 glances between them.

In the meantime the god, Quetzalcoatl, who had been overseeing the Itzas and the construction of a new empire with an understandably jaded eye (a puff of Spanish wind for godsakes!) decided that direct intervention was necessary to deal with this Old World menace. He called forth all his snakes to attack Thomas Goff. The fer-de-lances released their holds on the slaves and slithered by the thousands into the clearing.

Tommy Goff, a small smile on his lips, strode forward to meet them.

And then all those gathered witnessed the most wonderful thing they had ever seen, for Tommy Goff touched not a single snake, and not a single snake touched him. Though they encircled him in their thousands, though they raced forward with venomous intent, fangs extended in the fury of their god's savage desire, the greatest child of Africa *danced,* and he danced around them, he danced between them, he danced over them and under them. He whirled, he spun, he moved in such sinuous rhythm that he became their master in motion and they his students.

Invisible in the sky overhead, Quetzalcoatl knew the wonder as did his children. And his rage, and his dreams of an empire reborn, disappeared inside the dance of Tommy Goff. The giant limestone blocks that marked the pyramid's foundation crumbled to dust. The Itza Brothers ran wailing into the jungle, perhaps—but only perhaps—never to be seen again. Quetzalcoatl descended from the heavens to weave his own dance of wonder around Tommy Goff.

In this time, other great dramas had occurred that became dances of their own. Ducat had stopped just inside the clearing, looking for the factor. At the moment she could not see him and oh how frustrating was that?

Mowbry approached the wig from behind and stared down at it. He hesitated.

The elephant had followed Tommy Goff as he strode into the clearing, having it in mind to stomp on snakes to his heart's content, the wig-creature forgotten for the moment. Upon hearing a horrifyingly familiar ululating cry behind him, the elephant whirled, and there crouched the !Kung hunter, spear in one hand, branch in the other.

All that stood between them was Mowbry and the wig, and it appeared to the elephant that neither had heeded the cry. The bushman began rattling the branch, inscribing strange patterns with it that seemed to hang in the air. The elephant stared at the branch, mesmerized.

(Something about that branch better not take my eyes off it oh God that branch! What's he gonna do with that branch?)

The hunter smiled.

(The branch always works. Now all I do is stick it in the ground right here and walk right up to him—he'll still be staring at the branch—and let him have it! Soup's on!)

And he crept forward.

At that moment Mowbry bent down and snatched up the wig. "This, y'damned cat, belongs to the factor! It ain't yours!"

Ducat froze, then she leapt high into the air in a blind rage, cartwheeling and thrashing about with all claws unsheathed. On her forehead Agent Six Gee Eff clung with all eight legs in mortal fear for his life. A thought darted through the spider's liquid brain—

(So, which is the better way to go? Like this, or being eaten by your wife?)

When Ducat landed, she was facing the bushman.

(Impossible!)

She snarled and fixed him, oh indeedy, with a savage glare of denial.

The hunter stared down at the cat, but it was not a cat that he saw. Rather, it was a red-skinned spitting demon with a tarantula plastered to its head and raw murder in its eyes. The bushman's spear flew straight up. He let out a single shriek, then was gone, running through the jungle, covering the fifty-one miles to the coast in three point seven seconds, the Caribbean and then the South Atlantic in two minutes fifty-one seconds, across most of Africa into the Kalahari and into his hut to fling himself into his wife's arms having left the scene at the clearing but three minutes past.

Meanwhile the elephant, frozen into immobile terror by the branch, suddenly snapped. With an ear-splitting scream of agony and rage he jumped into the air, came down on the branch with all four feet and promptly broke the earth's crust. He passed through the world in the blink of an eye (the left eye), and burst from the Indian Ocean not fifty yards from a fishing dory occupied by a lone Sri Lankan who thought, for a brief moment, that he had the catch of a lifetime. Then the elephant came back down with a big splash, and the fisherman came to his senses. Seeing the massive wave approach, he hastily tossed a life preserver in the elephant's general direction and began rowing like mad.

In the clearing that would one day be called Quashie Trapp, all was returning to normal. The snakes had dispersed with dreamy sighs. Quetzalcoatl slept an enchanted sleep of love and peace, Ducat had calmed down and was reunited with a strangely hesitant factor, the slaves were free to begin a life of corsairing, and Mowbry and Tommy Goff were in deep conversation.

At around this time Red made a landing in Norway. When she stepped out of the bathtub she gave it a single vicious kick, then stalked away without a backward glance. She was adopted by a colony of Norwegian rats who set her up as a divine oracle, and they would, one by one, descend ceremoniously into her sanctuary and ask her profound questions about the universe, though mostly they voiced one particular question: "So, is this boat I'm sneaking onto tomorrow night gonna sink, or what?" And the answer that came from behind the screen was always the same: "If it's a tub, it'll never sink!"

BACK IN QUASHIE Trapp, Mowbry and Tommy Goff went into partnership, a business agreement, aye, opening up the first of what would soon become an ubiquitous establishment in British Honduras: the Blacklight Bar, and with a click of the lights the posters on the wall behind the huddle of official irregulars comes alive—the glowing eyes of Che Guevara, the incandescent shark-teeth necklace and Stratocaster guitar of Jimi Hendrix, the gathered shining smiles of Led Zeppelin, and the spot of bright white that marks the half-open mouth of Margaret Thatcher.

And this Friday night (since there are more tales to come, aye) all are welcome to visit Mowbry and Tommy Goff's Quashie Trapp Blacklight Bar, and with a little coaxing, maybe, just maybe, Tommy will make an appearance, coming out from the back room, taking the center of the floor, and dance with a snake.

There's a charge for the privilege: fifty cents Belize, pay at the door, mate. There'll be no one there to receive it, or even check that you paid at all, but it's advised. You see, if you don't there's this hairless cat with a tarantula on her forehead—you saw her eyes from the sprung seat of the chair—and she'll fix you with a baleful glare of intense concentration. And as you step into the bar, you might find yourself feeling a tad... insubstantial, rather... light-headed, and before you know it, mate, you are *gone*.

About the Authors

A winner of the British Fantasy Award, **Mark Chadbourn** is the author of eleven novels and one non-fiction book. His current fantasy sequence, *Kingdom of the Serpent*, continues with *The Burning Man* in February 2008. A former journalist, he is now a screenwriter for BBC television drama. His other jobs have included running an independent record company, managing rock bands, working on a production line, and as an engineer's "mate." He lives in a forest in the English Midlands.

Through her combined career as a novelist and her background in the trade as a cover artist, **Janny Wurts** has immersed herself in a lifelong ambition: to create a seamless interface between words and pictures that explores imaginative realms beyond the world we know. She has authored seventeen books, a hardbound collection of short stories, and made over thirty contributions to fantasy and science fiction anthologies. Novels and stories have been translated worldwide, with most editions bearing her own jacket and interior art. Recent releases include a stand alone fantasy, *To Ride Hell's Chasm*, and her latest Wars of Light and Shadow novel, *Stormed Fortress*. She lives in Florida with a husband, three horses, four cats, and all manner of wild things parading through the backyard.

James Maxey lives in Chapel Hill, North Carolina. He is a graduate of both the Odyssey Fantasy Writer's Workshop and Orson Scott Card's Writer's Bootcamp, and the winner of the Phobos Award for his short story "Empire of Dreams and Miracles." His novels include *Nobody Gets the Girl* and *Bitterwood*, and his short fiction has appeared in *Asimov's Science Fiction*, *Orson Scott Card's Intergalactic Medicine Show* and *Prime Codex*, among many others.

T. A. Pratt lives in Oakland, California, with his wife, Heather Shaw. Tim's fiction and poetry have appeared in *The Best American Short Stories: 2005*, *The Year's Best Fantasy and Horror*, *Strange Horizons*, *Realms of Fantasy*, *Asimov's Science Fiction*, *Lady Churchill's Rosebud Wristlet*, and *Year's Best Fantasy*, among many others. His most recent books are the collection *Hart & Boot & Other Stories* and the novel *Blood Engines*, which takes place in the same urban fantasy setting as "Grander than the Sea."

Hal Duncan was born in 1971 and lives in the West End of Glasgow. A long-standing member of the Glasgow SF Writers Circle, his first novel, *Vellum*, was nominated for the Crawford Award, the British Fantasy Society Award and the World Fantasy

Award. The sequel, *Ink*, was recently published, while a new novella set in the same world is due out in November 2007. He has also published a poetry collection, *Sonnets for Orpheus*, and had short fiction published in magazines such as *Fantasy*, *Strange Horizons* and *Interzone*, and anthologies such as *Nova Scotia*, *Eidolon* and *Logorrhea*.

Jeff VanderMeer's book-length fiction has been translated into fifteen languages, while his short fiction has appeared in several year's best anthologies and shortlisted for *Best American Short Stories*. A two-time winner of the World Fantasy Award, VanderMeer has also been a finalist for the Hugo Award, the Philip K. Dick Award, the International Horror Guild Award, the British Fantasy Award, the Bram Stoker Award, and the Theodore Sturgeon Memorial Award. His most recent books have made the year's best lists of *Publishers Weekly*, *The San Francisco Chronicle*, *The Los Angeles Weekly*, *Publishers' News*, and *Amazon.com*. In addition to his writing, VanderMeer has edited or co-edited several anthologies, including the critically acclaimed *Leviathan* fiction anthology series, *Best American Fantasy*, and *The Thackery T. Lambshead Pocket Guide to Eccentric & Discredited Diseases*. He also writes for *The Washington Post Book World*, *Publishers Weekly*, *SF Weekly*, *Bookslut*, *The SF Site*, *Locus Online*, and many others. He lives in Tallahassee, Florida, with his wife, Ann, and three cats.

Christopher Barzak grew up in rural Ohio, went to university in a decaying post-industrial city in

Ohio, and has lived in a Southern California beach town, the capital of Michigan, and in the suburbs of Tokyo, Japan, where he taught English in rural junior high and elementary schools. His stories have appeared in many venues, including *Nerve.com*, *The Year's Best Fantasy and Horror*, *Strange Horizons*, *Salon Fantastique*, *Interfictions*, *Realms of Fantasy*, and *Lady Churchill's Rosebud Wristlet*. His first novel, *One for Sorrow*, was published in the fall of 2007. Currently he lives in Youngstown, Ohio, where he teaches writing at Youngstown State University.

Chris Roberson's novels include *Set the Seas on Fire*, *Here, There & Everywhere*, *The Voyage of Night Shining White*, *Paragaea: A Planetary Romance* and the upcoming *Dragon's Nine Sons*, and he is the editor of the anthology *Adventure Vol. 1*. Roberson has been a finalist for the World Fantasy Award for Short Fiction, twice for the John W. Campbell Award for Best New Writer, and twice for the Sidewise Award for Best Alternate History Short Form (winning in 2004 with his story "O One"). He runs the independent press Monkeybrain Books with his partner.

Juliet E. McKenna has been fascinated by fantasy, myth and history since she first learned to read. After studying Greek and Roman history and literature at St Hilda's College, Oxford, she worked in personnel management, continuing to read SF, fantasy, crime and historical novels, thrillers and literary fiction and anything else that looked interesting. After a career change to combine motherhood and book-selling, her debut novel, *The Thief's Gamble*, was published in 1999. This was the first of *The Tales of Einarinn*, now translated into more than a dozen languages. Her ninth book, *Eastern Tide*, concluded The Aldabreshin Compass sequence in October 2006. Also the author of assorted shorter fiction, she works from time to time as a creative writing tutor, keeps a keen eye on book trade issues and is one of the leading lights of the Write Fantastic, an authors' initiative promoting the whole gamut of speculative fiction. Living in Oxfordshire with her sons and husband, she fits in her writing around her family and vice versa. She's currently working on her third fantasy series.

Mike Resnick is the author of over fifty science fiction novels, 175 stories, twelve collections, and two screenplays, as well as the editor of more than forty anthologies. He is the winner of five Hugo Awards, and according to *Locus* is the leading short fiction award winner in science fiction history.

Steven Savile has edited a number of critically acclaimed anthologies and collections, including *Elemental*, *Redbrick Eden* and, most recently, the Doctor Who anthology *Destination Prague*, as well as *Smoke Ghost & Other Apparitions* and *Black Gondolier and Other Stories*, the collected horror stories of Fritz Leiber. Steven is also the author of the Von Carstein trilogy, *Inheritance*, *Dominion* and *Retribution*, set in Games Workshop's popular

Warhammer world, and has re-imagined the blood-thirsty Celtic barbarian, Sláine, from *2000 AD* in a new duology of novels. Steven has written for Torchwood, Star Wars and Jurassic Park as well as his own novels and short stories, including *Houdini's Last Illusion* and *Angel Road*. In his copious spare time, Steven... erm... writes... He was a runner up in the British Fantasy Awards, and a winner of a Writers of the Future Award in 2002.

Jay Lake lives in Portland, Oregon with his books and two inept cats, where he works on numerous writing and editing projects, including the World Fantasy Award-nominated *Polyphony* anthology series. His most recent books are *Trial of Flowers* and *Mainspring*. Jay is the winner of the 2004 John W. Campbell Award for Best New Writer, and a multiple nominee for the Hugo and World Fantasy Awards. Jay can be reached through his blog at *jaylake.live-journal.com*.

Conrad Williams is the author of three novels, four novellas and a collection of short stories. "O Caritas" is a sequel to his 2004 novel, *London Revenant*. He lives in Manchester with his wife, the writer Rhonda Carrier, and their two sons. His latest books are the novel *The Unblemished* and the novella *Rain*. His website is at *www.conradwilliams.net*.

Scott Thomas is the author of *Cobwebs and Whispers*, *Shadows of Flesh*, *Punktown: Shades of Grey* (with Jeffrey Thomas) and *Over the Darkening Fields*. His fiction has appeared in a number of anthologies, including *The Year's Best Fantasy and*

Horror, *The Year's Best Horror*, *Sick: An Anthology of Illness*, *Leviathan 3*, *Of Flesh and Hunger*, *Deathrealms* and *The Ghost in the Gazebo*. Thomas is fond of old houses, cats and the music of Corelli. He lives in Maine.

Lucius Shepard is one of America's pre-eminent writers of literary science fiction, fantasy, horror and magic realism. His recent novels *Trujillo*, *A Handbook of American Prayer*, *Viator* and *Softspoken* have all received critical acclaim and his new collection, *Dagger Key & Other Stories*, assembles much of his important work from the last two years. He is the recipient of the John W. Campbell Award, the Nebula Award, the Hugo Award and the Rhysling Award. He lives in Vancouver, WA.

Steven Erikson is the author of the Malazan Book of the Fallen novels; and has also published shorter fiction. Steven worked as an archaeologist for eighteen years before pursuing a career in fiction. He attended the Iowa Writers' Workshop, from which he graduated in 1990. He has published other fiction under the name Steve Lundin. He lives in Victoria, Canada, with his wife and son.

"Horatio Hornblower meets H.P. Lovecraft."

Revolution SF

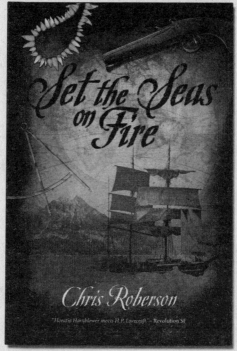

ISBN: 978-1-84416-488-2

1808. The *HMS Fortitude* patrols the sea lanes of the South Pacific, harrying enemies of the British Crown. When a storm drives the ship off course the crew find themselves aground on an island in uncharted waters. Whilst they struggle to rebuild their damaged vessel an encounter with the island's natives leads to a discovery of a dark and terrible secret that lurks behind the island's veneer of beauty...

www.solarisbooks.com

 SOLARIS FANTASY

"For the sake of humanity, join in Bitterwood's revolt."
Kirkus Reviews

JAMES MAXEY

BITTERWOOD

"For the sake of humanity, join in Bitterwood's revolt." – Kirkus Reviews

ISBN: 978-1-84416-487-5

It is a time when powerful dragons reign supreme and humans are forced to work as slaves, driven to support the kingdom of the tyrannical ruler King Albekizan. However, there is one name whispered amongst the dragons that strikes fear into the very hearts and minds of those who would oppress the human race. Bitterwood. The last dragon hunter is about to return.

www.solarisbooks.com

SOLARIS FANTASY